# A Matter
# of Marriage

Lesley Jørgensen

BERKLEY BOOKS, NEW YORK

**THE BERKLEY PUBLISHING GROUP**
Published by the Penguin Group
**Penguin Group (USA) LLC**
**375 Hudson Street, New York, New York 10014**

USA • Canada • UK • Ireland • Australia • New Zealand • India • South Africa • China

penguin.com

A Penguin Random House Company

A MATTER OF MARRIAGE

Berkley trade paperback ISBN: 978-0-425-27289-3

An application to register this book for cataloging has been
submitted to the Library of Congress.

PUBLISHING HISTORY
Originally published by Scribe Publications Pty Ltd as *Cat & Fiddle* / 2013
Berkley trade paperback edition / December 2014

PRINTED IN THE UNITED STATES OF AMERICA

10  9  8  7  6  5  4  3  2  1

Cover design by Danielle Abbiate.
Interior text design by Tiffany Estreicher.

*To my parents,*
*Margaret and Allan Jørgensen,*
*for the moral and practical support without which this book*
*would still be an unfinished manuscript.*
*With love and thanks.*

# One

How CAN A good wife and loving mother end up with not one but three unmarriageable children? Mrs. Begum rocked back on her heels on the sitting-room floor, in the middle of a patch of late-afternoon sunshine and with the comfortable sound of Dr. Choudhury's newspaper behind her, and chewed contemplatively on the wad of paan tucked into her cheek. She patted the photos spread out on the carpet. How handsome-clever they were. At least she could say that, for all the pain they had given her mother's heart. They could not have grown so beautiful for nothing.

She picked up a photo of Tariq, in his robes on graduation day, and sighed with pleasure. Like a young Shah Rukh Khan he was, so proud and handsome, despite that dirty beard. Tall and light-skinned like his father, but her own face, not his father's, *Inshallah*. And book-clever like Dr. Choudhury but without being a fool in the world.

Except for that fundamental business. Dressing like a village elder and talking that way too. "No smoking," he had said to his father. "It's a drug, against the Qur'an, as bad as alcohol." His own father.

"How about honor your father and mother then, boy?" Dr. Choudhury had said. Not that the boy knew the first thing about that, going off to South Africa almost two years ago now. Not a visit for all of that time. What had they come to UK for, if not for him, and then he leaves them to go somewhere else. No wonder she had a hole in her heart.

Ten months you carry them in your womb, then they turn around and stab you in your heart. A mother's lot, yes, she understood that, but why did he have to abandon them? What did it say about the love in their family, that it could not hold him close, stop him from flying away from them all as if they had died?

Mrs. Begum sat back on her haunches and sucked noisily on the paan, feeling the betel nut's relaxing buzz start to run through her blood. Yes, she knew all about pain, from her own children. She stroked the line of light in the photo that followed Tariq's perfect, straight nose, just like her own. What a lucky boy, not to have his father's nose. Or sticky-out ears like Prince Charles. The Queen had done the best she could for Charles, the first time. Just a pity she had not managed Diana a bit more. Of course a motherless girl neglected by her husband was going to go off the railways—she could have told the Queen that. Warned her.

She looked up, toward the sitting-room window where, even from the floor, Bourne Abbey could be seen, balancing its bulk on the hilltop opposite. As big as Masjid al-Haram that one, and twice as much trouble, taking them away from their little house in Oxford and the Bangla community there. Though, given the curse that this family was under, probably a good thing that there was no community here.

Mrs. Begum turned to the other photo of Tariq and gave a heavy sigh. This was one of Mrs. Guri's nephew Hakeem's artistic efforts, with Tariq a few years younger, clean-shaven and much less stern, wearing his best deep-blue *sherwani* with the silver embroidery and looking dreamily past the photographer. That was his first year away at Oxford, before he became so angry about Dr. Choudhury's occasional pipe and Rohimun's blue-jeans.

Mrs. Begum, still squatting on the carpet, put Tariq aside and turned to the pile of eligible matches in front of her, each with its studio photo attached. Everyone now gave out these fancy ceevees, just like Hakeem had said: age, height, favorite Bollywood heroes.

And the boys too: favorite sports, good jobs, what car they drove. Inky, ponky, poo . . . how does one choose? All nice girls and boys, all looking the same.

Soon Tariq would be back at last from those godless South Africans. What better time, when he would be feeling the first full rush of family love, to talk quietly one night of future plans, just mother and son. To say, how nice-nice it would be to see him happy and settled, now that she was beginning to feel her age. And then she would get up to make chai, leaving the photos and ceevees of all these pretty girls on the table. What man could resist a peek? Planting the seed, that was the important thing.

And Shunduri, her baby, look how stylish she had become, what a modern girl with her good bank job and studying still at the polytechnic. Surely she would be finished soon. And then a good boy for her, someone to keep her busy with lots of babies and a nice house. Not too near: it must be visits for a week or a month, not this next-door-just-a-cup-of-tea business.

Mrs. Begum picked up Shunduri's photos, a whole bundle: each time a different sari, different jewelry. No smiles, chin as high as the sky, eyes half closed, breasts thrust forward. What had Hakeem been thinking of? Only one or two of them were suitable for a marriage ceevee. It was all her father's fault. Calling her Shunduri, Beauty, was asking for trouble, and Dr. Choudhury should have known better.

Mrs. Begum selected the photo of Shunduri that most closely approximated maidenly modesty and thrust it up and behind her. It smacked into Dr. Choudhury's wall of newspaper, and she felt his knees jump.

"What a beautiful daughter, nah?" Dr. Choudhury hurrumphed, and Mrs. Begum felt the photo pushed back into her hand. She thrust it up again. "*Beautiful*, nah?"

An irritated cough. "Yes, yes."

She could hear the newspaper being put aside now, so she swiftly retracted Shunduri's photo and picked up one of Tariq's. "What a handsome boy. A *good* boy."

Silence. An annoyed-but-listening silence.

She held up one of the prospective brides' photos next to the photo of Tariq. "Mrs. Guri, you know, Hakeem's auntie just here yesterday, said this girl very homely, does not go out. A good family."

"Why are they wanting to send their daughter to South Africa then?"

She huffed sharply and turned to face her husband. "Tariq is coming home any day now. Any day."

"Any day, any day for months now."

"He called, two-days-ago-now. He said soon."

Dr. Choudhury leaned toward her and tapped Shunduri's photo with one long finger. "And what is the community going to think of this number-one silly girl? Maybe she thinks if she looks like a Bollywood actress she will get a hero in Mumbai." He snorted at his own humor and sat back, reaching for the newspaper.

Mrs. Begum's quick retort—"How could you say this of your own daughter?"—was lost as her paan was swallowed prematurely. By the time she had finished hawking, Dr. Choudhury's newspaper was held firmly in place, in a manner designed to resist further photographic incursions.

Well then. She turned her back on him once more and pulled out a manila envelope from underneath the other photos. She gently slid its contents partway into her palm, trying to ignore the burning lump that the paan was becoming, just below her breastbone. More eight-by-ten glossies, these of a pretty young woman, short and slight, with long rippling dark hair, but no Bollywood poses here.

Her Rohimun, Munni, her first daughter, Tariq's favorite sister, the other knife in her mother's heart. Half smiling, half frowning, her *chunna* crooked and her fingers hooked into her bracelets as if she was trying to pull them off. As she probably had been. Mrs. Begum blinked tears and pressed her lips together. Look at Munni's nails: broken and dirty as if she'd been planting rice in the paddies, not studying at that expensive royal college. Fine arts indeed. More like dirty arts: stinky oil paints that ruined good clothes, got in her hair and made her smell like Mrs. Darby's port-and-stilton.

And what did that oh-so-so-big Royal College of Arts scholarship get Rohimun in the end? Her face in the papers like some pub-girl, laughing with men. Ruined for marriage, lost to her family, a blight on Shunduri's prospects and maybe even Tariq's. The pain in Mrs. Begum's diaphragm climbed higher, and she burped quietly. She must put less lime powder in her paan.

There was a faint rustle behind her, and she sat perfectly still with Rohimun's photos fanned out in her hand. The little room with its briar rose wallpaper, Taj Mahal clock and peacock fan fell silent. Nothing was said, but she knew that he had seen, and that nothing would be said.

After a short while, Mrs. Begum slid Rohimun's photos back into their envelope and wiped her face with a corner of her sari. She bundled up Tariq, Shunduri and all the eligibles' ceevees and stood up briskly. No more spilt milk, as Mrs. Darby would say. Time to make a curry of what remains. She would talk again to Dr. Choudhury.

When the ceevees were back on her recipe shelf nice-and-tidy, Mrs. Begum loaded up the pandan tray, her pride and joy, real silver, so heavy, nah? With its eight (eight! No one had as many!) matching silver bowls, brimming with their separate loads of fresh betel leaves, cumin seeds, aromatic cloves, dried tobacco leaves, pink perfumed sugar balls, acrid lime powder with its own lid and silver spoon, finely chopped betel nuts and, last but not least, the whole betel nuts, with the deadly little betel knife lying alongside.

With arms at full stretch, she hauled it from kitchen to sitting room, laid it on the tiny, twisty-legged occasional table next to her husband's chair, and only then saw the photos of Rohimun on the floor, tipped out of their envelope. Dr. Choudhury was turned away from them, his shoulders drawn up and his fingers plucking at trouser corduroy as he stared unblinking at the wallpaper. Mrs. Begum thought suddenly of her uncle the tailor who had been so thin when he died, and drew close to her husband's chair.

"I have made *hidol satni*." His favorite. "And dahl."

He was silent, and she drew closer. She could see the top of his head: the white hair that ran straight back from his forehead was overlain by a few longer strands that crossed from left to right, and some of these had been displaced, exposing small squares and rectangles of scalp. Mrs. Begum's right hand crept out and started to order them and then her left hand came as well, to smooth down. Dr. Choudhury did not appear to notice, but after a while he withdrew his gaze from the wall and picked up the latest *Roopmilan-Mumbai* sari catalogue. His shoulders relaxed, his head tilted back to rest against a chair wing and he looked up from the pages.

Her hands moved to adjust her bracelets. "I will make you a hot salad too."

The phone shrilled, and Mrs. Begum was in the hall before her husband had even managed to uncross his legs. At the telephone table, she stopped, took a breath and re-tucked the front pleats of her sari. It might be the Women's Institute. But then Dr. Choudhury arrived in the hall, and she snatched up the handpiece. This call was not going to be answered like some fresh-out-of-the-village type, waiting for the caller to speak.

"Windsorr Cott-hage." She paused. Mrs. Darby didn't know everything. "*Salaamalaikum.*"

"*Alaikumsalaam*, Amma. Amma, I'm so tired like you wouldn't believe. And the weather in London's bin so stinking hot, yaah?"

"Aah, Baby!"

"Amma, what's happenin' wiv Affa, big sister? Have you heard from her? She was in the papers again! She was at some *party*, yaah . . ."

"What are you eating? When are you coming to visit your father?"

"Nah, Amma, the *newspapers*. Have you seen dem?"

"Papers-papers. What does your mother want with papers, when no one visits us as they should? We are getting old on our own while you are a Londoni modern girl."

"Amma, I'm busy here like you wouldn't believe: the bank, yaah . . ."

Mrs. Begum saw her husband reaching out to take the receiver and sidestepped to the right, still holding the phone. He followed, but in doing so was left square in front of the hall mirror and seemed to become distracted. She thought quickly, her desire to see her youngest child at war with her need to protect Rohimun from Shunduri's loose tongue. Surely she could manage both.

"Aah, Baby, so much has been happening here. Too much is happening to this family . . ."

"What? Amma, what's happenin'? Amma!"

"Your father is a wreck . . . What will the community be saying . . ." Mrs. Begum ended her disjointed hints with a convincing sniff and passed the receiver to her husband. Shunduri would not be able to resist coming down now, her mouth wide open like a little bird, for family drama, tears and shoutings, especially if it was Rohimun who was in trouble.

Dr. Choudhury grasped the phone and spoke absently to the mirror. "Aah . . . Baby . . . yes . . ." He slid his thumb between tie and shirtfront and slowly stroked his fingers down the length of the tie. "How are your studies?"

Mrs. Begum watched him closely, fairly certain that he would say nothing that would make Shunduri stay put in London. She hurried off to the kitchen, his voice echoing behind her.

"No, your mother may have. I only take *The Times* . . ."

-----

Mrs. Guri's other comments, the ones that Mrs. Begum hadn't repeated to her husband, came back to her now. They had been made without preliminaries as Mrs. Guri sat in Mrs. Begum's kitchen yesterday, with as much eyelid-drooping and table-pointing as if she had been asked for her matchmaking advice.

"Oh, Mrs. Begum, your daughter Shunduri, she is so *busy*, nah, I wonder she has time for her studies."

Mrs. Begum had smiled and wrapped another paan leaf, with consternation in her heart. "Yes, yes, a very busy girl, a good girl, the bank . . ." Mrs. Guri had leaned forward, close enough for Mrs. Begum to smell the thick smear of Vicks under her nose. "Oh, Mrs. Begum, I *know* she is a good girl. A *beautiful* girl. But . . ."

*Trouble follows beauty.* Mrs. Begum finished the saying in her head, smiled and thought how Vicks would be of no help to Mrs. Guri if she was kicked in her fat face. What had she seen or heard to be giving such a warning?

"Have you thought, has your husband thought . . . There are so many good families looking for their sons now." Mrs. Guri waited.

"We are not an old-fashioned family to be rushing her before she has finished her studies."

"Such a lovely girl. So many friends. Do you know her friends?"

Mrs. Begum sat up a little straighter. "She is coming down this weekend."

Mrs. Guri nodded, her cheeks jiggling a little. "That is as it should be. You are a very lucky mother to have her come to you at this time . . ."

*Before it is too late.* Mrs. Begum knew exactly what she meant, but smiled at the old gossip as airily as she could over the tightening in her stomach.

Mrs. Guri glanced at the clock and swallowed the last of her chai with finality. Selecting a paan, she tucked it into a corner of her cheek and dipped into her Harrods bag for a touch more Vicks before announcing she must go as Ahmed would be back now.

Mrs. Begum walked the fat, matchmaking, troublemaking cockroach to the door with fear in her bowels. If Mrs. Guri, knowing everyone in Brick Lane, in Tower Hamlets, was telling her this, what was it she knew? Or, rather, who? One last effort must be made, despite her anger.

"In London . . . is everyone . . . your daughters and their families well?"

Mrs. Guri slowed but was not so silly as to give a triumphant smile. "All well."

"*Inshallah.*" Both women spoke at the same time, and they smiled as they walked outside and down the garden path. Across the road, Mrs. Guri's son-in-law Ahmed was crouching by his car, rather forlornly wiping at a crumpled bumper with some paper towels.

They were almost at the gate now, and Mrs. Begum was growing desperate. She did not have Mrs. Guri's London connections and her knowledge of the families and of reputations and rumors. She put her hand on Mrs. Guri's upper arm, and her fingers sank in as if it was Mrs. Darby's chocolate mousse.

"Perhaps you could let people know, that Shunduri is ready . . ."

Mrs. Guri, visibly gratified, stopped at the gate and rested against the post. She was waiting for more. Ahmed straightened when he saw them, then went back to trying to smooth the dent.

Mrs. Begum clasped her hands together. "I . . . a mother always worries . . . and London is so far away . . . You know all the best families."

Mrs. Guri looked back at the house, and Mrs. Begum turned to look with her, at the *Windsor Cottage* brass plate that she had put up only this morning: just the right size, not too big, not too small, and with that veneer of hastily acquired verdigris, so hurtful to her house-proud instincts, but on a sharp-eyed walk through the village, apparently so necessary for the proper country look. She cursed country-look in her thoughts as she followed Mrs. Guri's eyes. Why did country-look have to be so different to town-look? Why this need for falling-down and dirty?

Nothing was said. Mrs. Begum again swallowed her pride. "Please."

Mrs. Guri nodded in gracious acknowledgement. "Mrs. Begum, you should never worry, you have good children." She paused, then spoke again, in a lower voice. "Niece Indra, you know, my niece, Hakeem's sister that married the doctor? She saw one night, Shunduri talking to a boy in his car. But it was dark, so easy to make mistakes . . ."

"Aah, yes," said Mrs. Begum bitterly. "So easy."

Mrs. Guri took a reviving sniff. "We all have these problems. These modern children, they think they must have everything . . . that they deserve happiness. What can you do?"

"Aaah," they both said.

Mrs. Guri's own eldest daughter—four children and two broken noses in three years and now on indefinite *nyeri*, family-visit, with her parents—was before them both, and Mrs. Begum's anger faded. What could any of them do for their children's happiness and safety, except pray?

Mrs. Guri touched Mrs. Begum's shoulder and said with genuine kindness, "We will do our best to find her a good husband."

"*Inshallah.*" Both women had spoken together again, this time with no animosity.

Mrs. Guri rested one hand on her stomach. "They are only safe in your womb, nah? Then your sorrows start." She brought one plump hand up to her face, pinched the bridge of her nose and squeezed her eyes shut, as if trying to recall. "He is a businessman, I think . . . Phones and cameras."

Tears sprang to Mrs. Begum's eyes. She had no pride left now, none at all. "Can you ask? Find out the important things?"

Mrs. Guri nodded heavily. "Yes, yes," and pushed her bulk off the gatepost. It did not spring back.

Likewise, the mood of the two women, as they walked together across the roadway to Ahmed's car, was unusually subdued. The current of strong emotions, genuine feelings, that flowed between them was not a comfortable thing, and so it was with some relief that Mrs. Begum, nodding and smiling, accepted her friend's parting shot (an offer of Brasso for Windsor Cottage's name plate) to resume the usual community hostilities.

---

MRS. BEGUM, STANDING in the kitchen and remembering every word of that visit, was aware that it would be a month, maybe more, before Mrs. Guri could return with news, and so much could happen in a month. If Mrs. Guri was telling her about one time, that meant many times, enough gossip to get her big bottom into Ahmed's car for a two-hour drive to give her this sorrow and receive the satisfaction of Mrs. Begum begging for her matchmaking help. Images of Mrs. Begum's own hasty marriage flashed before her eyes, and she gave a little moan. Baby. Shunduri must be brought back home before it was too late.

Phones. Businessman-businessman. Every *gundah*, yob, in the community was a *businessman*. All it meant was that there was no job and no family occupation, no restaurant or shop for them to attach themselves to. That they were boys alone and liable to go off into any direction. And Shunduri. She thumped the rice saucepan down hard on the stove and blue flames bellied. *So busy with bank.* Did Shunduri think her mother was born yesterday? This boy must be made to realize that Baby was not a girl without family.

And if he was halfway eligible . . . Mrs. Begum stirred the basmati vigorously. Rohimun's antics had ruined this family. If he was one *grain* eligible, then pressure could, *must*, be brought to bear. Mrs. Guri had not acquired her reputation as a matchmaker through her sugar-cane sweetness. Mrs. Begum had heard here in UK of *funchaits*, the community councils of elders, being called, with the attendant beatings, to force love-match couples to wed, and of the girls who were getting too modern and were shipped off to Bangladesh to be married to traditional men who controlled their wives with traditional methods.

This phones-businessman, whoever he was, would be no match for the combined forces of Mrs. Guri and herself. The way things were going, Baby would be the only Choudhury daughter to marry within the community. And if this could be managed, the damage to the family's reputation caused by Rohimun would be partially repaired. Even if it meant a *funchait*, this would be done.

Look at Princess Margaret when she was young: what a mess cleaned up there with just a little pressure from her *affa*, her big sister the Queen. Not a first-rate marriage perhaps, but the royal family would have known not to expect first-rate after that fuss with a man who had been married before. She must speak again to her neighbor Mrs. Darby, with her knowledge of all things royal, about how it had been done.

As for Rohimun . . . Mrs. Begum abandoned the rice and began to chop onions, tears filling the corners of her eyes. Perhaps marriage was possible if it was outside the community. Dodi and Diana. Yes, Dodi and Diana: such a thing could be managed. She just needed to be more practical, more accepting than the Queen and Prince Philip had been. Yes, it was for her, Mrs. Begum, to learn from their mistakes and acknowledge that, for Rohimun, even a mixed marriage would be a blessing. Rohimun was like that poor foolish girl Diana in other ways too: she needed a marital anchor, otherwise she was likely to drift into dangerous waters. As indeed she had.

Mrs. Begum scraped the onions into a saucepan and threw in a pinch of the big rock-salt crystals that Tariq had persuaded her, years ago now, to use instead of the fine-ground salt that everyone so admired in Bangladesh. Sons were always less predictable: they had more choices, more freedom to get away from family influences. With his looks, she had expected love-trouble at university as a certainty, yet all Tariq's love then seemed to be for family and for Allah, peace be upon Him. And his precious art pictures. And it had turned out to be Tariq rather than her daughters who had been so sick for home at that time. Although of course he had been away in South Africa these last one-two years with no such yearning.

Twenty-seven was not too late for a man to marry in UK. Look at Prince Charles. Tariq just needed to be steered, no, nudged, very slightly, in the right direction. A nice homely girl. Someone to keep her mother-in-law company, be interested in the garden and the kitchen. Such a girl was considerably more likely to give her grandchildren than Rohimun or Shunduri. Tariq would be home soon, she could feel it in her stomach, ever since that phone call two days ago: the first since he'd left. Family was becoming more important to him.

And if there was a secret there, in the background, it could be managed. Camilla had not wrecked that royal marriage; it was Diana's loneliness and lack of family help—Mrs. Darby and Mrs. Begum both agreed on that. A second wife, or mistress as they called her in UK, could stabilize an unhappy marriage, give a difficult husband someone else to bother, give both women a break. It could even have its own harmonies, especially if one of the wives, for some reason, was barren.

Mrs. Begum bent over the hissing onions and sniffed. Something was missing. *Haldi.* She took a generous teaspoonful of the golden turmeric powder, spice of weddings and all things fishy, and scattered it over the onion. Time to blend all the ingredients together now, and then wait, while the onions caramelized and the spices roasted, for the hidden flavors to reveal themselves.

## Two

BABY WAS LOOKING good tonight. Shunduri stood back from the mirror and tossed her hair, tilted her head and affected to stare blankly as though at an admirer, conscious of length of leg and height of breast. She was never going to be one of those Asian girls who lost the plot as soon as they were married, getting fat and not doing their hair or nails; spending all their time watching Bollywood movies and filling their faces with samosas and pick 'n' mix. When she married, she was going to be like Posh Spice, getting thinner and younger and better dressed every year, handsome rich husband, a flash car of her own. Yaah.

Affa, big sister Rohimun, had been stacking on the weight and not even betrothed yet. And probably never, now that everyone knew she had a *gora* boyfriend. Shunduri sniffed and tossed her hair again, watching its glossy swing under the bedroom light. Served Rohimun right, always criticizing her taste in clothes and friends, telling her she shouldn't read rubbish, dissing her London *Vogue* and her Desi and Bollywood mags. *What you need is serious reading to improve your mind, Baby.*

Shunduri held her hands out in front of her: baby-blue nails, tipped in silver glitter. Perfect. As they should be—she'd only just finished doing them. She looked in the mirror again. Sass & Bide leggings in the same pale blue as her nails and a tight scarlet *choli*, the blouse taken from her latest sari. Scarlet stilettos, and blue and silver toenails. Without taking her eyes from the mirror, she picked up the matching veil from the bed, tucked one corner into the top of her leggings, wrapped it once around her waist then draped it diagonally across her torso, pulling it tight across her breasts before pinning it on her shoulder.

Shunduri turned sideways to admire the five feet of veil that hung down her back and the neatness of her bum in the shiny pants, visible through the draped chiffon. Then she grabbed her hairbrush, tipped her head over and brushed her hair vigorously before straightening up and enveloping herself in a cloud of Silhouette extra-strong hold.

Why hadn't she gotten Mum's hair? It was so unfair being stuck with Dad's fine strands, though no one could say she hadn't made the most of them. Not that she'd ever wanted a great big rope of the stuff like Affa had: just a bit more thickness, so she could grow it to her shoulderblades and not have to use hot rollers every time she needed a bit of volume. Affa had the hair alright, but what a waste. All she did was wear it down in a tangled mess, no styling whatsoever, or plait it back like a village girl. Shunduri would never let herself go like that. It was just a matter of making an effort, not being lazy. No one likes a slob.

She stared in the mirror again. Her legs were looking even longer tonight in leggings and three-inch heels, not to mention what the balconette bra was doing to her bust. Nothing much in the waist department despite all her dieting, but her stomach was as flat as a board, unlike Rohimun's. Why she'd let herself go now, Shunduri couldn't understand. Just when she was getting herself into the papers too. If she'd played her cards right with that blue-blooded boyfriend of hers, she could have been London's first Desi It-girl.

Not that he was her type. She, Shunduri Choudhury, would never go out with a *gora*, a Christian: she was a true Muslim girl. But despite that, she'd done her best for Rohimun when she'd turned up that time. No money in her purse, not even a change of clothes, and crying on her doorstep as if Shunduri was the big sister. She'd looked after her, gotten in takeaway and fed her, put sheets on the couch and found some clothes that fit her (no easy task). And then Shunduri had called Simon, just to let him know the score, that Rohimun had family who cared, yaah, and then, before you know it, they were back together again. Not that Rohimun'd ever thanked her.

Just went to show, Affa knew nothing about men. About relationships. If she wasn't careful, she'd lose Simon, and then who'd marry her? Shunduri stalked into the bathroom and found the tube of lip primer that she had bought earlier that day, unscrewed the cap and rolled it on the way the salesgirl had shown her. Something still wasn't right though. Mum was throwing out these hints, and Rohimun hadn't phoned since she'd left with Simon, ungrateful cow, and now she'd had her picture in the papers again.

Shunduri made smacking sounds with her lips and counted in her head to twenty to let the primer settle in, before applying lipstick in a vivid red. She clicked the lid back onto the lipstick and looked at her face in the mirror with complete satisfaction. That really finished her off. Yaah. Kareem was one lucky man.

---

SHUNDURI SWANNED INTO the cafe, head high despite the butterflies in her stomach that always clustered at these moments, striding from her waist the way the modelling course had taught her, stopping herself from making any of those giveaway touches to hair, clothes or face that advertised self-doubt. They'd also told her to say *brush* just before entering a room, to give the appearance of a natural smile, but Shunduri didn't follow this advice. It was more dignified not to smile, cooler. Look at Posh Spice.

Only problem was, walking in like this made it hard to look around for her posse. But no matter, they would find her. Shunduri leaned on an empty chair to pull at a stiletto strap, and the next minute Amina and Aisha were by her side with hugs and air kisses and "Baby!" and the usual gasps and compliments for her outfit.

Soon they were all lolling back in cafe chairs, facing the street for maximum exposure, and Shunduri rearranged her veil and swung her sleek, shiny bob a little, well pleased with the reactions. She was still showing her posse how to dress, and from the looks other tables and passersby were sneaking, they weren't the only ones.

Her cream-coffee, when it came, was in a deep red cup that contrasted beautifully with her nails, and even dear Amina and Aisha had decked themselves out in pastels, which made them fade into the pinkish walls of the cafe almost as much as she stood out. What good friends they were. Amina and Aisha oohed and aahed, telling Shunduri who was walking in the door and who was looking at them, and she half closed her eyes and took microscopic sips and pretended not to be interested.

Where was Kareem? She wanted him to come and see her like this: Queen of the Cafe, surrounded by admirers. She could just imagine what Affa would say, seeing her here. *Empty-headed.* Why, her head was crowded out with thoughts and plans and schemes for the future. Most of them involving Kareem, her man, who made her look so good and treated her like the princess she was.

Look how well she was doing at the bank: always on time, never a day off, quicker on the keyboards and with the money than some of the women who'd been there years. Promoted onto the money transfer and currency exchange counter after only three months, already seen as the one to sort out difficulties and assist the manager with end-of-month problems. Self-possessed and decisive, her last review had said. Looking good in the uniform too. You had to think ahead in this life, think ahead all the time. She was the most go-getting girl she knew, and the most sensible, the most rational, leaving nothing to chance. She knew what she needed to succeed in life: a good job, good clothes and a man like her—ambitious, successful, stylish.

Shunduri glanced at her besties, heads together and giggling over some text message. Where were they going to be in three years' time? Wherever they were pushed. Amina's parents were already looking for her: a good Hindu match. They wanted a nice accountant from the Punjab, but with Amina having dropped out of college without a degree, they were changing the bio data on her CV to read "traditional homely girl, loves children and cooking," which was playing very risky, maybe ending up with a traditional man who would never let her out of the house and would want babies straight away. And what a shock he'd get. Nails longer than her smokes and wouldn't know what to do with a saucepan if it jumped out of her Louis Vuitton knockoff handbag and smacked her.

Aisha was no better: still hanging on by her toenails at the poly like Shunduri, doing one subject just to keep the accommodation going and to stop her mum and dad bringing her home. Being Christian, her parents were no help at all finding a husband, instead putting all the pressure on her to find herself a match and give them grandchildren. And where do you start? All the decent Asian Christians were in India, not here. And even if they weren't, Aisha's parents were so determined to integrate that they only spoke English at home, never met up with their neighbors at Diwali or Eid, knew no one. Aisha was already talking about putting her own ad on the Internet, was at her wits' end trying to find a husband who was Asian but would speak to her parents in English, was Christian but not a pubman, street-cool but with a good job.

Shunduri knew she was the best-looking, the best-dressed, the standout in her crowd—and always had been—but that knowledge had started to pall. Mirrors, once her friends and able to be turned to at any time for a shot of confidence about her future, had become temperamental oracles that she only approached after careful preparation and proper lighting. Twenty-three. She wasn't some *gora* career girl who only married in her thirties, if at all. Desi girls were seen as over the hill by twenty-four unless they were film stars or heiresses. She'd started to hate going to other girls' betrothals and weddings. It didn't matter, she'd discovered, if you could out-dress and out-dazzle the bride-to-be. You were still not the bride.

A black Golf cruised past. Was that Kareem through the tinted glass? She felt a surge of excitement, but the car continued on, and she affected boredom and recrossed her gleaming blue legs. At least Mum and Dad weren't putting the pressure on and lining up prospective grooms right, left and center. This was probably the last year she could swing it living in London, with her one subject due to finish soon. Working full-time at the bank on top of her college allowance, she'd been able to keep herself in Dolce & Gabbana and good Versace knockoffs. And surely Kareem would be giving her the word soon: he'd be a fool not to, with no real family here and money to burn. Girls like her didn't come along every day.

She remembered that day in the bank when Kareem had sauntered in, suited and smiling. She'd tilted her head back and looked at him, eye to eye, deadpan.

"How can I help you today, sir?"

He'd just continued grinning right back. "Nice day, innit?" he'd said, as if she had all the time in the world, was working in a takeaway and not on the international money transfer counter of the biggest bank in Britain. The bank that likes to say yes. She touched the company scarf at her neck, tied and angled perfectly, to make the point.

"Yes. How can I help you?"

He smiled on, looking her in the eyes and pushed a bundle of notes, one hundred and fifty pounds' worth, under the Perspex barrier. "For my family," he said. "In Bangladesh. You from dere?"

"None of your business," she said calmly, taking the money and counting it as rapidly as the machines, red nails flashing.

"Have you filled out the transfer form?"

"Nah. Bein' an ignorant Desi boy, I was hopin' you could help me wiv dat," he said, and she knew even then that he was playing up his East End accent, playing the peasant for her.

She picked up a pen. "Name?"

"Kareem Guri. And you are Shunduri Choudhury, right there on your badge. I think my auntie knows your—"

"Full address, please."

"I'm a Brick Lane, Tower Hamlets boy, of course. Can't you tell?"

"Oh *yaah*," she said, heavy on the sarcasm, using the ID he'd pushed under the grille to complete the form.

The transaction was over in a few minutes and she'd been expecting him to try to hang around, try to chat, but instead he'd said, "See you next Monday, Princess," and left before she'd had a chance to ignore him.

Next thing she knew, she was running into him all the time: at the clubs and the big Brick Lane *melas* for weddings and betrothals, and even on the street. They'd been together for six months now, but keeping it real quiet. Word was going to get around about the two of them, she knew it, and Kareem had been telling her that he loved her, she was the girl for him, but he didn't deserve her, no, he didn't, until he'd shown her what he could really do and pulled off a certain business deal first. For their future. Then he'd get Uncle and Auntie to speak to her parents, make some arrangements.

But it was June already, and Kareem was still planning the big business deal, still talking it up, and she was . . . well, she'd given him everything and she wasn't one to cry about it, but he had to come through now. He had to. How had she gotten herself into this position, where if Kareem were to fail her she would be ruined?

There was a flurry of oohs and aahs from the ever-reliable Amina and Aisha, and Shunduri looked out the cafe window to see a car stopped at the front and a figure emerging from the back of it, clad head to toe in a flowing Saudi-style *abaya* and *niqab*, as black as night. A man in the driver's seat, in an oversized American football jersey and several necklaces, was glaring at the cafe crowd. The woman approached the cafe door, and Amina gasped.

"It's Shilpi, it's Shilpi, innit!"

Aisha stood up to stare. "It's Shilpi. Oh my God!"

They tottered to the door to greet her, and within minutes half the cafe was clustered around her with *salaamalaikums* and Shilpi-is-that-yous, and Shunduri was left on her own, sitting at the table, her graceful slouch feeling a little stiff. No one was looking at her. She felt invisible. Shilpi, for it was her, was replying to the crowd in a muffled voice and waving one hand encased in a black satin glove, in a dignified sort of way. In fact she looked more dignified and more substantial than Shunduri had ever seen.

"I can't stay for long, yaah," she was saying to everyone. "My baiyya, my big bruvver's just dropped me off for half an hour, den he's pickin' me up again, for evening prayer."

"Wow, Shilpi, you look amazin' . . . I never thought . . ." Aisha ran out of steam in a dazed sort of way, and Shunduri thought to herself, No, you never do think, do you, dear friend that always follows whatever is newest. Some friend you are. So shallow. She tossed her hair again, recrossed her legs, but this time no one noticed. The changed atmosphere in the cafe was affecting everything. Shilpi's dramatic monochrome presence made Shunduri feel gaudy and obvious, and she noticed that the polish had started to peel off the nail of her right index finger. She hid it under the table.

Next thing she knew, an escorted Shilpi was lowering herself gracefully onto the chair opposite her, flanked by Amina and Aisha, whose pastel *salwars* now looked delicate and feminine next to the black microfiber. Not an inch of Shilpi's skin was to be seen, except between cheekbone and eyebrows. The edge of the *niqab* around Shilpi's eyes and across her nose was decorated with small black beads in a pattern of interlocking zigzags, and the same pattern traced the cuffs of her sleeves. Her eyes, thickly lined with kohl, flashed large and round in their bead frame, drawing the light.

Good move, thought Shunduri. With Shilpi's bad skin and dumpy figure, of course covering would be an improvement.

But it was more than that. Shunduri had noticed the growing group of girls at college who were covering. Some did it with a swaggering *fuck you, I'm proud of who I am* attitude. And some did it because being a born-again fundamentalist was suddenly cool. Those girls formed their own cliques: walking and sitting together and avoiding contact with Shunduri and her friends in such a way that made it clear that they saw themselves as morally superior to the Asian-princess crowd and the coolie-girls.

And despite joking about them, calling them ninja chicks, everyone's behavior toward them seemed to acknowledge it. College lecturers were disconcerted by them, library staff and security guards looked at them askance but never challenged them. And everyone made way for them when it was time for *takbir* or a rally.

Shunduri's coffee was cold, and she felt flat and sour. Eight people were at their little table now, and all of them were focused on Shilpi, on her news, her movements. Before she'd covered, Amina, even Aisha, would scarcely have given her the time of day, let alone have asked her opinion of the latest Bollywood movies, which kohl she used and whether she was going to Rukhsana's wedding. Shunduri couldn't take it anymore. She stood up, straightening to her full height, tucked her hair back on one side to show off one of her diamond earrings (presents from Kareem to match his, one carat each) and flicked her veil. No one even noticed.

"Eh, Princess."

She turned and Kareem was there behind her, and he too was staring at the woman in black.

"Who's dat?"

Shunduri glared at him. "Shilpi. You remember Shilpi."

"Ahh, yeah. Course I do." He frowned, then snapped his fingers and gave a laugh of recognition. "Eh, she's a ninja chick now. A funda-woman-talist," he said, nodding and *salaaming* Shilpi when she caught his eye. "Just a tick, Princess."

And Kareem left her, just like that, to cruise through the cafe doing his meet-and-greet with each table, letting people know where he was going to be tonight and when: which club and which kebab shop. Shunduri watched him through slitted eyes. All fuckin' Muslim men were the same then. The more you covered up and denied access, the more they wanted you. So where did that leave her?

There was no point in staying now. She moved away from the table, then made the mistake of looking back. Someone had already taken her chair, and Shilpi was holding court with a poise that she'd never had in her *salwar* and chunky platforms and too much cover-up on her spots.

It was so unfair, after all the effort Shunduri had put in for tonight.

It was like someone had changed the rules without telling her. She picked up her handbag, stalked to the toilet and locked the door. She started to reapply her lipstick, but then stopped and put it back in her bag.

She pulled the free end of her veil over her head, wrapping it across her nose, and stared at herself. Mysterious, fascinating. She would look better in a *niqab* than Shilpi ever would. She tissued off her lipstick until there was just a hint of color, found some eyeliner in her bag and, bracing her elbow against the wall next to the mirror, ran a cool wet line along the tops of her eyelashes, flicking it out and up at the ends. There. It was all in the eyes.

When she came out of the Ladies', Kareem was at the counter, paying for her table's coffees. She ignored him and hugged and kissed Amina and Aisha goodbye, arranged to see them at Aisha's dorm room in a couple of hours to oil each other's hair and watch Sky Asia's premiere movie. She ta-rah'd Shilpi and the others with a wiggle of her fingers.

Shilpi gave her a pompous little wave. "*Salaamalaikum*, sister. See you round."

Shunduri bared her teeth in what was almost a smile. "*Inshallah. Alaikumsalaam*, sister." Pious ninja bitch, just doing it for the attention. Two could play at that game.

Kareem was right behind her, moving toward the door, holding it open. As she passed by him, he whispered, "Princess," and his breath was hot on her neck. She felt a spurt of pleasure in her stomach and fought back a smile. No one called Shilpi that. And only Shunduri had Kareem. No one else had anyone like him: handsome, street-cool, going places, with his own council flat on the side, for business. And privacy. Everything was going to be alright.

They walked down the street together, Shunduri acutely aware of his rolling walk, the swing of his shoulders. He would never touch her in public, no Muslim couple would except maybe modern newlyweds, but Kareem's tone, his stance, promised intimacies later. An image of the bridal sari in the main window of Mumbai Magic floated through her mind: deep pink with red-gold embroidery over stiff gold gauze.

If he wore the biggest wedding turban, she could wear three-inch heels and he would still look taller than her.

Kareem took her around the corner, down an alleyway, and tucked her hand into the crook of his arm.

"I've got to go round the clubs later—Varanasi, Rome and Salem tonight—but there's something I want to show you first."

"What?" She forgot herself enough to clutch his arm and tried to see if he was holding something in his other hand, had something in his pocket.

He laughed and pulled her closer, squeezed her against his side. "Look, Princess. Whaddaya think?" He gestured with his free hand at a large black SUV parked up at the rear of the cafe.

"A car?"

Its lights blipped on, and Kareem steered her around to the front passenger seat, urging her inside, up a high step and into a cabin that smelled of newness and leather and luxury. She sank into a seat as large and soft as the rocker-recliner at Amina's house that only her dad was allowed to sit in. Kareem shut her door and went around. From the driver's seat, he reached across and fastened her seatbelt, brushing his arm across her breasts as he did so.

"How about I take you for a drive tomorrow? A long drive, like for the day, out of London, see what this baby can do?"

She stared at him, still caught up in that moment where she'd thought he was going to give her a present, or perhaps something even better.

He seemed to recognize the disappointment in her eyes and took her hand and kissed it, watching her. "It's all for you, Princess, you know that." He started the engine, which thrummed and roared. "That's Jag V8 direct injection that Rover use. Classy and powerful: like you and me, yeah. And Rover's been bought out by Tata, so it's a real Asian car, man."

A car. He had bought a car. What did he think that was telling her?

Kareem was pointing at the dials, saying something about the features. "See, Princess? We're in the money now, and this is just the beginning. I'll take you for a drive—anywhere you like."

Shunduri looked at him, challenge in her eyes. "I haven't seen Mum and Dad in ages, yaah."

He fiddled with the stereo, then smiled brilliantly at her. "Yeah. Anytime you want."

She pressed her advantage, smiled back at him just as brightly. "Tuesday? I've got a lieu day from the bank."

Kareem's hesitation was more obvious now. "We'd have to go early, Princess: in the morning. I've gotta be back for business, yeah."

"*I'm* up to start work at nine every day, yaah. You're the one who lives on Asian mean time."

"Alright, first thing, yeah. I'll be round at the dorm."

Maybe ten if I'm lucky, she thought. Her palms felt clammy and, as Kareem drove them back to his flat, she slid her hands under her thighs, like she used to do at school when she was trying not to bite her nails. As an unrelated male, he could only get away with driving her down to see her parents once. Once would be an exception, able to be overlooked provided he showed them enough respect, kept his distance from her, and never did it again.

Or became an official suitor.

And then what? He would have to speak to Mr. and Mrs. Guri about them soon, or they would have to elope. And there was no way she was going to be one of those couples running off to Brighton, parents disowning them, brothers and uncles looking for them to beat the shit out of them or worse, and a *funchait* to force her marriage, as a ruined girl, to a reluctant Kareem.

No, she wanted a proper wedding with all the trimmings: the betrothal party, then the full *nikkah*: the proper Muslim ceremony, with her in a sari stiff with gold thread, weighed down with gold jewelry, at least two kilos' worth, seated upstairs in Mum and Dad's bedroom and all the women around her, saying *Nah, nah*, to the mullah, and then the third time he asks, "Do you consent to marry

Al-Mohammed Kareem Guri?" Mum prompting her to say, with every appearance of reluctance, *Jioii*. Yes. Then the *haldi mendhi* for her and all her friends and female relatives with music and dancing and singing going all night, and Shunduri in green and gold having her feet and hands rubbed with turmeric. Then the visit to the registry office to do the *gora* legals, perhaps in a hot pink *lehenga* and gold veil, and Kareem in one of his Savile Row suits.

Then off to the *rukhsati*, the reception, to sit on the red and gold thrones on the stage in Oxford's grandest reception center with Kareem in a white and gold *sherwani* and matching turban, with everyone sliding rings on her fingers and bracelets on her wrists, her head bowed down, her expression sweet, modest, a little sad. And, after the reception, the tears and clinging to Mum as she is torn away from her family to start a new life with this man, subsiding tearily into the stretch limousine and the protective concern of her new husband and the chaperones.

And a full *walima* for the newlyweds a week later, where she is allowed to smile as much as she likes, as she accepts everyone's best wishes and compliments as to how much married life is agreeing with her. And not to forget all the visits she would be making as a new bride, wearing all her finery, to drink the pistachio and sherbet at the houses of all their wedding guests for months and months afterward . . . She wanted it all, every bit, including the astonishment and envy of her friends, the pride of her parents, and the look in Kareem's eyes when he sees her in her wedding sari. Shilpi would just die.

"Eh, Princess, we're here, my place," Kareem said softly, undoing her seatbelt.

Shunduri blinked and turned to open the car door. There was a tearing sound. The end of her veil had caught on Kareem's buckle, and her careless movement had resulted in a long slit in the chiffon. He dropped the end on her lap.

"Sorry, Princess. I dunno if you can fix that."

She bundled the torn end out of the way. "Mum'll know what to do. I'll give it to her when we visit."

Kareem came round to her side of the car and, since there was no one in the car park, she slid into his arms.

"On Tuesday," she said.

"Eh?"

"The veil. I'll give it to Mum on Tuesday, when we visit. You promised."

"Oh yeah, yeah, yeah," he said, kissing her neck and shoulder. "You look so hot, Princess. Did you dress for me tonight? Did you?"

"Oh *yaah*." Shunduri caught hold of his tie and pulled hard. "As *if*."

"Eh, watch the tie, man!"

She tugged the silk knot tighter. "Desi boy, think I'd dress on your account?"

Kareem carefully lifted each of her fingers off his double Windsor and pushed her hand down, past his belt buckle. "Come upstairs. I'll drop you back to college when I go to the clubs."

She pulled a face. "Why can't I go with you?"

"It's work, Princess. And your friends're expectin' you, innit?" She rolled her eyes, and he smiled, ran his hands over her bottom and squeezed it gently. "I'm only thinking of you, you know. Taking care of Princess's reputation, yeah."

"I can take care of myself." She slid her fingers under his jacket and pulled him closer so that they stood eye to eye, nose to nose. With her heels on, they were the same height, and she tried to fix his gaze.

"Nine o'clock Tuesday, yaah? Nine."

"Yeah, Princess. I'm all yours. I'll be there."

Only then did Shunduri let him kiss her on the mouth and, by degrees, urge her to the stairwell and inside.

# Three

THE DOORBELL RANG and then, as Rohimun was halfway down the hall to answer it, Simon's key crunched in the lock. She diverted sullenly into the spare bedroom where her easels sat, and that god-awful mess on the two large canvases, gathering dust.

She turned around and went out again, trying not to breathe in the smell of linseed oil and turps. Shutting the door hard, she bumped into Simon, whose arm fell around her and pulled her against him, pinching the skin at her waist.

"Wotcher, love," he said in a parody of a working-class accent, and laughed at his own joke.

He smelled of wine and cigarettes over expensive aftershave, and she thought to herself, I'd rather the turps. He dragged her along with him as far as the kitchen, then seemed to lose interest, dropping the mail he was carrying on the counter and getting out his smokes. Rohimun edged away discreetly, reaching to pull out an envelope from the pile of junk mail and bills. It was large and square, with *Rohimun Choudhury* written in sprawling, elegant handwriting diagonally across the envelope. But Simon, cigarette already wedged between his first and second fingers, twitched it out of her hands.

"What's this, love?" Without waiting for an answer, he tore the envelope so that it ripped halfway through her name, and pulled out a crimson card with black gothic lettering. *Victoria & Albert: Portraits and Studies.* "Ooh," Simon said, his Eton accent taking on a camp *Coronation Street* edge as he looked at the back of the invitation. "*Tommorer. Eye-talian rooms also open.*"

Rohimun was silent. He would only taunt her if she tried to take it back, so she folded her arms and pretended to ignore him while he drew on his cigarette and continued to hold the card out in front of her and read it at his leisure. The new portrait exhibition. Who could have sent it? She'd thought no one at the RCA knew, or cared, where she was now. Old teachers and friends would be there. Hopefully not her former agent, *Inshallah*, for what could she say to him now?

Simon tossed the card in the bin and moved around the counter-top toward the sofa.

She busied herself making tea for them both, but once Simon was lying on the sofa, his second home, a perverse instinct drove her to pick the card out of the bin, place it on the mantelpiece and stand by it, waiting for him to notice. And when he did, he didn't get off the sofa and tear it up, or even say a word. Just turned his face away so that his cheek rested against the sofa cushion, pretending that he hadn't seen a thing.

The TV went on, and Simon popped a downer with his whiskey and talked about his day like he always did, while Rohimun half-heartedly wiped things down in the kitchen. Her eyes kept flicking to the invitation; she knew better than to indicate any desire to attend.

In the end, to escape the boredom, they headed out to the pub to meet up with Simon's friends, Rohimun agreeing for the first time in weeks to tag along, because of a vague idea of larger battles looming. As soon as they arrived, Simon was transformed into the old Simon: public Simon with his porkpie hat tipped over one eye, full of laughter and good cheer, at the center of things. But it was a magic circle that she no longer wished to enter, so Rohimun, relieved to be away from the atmosphere in the flat, balanced on the outer edge of the snug, making small talk to new or less familiar arrivals.

Now that they were out together, she was his *love* as if he meant it, and he was talking about how much he missed her when he was at work, and how they were going to go away together soon, to Amsterdam or Morocco, just the two of them; and his friends were laughing and saying *Never thought you'd settle down* and *Simey, what a sweetie you are, isn't he?* Especially as he was putting his card behind the bar like the big man he was.

He pushed a second double G&T in front of her, and she shook her head, not quite looking at him.

"Oh, *love*," he said, concerned, and put his arm around her, sliding his fingers under her top and pinching the tender skin beneath her breast. She tried not to jump. "Drink up fast, love. You're getting behind."

When she picked up the glass, he kissed her cheek with a hard, smacking motion, and leaned back to laugh at something someone else had said.

Rohimun took a small sip of her drink, then another. Nothing was real here. She could see, more clearly than the blurred faces around her or the ashtrays and dirty glasses collecting on the table, the V&A invitation waiting in the flat, like a drugged-out guest from the night before, or a bill that they had no money to pay.

When they returned home, the thing was still not mentioned, but lay between them as they fucked joylessly, looking past each other. Afterward, she lay awake with her eyes closed. Perhaps it was just a phase they were in now, after the early, heady, can't-keep-their-hands-off-each-other times, the will-do-anything-for-you times, when she'd been so grateful to defer to Simon all the vexed decisions, from how to deal with her agent and what invitations to accept, to what to wear to *gora* functions with their infinite gradations of dress, and when to arrive and leave. It had been so easy to let him steer her from group to group, to hang out with his friends who never asked her why she wasn't painting anymore.

She had never thought, when she'd met him, that she could have been lonelier than she was then, when Tariq, her big brother, two years older and her best friend, had dropped out of her life, all their lives, with no word of warning. From her very first day of primary school, through to those scary early weeks at the RCA, living away from her parents, he had always been there for her, sticking up for her, then supporting her choice of a fine arts degree, the two of them standing firm against Mum's marriage plans and Dad's criticisms.

For Tariq to have gone fundo like that, then disappear altogether, soon after her graduation and the first euphoria of positive reviews and acquiring her own agent and a list of commissions that seemed to be a mile long, had felt like the worst of betrayals. Perhaps he'd thought she no longer needed him. Or perhaps his favorite sister just wasn't that important anymore.

The last time she'd heard Tariq's voice was in a phone message that she'd discovered late the night before her first solo exhibition. She had not recognized his voice at first, the high-pitched, too-loud tone in which he spoke, almost gabbling the words, as if he was on a time limit.

"*Salaamalaikum*, Rohimun, I bid you farewell. I have joined the legion of the soldiers of God, the mujahideen, for the holy jihad. It is the duty of every Muslim and, Rohimun, listen, you must listen, your painting is idolatry and must be put away, you have to cover, live a pious life, and you must tell Mum and Dad, tell them . . ." A wave of static engulfed the line, then cleared. "I have to go. Tell them I've gone away to study. Overseas. Africa." There was a rapid despairing gasp, as if he had run out of air, and the connection severed abruptly.

When she had tried to call him back, all she could get was a mechanical voice telling her that the number was not available. She'd sat in bed and listened to his words again and again, with that terminating gasp, until she found herself breathing with it, gulping for air as it clicked off.

The next day, when she should have been checking the hanging of her pictures, she'd wandered around in a daze. It was with only an hour to go before her first solo exhibition that she'd managed to dress and get out of the flat. How could he do this to her now. Now that she was having doubts, having second thoughts about these paintings of hers that were so popular, so well reviewed and so quickly sold.

She'd turned up late for her own show, shamed by the staring of strangers and resentful at her agent's hissed queries and the expectation that she stand next to her paintings for photos, like a mannequin or a statue. Who was she without her brother to lean on, to tell her that her paintings were good, better, best; to deflect the needy and resist the pushy; and to laugh at this rent-a-crowd who talked to each other with their backs to the artwork and kissed each other without touching.

She felt like she was drowning. Tariq, one of those crazy fundos who went to fight in foreign wars. Pressure, responsibility, loneliness and no one to help her.

Then a man, dark-haired and with Tariq's slender build, breezed into the gallery, half hidden by the crowd, and for an instant she'd thought it'd never happened, here he was. But he came closer, and it wasn't Tariq at all. He was *gora*, not Asian, as pale as a night-worker and walking with a cocky air, as if the crowd was there to see him, looking like a musician or an artist in his tight black jeans and t-shirt, pointy-toed black boots and porkpie hat. He caught her staring at him and held her gaze, kept walking until he was at her side then stood as if he belonged there and called her Princess Jasmine, making her laugh at the Disney reference. He beckoned a waiter over with a salver of glasses holding very yellow champagne, lifted one off and pressed it on her.

"What are you doing here?" he asked.

She didn't say, I'm the artist, these are my paintings—didn't want to say that. She wanted nothing to do with those daubs on the walls with their spreading pox of little red stickers. She was sure he could tell they were rubbish, like all the people there, who were either just being polite or were too stupid to know.

"I'm Rohimun."

"Simon. Drink up, love," he said, with the casual authority of an expert in these matters, and she had drunk then, automatically obedient to his confidence, his sureness of touch, the waiter's deference to his Eton accent. She drank the whole glass down, as if she was a patient in casualty told to take her medicine, or a bride swallowing her sherbet drink, and the yeasty bitterness made the wound of Tariq's condemnation and abandonment throb more softly, for a while.

Simon watched her empty her glass, laughed in the face of her agent's disapproving stare, then spoke softly, close to her ear. "Let's go, love. Let's get out of here. Fuck them, you've had enough of this function."

"I can't."

"Love, you can do anything you want: it's your show. Come with me. They've had enough of you, those vultures."

And he gave her a wide, can-do-anything grin that was surely sympathetic, and she had felt suddenly released from a great burden, flying upward like a diver who had slipped a weight belt and was rising irresistibly to the surface of things. Why should she stay when she hated it so much, felt so uncomfortable?

Afterward, Rohimun had never given a thought to going back. Not even on that first Monday morning when she lay in Simon's bed and watched him put on his suit and transform into a city stockbroker. Not when, a mere two weeks later, Simon, high as a kite, left her at a party while he was chasing some deal and forgot to come back. What was there to go back to anyway? A lonely merry-go-round of more second-rate paintings and more rubbish commissions, or going home to Mum and Dad and letting them marry her off to some Desi optometrist or accountant. She'd made her bed.

If Tariq had been there, the old Tariq, perhaps at least she'd have been able to see the differences between him and Simon. Whatever they were. But then, what was worse: the humorless judgemental fundo prick that Tariq had become, or the revelation of Simon as a snob and a *casra charsi*, a dirty addict? Or indeed, herself: a painter who couldn't paint, a fat whiny girlfriend, a *casra sudary*, dirty slut.

---

WHEN ROHIMUN WOKE late the next day, Simon was still in bed. She should have known that he would take the day off, to keep an eye on her on the day of the exhibition. For the rest of Friday morning, she lay on the very edge of the bed with her eyes closed, feeling the grittiness of unwashed sheets and the thick itch of dirty hair. While she pretended to sleep, tried to ignore Simon's hungover body weighing down the mattress behind her, she thought about the invitation and what it meant. But then he rolled into her back, and she held on to the side of the bed and feigned lumpish unconsciousness as he fumbled with her halfheartedly, trying to jam his half-soft cock between her legs from behind. He soon gave up, giving her one last mean shove before getting up and going into the kitchen.

The sucking kiss of the fridge door and the rattle of ice against glass announced that he was not coming back to bed. She thought of who would be at the V&A tonight, and what she could wear that would not cause trouble, and why she was suddenly so willing to court it at all. The creak of sofa springs from the sitting room was drowned out almost immediately by the staccato cheeriness of television ads, then the thoughtful, reasoned voices of two men.

*There go the seagulls . . .*

*The crowd certainly enjoyed that. And who knows what surprises this player might be bringing to the field today . . .*

*Those seagulls are settling again.*

*Yes, raw talent here, up against a fair bit of aggression . . . could put the selectors off though.*

Rohimun opened her eyes, then squinted, trying not to see the room just yet, instead focusing on a point midway to the window, on the sifting beams of sunlight, in which floated thousands of particles of dust. Wasn't it meant to be skin?

*And there go the seagulls, rising and wheeling to the east . . .*

Thousands and millions of parts of herself and Simon mixed

together and drifting aimlessly. White lead mixed roughly with titanium and barium yellow would give that hazy gleam, with a dry roller rolled softly over the wet paint to break it up, make it both more and less solid.

*I don't know about that first ball. Shades of Murali, if you know what I mean. But the umpire's ignoring it for now.*

How had they come to this? Food going off in the fridge and clothes piling up unwashed because, even though the days seemed endless, there never seemed to be enough time or energy to sort things out.

*It's a perfectly clear blue sky here today at Old Trafford.*

Was their life now, full of daytime TV, takeaway, late-night calls and taxis to meet Simon's dealer or to get the money to pay him, just a temporarily not-so-good phase?

*The test will be the second ball. I don't think the umpire could ignore a second ball like that.*

Now that she looked back, their frantic need to be together, for which she had given away her painting and everything else, seemed to have segued straight into this loveless, grey existence. The wonderful bright joyousness of painting all day, and going out at night with her RCA friends and even the odd one from Brick Lane, had turned into a flat that she felt she hardly left. Simon usually went out on his own now, to meet up with his friends: a lot of Hooray Henry brokers and trustafarians. And she refused to go with him on his twice-weekly visits to the one friend, the essential man, who always answered his mobile, who always had what Simon needed.

*My mistake. It looks like there's just one small cloud here in this blue sky, directly over the batsman in fact, from our point of view in the commentary box . . .*

And no painting at all, because she just didn't seem to be able to begin anymore, and anyway, she had been so stressed in that existence, after she got a name for herself and Tariq went fundo and stopped visiting, and before she and Simon had gotten together, hadn't she? Not knowing how to cope with gallery owners and agents, all the invitations and phone calls. All the trappings of success. Not such a problem now, that was for sure.

*This almost wraps things up before lunch . . .*

Simon had recently started to do a line before leaving the flat on Monday mornings and, from the scraps of foil she found in his jacket pockets, she suspected that he was now using at work as well, perhaps before big meetings or tricky interviews.

*Memories of that brilliant century by Tendulkar . . .*

And for some reason, even when he was at work or asleep on the couch, she could no longer paint, although since yesterday, when the invitation had arrived, she'd found herself pining for it. Like she used to.

*An untraditional choice for the selectors: a high-risk choice, even. Team players have usually been preferred . . .*

She hauled herself to a sitting position just as the televised crowd roared approvingly: someone must have hit a six. She considered going straight to her easel, but she'd already thought about it too much, so she dressed, squeezing into too-tight jeans, then trainers and a hoodie. She walked into the living area, thumped down in an armchair next to the television and contemplated Simon, wanting him to react.

*That cloud's getting bigger . . .*

His left arm was curled around an ashtray on his chest, and from where she sat, she could still smell on him the beer and ash of last night. He stretched out his right hand toward her and beckoned her forward, for a cuddle or a fight. She ignored it and stared at the ashtray.

His other hand moved then, to pull on his cigarette and tap it delicately into the ashtray, a heavy glass one with *Cat & Fiddle* stamped around its sides. *Cat & Fiddle.* Simon must have lifted it from the pub last night. He smiled at her suddenly, and her stomach tensed.

"Catholic and Infidel, eh? I don't forget what you tell me. I don't forget anything."

"I never told you to take it."

"Thought you'd appreciate it. Old times," he said, drawing out the last two words as breathily as if they were the title of a Mills & Boon novel.

*Richie, this day will truly be one for the history books.*

The crowd roared again.

Rohimun could remember, at the beginning, holding forth to Simon, just like her father, about the political significance of old English pub names, how some of them went back to the Crusades and earlier, but she hated to remember talking to him like that, so freely and enthusiastically, how starry-eyed she'd been, how much she'd assumed about his interests and his values. She tried to dispel the memory, the sense of unease and disappointment it evoked. She'd far rather be angry.

She got up, trying to look purposeful, crossed onto the kitchen lino, and opened the fridge door.

"I'll get some milk." She despised herself for needing to say something to ease the tension, give herself an excuse to leave.

"Some smokes too, love." Simon spoke around his cigarette without missing a beat, as if he'd known exactly what she had been going to say before she'd said it.

*Get them yourself, you bastard.* She picked up her purse and shuffled out of the kitchen. *Love* was for charladies and barmaids. She knew now that he'd never call any of the women in his crowd that. Just went to show, didn't it. But Rohimun didn't really want to think any more about what exactly it showed, just wanted to get out into the fresher, cleaner air of the street.

As she turned into the passage, her eyes flicked involuntarily, covetously, to the reassuring, shining square of the V&A invitation above the empty fireplace, like a talisman. Mum was always safety-pinning one of those onto Rohimun's vest before she went to school, especially before exams, or in winter if she had a cold. Little flat boxes of beaten silver sealed with wax, dangling from one of Mum's big nappy pins with a yellow teddy or pink duck on it, pulled out of the pleats of her sari at the last minute. The little boxes held a favored *surah* from the

Qur'an that had been blessed by some village mullah back in Bangladesh and were supposed to protect you from harm, bring good luck. But if it was a PE day, once they were on their way to school, Rohimun would fumble it undone and tuck it in her pocket, to save herself embarrassment in the changing room.

She hesitated at the front door, wanting to go back and pick up the invitation, feel its stiff pasteboard safely between her fingers. But then Simon shifted on the couch, and she stepped out quickly and shut the door before he could decide to keep her company.

Outside, the air was warm, although the sky threatened rain later. Rohimun wandered past the park and the local shops, enjoying the midday dawdling as long as she could avoid the Desi shopkeepers. When she reached the local shopping center and saw the hairdressers just within the entrance, she ducked inside.

They could fit her in. She just had to wait her turn, so she sat and flicked the pages of a magazine, grateful for the clutter and activity. Older women complained comfortably about husbands, and teenage girls with dazzling fluorescent nails bitched about bosses and boyfriends. The hairdresser washed Rohimun's hair, joking about not having a sink big enough, needing a forklift for this lot.

After she muttered something about a wedding, the hairdresser dried it and pulled it back tightly and smoothly in a way Rohimun had never mastered, and coiled and pinned and sprayed it into a monstrous chignon, almost as big as her head. Its tight stiffness was loathsome, but should keep Simon happy, and would be one less thing to worry about tonight. And a clear announcement of her plans.

She spent the rest of the afternoon wandering around the streets trying to avoid her reflection in shop windows, her stomach gradually tightening as the day wore on, and she walked and walked, too on edge to while away the time sitting in a cafe. I don't care, she kept saying to herself. Today is my day, and tonight is going to be mine as well.

## Four

"It's your brother on the line . . ."

Susan's invisible, inimitable voice was hesitant, its pitch rising with the tonality of a question. Very different to her usual brisk neutrality.

Richard Bourne looked at the clean expanse of his desk: only four briefs sitting patiently in the far left corner, a half-full in-box and the desk clock at three forty-five. For the first time in a while, he had no good reason to put Henry off. The hint of judgement from his Chambers' longest-serving secretary gave Richard an extra frisson of irritation. Knowing Henry, he'd have Susan thoroughly onside by now, had probably been sending her birthday cards and asking after her children. If she had any: Richard couldn't quite recall.

"Thank you, Susan." His hand stretched out automatically to put the caller on speaker, then he changed his mind and picked up the receiver. Henry hated speakerphone and always ended up shouting as if he were calling his dogs across a field.

"Richard!" The line sounded as if his brother were in a roadside phone booth in some Third World country, rather than two hours' drive away.

"Henry. How are you? How's the new grant application?" Richard said, pulling the blotter toward himself and flattening its curling edges with his free hand. Amazing how restricting it felt, not having both hands available to fiddle with something.

"Oh, I didn't call about that. But, ah, as you mention it, perhaps you could, you know, when you next come down. The National Trust are so picky . . ."

How Henry had ever finished his degree, Richard did not know. "Shoot the details through to me and I'll get on to it."

The blotting paper was tired and grimy, covered with illegible notations and calculations from his last trial. Richard propped the receiver under his chin and used both hands to edge each corner of the paper out from under its leather frame.

"Why don't you pop down in person this weekend? Or if that doesn't suit, maybe next. It's been a while. You'd want to see what's been done with the Abbey outbuildings. All the lath and plasterwork completely restored, using all the old methods. Absolutely brilliant."

"I've seen the plans: they're looking good, all credit to you. And the builders' report."

The old blotter was completely free now. Richard folded it on his knee one-handed, as quietly as he could, and wedged it into his waste-paper basket.

"Nothing like seeing it in the flesh though. And the sunken garden is amazing: looks like there used to be a well in the middle. Come on, Richard, you deserve the weekend off. Thee and the boys, they haven't seen you in ages."

Richard picked up his fountain pen, wiped the sides of its nib on the pristine blotter, and started to turn the resulting smears of deep-blue ink into something more symmetrical. His recent run of back-to-back trials had finished, and the current briefs could be put off easily enough.

"Is Deirdre still around? You could bring her too, you know, or whoever. We could make do, and use the put-me-up. Or just come for the day."

"It's not really Deirdre's thing." To put it mildly. Deirdre in the country, Deirdre sleeping on a camp bed, Deirdre sharing a family bathroom were things unimaginable. Richard raised his eyebrows at the thought. "Look, I'll think about it. Perhaps I could manage a day. How're the boys?"

"Fantastic. Never better. Jonathon's going to be as tall as you, I think. And Andrew's turning into a killer footballer. So, you'll come?"

"I'll let you know."

There was a small uncharacteristic pause: Henry was usually so keen to fill in every conversational gap.

"Thee's missing you too, you know. She always perks up when you come down."

The line was tinny and faint, but even so, Henry's voice seemed to have gone unusually flat. Richard frowned and lifted his gaze to the blue and gold Persian rug on the wall opposite: Bourne Abbey's only contribution to his Chambers. Beautiful—though it had never looked entirely comfortable with the cool minimalism of the rest of the fittings.

No point in asking Henry if anything else was wrong; he was never one to come to the point, particularly over the phone. He would just warble on about the weather and the dogs and what was nesting in the hedgerows. If there was anything awry, Richard would have to visit in person. And he had been remiss lately.

"Look, I'll try to get down this month. Or thereabouts." He heard a breath taken in: Henry wanting to pin him down, lock in a definite date. He quickly cut in. "I have to go, Henry. I'll call you next week."

Henry didn't object, but after Richard had hung up he left his hand sitting on the receiver, wondering if he'd been too abrupt. It was true: his trips home were getting to be rarer, more easily put off. Maybe he would go down next weekend. Depending.

The phone rang again, just as the clockface flicked to 4:00. Susan's calm tones echoed slightly on the speakerphone.

"Richard, I have Felicity Harporth holding for you on the Reid matter. This is the third time she's called today. Would you like me to take a message?"

Richard suppressed a sigh. Some instructing solicitors were needier than others, and Felicity was a wonderful example of that genus.

"No, thank you, Susan. Put her through."

"Richard, thank you *so* much for giving me a moment so late in the week: it's in relation to the Reid Family Trust matter. We just received your formal advice this morning and the Reids have already been in to discuss it. They are *very* keen to reduce Trust payments to their son to the minimum, as soon as possible. I was hoping to meet with you regarding what, ah, what you think the minimum would be, given the family. The rich are not like the rest of us, you know."

"I'm happy to do that. Perhaps a meeting with the Reids present as well?" Felicity did sound more than keen to pass him this particular hot potato.

"That would be *most* satisfactory and—"

"I'll leave it to the capable Susan to organize the time. I'll look forward to seeing you then." He paused. Some further direction was needed, especially as Felicity tended to be driven by her clients. "I would agree with you that this is a very difficult situation for the Reids: they will need to be considering all the implications, legal and otherwise, of any decision that they may make."

"Oh, yes, but they're *so* happy that—"

"Yes. I'll look forward to meeting with you all, at that date to be fixed."

"Thank you *so* much, Richard. The clients are *most* happy with—"

"You're welcome, Felicity. Enjoy the weekend. Goodbye."

That must be some kind of a record for getting Felicity off the phone. The Reids were messed up as only the rich knew how, as Felicity herself might have said. And even now, with all that had happened, thinking that if they paid out enough money, held the purse strings tightly enough, that they could somehow fix their son up into the man they wanted him to be, rather than the well-dressed parasite that he was.

Four demands for additional funds the son had made in the last six months: all granted because the old family solicitor was as weak as dishwater and far too in awe of the family to say no to anything. At least Felicity was one step up from that. But she was clearly not managing her clients' expectations, so he was going to have to do it for her: ensure that the Reids were fully apprised of the fact that this was a lose-lose situation, however much was paid to solicitors and barristers.

The bad news coming from him would probably be taken better and be less likely to taint the solicitor–client relationship. He would have to think very carefully about moving the Reids' focus away from his own initial, purely legal advice that they could make all further extra Trust payments conditional upon their son's attendance at some expensive private rehabilitation center. And shift it to the extra-legal consequences: that, chances were, the fashionable rehabilitation center attended under duress would become a revolving door, leading inevitably to further demands for money, escalating threats from the parents and then complete estrangement.

*He is lost to you either way*, was the thing Richard could not say. *You can't save people from themselves. I should know. The Trust money, whatever you do with it, fixes nothing.* He thought of the young man who was the sole beneficiary of the Trust. *You will be fielding abusive phone calls from your own son, or hearing how he lied to and stole from your friends and relatives to feed his various addictions, and then be reduced to fighting him through the courts for the Trust money.* Just goes to show: family can be productive of the greatest misery of all.

Enough. He was leaving early today. He swept the mail into his bag, locked his room and took the long way out, strolling through the muddled privacy of courtyards, laneways and mews that made up the Inns of Court. He would pick up a cab to South Kensington and meet Deirdre for drinks at Bluebeard's, a new wine bar she'd heard about down that way.

Richard stopped by one of the Middle Temple's grassed areas, dropping his bag on the gravel to light a cigarette and lean on the heavy iron railing. Nice to see a bit of green. It was not often that he felt like a break from London, but this latest run of briefs, all dealing in one way or another with family schisms over debt and infidelity, had left him feeling sour and stale. What a walking disaster some families were. Maybe all families, once you scratched the surface. He straightened up and flicked the half-finished cigarette onto the gravel. Time to go: he'd said five and it was just past, and redheads would spoil if kept waiting too long.

————————

BY THE TIME Richard arrived at the wine bar, it was clear that, despite the early start, Deirdre had already had a few drinks. As usual, she was at the center of her crowd of gallery owners and art aficionados and the odd city suit. Her head was tilted back, and she was laughing at something with every appearance of abandon, but still managed to reach out a long arm to snag his, saying, "Doubles, darling. Late as usual and I've such a thirst on me."

Since their last Friday, she had changed her hair. It was the same brilliant artificial red but now in a high bob that made her white neck seem even longer. In leggings and boots and a white smock belted on the hip, she looked like a cross between a flapper and a cutting-edge Joan of Arc, out to conquer the philistine hordes. Or at least sell them some art. Deirdre was using a cigarette holder, to great effect, if the mesmerized gaze of a couple of the suits was anything to go by.

She looked eminently fuckable, and Richard willingly gave the requisite public kiss, full on the lips but not hard enough to disturb the lipstick. Some of the men, but not all, moved back a little in acknowledgement of the kiss, and Deirdre stretched out a leg and hooked a barstool for him. He shook his head. This was not the place to be for more than one drink. There was totty moving in on the stockbrokers at the other end of the bar, and he was fairly sure that he could recognize an instructing solicitor, who had pursued him for dinner to the point of embarrassment, working her way toward him.

But Deirdre's glossy mock pout made it clear that she was not to be budged. Drinks were almost always work for her dealership as well as play, and some important artwork sale was clearly afoot or being celebrated. Or she was wanting to warm them up into a purchasing mood for the V&A exhibition. He hadn't asked Deirdre if any of her artists were exhibiting, or schmoozing, there tonight. Either way, dinner looked to be some time off, and he was hungry. Or perhaps just bored. He balanced his drink on a high table and buried his hands in his pockets to hide his irritation at the commitment he had made to attend the exhibition. Even if they only stayed an hour, it would be well after eight o'clock before they could leave. And Deirdre being Deirdre, she would be reluctant to leave until the bitter end. He had visions of relying on canapés and cocktail olives for his evening meal, and his stomach gave a dissatisfied rumble.

After another round of drinks and anecdotes, Richard pulled out his cigarettes to make a temporary escape. But Deirdre, suddenly amenable, announced to all that it was time they headed off, and followed him outside, trailed by some of the suits. She stole his lit cigarette as they began to walk the few blocks to the V&A.

"Anyone special in this exhibition then?"

"Not really, darling. There's one artist I'm hoping to catch up with. I delivered the invitation to her flat myself yesterday, but she's just the type to leave early if she comes at all. I've heard Nigel dropped her from his list. If I can commission something from her direct for some of my buyers, I'll save myself thirty percent."

Richard half listened as Deirdre talked on through the swishing of rush-hour traffic on wet streets. A misty rain was falling, and by the time they could see the main entrance of the V&A, the only spot of color was a yellow awning over a distinctly soggy red carpet.

He threw away his cigarette and ducked his head under the awning's lip to join the queue, then realized that the main doors were not even opened yet. They were half an hour early, which never happened with Deirdre. When he looked around, she had left him to chat to some people further up the line. He watched, caught between amusement and irritation, as she took the long way in order to go past the bank of photographers waiting stoically just outside the awning's shelter. He put his hands in his pockets, bracing himself for the rising grey tide of boredom. Why was he here, again?

# Five

WHEN ROHIMUN HAD returned from the shops, as late as she possibly could, Simon was still lying on the couch, a whiskey glass next to the ashtray on his chest, watching *Countdown* in a fug of ganja smoke. She'd walked past, with her head up, bracing for his comments, which never came, then continued awkwardly to the bathroom, her jaw aching with tension, the retorts she had been holding ready for him trembling in her mouth. "Well, fuck you, I'm going," she'd whispered to herself as she quickly showered and began dressing in the bathroom with the door locked. "You can't stop me."

But here she was, still carefully choosing the kind of clothes that Simon would be least likely to object to: a black cocktail dress that he'd bought for her ages ago, and high heels. The dress was far too tight, she should have known, and she could feel herself starting to get warm as she scrambled into it, anxious about the time. So close now.

Finally, Rohimun stood up straight, sucked in her stomach, took a firm hold of the dress's side zip, gingerly pulled it upward and for once it ran smoothly from hip to underarm. She felt hot and uncomfortable and exposed, but if it avoided any arguments and got her into the V&A without a drama, it would be worth it.

When she came out into the sitting room, Richard Whiteley's audience still screamed and cheered, but Simon was gone, thank god, probably to the pub. The invitation remained on the mantel, and Rohimun kept her eye on it as she picked up the phone and ordered a mini-cab. But as she put down the receiver, Simon swaggered out of the bedroom, cigarette smoke swirling around him like a pantomime villain. He was in his dinner jacket, freshly shaved and with his hair spiked. Her heart jumped in her chest, and she retreated to the kitchen and pretended to wipe the counter.

He started to move in her direction, and she froze, clutching the cloth in one hand, while her other hand, down by the cupboard door, clenched into a fist. Was it one of Tariq's friends that had told her, years ago, always tuck your thumb under your fingers if you're going to punch someone? She couldn't remember.

"You ready then, love?" Simon diverted to the mantel, plucked the invitation, then moved to the other side of the countertop and looked at her with reddened eyes, posing theatrically with the spliff-end held up between his fingertips. He flicked it toward her.

She met his eyes and refused to flinch as it flew and fell, just short of her, into the kitchen sink.

He gave an odd, angry giggle. "You're trussed up like a Christmas ham." He leaned forward, still staring at her, and hawked noisily and spat on the spliff-end.

She was gripping the cloth so tightly that it was dripping water onto her foot. This was it. She took a breath, to finally tell him that she wasn't scared of him, that he was a *casra charsi*, a sponger on his parents, the son of a dog. But then she felt a movement under her arm and looked down to see the zip, still closed, tear away from her dress's seam from bust to waist. Her flesh, imprinted with the fabric's tight ruching, bulged immediately and triumphantly through like a rising omelette. Simon started to laugh but stopped, as if overcome by tact.

"It's all that butter chicken, love. Look, dressing up's just not your thing. Why don't you put your jammies on and watch the box." He rested one hip companionably against the countertop, his voice gentle, mock-understanding, as he picked a fleck of cigarette paper from his lip. "I'll go on ahead, love, tell you all about it."

Rage rose in her, but she had lost the words that she was going to say. She could see the invitation's red slash above his black-jacketed heart. Simon was looking elsewhere, lighting a cigarette and brushing some ash off his lapel close to the invitation, as if by coincidence. She dropped the cloth into the sink and walked to the bedroom with as much dignity as she could muster. As she reached the bedroom door she called out, "I'm still going." Her voice sounded half strangled, but at least she'd managed to get the words out.

As soon as she was inside, she crossed her arms, seized the bottom hem of the dress and pulled it straight up over her head. It stuck half-way off, and she thrashed and pulled at the fabric, surrounded by ripping sounds, until it came loose, her chignon raining hairpins and shifting to the side of her head. In the mirror she looked like some kind of demented conjoined twin. She swore again, dropped the dress on the floor, kicked off the stilettos and started to rake her fingers through the remains of the ruined chignon, pulling it to pieces. Fuck him, and fuck this shitty *gora* hairstyle. Hairsprayed chunks of hair stood up at unnatural angles and crackled as she brushed fiercely. Now she looked like Bride of Frankenstein. Her fingers flying, she plaited it into one long thick braid and snapped a hair elastic over the end. Done.

She ransacked the wardrobe, then the chest of drawers, for something, anything, that she would still be able to fit into, but everything was too casual or too dirty or too small. How ridiculous that she of all people was having a clothes crisis. In despair, she spotted an orange and pink sari and blouse of her mother's, at the bottom of her old college duffel bag. God knows how long it had been there, but it wouldn't need ironing, or squeezing into. And she could lose the too-small strapless bra that burnt like fire across her back.

Rohimun's hands shook as she fastened the hooks and eyes on the blouse and folded the sari pleats. She pinned them flat with one of Mum's yellow, duck-shaped nappy pins, found lying at the very bottom of the bag, and which brought tears to her eyes as she tucked it inside her waistline. She couldn't face putting the heels back on, so slipped on her everyday flat Indian sandals. That would have to do.

When she came out, Simon was standing by the open front door, methodically kicking it with the toe of one shoe so that it rattled against the wall. He stared at her, swinging her handbag on his forefinger and chewing gum with a rapid, unceasing, almost violent motion.

"You going to bring some takeaway? Hand out the pappadams while we're there?"

She ignored him and edged past, gingerly retrieving her bag and trying not to think about what else he'd taken while she was changing. Just let her get there tonight.

Outside, a dirty orange mini-cab was waiting. The driver, a big Rasta in Adidas, was filling most of the front. Not Asian or Muslim, thank god. Simon could pick them as easily as her now, loved their reaction when they saw him with Rohimun, would goad them with references to bacon breakfasts and getting pissed. Then she would try to ignore their open contempt or, even worse, their efforts to bring her back on the true path of Islam, sister, while Simon would listen, his forehead wrinkled with simulated sincerity and concern.

The mini-cab ride was tense and quiet, except for Simon blowing contemplative raspberries between bouts of chewing. His left arm lay all the way along the top of the seat, so she could not lean back. In that hand he was holding the invitation, and every so often he flicked it so that its edge dragged against the back of her neck. Rohimun tried not to think about making a grab for it and perched forward, balancing against the car's cornering.

At a red traffic light around Soho, she stared out the cab's windscreen, past the driver's eyes in the rear-view mirror. Ahead on the left was a recessed doorway partway down an alley, perhaps a nightclub entrance. Above it a neon light shed a dirty yellow, the color of old urine, its looping script spelling out *Mecca*. For that shade, deep cadmium yellow mixed with a smudge of lamp black, put on with a thin, dried-out brush so that the texture was flawed, scratchy. The card flicked against her nape and she could not suppress a shudder.

"What is it, love? What's the matter?"

The cab moved on, and soon they were out the front of the V&A, and Simon was in a hurry to get out. He left her to pay the driver, then wriggle awkwardly out of the back seat, sari skirt wrapping around her sandals.

He was holding open the door of the cab with the tips of two fingers but would not acknowledge her, was waving instead at a group further on: some of his stockbroker mates were here in their perfect dinner suits, with their perfect blonde girlfriends that always seemed to be at these things. Well, fuck you, fuck all of you, she thought. She'd go in on her own. But then she remembered that he was holding the invitation so she was stuck with trailing behind Simon as he caught up with his mates. She exchanged fake smiles with a lot of tall skinny blonde *gora* totty girlfriends—well, what other kind of totty was there—she being the ethnic mascot for the night.

She hung back on the edge of the group as they chatted and laughed, looked longingly toward the main entrance. The doors weren't open yet, but the red carpet, already dark from the rain, had been laid in one wide strip from the road and up the middle of the steps to the main doors. It was partially covered by a yellow plastic awning, bright under the streetlights. More people of Simon's type, men in suits and dinner jackets, and long-legged women in silver and black and grey, wandered under the awning in apparent disregard of a small group of dishevelled men sitting on deckchairs taking photographs.

Something was digging in under her blouse: it felt like one of Mum's spare safety pins. She turned away from Simon and his lot, trying to run a finger under the shoulder of her blouse without being too obvious, and caught the eye of one of the security guards, a Sikh, looking at her like she was from another planet. Thanks, she already knew that.

Flashbulbs were going off: someone must have arrived, and now Simon and his posse had disappeared. Rohimun scanned the gathering. There they were, almost inside, all heading up the steps together. Despising herself, she scuttled after them to catch up, her bag banging unrhythmically against her bottom, but as she ran, another group of people moved in front of her, blocking her way. The crowd on the red carpet had become a queue for the doors, opened now, and she stopped and rose awkwardly amongst them on tiptoes, just in time to see Simon present her invitation to security and disappear inside. Blank backs hemmed her in, and she whispered *you bastard* as she stood her ground, angry and at a loss.

But then the group just in front of her exploded into noisy meet-and-greets with another group and she, blessing her shortness for once, edged forward with them, past the security guard and inside. The crowd had seemed large before, but within the first exhibition room, it was diminished by the room's enormous proportions: oompa-loompas in a room for giants. People spread out and started to cluster into small bands, kissing and laughing.

The roiling anger in her gut that had seen her through the taxi ride and onto the red carpet seemed to have subsided and she felt oddly lighthearted. *Seize the day*, as Tariq used to say. Rohimun lifted her eyes to the room's vaulted Victorian wedding-cake ceiling, eighteen feet high, scrolled and curlicued and coved and acanthused in a multitude of whites: zinc white, antique, palest violet, ivory and cream; a tumbling shadowed richness of tones and shades that leapt up from the deep red walls like seafoam on blood.

And then there were the paintings. Rohimun started to walk around the edges of the room, avoiding the cocktailed people trying to compete by volume alone with Crivelli, Raphael, Michelangelo. Monumental figures lifting, straining, stretching, bulging eyes focused on the utterly immediate or the unutterable vision. This was where she belonged. Flesh was everywhere: huge muscled arms, backs and thighs. The women were no less monumental: gigantic pearly or tawny stomachs, breasts and buttocks, their hair curling and cascading. Nakedness was the obvious and inevitable state. Clothes were an unrestricting, almost ephemeral afterthought: ready to tear apart, fall off, drift away at the slightest movement or, indeed, even an excess of emotion.

Rohimun sighed. Not one thin, hair-straightened blonde amongst them. Or a single skinny-bottomed stockbroker. She wandered further, into the next room, her sandals making pleasant shushing slaps on the marble floor.

The portrait exhibition was not yet open, but she was more than happy to see these paintings first, her old friends. Bodies as landscape, rolling hills of flesh, clouds of hair, the fishy gleam of bulging, still-life eyes. How tired she had been, still was, of her own portraits, of London It-girls, gap-year royals, young MPs with an eye on posterity. She was tired of mixing white lead and yellow ochre and red oxide for rosy or pasty skin tones, then puddling white lead and interference violet for shade. She was tired of long arms in custom-made shirts, little pointy noses and puffy lips that had been made not born, tailored suits and the one discreet piece of "statement" jewelry. *Statement, my arse.* This was not Raphael or Michelangelo, where the body was a natural wonder. This was painting as décor, faces as Plasticine. She may as well have been putting Vaseline on a camera lens. No wonder she wasn't painting anymore.

When Rohimun had had her fill, she walked slowly back to the first room. Simon had his arms tucked around two of the totties, posing for a photo. The camera flashed as all three did the half-gasp so beloved of fashion wannabes. Rohimun grimaced: cameras brought out more fakery than a paintbrush ever did. Or maybe it was just harder to maintain the illusion for the multiple sittings that her portraits took. Something real was bound to show itself in all that time. Although the end result was still largely rubbish.

She turned back to a favorite Raphael, painted in reverse for a Sistine tapestry. The disciples were portrayed as rough and solid fishermen, pulling on nets and gobsmacked by the size of their haul. The delicate Christ figure sat passively at the end of one boat, knelt to by sunburnt, muscled peasants. She remembered this story from school:

the prophet Christ telling his disciples to become fishers of men. To leave their livelihoods of honest toil, their families and traditions, for lives of isolation and suffering, glory and miracles.

Did Raphael ever miss the village in which he'd been born, the dialect of his childhood, as he lived in the holy city and painted to order for the Vatican? What had he, the son of peasant farmers, thought of the corrupt wealth of cardinals? Rohimun thought of her mother, wanted to ask her how she'd felt about what she'd left behind, if it had all been worthwhile.

And what of Rohimun's own pilgrimage? To London and commercial success as a portrait painter. Had this path led inevitably to Simon and his kind? To burning out as an artist? It hadn't happened to Raphael. Not that she knew. He'd painted his best after he achieved success, had never returned to the village of his birth. Not that was recorded, anyway. She sighed again. *Fuck the Masters. I must paint like Rohimun Choudhury at her best. If I can paint at all.*

---

RICHARD HAD LOST Deirdre in the crush immediately inside, but was quite happy to avoid the air-kissing hysteria of the first fifteen minutes of Deirdre's arrival anywhere. Rent-a-crowd would be off in half an hour anyway, especially as the word seemed to be that Lucian Freud was a no-show to open the exhibition, and some arts administrator in Chanel and a stiff blonde bob was standing in for him. Predictably, all Richard could think about was a nice quiet smoke. Why had he ever agreed to this? The numbers around the doors were thinning now, so it would be easy enough to head outside. By the time he got back to the main entrance, it was empty except for a turbaned security guard, who nodded at him as he passed outside.

It was raining properly now, but there was a sheltered spot a few feet to the right of the main doors. He lit up a smoke, noticing that the guard was also enjoying a discreet cigarette. The air was cool and sweet, and cars hurried past, gleaming darkly. He considered his options, thought about when he would have to return and get caught up with Deirdre's crowd again, and tried to calculate just how pissed off Deirdre would be if he didn't go back in at all.

––––––––––

A HAND LANDED on Rohimun's neck, squeezing the flesh, then pinching the little hairs on her nape.

"*Love.*"

She froze, made herself keep looking at the Raphael. In a light summer sky, ravens circled. Faded by time of course. They would have been much darker, more dramatically contrasting, when freshly painted.

"Give me your purse," said Simon. "That's a bloody awful hairdo. You could clean the toilet with it."

She turned toward him as he took hold of her handbag. His eyes were bright and his top lip, near the nose, was pinkish and glistening. She felt a surge of disgust. He must have done a few lines just now, in the cloakroom or the toilet, having stashed the rest in her purse for later. *Her* purse. Without thinking, she pulled back viciously on the straps of her handbag and stepped away from him.

"You fuckin' *bitch*," he shouted, making her jump, his face suddenly much closer to hers, dark red and screwed up, like a shrunken, concentrated version of himself.

He put his other hand on the bag as well and hauled her toward him. Her soft sandals struggled for grip on the floor, and Rohimun twisted away. Then the strap broke, and she lost her balance and would have fallen but for Simon's arms yanking her against him and spinning her around in some kind of monstrous waltz.

She could hear the rustle and shift of attention in the room, and with a surge of shame leaned into Simon. His head bent down as if to whisper endearments, pale blue eyes focused on hers. Then he let go of her and pushed her hard with the heel of his hand on her sternum. She staggered sideways and came up against a man's shirtfront. He grasped her forearms, held her up, and she looked up into his face. Tariq.

Gasps and smothered laughter ran around the room, along with a comment about it being a bit early for a domestic.

Simon's voice, shrill with need and anger and self-justification, rose above it all. "She's pissed!"

Baiyya, big brother, clean-shaven and in a dinner jacket as she'd never seen him, while she was dishevelled and still reeling from Simon's pseudo-embrace. Tariq turned his gaze away from her and toward Simon. She felt sick to her stomach. After almost two years away, Tariq comes back now? For this?

Slowly and awkwardly she sank down, until one knee, then the other, was on the checkered marble floor. She stared at the two men. Such stillness, with Simon standing in front of the avid exhibition-goers, and her beautiful, beardless brother to one side of him, an arm outstretched toward her, though his eyes were turned away. For one strange second she was outside of it all and could see their trio with her painter's eye: a tableau, classically balanced, with all the whirling color and activity of the red-carpeted arrivals visible behind them.

———

THE BUZZ OF the exhibition crowd, audible to Richard through the open doors, suddenly quieted then was broken by an angry shout, followed by the rising murmur of people with something to talk about.

"Oh, man," said the guard. He looked at his half-finished cigarette, then dropped it onto the flagstones and walked quickly toward the main doors.

Richard followed, telling himself that another hour of the opening was still preferable to spending all Saturday placating Deirdre. Once inside, the guard pushed without hesitation through a wall of backs. Richard stopped near the door, keeping the guard in sight. From where he was, he could see over people's heads to the two men that the crowd had circled.

An Asian man in a dinner suit, his face set and angry and as impossibly handsome as a magazine model's, was standing over a young woman on the floor. She sat awkwardly on one hip, an orange and pink sari piled around her, breathing quickly, her soft features blank and slack-looking. One hand gripped a thick braid that hung over her shoulder, its end brushing the floor. Richard edged forward without thinking. Was she hurt? Sick? The other man was shorter, with gelled hair, his face flushed and angry-looking. But the guard was watching the Asian man, as if he were the greater threat but also almost as if waiting on his word to act. The crowd had stilled again, waiting also.

Someone's mobile phone beeped, and then all was noise and motion. Gelled-hair turned toward the girl and, just as Richard took another step, the Asian man moved swiftly, his shoulder colliding with gelled-hair with enough force to make them both grunt, and to knock the shorter man off-balance. He crashed to the ground on his back, his face, white as paper now, framed by a black tile. Someone in the crowd called out in an encouraging way, as if this were the entertainment for the night. The guard put a hand to his radio, watching the two men intently.

The Asian man pulled the girl up with one quick movement that also seemed to propel her, sliding and skidding on the marble floor, through the parting crowd and toward the main doors, keeping a tight hold on her all the while. Short and plump, she only came up to his shoulder, and was struggling to keep up with his long strides.

Richard followed just behind them, the guard catching up with him at the doors.

"Aah," the guard said warningly, one hand patting the radio on his shoulder, which was squawking like a fractious baby.

"That's family trouble for sure. Best to let them go, man."

The couple ran down the carpeted steps as if pursued, and for a second the girl looked back over her shoulder, her face, lit up against the darkening sky by the light through the glass doors, distraught and fearful. Beneath the yellow awning, the sari's colors brightened, and the fabric's loose end rippled and flew back from her shoulder toward him.

As they left the carpet for the pavement, she seemed to stumble and the man half picked her up, swept her along past the few remaining photographers, flashbulbs going off, and they disappeared down the street.

Richard followed in their wake until he reached the photographers, who were packing up their equipment. One of them was trying to wave down a taxi. When he saw Richard looking down the street, he shouted, "They're long gone, mate. He had a car."

Richard offered him a cigarette. "Do you know who they were?"

The man waved energetically at a taxi that drove past without stopping, then shook his head in disgust. "Nah. Gatecrashers, maybe. Protesters. Somethin' like that. Jaysus, what does it take to get a cab."

Another photographer appeared, younger than the rest, coming back from the direction in which they'd gone. "That's that Paki girl-friend of one of the Trust-fund boys, I fink. Took a shot through the side window."

"Well, aren't you the lucky one," one of the other photographers jeered. "That'd be worth a bit, Asian girl in a car. Never seen that before."

"Just fuckin' jealous you are. Too old and fat to run for it now."

Richard turned away and retraced his steps, unsettled by the quick drama and mystery of it all. The guard was still at the top of the stairs, drawing on a fresh cigarette with a contemplative air. Richard stopped near him, unable to let it alone. "What do you think happened in there? To start the fight."

"It was over that girl, yeah."

"So they weren't gatecrashers?"

"No, no." The guard gave him a reproachful look. "All invited." He turned and went inside.

Richard stayed outside to finish his cigarette, mildly disgusted at his own nosiness. Was his own life so boring that he had to stick his nose into other people's now? The girl was probably fine. Her face flashed into his mind again, as she'd looked back, her round face, the full bottom lip, with its deep central crease. He walked toward the entrance and into a burst of laughter and talking, and Deirdre on her way out with a couple of her stockbrokers in tow.

She gave a small shriek when she saw him. "Darling, how clever of you! I'm famished, *so* ready to eat something after all that excitement. There's nothing left to wait for now, and I know *you're* starving." She walked him back outside and, after waving the suits into a taxi, skipped over to him. "How about a curry? On second thoughts, all that *fat.*"

She waved again at the departing taxi, which appeared to be receiving conflicting directions.

The taxi sped off, then braked and performed a U-turn before passing them again.

Deirdre's long fingers hooked into his arm and pulled him out from under the awning. "So, Japanese, then? I know this *darling* little place."

Richard turned to face her, took her other arm and walked her backward until she was up against the gallery wall, in the shadows, and pressed to him hip to hip. He reached behind her and hooked his hand under her bottom to pull her against his groin, then slid his hand under the hem of the smock and against her crotch. Her mouth opened, and he kissed her hard, spreading the lipstick.

"Takeaway, your place. Let's get a taxi."

His fingers were inside her before the taxi had gone a block. The urgency of his desire almost kept them in the lift and, then again, against the door to her flat, only prevented by her leggings.

When the key was finally fumbled into the lock and they staggered inside, Deirdre pulled away, wanting to shower, to slip into lingerie, her usual routine, wanting the latest purchase praised, but he didn't let her.

A swift upright fuck with her legs around his waist followed in the entryway, with Richard almost instantly dissatisfied, wanting more, trying to carry her into the sitting room. But as he stopped to disentangle himself from suit trousers and shoes she fled laughing to the bathroom. He stripped off and followed her, but by then she was in the shower. She beckoned him in, but the sight of her body leaning against the glass, attenuated by the steam to a minimalist sketch of womanhood, strangely only made his desire fade. He padded out to the kitchen, wondering whether he would have time for a smoke before Deirdre had finished her shower, primed herself with moisturizer and perfume, and climbed into the newest bit of satin and lace. As it turned out, it was two cigarettes and a coffee before she returned, in latex.

## Six

TARIQ DROVE THE rental car hard, his arms straight, going fast now that they were on the motorway. Dashboard lights drained color from his face and forearms, and made Rohimun remember a scene from some old black-and-white movie in which the hero was slowly descending an endless ladder into a bottomless pit.

She shivered, but could not bring herself to turn on the heater. Her sternum and right hip felt bruised and tender. The important thing was to be still. And quiet. If she didn't say or do anything, nothing would happen. Baiyya, big brother, wouldn't ask anything of her, tell her what he thought, what he was going to do with her. They would just keep driving through the darkness, getting further and further away from London.

When they'd left the V&A, she'd been faint with shame and fear, utterly unable to think what would happen to her next. Tariq had dragged her to a shiny white car and bundled her into the front passenger seat and slammed the door behind her.

As Tariq had got into the driver's seat, there had been a blinding double flash through her window: a photographer must have caught up with them. Her brother had thrown the car into gear and accelerated away, and had not spoken or looked at her since.

It had taken them forever to get out of central London, caught in the web of Friday-night traffic, and she kept thinking that Simon would be at the next intersection. But when they eventually merged into the constant swinging speed of the motorway, it brought her no relief.

Now Tariq was saying something about coffees, and he pulled into a service station and got out before she could say, no, please don't leave me. As soon as the driver's door closed, she central-locked the doors and shrank down in her seat, keeping her eyes on her fingers, which she clenched on her lap, then spread out, then clenched again.

The angry rattle of the driver's door handle made her jump, and she leaned across the car to fiddle hopelessly with the handle before she remembered she'd locked it. Tariq slid back into his seat, a steaming polystyrene cup in each hand.

"Munni," he said. "Take these."

Her pet name, little Munni, from ever since she could remember. God, how long since she'd heard that from him.

"Munni. The coffees." Tariq fished in his pockets and pulled out a handful of sugar sachets, tearing them open and emptying three or four into her cup, then the same into his. He never used to have sugar.

He drank his coffee quickly, holding the cup in his left hand as if in the habit of keeping the right hand free. Rohimun watched him as she held her coffee, still far too hot to drink. Tariq here, back in the UK, after so long. Had he known she would be at the V&A tonight? Had Mum and Dad sent him? She shuddered again, pushed the thought away.

Tariq had lost some puppy fat along with the beard, looked taller and thinner, but fit. Wiry, that was the word, with his face and hands darker, more weathered. His alertness, the impression that he gave of physical readiness, was also new. Perhaps this was manhood, after so many years of being a student. His old impatience was still there though, not far below the surface: one quick drum of his fingers, which he then suppressed until she managed to finish her coffee.

No more words were exchanged until after they had set off again.

"So, you knew him, yeah?"

"Yeah." She forced herself to sip the coffee. Despite the burning shame, some *shaitan*, some devil inside her would not let her lie. He may as well know the worst. "He was my boyfriend."

"Jesus."

He glared at the windscreen, shifted up a gear and merged from the slip road into the busy motorway traffic. Rohimun swallowed, her palate sore from the scalding drink, wrapped one hand around the sash of her seatbelt, the other protectively across her stomach, and waited for what she knew was inevitable. The explosion of rage, the slaps, perhaps a beating.

Lubna from school had lost the hearing in her left ear after her father had caught her sitting in a cafe with a boy: he had driven her home without a word, taken her to the landing and thrown her down the stairs. Tariq, unlike many of his friends, had never raised a hand to his sisters. But there had never been a matter of family honor before. He couldn't do much while he was driving, though. It would be stopping that would be dangerous. Oddly enough, the thing that scared her most was the thought of Tariq taking her back to Simon. Or Simon finding her. She felt sick at the thought of that photographer, of the scene at the V&A; that would surely mean payback.

Tariq glanced at her, then away before she could meet his eyes. "This is going to kill Mum and Dad."

The relief: he was taking her home. The shame. Rohimun felt her eyes well up, and she started to search fruitlessly for a tissue.

She heard Tariq puff out a sigh. "Munni. I didn't mean it like that."

"It's alright. You're right anyway, Bai." Rohimun found a paper napkin and pressed it against her eyes. "I don't know . . . I can't think what to say." God, how could she face her parents?

"I'll talk to Dad. Mum will want to talk to you though."

"No. Not tonight." She shivered and pushed her body further back into the seat. "I can't talk about this. I can't, I can't. Couldn't you talk to her? Please, Bai?"

He frowned, but his eyes were glittering and liquid.

She reached out, hope in her heart, and awkwardly brushed her hand, sticky with her own tears, across his fingers on the gearstick. "Please, Bai. I just can't face Mum tonight. You know what she's like. Please."

They were off the motorway now, and the narrow country road was bounded by ditches of featureless, deepest black that made her feel as if the roadmetal on which they travelled was detached, floating above the countryside through which they passed. The road itself had become a series of sweeping blind curves, unlit except by the head-lights. She shivered again, and this time Tariq reached out and flicked the heater up.

"I just wish I'd had some idea. All this time away . . ." He hit the steering wheel with the heel of his palm, and she could not stop herself from flinching. "I don't understand how this happened. It's not like he's some village *gundah* straight out of Bangladesh. Or a pub-man. He looks like an educated boy, high-class family."

"Yeah, very high class. High-class bullshit." She winced at Tariq's startled look. "Sorry, Bai."

"So why didn't you just leave him?"

"I did, a few months ago. I went to Shunduri's flat. I couldn't cope with going to Mum and Dad's."

"Baby's in London now? Jesus. What'd *she* do?"

"I told her we'd had a fight, you know? But he was there within a day: I think she called him. And then they did the story on him in that magazine." Rohimun felt her face burn.

"I've been out of the country, you know?"

She swallowed. It gave her a sharp pressure in the chest to tell her brother, almost as bad a pain as when Mum had left the awful message on the answering machine after the magazine article came out. Nothing but *Munni, Munni*, then crying until the machine cut out. Rohimun never answered the phone after that.

"He's a society boy, yeah? So the magazines, the papers, they were interested in him, in who he was with." Rohimun swallowed again and went on, very softly. "He told them I was living with him, and they printed it."

There was silence in the car now, but Rohimun could see that Tariq was crying. So Mum and Dad had told him nothing. She may as well have stabbed him. She forced herself to continue. "After that I knew I couldn't go home."

She didn't need to tell Tariq her other great dread: that when they got home, the door would be closed to her anyway. That Shunduri was their only daughter now.

In the silence Tariq drove on, the headlights illuminating a continuous tunnel of black hedgerows.

She closed her eyes and drifted into a doze, broken now and again by panic and the conviction that it was actually Simon driving, or that Simon was behind them. Then Tariq was on his mobile, speaking quietly in Bangla. She hadn't heard it in so long, she could feel the tears start again.

When he finished, he turned to her. "Mum and Dad aren't living in the community, the Oxford community now. Don't forget that. It's not like they've got neighbors watchin' their every move anymore, yeah. It's a *gora* village in the countryside."

At least he could still speak to her. "Have you seen them then? Since you got back?"

"Nah. I only got back from Jo'burg a week ago. Been looking for you."

She tried to swallow the lump in her throat. So they hadn't sent him. "It won't make any difference, Bai. I mean, they haven't changed that much. They'll never take me back. And what if a reporter turns up, or a photographer comes around, yeah. What Dad's precious stately home will do then, I don't know. Sack him maybe."

Tariq gave a sudden grin. "Put him in the stocks, more likely. Look, I'll think of something. Mum and Dad'll come around. They just need some time."

"Bai, they'll never—"

"Of course they will. You're Dad's favorite, yeah?"

"They *won't*." Rohimun startled herself with the force of her tone, and they both fell silent.

Then Tariq spoke, his voice tight. "They've fucking got to, alright? They're all we've got." He cleared his throat. "If they can't forgive, I won't leave you here. You could come back to Jo'burg with me."

She stared blankly at him, but he kept his eyes on the road.

"Just let me worry about it for now, right?"

South Africa. He wanted her with him, even if it meant breaking with Mum and Dad. He knew about Simon, and he didn't care. He wasn't turning the car around and driving back to London to sort things out with a *funchait*, or even shouting at her about the family honor, telling her that she'd made her bed.

She dipped her head and looked at her naked wrists. It'd been so long since she'd worn her bracelets. How long ago had Tariq discarded beard and topi? He was clearly no longer her fundamentalist big brother home from university, who repelled her confidences, threw her precious jeans in the rubbish and told her that she should be wearing a burqa. She stole another look. But neither was he the old Tariq, carefree enough to take her hand at the school gates and walk her home, laughing and teasing and talking with his friends, as she towed along a whining Shunduri with her other hand.

"Do you really mean that, Bai?"

"Do I mean that? Do I mean that?" His voice was loud and harsh, as he braked hard, gearing down the car to steer it into a lay-by.

"Jesus Christ, Munni." He was shouting now, as he switched off the engine and turned toward her. This was the Baiyya she remembered from university, always angry. Rohimun felt her ribs constrict. "Do you think I would lie to you, after what I saw? My own sister?"

She felt her head shaking. "I don't know, I don't—"

"Do you think I wanted to be away? For eighteen, nineteen fucking months, no family—"

A sudden roar of engines behind them shook the whole car and seared the interior with light, while a large vehicle drew up alongside. Simon. He'd found them. Rohimun gave a long moaning indrawn breath, her left hand scrabbling between the seatbelt and the door catch.

"It's a lorry. Shit. It's just a lorry, Munni."

She couldn't breathe out, only little gasps in and in and in, ratcheting up a bubble of pressure just under her diaphragm, rising and swelling and pressing on stomach, lungs, heart. Pins and needles rippled up both arms. Tariq was swearing gently, in Bangla this time, as he got out and came around to her side of the car. There was a wave of cold air as he opened her door and fumbled around her feet, and she felt the slimy rim of the polystyrene coffee cup circling her nose and mouth.

"You're breathing too fast, Munni. Try to slow it down, yeah? Just slow it down." He put his hand on her forehead and stroked it backward, a little way over her hairline. "It's alright, yeah? We'll work it out. I won't leave you, Munni. I won't leave you again."

She closed her eyes against the glare of the light and the dreadful bubble in her chest. The pressure inside was easing, with the warmth and weight of his hand and the murmur of his voice, speaking in Bangla, like years ago, when she used to climb into bed with him after a nightmare and he would let her snuggle in close and just talk and talk softly about what he was going to do when he grew up and the names of the planets and how clouds filled up with water. What terrible tiredness now.

---

Tariq watched her, bracing her forehead with his hand as he dropped the coffee cup onto the floor. She had fallen asleep so fast after hyperventilating, it was almost a faint, but her color wasn't so bad now, and she was breathing more slowly. He pulled a wet tissue from her fingers and wiped her chin and the bridge of her nose where the coffee cup had rested, then leaned awkwardly in, searching for the lever to recline the seat. Her feet were icy in her sandals, and it took him almost a minute to tease out the fine leather loops from around her big toes before they could be removed.

He put his hands around an instep to chafe some warmth into it, but Rohimun turned and tucked her other foot into his hands as well. Tariq, still squatting on the verge next to the car, found himself cradling her feet as he looked up at her unconscious face. The traditional posture to beg for forgiveness.

"*Allah rasta, shunnah Munni*," he said. *May God help you forgive me, precious Munni.* For all the selfish lies, and the selfish absences. None of this would have happened if he'd been around for her. God knows why she still called him Baiyya: some big brother he'd been.

Tariq dropped the sandals in the back seat and stood to take off his dinner jacket, then slid it under her seatbelt to wrap it around her. He ached with tiredness. The lorry was gone now. They would stay here for a couple of hours, have a nap, prepare themselves for the onslaught at home. It was less than an hour to go on these back roads, if he could remember the way, before having Mum and Dad to deal with. *Inshallah*, God willing, she would sleep till then, though only God knew how things would go from there.

He carefully closed the passenger door and stretched backward as far as he could. He was stiff with post-fight tension, and his eyes stung with fatigue. This was not how he'd planned his return to his parents. Not that he had done any planning: he'd managed to avoid thinking about it pretty much, what with the last-minute rush of leaving Jo'burg, where no sooner had he settled in that city than the old ache of family and home had started up as it never had in the desert.

It was only after he'd fought his way through the claustrophobia of Heathrow and sighted the queue for taxis that he'd realized the impossibility of simply coming home: that every expectation would be that he was ready to marry. He was twenty-seven, no longer a student, and back at last. There were no more barriers to arrangements being made.

While away he'd missed Rohimun most of all, missed her with a terrible ache; part love, part loneliness, part guilt, all the worse for not having realized it till then. He'd changed some money and called her on her mobile, but it was disconnected. It was only then that he'd called his parents, let them think he was still away, but said that he'd be home in a couple of weeks—*as soon as I can, yeah*—and asked for Rohimun's number and was told by his father that she no longer existed and by his mother that she was gone, gone, no one knew where.

He'd hung up in despair and could not think what to do next except what he'd been flown over for: chase the artists and artists' agents for the Goodman Gallery. But almost as soon as he did, he found his sister's name on the lips of the London dealers and curators, their memories fresh of her sellout exhibition and the disappearing act she'd pulled on its opening night.

Most of them wouldn't touch her with a barge pole now: unstable and unreliable, Rohimun's old agent Nigel had said, in the course of bitching, unknowingly, to her brother about commissions not filled, calls not answered and deposits he'd had to return. Her old teachers at the RCA were no help either, and in the end Student Services had asked him politely to leave. *We can't help you anymore. Really. Try the police, try Missing Persons.*

And then, as he had stared despairingly at one of his sister's portraits, on show in an upmarket Soho gallery, the dealer, piqued by his interest, had, in her elegant drawl, repeated to him the story of Rohimun's disappearance. She'd seen his expression and touched his arm and said, "Look, there's a chance she might be at the V&A tonight. Not that she's showing anything of course, but it is her thing. Best of luck, darling."

He'd acted quickly: asked the woman outright to organize an invitation for him. She'd laughed at his cheek, but said, "Here, darling, take mine, they know me there." He'd thanked her and flown out the door, already calling the assistant curator whose couch he'd been crashing on, to beg the loan of his dinner jacket.

Tariq had arrived at the V&A out of breath, just in time to follow the last straggler in. Then he'd seen Munni, behaving like some *gora* slut with that man. It was Allah's judgement on him, without a doubt.

He sighed. Dew was everywhere: condensing on the bonnet of the rental car; sparkling on the low hedge nearby. He rubbed his eyes and yawned. How soft and wet England always was, even in summer. In

South Africa, dew was a winter thing, and in the deserts further north, a nightly visitation with nothing soft about it. He walked around to the driver's side and sat heavily, closed his eyes. He'd become a good catnapper.

———————

ONE A.M. AND Richard was tired out from fucking but too hungry to sleep, and the moon was shining cold and clear through Deirdre's white plantation shutters onto his clothes on the floor. He started to search for his cigarettes, but they were nowhere to be seen. Deirdre's Silk Cuts and a lighter were lying on the kitchen counter, so he took them out onto the miniature bedroom balcony.

It was becoming less satisfactory, staying over at Deirdre's place. Perhaps their officially casual arrangement was becoming too routine. But Deirdre wasn't like Thea had been, wanting to start her own family, move to the country. She'd never made demands on him he wasn't comfortable with, save the odd bit of pushiness when it came to selling art to his friends, and they could look after themselves.

Postcoital tristesse? Deirdre's body was made to please. Richard turned to look at her sleeping in all her glossy, hip-jutting perfection, like a shop mannequin that had somehow fallen onto the bed. With a wig. Maybe he should go back to bed right now, slip his hand between her legs . . .

He flicked ash over the railing, which glittered, spun above him, then vanished. Like that Kipling poem, about the sparks flying upward to nothingness. Surely he was in a good place now. He was no longer carrying the debt he'd taken on to free himself from the Abbey. He was in a first-class Chambers and in the running to take silk and Queen's Counsel before he was forty. He was free, completely free, of the morass of burdens and obligations that had sunk his parents' marriage into the ground.

And he had Deirdre, no strings attached. Henry probably envied him. Richard's friends certainly did. Her body, so lean and clean, her business sense, the androgynous, quirky haircuts and clothes, put her streets ahead of the wives and girlfriends of his set, with their "fun" jobs, conservative outfits and family jewelry. Had the novelty worn off? The cigarette was spent now, and he had a foul taste in his mouth.

Back in the bedroom, sleep was impossible, and the ultra-mild cigarettes had left him wanting something with more taste and body. There was enough moonlight to sort out his clothes, and he could dress in the sitting room. From here he could walk it to his flat in forty-five minutes and pick up cigarettes on the way. He'd been sitting on his arse all week; it would do him good.

————————

Tariq woke, stiff and sore, and stared disbelievingly at the dashboard clock. Four a.m. How had he slept that long? He started the engine and pulled back onto the road as smoothly as he could. No more delays: Rohimun needed to be in a bed. Time to head home and deal with Mum and Dad. Amma and Abba.

Mum and Dad's new home and its distance from the Oxford Bangladeshi community could only be a plus. He could just picture all this happening in their old house. Ten Auntie Jiis in Mum's kitchen cooking for the disgraced family, as if there'd been a death. "What a pity! What a tragedy! And who would have thought! Such a nice girl . . . They'll never get a good match for Shunduri now . . . This is what comes to these hi-fi modern families . . . asking for cream-coffee and next thing they're too good for the community-center's *melas*."

And the male elders in the sitting room drinking chai and chewing paan and telling Dad it's all about respect, and she will have to be sent back to Bangladesh so as not to taint the family, and this is what comes of leaving your roots.

And, thanks to this magazine article, the focus would be squarely on Munni, not the prodigal son who'd barely written and never called in eighteen months away. So much for all his debating about how to handle his own story, what to tell them and when. Anyway, they would have enough on their plate with Rohimun's return, which, *kunu oshibidah nai*, would be no hardship in comparison. Funny how the words were coming back.

His jaw clicked with a gigantic yawn. He could really do with a Red Bull for this last stretch, but stopping now, Munni perhaps waking while he was out of the car, was too big a risk. He'd seen how freaked out she was the last time he'd left her. What had that fucker done to her? God, he needed some music. He massaged the dial of the car radio. Maybe the upbeat drumming of a Bhangara station: those Sikh boys were always on somewhere. Even some of the more upbeat Bollywood tracks would be better than nothing.

He remembered Hussein from down the street before he too went fundamental, going on about the racism of the music industry in England, how Asian music CDs were outselling *gora* CDs almost two to one, but the compilers of the top one hundred and the producers of mainstream radio and television shows having a blanket policy of ignoring sales figures for Asian music. Nothing had changed: Asian music was still a joke unless it was Ravi Shankar or Nusrat Fateh Ali Khan at the Albert Hall; too refined, too "ethnic," to be a threat. Too distant from the masala of influences that produced Anglo-Asian bands like Fun Da Mental and Asian Dub Foundation.

But some things had changed forever. Those passionate arguments they'd managed to have, despite all being on the same side, would never happen again. Football-mad Hussein, always bouncing on the balls of his feet ("Good for the calf muscles, man!"), Tariq had last heard of training in Pakistan; stocky little Ali, like a baiyya to them both, missing in Afghanistan before his son was born, both men probably dead. They were the only ones he'd been able to keep in touch with: outsiders like himself, asking the big questions.

And the rest of the old crowd, he could guess well enough. Arranged marriages that had probably lost their luster by now, driving taxis and double-shifting in restaurants to support parents, in-laws and the new baby every second year, younger sisters' dowries and the endless pleas for help from the family village in Bangladesh. And what flood and pestilence in the old country didn't take, age and loss of hope here in England would.

The rush of hedgerows slowed as Tariq began to concentrate on road signs. Dad's directions, so English with his "go around a bit" and "up a bit," no left or right, the only certain landmarks being the different pubs: The Weeping Maiden, The Weary Traveller and, of course, The Saracen's Head. Surely he was getting close now.

Tariq slowed further and made another attempt to scan for something decent on the radio. He paused on the dial, recognizing the title song of the 1970s Bollywood movie *Sholay*. Two friends as close as brothers, enduring adversity together and sticking by each other, no matter what. But the song was cut short before the final chorus and succeeded by the imam's wailing call: *Allaahu Akbar, Allaahu Akbar* . . . The *azan fajir*, the call to dawn prayer. Tariq's hand snaked out and flicked it off, and silence filled the car as he swung the steering wheel left. They had arrived.

## Seven

IT WAS EARLY on Saturday morning, and Dr. Choudhury, bleary-eyed, had just nodded his assent to Tariq's leaving the house to make the necessary arrangements, when without further ado, his wife whirled from her station at the kitchen sink and fell to her knees in front of him. She reached for his feet, but he, too quick for her, tucked them under his chair.

Despite this, she stayed there on the floor, staring up and trying to fix his eyes with her own. He determinedly looked over her head, and stirred more sugar into his tea.

Mrs. Begum spoke softly, as if praising him. "The father of my children is a loving father, the best of fathers, and I know, I know in my heart, of his love for his Munni, his first daughter."

She paused, but Dr. Choudhury, not deceived, kept his eyes on the kitchen door.

His wife spoke again, her voice now a little less soft. "She has suffered enough, she is a good girl, she loves her family, she wants to be forgiven. How can anyone live in this world, without their family?"

He hurrumphed to clear the tension in his throat. "Nothing can be done. That girl has ruined her own life." No one could have been a better father than he. He could hear Mrs. Begum's grunted exhalation as she sat back on her haunches and knew from the heat on his skin that she was still staring at him. That feminine stubbornness that brooked no ignoring. "If you must punish someone, punish me. I am her mother! I taught her, disciplined her . . ." She began to sob.

Dr. Choudhury switched his gaze to the tabletop. Someone had to uphold proper standards, proper behavior. Sacrifices, great sacrifices he had made for these things. Why should it be only him? "She has ruined more than her own life. She has shamed us all."

"Was I ruined too, then, husband? Do you not remember what we did?"

He jumped up, half in fright at her bluntness, pushing his chair backward to escape.

She followed him, still on her knees. "*Lal Abba*, most loving father," she said, as if reasoning with him. "Your first daughter, your Rohimun. She was young and stupid and in London on her own. With Tariq away, with no family with her, she fell."

An aggrieved tone crept into his wife's pleading then, and she did not reach for his feet anymore, but rested her hands in her lap. "This would never have happened if I had gone with her, if her whole family had been with her. I could have looked after her, made sure she was safe. You let her sleep here, she is upstairs now. Why make her go to the Abbey? She has suffered enough. Surely you could let her stay near her mother's arms. We are not in the Desi community here. And what would the Bournes think of your daughter if they find her up there, in the Abbey, on her own?"

Dr. Choudhury stepped around her to the kitchen sink and stared out the window. His wife would never have spoken to him like this before they had come here to this village, away from the community and into the arms of that woman, that Mrs. Darby. A woman like that, both widowed and independent and virtually next door, was bound to bring trouble to a traditionally minded woman like his wife. He continued to look out the window, but Mrs. Begum's vegetable garden was no help. Where had they gone so wrong in the management of their two daughters? One had all the looks, the other all the talent; and virtue, he suspected, belonged to neither.

He, unlike her doting mother, could see Baby with clear eyes: her vanity, her insecurity, her self-absorption. Where these traits had come from, he could not tell. As for Rohimun, there was bound to be trouble when both temper and talent were given to a woman. Look at what had happened to his own mother. Painting until his birth, then dead by his seventh birthday, no one would tell how. Perhaps that had been the inevitable result of her sex ruling and limiting her creative life: such women perhaps should never marry.

But even so, what Rohimun had done to this family: the pain and sorrow she had caused, the damage to the reputation of all of them, her recklessness, her refusal to think about the consequences of her actions . . .

"This cannot be simply set aside." He wiped a finger across his upper lip. "She would taint all of us, were she to return. After what she has done, what has been said about her. You cannot move me. And be clear on this, Mrs. Begum: Bourne Abbey is not Windsor Cottage. Into one house in this neighborhood, she shall never be welcome. That cannot change."

He moved to the kitchen door, eager to escape the sense of entrapment and failure that were as tangible in this kitchen as roasting spices.

Mrs. Begum scrambled to her feet, pulling at the *pallu* of her sari to wipe her face, and held out her hands, like a child showing an uncle or a father that they were clean. "How, tell me, how can she ever marry and clear her name if she is not allowed back in this house? You are cursing her. She cannot hide at the Abbey forever. You are giving her no choice but to go upon the town, to become someone's girlfriend, someone's mistress, again. Your own daughter."

He averted his eyes from her empty arms with an effort that made his tone harsh. "What is done cannot be undone. Who would marry a girl like that? No one we would want in our family. She must be gone from here today."

His wife gasped with the pain of his words, and he escaped into the hall, shutting the kitchen door on her cry. Truly the sins of the parents were being visited upon their children. Surreptitiously he bit down upon the fingertips of his right hand to ward off the further bad luck that must surely be coming.

Walking almost on tiptoe, Dr. Choudhury hurried to his study, locked the door behind him, went to the sari cupboard and opened it. He reached in and ran his hands across the folded stacks of silks, microfibers and brocades, breathing in their familiar scent, and saying under his breath the first line of the first *ayah* of the *Surah Al-Fatiha*, the old formula of prayer and protection. *Bismillah ar-Rahman ar-Raheem*. In the name of Allah, the infinitely compassionate and merciful. In the name of Allah.

But this morning neither saris nor *surahs* could soothe him, and he closed the doors of the cupboard and sat down in his study chair and swivelled it from side to side, trying to rock himself into calmness. Where could she go? Where would she go when she could no longer stay at the Abbey? How could he be a good father in this?

He pulled open his desk drawers searching for something to eat, but they were so clean and empty that it looked as if Mrs. Begum had dusted their insides. He slumped in his chair, let his hands drop between his legs and stared at his so-so-clean desk. All come to this.

---

ROHIMUN WOKE TO the sound of familiar household noises drifting up from downstairs: the clash of pans on the stove or in the sink, running water, the *bong-bong-bong* of Mum hitting a wooden spoon on the side of a pot after stirring, the kettle's whistle cut short, cupboards shutting, and the murmur of a male voice that could have been Tariq's or Dad's. There was bright sunshine in the little room and her first thought was that she'd overslept and was late for school.

She sat up, remembering, then lay back intent on misery. But soon, somehow distracted by the fresh smell of the sheets, the narrowness of the bed and the sound of birdsong, she drifted back to sleep.

Sometime later she woke again, but now the sun was slanting through the dormer window at a higher angle, and her mother's warm hand was patting her face and telling her to be up now, it was time to go. Old fears rose in Rohimun's throat then, as she remembered her arrival in the grey dawn light and her mother silently helping her to take off her sari and putting her to bed in her blouse and petticoat. Her breath caught as she tried to speak, to ask for one more sleep in this child's room.

Her mother's arms went round her, and she whispered in her daughter's ear, "Nah, nah, nah, my Munni, my precious one. Don't worry, don't cry."

She was dressed and walked downstairs and into the kitchen and quickly fed, taken out, past the shut study door, to Tariq's car where she was once again put into the front passenger seat. There, great tearing sobs rose up, hurting her ribs and pulling her forward jerkily against the pressure of the car's acceleration, drowning out Tariq's words.

At least a minute passed before she could hear him and understand that she was going somewhere else, just for a while, somewhere close, until everything had been sorted out. She looked around and realized that she was not on the A road heading for the motorway, but on a narrow lane that travelled downhill toward the bend in a sparkling river, then climbed up again, past stands of mature trees.

"It's the Abbey that Dad's been working on, Munni. You'll be safe there and I'll visit you every day: it's just till I've sorted out Dad, you know? Just for a few days and then you'll be back home, I promise you, yeah. I promise."

The Abbey loomed then, and Tariq's little rental car zipped up and around the back, away from the scaffolding.

"No one's here on the weekend. I made sure. Come on."

---

AFTER TARIQ HAD walked her up the crooked dark stairs at the rear and shown her into the room that Dad had chosen for her, he left to run back down to the car for some more of her things. Rohimun walked forward slowly, a little shocked by the room's size. She'd expected something like the bedroom that she shared with Shunduri at the cottage, but this was gigantic: big enough to be a basketball court or a dance studio; and flooded with light, from a large bank of mullioned windows at the far end, and above those, just below the ceiling, a row of high square windows that made the room bright despite the dark oak paneling and the green curtains that surrounded the lower windows as well as the bed.

Long rectangles of sunshine lay across the floorboards like carefully spaced beach towels. The bed, a massive four-poster that must have been built in here, dominated the room. A leather-bound trunk rested under the windows on the far wall and a 1930s-style veneered cheval mirror sat in one corner between the massive bed and the stone fireplace, looking flimsy and disposable in comparison. Her easel from school rested on the ground, along with the old carpenter's tray full of paints and brushes and rags, and a battered sketchbook, as if she'd just dropped them there, home from college for the holidays. She walked to the windows: trees, hills, and to the right she could just see the river they had passed. This building must face it.

Tariq came back in with an army kitbag and a toiletry bag, placed them on the bed and nudged the easel with his shoe. "It might take me a while to get your stuff from London, yeah. I found these in Mum and Dad's shed, just for now."

"Oh."

"Thought it would keep you busy: you know, for the next few days."

She hadn't told anyone that she couldn't paint anymore, had hardly picked up a brush for almost twelve months. Tariq's obvious pride in his find kept her quiet. She mumbled something, and after he had fussed around some more, giving her a three-tiered tiffin container from Mum and showing her how to stow the kitbag and his old Scout camp stretcher under the big bed, he left. She listened to his steps recede down the hall with a mixture of desolation and relief.

———

TARIQ SLID INTO his car, shut the door and found a tissue to wipe his eyes and nose. He'd promised Munni he'd never abandon her again, and what was he doing to her now, less than a day later? No one could live without family. He'd learned that the hard way.

Growing up in the Oxford Bangladeshi community, a respected

captain of his school and his school's soccer team, with the occasional dip into Christian life with one of his father's university dinners, he had seen himself as confident and worldly for his age compared to his school friends. But once he was at Oxford University, living at college had been a shock. He had not realized how different his life would be without the rounds of visits to friends and relatives, the name days, the celebration of new babies, circumcisions and Eid, the glory of visitors from Bangladesh, community-center *melas* for betrothals and weddings, and the great duties of laying out and burial.

There was so much empty time. All his habits of hospitality that he had taken for granted, of feeding his guests before himself, always paying for their coffees, were inappropriate or laughable. He was a sucker for always buying and never drinking; a try-hard for cooking people meals, giving lifts, helping out with assignments.

Few reciprocated; no one understood his big-brother kindnesses. And no one visited your room, called or dropped in to see how you were going, unless it was with an agenda: they needed a meal, a lift, to borrow an essay or a smoke, or to see if they could tick off sleeping with a Paki on their must-do list. He was completely unprepared for the loneliness of student life, disconcerted at how much he missed friends and family.

All his Bangladeshi and Pakistani friends, without his "in" into Oxford, had disappeared off to red-brick universities to do all the usual Asian courses: optometry, pharmacy, engineering and medicine. They were sharing apartments and houses, cooking, cleaning, smoking and talking together in their own little enclaves.

The few Asians at Oxford were coconuts, Bounty bars: only brown on the outside, and in every other respect living the *gora* lifestyle, drinking alcohol, eating *haram* food and squiring around white girls. They were embarrassed to be seen wearing or eating anything too ethnic, or even associating too closely with those like themselves. They seemed to his eyes to have acquired the status amongst their white friends not of equals but of mascots, secure only if they were the only one.

His choices of art history and philosophy of aesthetics, of which he'd been so proud, not running with the usual Asian ambitions, had started to feel like a curse, and Oxford itself a mistake. He was singled out in all the tutorials, having to explain who he was and where he was from, before the usual interactions were allowed. Then, when people started to relax around him, the jokes they were too inhibited to tell before, about being good at cricket and not seeing him in a dark room, would start to come out.

That was okay, he wasn't naive, had endured much worse at school, but here, somehow, he'd expected better. At school, acceptance of a sort was inevitable, and he was no great novelty. At Oxford, he remained an exotic oddity, like the Rhodes scholars hosted from far-flung countries. No one wanted to know what made him the same as them: if anything there was a sense of disappointment that he was not exotic enough with his jeans and his local accent; not wandering around in Punjabi-pyjamas, or smoking a hookah in his study. These people, England's intellectual elite, still saw him through the lens of Tom Brown and Billy Bunter.

And everyone he saw seemed to be dating, holding hands with girls, kissing in public, living with them, breaking up, kissing some-one else. The *goras'* relationships disgusted Tariq with their irrespon-sible, often alcohol-fuelled self-indulgence, seemingly devoid of tenderness and respect. And he also recoiled from his old Asian friends' relationships, with their moonish hypocrisy. All that swearing of true love and eternal fealty in the full knowledge that, after gradu-ation, they would each dutifully walk the prescribed path into sepa-rate arranged marriages, and never see each other again.

So he had become a minority on two fronts: not only an Asian Muslim in England's whitest university, but a man with no *lalmunni*, no sweetheart, however temporary, to yearn for and protect. He became preoccupied with thoughts of his family, how much he missed looking after his sisters and being looked up to by them, how dear their innocence and admiration was. In that first year, his weekend trips and phone calls home had had all the frequency that even a Bangladeshi mother could desire. And he felt that his special bond with Rohimun, where, childlike, she still told her baiyya everything and asked his advice and opinion on all matters, was most precious of all.

But gradually he went home less and less on weekends, and Rohimun headed to London to study at the RCA. He withdrew into his studies and worked ferociously, achieving academically as he no longer seemed to be able to socially. The walks to lectures and to the library became solitary. He started to avoid the college bar and eat in his room instead of the hall, with only his books for company. His loneliness became terrible, deforming.

Jesus, what a mess he'd been in then: even worse than what Munni was in now. It was up to him to fix it, fix himself, fix everything, make them all a family again. He ran his hands through his hair, started up the car and headed back to the cottage.

----

ROHIMUN SAW TARIQ again that evening, carrying a full tiffin container and a bottle of water as well as a shopping bag packed with other things that Mum had thought of in the meantime. And he came again on Sunday morning, with more food, staying to chat, but with an uneasy manner that spoke of continuing hostility at home.

In the afternoon though, it had, to Rohimun's shock, been her father who'd delivered the tiffin. She'd heard a knock and opened the door to find him standing there. He didn't come in, or say a word, just stared over her into the room behind her, then passed her the tiffin and left.

Yet he must have seen more of her boredom and loneliness than he appeared to. Soon after noon on Monday, Tariq turned up with a full set of Winsor & Newton oil paints, bought in London early that day to replace her old paint set from school, telling her it was Dad's idea. And then, pride and pleasure in his face and his voice, Tariq lugged into the room a large raw stretched canvas, about six feet by four.

"I got this myself. Saw it at the HobbyCraft in Swindon."

She folded her arms and scuffed the floor with the tip of her sandal, refusing to look at it. "Thanks, Bai."

But after he'd left, she could not help eyeing it, though indirectly, like a passerby trying not to stare, wary of the hopelessness that had gripped her whenever she had looked at her canvases in Simon's flat. After a while, and just for something to do, she primed it, taking her time to make the job last, enjoying the feel of painting without the pressure of creation, but eventually the job was complete. After an equally elaborate cleaning of brushes and folding of rags, she was left again with nothing to do.

Rohimun still couldn't bear to think of her disastrous Thames series attempts, sitting in the London flat: the only other big canvases she'd ever worked on. She had a creeping feeling, when she looked at this large, pristine canvas, that her studies of that cold river had been generated more by her agent's comments about the corporate need for foyer-size paintings, than anything more visceral. And it had been obvious: sweeping landscape was not for her.

But neither could she bear to revert to painting some version of the society portraits that had made her such a success in London. The very thought sickened her. And she had never been drawn to abstraction: it had to be figurative. But of what?

After hours of trying to ignore the canvas completely, her toes curling with boredom, Rohimun accepted that the cheval mirror was showing her the one subject that she had never attempted, never wanted to attempt, in all her years of training and practice. She didn't want to analyze why this had been so: it was enough to grapple with exactly what, or who, she was intending to paint just now.

Initially it was a process of elimination. It would not be the old Munni who hated photos and tradition and dressing up, and worshipped her brother. And certainly not the lumpish, resentful woman, Simon's *love*, who only wore Western clothes and couldn't manage without him. Someone different again, still forming perhaps. Well, then, it wasn't going to be a real portrait: just a painting with her in it. And she wouldn't even go full-faced or three-quarter: profile only. The real subject would be something else entirely. For a while Rohimun was stuck again.

The night was warm and still, and the darkened room with its oversized furniture and heavy drapes, felt claustrophobic after a day of doing nothing, with no television to lose herself in.

Finally, with her heart in her mouth, and jumping at every noise, Rohimun crept down the pitch-black stairs and unbolted the outer door. With the night air on her skin, she went for a cautious wander and found a walled garden area at the side of the building. Inside, an enchanted place, hidden from the world by its outer walls and further divided inside by little tiled streamlets. A garden out of Rossetti, or an illustration in a medieval hymnal. It reminded her of something else too, just outside her grasp.

She smelled the roses before she saw them, surprised by the strength of their heady night-scent. The roses themselves, bleached by moonlight into silver and grey, were far less spectacular than their fragrance, but for the sake of the exotic perfume she worked her nails into the thick stem of a two-headed specimen until it broke free, and carried it back to her room to sit in her water bottle.

When Rohimun woke the next morning, her roses revealed themselves. The outer half-inch of each petal was a coppery yellow that deepened to apricot and finally a dark, almost burnt orange at the center. She had her real subject. Rohimun stood at the window and slowly pulled apart one of the blooms, petal by petal, down to the stamen and beyond, examining each piece, then laying it on the sill. Each petal was a work of art in itself. She remembered the injunctions the RCA first-years had been constantly given: to look properly, to really see. She'd always applied it to people's faces, their hands, how they sat and stood as indications of character and personality: never to nature.

The diaphanous quality of each petal, combined with the reflected internal light of the whole: how could this be painted? She wished she'd paid more attention to van Aelst and Redouté, those masters of the rose, and tried to re-create in her mind's eye some of their paintings: how they showed both the fragility and the depth of the bloom, its pigmented translucence.

For the first time in more than two years she felt excited about painting, and when her father unexpectedly arrived again that morning with his mournful, averted face and her tiffin, she passed him last night's supper container with a note tucked into its lid that listed the additional paint colors, mediums and brushes that she would need. He opened it, and she saw his face startle before returning to its resting expression of noble suffering.

"For Tariq, Abba," she muttered, embarrassed when she realized that he had expected something else: an apology, perhaps, for everything. Not likely. She was beyond that now. Not sure where exactly, but not there.

# Eight

KAREEM's GPS HAD been silent for the last half-hour except for the occasional plaintive *No signal connection* and *Unable to calculate.* Dark clouds covered what sky could be seen between the trees, and the *weep weep* of the wipers were an unwelcome reminder of the sunny weather that Kareem and Shunduri had left behind in London. Even the stuffed peacock in the back seat, a gift from a new supplier that Kareem had decided at the last minute would do as a family present, seemed uneasy as it gazed out the left side-window with tightly closed beak and beady eyes.

For the past few minutes, ever since the rain had begun, Kareem had been driving steeply downhill on a winding single-lane road with no visible signposts, so crowded by trees and bushes on both sides that there was nowhere to turn around. But his princess, put into the back seat with the peacock fifteen minutes ago for reasons of respectability, did not appreciate this point.

"It's an all-wheel drive, yaah?"

"I'm not getting dis car dirty for anyone, Princess. Know how long it took to shine up?" And all done earlier this morning than any Asian man should ever be getting up, due to Shunduri's multiple texts telling him to get up.

"What are you going to do, then?"

He shrugged irritably, concentrating on keeping all four wheels of the large vehicle on the narrow strip of tarmac and away from the reaching arms of the undergrowth. He'd have to go over everything with a chamois once they were out of this wilderness. "We just keep going, innit?"

"What, so we just keep going on down like this for evah, yaah? Me and this stupid bird?" Shunduri sniffed, and he could see in the rearview that she had folded her arms and was staring at the peacock with a kind of competitive hostility. "I don't *think* so."

As she spoke, the dark road started to twist and rise, then they passed between two stone statues: a wolf and a lion. It looked like private property to Kareem, and he adjusted his shoulders uncomfortably, tense from holding the car positioned in the middle of the road and from looking for a way out. He must have been dreaming to have gotten himself this lost.

But just as they encountered another statue on their right, a leopard or cheetah, and he was readying himself to ask whether there was some kind of safari park near her parents' place, the tarmac gave way to a broad sweep of creamy gravel with a gigantic grey stone building at its end. He leaned forward and stared up through the windscreen. Jesus Christ, it was as big as Buckingham Palace. Some kind of hospital, or country club, maybe. He turned off the engine and started to fiddle with the GPS.

"Somefin's wrong wiv dis, for sure."

Shunduri bounced in her seat. "It's the Abbey. Bourne Abbey. Look. We must've come up the back way." She pointed at a small white sign stuck into the lawn right in front of the building, and he twisted around to read it.

*Bourne Abbey Tea Rooms, National Trust, This Waye*, and a gothic arrow that pointed away from them. No one was to be seen, and it was very quiet. Even the rain had stopped.

"Dad knows these people," she said.

"Your dad?"

"Yaah. He's been advising them. On the building, fixin' it up an' that, for years now. That's why they moved here from Oxford."

What appeared to be the main entrance was deep in shadow and, with its iron-studded door, it looked straight out of a *Dracula* movie. All it needed was a creepy butler squeaking it open. He leaned back in his seat, feeling observed, despite the car's tinted windows.

"They *live* here?"

"Mum and Dad? Nah, they moved close to here, in Lydiard. The village. That's where we're *supposed* to be."

Kareem started up the engine again.

"What are you doing?"

"Turning round, innit? Plenty of room to turn round here."

"Forget that. I'm gettin' out and asking for directions. Seein' as your GPS is so fine."

"Eh, Princess, no need for that," he said faintly. Hadn't she seen any horror movies? They had half a tank of petrol and no need at all to hang round here. Next thing, she'd go missing and he'd have to go looking for her. Straight out of *Hammer House of Horror*. Never go exploring, never split up. Didn't she know anything?

But she was already unclipping her seatbelt, and Kareem, doomed, gave one last despairing rev before switching off the engine.

"We're not splitting up, yeah? I'm comin' wiv you."

Shunduri stared at him, clearly irritated. "What are you talkin' about?"

Lightning flickered, putting the Abbey into silhouette behind her, and he bit his fingertips to ward off the evil around him.

---

"Oh," said Thea. "Very *Mission Impossible*. But who would turn up at the Abbey now? No one knows we're here except the decorator."

She and Henry had risen from the National Trust guidelines, fabric swatches and paint chips spread out on the sitting-room table, and were spying through one of the rear-facing windows, drawn by the sound of a car turning onto the gravel outside. She'd wanted to get to the Abbey early before the decorator came, but who could this be?

The shiny black SUV had stopped, facing the house, but no one got out. Thea had to resist an urge to press her nose against the glass.

The car windows were so dark that she was unable to see inside, and the effect was such that the car seemed to be looking at them. She could hear Henry just behind her, fidgeting restlessly.

"It must be the decorator. Why doesn't she get out?" he said.

"The decorator's not coming till later."

"I thought we were meeting her this morning. That's why we're here . . ."

She didn't recognize the car. Were they trying to force her and Henry to come out to greet them? Was this some kind of power play?

"I wanted to get here early so we could look at the fabrics and paint samples in this room and make some decisions. Then the decorator for lunch at one, then we work, then afternoon tea before she leaves. That's why Audrey's here. I can't do everything myself, you know."

Henry made his nervous, throat-clearing sound. "Do we know them? Are they, ah, family?"

"You mean *my* family when you say that, don't you?"

"I'm just caught a bit by surprise, Thee. You know me."

She did not deign to reply. The SUV's side passenger door swung open and, in one twisting, sinuous motion, a figure emerged and slid to the ground. She wore a long-sleeved, boat-necked black dress with ruched sides, sheer black stockings, black three-inch heels, black gloves, a black headscarf tightly bound and knotted around her head and neck, and sunglasses that obscured most of her face. She looked like a negative print of Grace Kelly. The woman paused, facing the house, then slammed the car door shut and started, with some apparent difficulty, to traverse the remaining loose gravel between herself and the back door.

At the first of the three steps up to the entrance, she stopped, one hand on hip and one outstretched diagonally behind her, as if reaching for something that should be there.

Thea stared. "Alaïa, I can just tell. Blahnik heels. I don't know about the glasses though. If they're not copies, that's that new Dior shape that even Pip can't get her hands on yet." She clicked her tongue.

"*Christos*. If tight from neck to ankle is the new silhouette, I'll have to lose twenty pounds."

"Ah, Thee." Henry took a step away from the window. "Is this some relative you haven't told me about? Because she looks cross and you know I'm not . . ."

Thea, still entranced, flapped her hand in negation. "Who *is* she?"

"She looks Greek. She's got that look." Henry's voice was lugubrious. "Remember your Auntie Alex? She wore black too. And no one told me she'd put a curse on me for taking you away from the true church. Remember? She said that if she'd had anything to do with the Kiriakis Trust, I'd have to pay back every drachma . . ."

Thea pressed her lips together. A pillar of strength he was. Without taking her eyes from the window, she reached behind her, caught Henry's sleeve and pulled him forward. "Look." She pointed with her free hand. "There's another one!"

And indeed, another figure, also in black, had descended from the driver's side of the car. This second figure was as clearly male as his companion was not. Dressed in a skin-tight, black Savile Row suit with a charcoal stripe, black shirt and tie, driving gloves and wrap sunglasses, his head was shaven, his ears glittered, and he had a boxer's broad shoulders, wasp waist and chicken legs. With no discernible hurry, he swaggered around the front of the car to his companion, who grabbed his sleeve and used it as leverage to pull herself, hobbled by the long tight dress, up the steps.

Henry gave a sigh partway between resignation and martyrdom. "I'll go to the door."

"No, wait. I'm not ready." Thea glanced at the mantel mirror, bent over and shook out her bob, and stood back up to comb it through with her fingers so that it flowed back from her face in a glossy black helmet. On tiptoe, she could just see reflected her favorite brooch, a cream-on-rose Helen of Troy cameo, circled with gold. Her fingers flicked it as she briefly surveyed the room. *This is my territory now.*

"Quick! Help me get the dust covers off the sofas."

As Henry folded the covers and dropped them, at her direction, through the doorway that led to the servants' passage, she took a quick look around. This room was presentable enough, impressive enough, for unexpected visitors, with its view over the Park and a fire burning in the hearth, and Colin's wife Audrey in the Abbey kitchen to look after them. Good thing she'd put on the McQueen cashmere this morning, with its breastplate design woven into the pattern. Very cutting-edge.

In the mirror she met her husband's eyes, and was startled into a smile when he grimaced at her seriousness. He came closer, and his hand brushed her shoulder. "Girding our loins?"

She shook her head at him wryly. Easy for you to say, she thought. No one questions your right to be here.

The doorbell pealed just as he opened his mouth to speak.

"They're *not* family." Thea knew what he had been about to ask. Again. "I've never seen them before." She took a seat at the table so as to face the double doors that led off the main hall, threw the Biro in the wastepaper basket and found the Mont Blanc fountain pen in her handbag.

"Oh." Henry walked to the table and shuffled the loose papers into disorder for her. "So, ah, we wait then?"

She could sense him hovering but refused to look up. "Yes." The doorbell pealed again.

Eventually Audrey could be heard on her way, muttering under her breath, to answer the back door. Thea waited, head down and fountain pen raised, as if confronted by a particularly tricky National Trust issue. Audrey's knock at the sitting-room doors was soon heard, followed straight after by Audrey herself, flowered pinny on and tea towel in her hand. Opening doors was not her job.

"Oh, that's where you be, Mrs. Kreekis," she said in a carrying tone, making her position on having to leave the kitchen clear. "There's a man an' lady."

Thea hesitated, torn between going too far with Audrey and a real need for information. "Did you get their names, Audrey?"

Audrey sniffed. "Summat *furrin*." She looked pointedly at Thea. "Couldna' make head nor tail ovvit."

Thea drew breath to speak, but Audrey slapped the tea towel against her flank and turned away to show that she had no intention of taking this front-of-house rubbish any further. "I'm showin' them in then," she threw over her shoulder.

Audrey returned almost immediately and proceeded to open only one half of the double doors that led into the sitting room from the hall. She flattened her bulk against the door with exaggerated care, waving the mysterious visitors past her with a flip of her tea towel. The woman in black stalked in first, brushing past Audrey without a second glance.

The man followed her, but he had to turn sideways to pass. Broad-shouldered but short, he was no match for Audrey's big-boned, farmer's-wife build, which gave her the necessary height to talk eye to eye with a reluctant Henry when his breakfasting habits got too messy. The man had made the mistake of facing Audrey to slip past, which put him at eye level with her massive floral bosom. Acres of cornflowers. For a second he froze, transfixed. She stared back at him unsmiling and, somehow diminished, he turned his head to the side and made his escape into the room.

"Here they be then. From Lunnon," Audrey said flatly, turning to exit, but not quite fast enough.

Thea, having learned her lesson, spoke at once. "Thank you, Audrey. Can we have coffee and cake, please. *Proper* coffee." She turned to her guests, rising from her chair and smiling, her voice slowing and smoothing to pure transatlantic caramel. "I'm so sorry. I didn't catch your names."

In the hurly-burly of first-name introductions, and talk of GPSes and roadworks detours, the obscuring sunglasses were finally removed, and Thea found herself staring at a young woman whose swarthy coloring, slim build and designer clothes were close enough to her own old London appearance to feel familiar, and whose head-high, nervy aggression also gave Thea the sharpest stab of self-recognition.

Here was fifteen-years-ago Thea, new to school in England, escaping a fractured, feuding family back in Athens. Trying to break into the little cliques that mattered, but always the shortest and darkest, always the accent that singled her out. And then, after the hiatus of her undergraduate years in Stanford, it was also ten-years-ago Thea doing the whole thing again at Oxford for her master's, always on the outside, always pretending not to care but, underneath, paddling frantically to catch up, to break into the magic circle of belonging.

Until she met Richard, born to everything she had ever wanted but wanting none of it. Their relationship had provided an entree to the very people, the very groups she had craved, first at Oxford, then when living together in London. He had teased her about it: how she hung on every word he spoke about friends and relatives, the efforts she made to meet and greet and eat with those very people whose phone calls he could not be bothered to return, whose social demands he told her he loathed. By the end of that time, she knew everyone, had been everywhere. She had cultivated all of the connections and contacts that he was so blasé about, even had her own inner circle. What efforts she had gone to, been happy to go to, to create a community of belonging: her contribution to their joint future.

After two years together, he had finally taken her home for a weekend, and she had fallen in love at first sight with a crumbling stately home and, especially, its last one hundred years of continuity and family. She had glimpsed a dream of an existence, and then he had told her he wanted none of it, not Bourne Abbey, not marriage, not children.

Audrey, with a swiftness that was commendable until Thea remembered that *The Archers* would be on in half an hour, wheeled in the tea trolley with Thea's favorite demitasse cups and Henry's mother's cake-stand, piled high with slices of halva and miniature baklava triangles. Audrey had used those tacky paper doilies again, as if she'd never been told not to. Clearly the only way Thea was going to stop that was to find Audrey's secret stash and throw it in the bin. But, Audrey being Audrey, she'd probably just put them back on the shopping list and plead ignorance.

And here was Thea's younger self still standing before her, insecurity coming off her like sweat off a racehorse, and so ready for the rejection that was bound to ensue, because it always did. For a moment Thea fancied she could see herself through this girl's eyes: older, frighteningly well-groomed and, most importantly, belonging in the setting of the Abbey. It didn't matter what the girl had to say: Thea knew what was really at stake. She felt all her initial competitive hostility melt away, and grasped the other woman's gloved hand.

"Do come and sit by the fire, Shunduri. Did you take the motorway?"

---

HENRY, STANDING WATCHING the exchange between his wife and the woman in black, had the distinct feeling that he'd missed plenty, but not the shiver of seeming recognition that had passed between them. Bloody Greeks. His fate was sealed. The main hall renovations, largely funded by in-law drachmas and never achievable on the National Trust grant scheme alone, were complete. And now they were coming to claim their piece of the action.

How often had Richard told him that, with money, there were always strings attached? What would it be? Installation of one of Thee's evil aunties or grandmothers upstairs, for life. She'd probably outlive them all, having made a compact with the devil already. Or maybe Thee's brother would arrive next, wanting the takings from open days to fund business expansion into England.

These two, maybe the family's Turkish branch, were just the outriders, the advance scouts for the full-scale invasion to come. Henry felt a little doom-laden frisson run down his spine, and smiled weakly at Kareem.

"So, ah, are you planning to stay long?"

"As long as my princess needs."

"Oh, ah, that's Shunduri then?" Henry had never, since school, felt more like a fool. Maybe she was Greek royalty. She certainly had Prince Philip's resting expression down pat.

"Yeah."

Henry squirmed on the inside. It was a horribly awkward situation, but he had to know. He drew Kareem away from the two women, toward Audrey's double doors.

"So, ah, whereabouts are you from, exactly?" He held his breath.

Kareem stared at him, all geniality gone as if it had never been. He extended his right arm, and shook his hand from the wrist in such a way that Henry could hear the knuckles crack. "I'm an East Ender, meself."

Henry felt a prickle on his neck, and became very aware of the ropes of muscle that rose out of Kareem's shirt collar. All those tabloid stories of drug gangs, ruthless criminals . . . He felt his chin drop and recede, as it always did in a crisis, and he blinked rapidly behind his glasses. "I'm sorry, I d-didn't mean . . . I thought you might be related to my wife . . . She's Greek, you know."

"*Greek?*" Kareem's eyebrows shot up. "*Ei hala kwai toni aliue!*" He laughed and shook his head, then pulled on an earlobe in which sat a fat diamond or diamanté or something. Thea was always trying to explain the difference to him. "Man, what are you thinkin'? I'm a Desi boy." He grinned at Henry's blank face. "Bang-la-desh."

"Ohh, so . . ."

"So I'm no Mirpuri Paki either."

"It d-doesn't matter." Henry always stuttered when he was nervous. "I'm just glad you're not Greek."

Kareem gave him a look that Henry remembered from school. A fifth-form, what-am-I-going-to-do-with-the-new-boy look. Kareem's fingers circled Henry's upper arm, and he was back in the Becksley Grammar School first-floor toilets, hands gripping him, his forced, skidding walk to the end cubicle and the brief sight of a toilet bowl before the backs of his knees were kicked in and his head was forced down and into the bowl, cracking his chin on the porcelain edge. The agonizing fight for breath amidst the emptying cistern, then shouts, running feet and the bang of the cubicle door before being left alone with ruined glasses and pissed pants.

"Hey, man, you alright?" Kareem was standing close, closer than before, and staring at him. Wanting to know if he was okay. Like an ideal big brother, always there when you need him.

He touched his glasses for reassurance. "Sorry, miles away."

Kareem spoke again, and his tone was almost kindly. "Come and see my new car, man. I only picked it up last week." He turned toward the two women. "You're not goin' anywhere else, are you, Princess? You're stayin' here?"

"Yaah. What do you think?" Shunduri spoke without looking at him.

Kareem, seeming satisfied, reached out again to Henry, this time putting his arm around his shoulders, and started to guide him out into the main hall.

Henry complied: how could he not? In fact, one part of him was surprised at how safe he felt in this stranger's presence. He ventured further. "So, ah, what's Mirpuri?"

"They're the poor Pakis, man. Not the rich ones from Islamabad and Karachi. The dirty peasants from Mirpuri province that come over here and clean your toilets and run the railways and set up restaurants and try to cook as well as us Bengali boys. Crap food. Tastes like shit. And do they love their bread, man. Always bread. Like you *goras*, you Christians, with your potatoes. I can't take it. It's no meal without rice, yeah."

As they walked outside, Kareem glanced back at the Abbey and spoke more quietly. "Does this place have dungeons?"

"Sort of, I suppose. Quite big ones, actually."

"Jesus."

"Well, cellars, really."

The car, beaded with raindrops, loomed over them, its windows impenetrable even from this close.

"Now this is my pride an' joy, yeah? The latest Rover SUV. Tata just bought them out, you know. It's not even in the showrooms yet. See that paint job? I had it T-cut last night, ready for me this morning. And now GPS problems. Man, I didn't expect that. Too many trees, or hills, or somefin', messing with the signal. But check out those aerials."

Henry looked in vain. Not an aerial to be seen.

Kareem steered him to the rear of the car, where he pointed to an LED cylinder just visible inside the back window. "They're embedded in the LED. One for family, one for my Princess, you know? And two for business. For clients. Got to be in touch all the time, otherwise, that's the thin end of the wedge. They'd be callin' someone else before you know it. No loyalty these days, man. Just the quick or the dead, you know?"

"So . . . but that would mean, you'd need . . ." His voice failed him.

"Yeah, four mobs." Kareem squeezed his shoulder again. "Never leave home without 'em, yeah."

"Where do you put them all? The, ah, mobiles?"

Kareem grinned and pulled up a trouser leg to show a strangely underdeveloped calf that narrowed to an ankle smaller than Henry's wrist. His sock bulged. "That's for family." Then he carefully unbuttoned his skin-tight suit jacket to show his shirtfront, which was crossed by a diagonal of shiny black fabric. "That's for my new clients, and my old ones."

Henry goggled. "Th-that's, some kind of holster?"

"Yeah, they're big now. It started with the Sikh boys, the religious ones, wanting to carry their daggers, but still look good in a suit, yeah? Started to get 'em custom-made, then the Pakis found out how good they were for mobs. If you're a businessman, you need more than one, yeah?"

It had never occurred to him. His telephone sat on the hall table, where it had always been. "I don't know whether I want to know where the fourth . . ."

"Relax, man! My trouser pocket." Kareem laughed, glanced at his watch, a heavy silver Omega that Henry instantly coveted, threw a careless arm over Henry's shoulder, and started to move back toward the house.

Henry laughed as well, with a weird surge of confidence. Nothing could touch him now. He felt like the newest, weediest boy at school who suddenly finds himself best friends with the rugby captain. A rugby captain from Mars. He and Kareem were about the same age, both apparently born and bred in England, yet they may as well have come from different planets.

"Look, I'll show you something. The, ah, rose garden. It's just been excavated, you know. It's just around here, by that hedge."

"It's not too far, den? I don't want to leave Princess on her own . . ."

"No, no, not far at all. See, there. When it was dug out, look, they found these channels in a cross-shape, and this in the middle. We think it's the remains of a well."

Kareem stopped on the gravel and looked dubiously at the muddy garden beds.

"You can see more if you—"

"Nah, nah, I can see it all from here, man. That's a fountain in the middle, innit?"

"Well, I suppose it could have been," Henry replied doubtfully. "But that wouldn't be very medieval, and I don't . . ."

"It's a Paradise garden," said Kareem, warming to this theme. "I've seen 'em on BBC2, like out the front of the Taj Mahal. And in Spain. They always have a fountain in the middle. And four quarters for the four corners of Paradise."

"Oh, right. That would be the Muslim Paradise then. I don't think . . ." He spotted one of the dogs, Colin's black Labrador, bounding toward them.

"Jesus Christ," said Kareem, stepping rapidly backward, his hands over his crotch.

Henry slapped the dog's sides and fondled its ears. "Hey, Devil. Where's Colin then? He must have let you off. Hey, boy." The dog moaned ecstatically, then glanced back, its ears pricked, before loping off toward the river. Colin must have whistled for him.

Kareem was nowhere to be seen. Henry gave a token shake to his muddied cords, then wandered around to the Abbey's front.

"Oh, there you are, Kareem. Thought I'd lost you."

Kareem must have moved very fast because he was already up the steps to the portico'd front entrance, and reaching for the door handle.

"So, ah, you've seen enough then?"

"Yeah, yeah, yeah."

Their footsteps echoed in the main hall, the smell of fresh wood and new paint easily detectable here, and Henry wondered for a magical moment if this was how the first abbot must have felt as he walked into his brand-new abbey with his cohort: fellow travellers from the Holy Land, perhaps.

Kareem was still walking away from him, and Henry wondered if he'd done something wrong. "Did . . . ah, did the dog worry you? You don't like dogs?"

Kareem turned to face him and grinned, shrugging his shoulders. He almost looked embarrassed. "I'm from Tower Hamlets Estate, innit?"

"I don't . . ."

"National Front's very active round there, man. They used to set their dogs on us kids. The Asian an' black kids on the estate." Kareem gave a mock shudder. "German Shepherds, man, barkin' like crazy two inches from your face when you're pissing your pants on the monkey bars, with nowhere to go." He shook his head. "Dogs ain't my thing, man."

"Good Lord," said Henry, horrified. "Children? Why didn't someone call the police?"

"Ha ha, right." Kareem slapped Henry's back and squeezed his shoulder again. "You crack me up. I like you, man, I really like you."

As they walked through the hall, the Henri Regnault portrait came into view, and Kareem froze. "Jesus Christ," he said, and his arm dropped from Henry's shoulder.

Not surprising, really: the more than life-size African executioner, standing over a headless body and wiping his scimitar on his robes, took a lot of visitors aback.

Feeling oddly bereft without the warm weight of Kareem's arm, Henry hastened to explain. "It's pretty gory, isn't it? It's called *Execution without Trial* or sometimes just *The Executioner*. It was bought by an ancestor of mine: the Reverend Bourne. Used to give me nightmares as a child. Mind you, I still prefer it to these others." He gestured at the hated Victoriana decorating the walls of the hall. "Must say, not my favorites."

"Why have 'em, then?"

"They've been purchased by the Kiriakis Trust. I've got no say there. Old Theo Kiriakis's taste. That's Thee's grandfather."

"Yeah. You can't mess wiv elders." Kareem eyed the various paintings of kittens, puppies and family scenes, his expression neutral. "Are they valuable?"

"Oh, not really. Some of them were used, well, painted for the Pears' Soap advertising campaign of the time . . ." He stopped himself, unable to say anything more about them that was remotely positive. *If you can't say anything nice*, as Audrey used to say when he and Richard were little.

"They don't really go with the pieces, innit?"

"Pieces of what?"

"Weapons." Kareem gestured at the swords, daggers and early muzzle-loaders scattered between the pictures. "The weaponry you got up dere."

"Oh. Oh quite. You're perfectly right there. Well put." Thee had never agreed with him on this, and Richard seemed to think he was spineless for allowing old Kiriakis's kitsch to be displayed next to the armory.

Kareem appeared to have regained some of his confidence, now that they were inside. He folded his arms over his chest and approached the executioner. "*That* goes with the weaponry."

"Yes, yes, indeed. In fact that, ah, bloodstained scimitar in the executioner's hand, we've got two of those on the wall. The ones with the curved blades, next to the kittens in a basket."

"Oh yeah. Like in *Aladdin*. So, ah, why do you have all the swords up there?"

"Oh, ah, just tradition, I suppose. Most of them are still in beautiful order: perfectly useable if I ever felt the urge, you know. Hah hah."

Kareem didn't laugh. A buzzing sound started up, as if a bumblebee had sought refuge inside from the wet weather. Kareem bent and fished an angry mite of a mobile phone out of his sock. Putting it to his ear and launching into what Henry assumed was Hindi or something, Kareem strode toward the back door, giving the armory display a wide berth on the way out.

Henry wandered tentatively into the sitting room, caught a glimpse of himself in the mantel mirror, round-shouldered and soft-bellied, and drew in his tummy for a second before giving up. He had always been more duvet than washboard; Richard had scored all the tall-and-lean genes.

Some of the curtains had been drawn against the cool day, and the women were sitting opposite each other, on the new cabbage-rose chintz sofas. The two dark heads were together, almost touching, and little wisps of steam were rising like smoke signals from the tiny, transparent, gold-rimmed coffee cups in their hands. They looked up at him simultaneously, startlingly similar, as if they were cousins or even sisters. He felt like an intruder.

"Well, well." He briefly stretched out his hands to the fire, then unstuck a piece of baklava from a doily, and sat down next to his wife. Shunduri stared back at him, casually hostile.

"Isn't this nice," he said. She must be Greek, even if Kareem wasn't.

Thea put a hand on his knee, and spoke to Shunduri. "We were both at Oxford together, Henry and I. That's how we met."

He suddenly relaxed into the squashy back of the sofa, and could have kissed his wife. If she didn't even know how they met, she couldn't possibly be a relative. They really must just be lost, like Shunduri had said. He took an unwary bite of the baklava then realized that Shunduri was still looking at him.

"You know my dad then? Dr. Choudhury?"

"Your . . . Oh, good Lord," he said with sudden comprehension, speaking with his mouth full. "I didn't realize. Shunduri *Choudhury*. Yes, yes, of course, lovely fellow. We couldn't have done without him at the Abbey, you know." He leaned forward, elbows on knees, smiling with relief. "You're down here to visit your parents, are you? And your brother. Good lord, of course! And you probably haven't seen that new bypass they've opened this last month . . . Ah, that's why you were lost . . ." He realized that he had just sprayed a bit of baklava, and subsided. Last thing he wanted was an interview with Audrey about who'd put honey on the new sofa cushions.

Shunduri nodded at him in a dignified sort of way and fiddled with the knot on her headscarf. "I've been very busy with college in London, yaah. Studyin'." She paused, before saying with a careless air, "Have you seen my sister, then? Is she, like, stayin' around here or somefink?"

Henry, trying to discreetly remove the remains of the baklava from the roof of his mouth, turned to Thea, who shook her head and spoke. "I don't think so, Shunduri. We were introduced to your brother—Tariq, is it?—just the other day."

"Oh," Shunduri said, as if Henry and Thea had failed some sort of test. "I thought she'd be . . . We came all this way . . ." Her voice trembled. "My own sister. It's not my fault." Then she burst into tears.

"Good Lord," said Henry again, standing up and taking an instinctive step backward.

"For heaven's sake, Henry," said his wife, moving to the other sofa to sit next to Shunduri. "Find something else to say."

But even if he could have, the bloody endless baklava seemed to have glued itself to the roof of his mouth. He retreated further, grabbed the tissue box on the writing table and scooted it across to Thea.

With masterly timing, Kareem appeared at the doorway and, understandably, paused. Henry felt a surge of sympathy for him, although he didn't seem that surprised by the turn of events and simply said, "Princess."

Shunduri hiccupped and wiped her nose on the proffered tissues. Then she broke into a rapid, high-pitched flow of their native language, periodically interrupted by little outcroppings of English.

". . . just not fair . . . always the last to know . . . no one will tell me anyfing . . . dropped everything to come here . . . always the favorite . . . what about me . . ."

Kareem said something to her, and she shook her head violently, then looked round at them all, her eyes swimming.

"I *called* her you know. I *called* her just last weekend, to say I was coming down and that *gora* Simon picked up. He said, "Your bruvver's took her and good riddance." But Mum and Dad won't say *nuffink* to me."

Kareem looked as if he was about to say something, but she plowed on, the pitch of her voice rising steadily.

"And when I called home last night to say what time I was coming, Baiyya wouldn't say nuffink *either*. I didn't do *anyfing* wrong. She's my *sister*."

Henry started to say Good Lord, but Thea caught his eye, and he stopped himself so abruptly that he had a coughing fit and had to retreat with his free hand over his mouth to prevent any more baklava escaping. Kareem, ignoring his host's struggles and seemingly unbothered by Shunduri's tears, took over tissue-box duties from Thea and stood watching Shunduri, his plan apparently being to just wait for her to wind down to silence, like some kind of clockwork doll.

Perhaps Kareem was used to this kind of thing happening all the time. Henry felt a wave of gratitude for Thea's cool pragmatism, which, while not exactly serene, was certainly never out of control. He couldn't imagine Thea losing it in public like this.

Shunduri let up for a moment, then launched into another wail. Henry eyed Kareem's unmoved expression with admiration. Imagine living with this every day.

The sound of thunder outside, then heavy rain, interrupted proceedings. Kareem flinched, took a hasty glance at his Omega, and turned to his hosts. "Time we was goin'. Shunduri's family . . ."

"It's pouring," said Thea. "Why don't you wait until it stops?"

Kareem shook his head. "Really must get goin'. She'll settle down once she's with her mum. Very nice to meet you both. Come on, Princess. Let's go see your mum and dad."

"Oh yes, of course," said Henry. "Look, I'll see you out. You can't miss it from here." He followed Kareem, who towed a sniffing and complaining Shunduri through to the main hall and toward the rear entrance.

As the rain increased in force, the lights flickered, glinting off the armory. Kareem sped up, and Henry had to break into a trot to keep up, saying to their retreating backs, "Just, ah, continue round to the front, then to the gates, then hard left."

He watched as Kareem helped Shunduri into the car's back seat, ran to the driver's door and jumped in. Perhaps she needs a lie-down, Henry thought, as he stopped under the doorway's sheltering arch and called out to them. "Just a summer shower, you know. It'll have passed by the time you . . . Just make sure you leave by the front gates: that'll take you past the Lodge—that's where we're staying—then the very next house you come to on the left, just before you hit the village proper, that's Windsor Cottage, and if you miss it, Mrs. Darby's is next . . ."

But his last words were swallowed up by the roar of the Rover's engine and the scream of flying gravel as the car turned tightly on the circular drive and accelerated away. He watched them speed off admiringly: he'd never have dared go that hard on gravel. He stuck a finger in his mouth to finally scrape the last remnant of baklava off a sore back tooth. Good Lord.

# Nine

IT WOULD BE impossible for any man, even one of Dr. Choudhury's mental powers, to relax or to concentrate while Mrs. Begum, fizzing with excitement like a just-lit firecracker, was rushing between kitchen and front door, kitchen and sitting-room front window, looking for the much-awaited, much-anticipated arrival of their youngest child. A red-letter Tuesday, indeed. Baby's favorite dishes were on the stove, her favorite hair oil was on the mantelpiece, and Mrs. Begum had completely disrupted his peace of mind by rearranging the occasional tables in the sitting room.

The paan tray was already on display, heaped and gleaming, and everywhere there was an unusual profusion of flowers in vases and plants in pots: that Mrs. Darby's influence, he was sure of it. Dr. Choudhury felt like he was in a particularly oppressive jungle, or a Christian funeral. To walk to the sitting-room window, he had to shoulder past a large drooping plant in a brass container. He shuddered and wiped at the plant's point of contact with his second-best jacket, a tweedy triumph in burgundy and green with a subtle yellow fleck. Plants belong outside, people belong inside. Where was Baby? She should be here by now.

He just happened to glance out the window again when a large, dark car drew up at the cottage gate. The growl of its engine triggered a shriek and a flash of color as Mrs. Begum rocketed past the sitting-room entrance en route to the front door.

In light of the importance of the occasion, he gave only the most cursory of glances into the mantel mirror to check his hair and his tie (lemon and gold: an Eid present from Baby), smoothing both of them fondly. Buttoning his jacket as he walked down the hallway, Dr. Choudhury hurrumphed himself into position just behind his wife, who had already opened the front door. Her yellow sari set off his jacket nicely, and his tie. She could call and cry: she was the mother after all. When the necessary female fuss had died down, he would receive his due as paterfamilias, from the youngest and stupidest of his offspring. He was in no hurry. How long it had been since their Baby had been home.

Shunduri was not visible through the tinted windscreen, but a young man, very well dressed, had jumped down from the driver's seat and hurried to a rear passenger door, which he swung open with a flourish before standing back in an elaborate display of physical contact avoided.

A figure stepped out, away from the shielding door, and there was their daughter in a tightly fitting long black dress and matching headscarf. The front of the scarf had been pushed back a little, revealing the front of a scimitar-sharp bob, which Dr. Choudhury recognized at once as the latest celebrity haircut.

Although much of her face was obscured by aviator-frame glasses, he saw with satisfaction that Shunduri looked even taller, slimmer and more polished than he remembered: a remarkable achievement, given the short-and-round-ness of her mother, who was sighing and muttering something about everyone starving in London.

The man disappeared around to the back of the car where he appeared to be unloading luggage. Shunduri turned to them and gave a theatrical startle before crying out "Amma! Abba!" and running with a slow high-heeled stagger up the front path and into her mother's arms.

Dr. Choudhury felt tears prick at his eyes and hurrumphed again, loudly. *He* had never felt a mother's touch since he was school age. It took some time for Shunduri to extricate herself from the maternal embrace, but then, sunglasses removed and gratifyingly teary as well, she made a token feint for her father's feet before being drawn into his arms and bursting into loud sobs. Baby was home.

---

TARIQ RAN DOWNSTAIRS and into the hall, just in time to see his parents disappearing into the sitting room and his youngest sister pause dramatically in the doorway, framed by a sweep of peacock feathers behind her. He held his arms out. "Baby."

"Baiyya!" Shunduri gave a little shriek and skipped toward him, gestured toward his feet and accepted his hug. "I've missed you soo much, Bai, like you wouldn't believe."

Despite the little-girl voice, she seemed much older than when he'd last seen her: older than Rohimun in fact. Shunduri's perfect make-up, slender figure and cinched-in, stylish clothes were those of the married, moneyed women he used to sell to in the Jo'burg galleries. He cleared his throat, feeling all the weight of older-brother responsibility.

"Yeah, me too, Baby. God, you've grown, yeah."

"Are you back for good? Where's Affa? Where is she? Are you going to sort her out?"

Before he could answer, the peacock feathers shivered and moved toward them, then swung away to reveal a short, broad-shouldered, shaven-headed man in a tight suit, carrying an entire stuffed peacock as well as a number of boxes wrapped in gold paper. Tariq stared at him, expressionless, and the man quickly piled the boxes on the hall-stand and approached him, smiling, the peacock still tucked under his arm.

"*Salaamalaikum*, Baisahib," he said, using the full, formal version of the honorary title. "Kareem Guri. I'm honored to meet you, man. I've heard a lot about you." He held out his hand. Fat diamond studs glittered in each ear, and Tariq could see the trace of a Nike tick that had been shaved into his right eyebrow and was now growing out, with the help of some kohl sketched into the gap.

Shunduri wound herself around her brother's arm, using her girly voice. "Kareem's grandfather knew Amma's uncle the tailor. Their wives were, umm"—Shunduri flapped a hand—"*cousins* and Kareem, umm, helped out with Uncle's funeral."

Tariq nodded but did not take Kareem's outstretched hand. Kareem, still smiling, withdrew it and patted the peacock absent-mindedly on its rump.

Mrs. Begum, eavesdropping, reappeared at the entrance to the sitting room, tears in her eyes. "My beloved Khalo, Uncle! Like a father to me he was, sending for me to join him in Dhaka, when I was left with no one, no one at all." She grabbed a corner of her sari and wiped her eyes, then gave Tariq's arm a squeeze. A don't-spoil-this-for-me squeeze.

He affected not to notice, and kept watching Kareem. After one last squeeze, hard—migod Mum must have been working out—she let go of him and put an arm around Shunduri, gesturing with the other for Kareem to join them in the sitting room.

Kareem dipped his head but stood back, making it clear that he was waiting for Tariq to precede him. He pretended not to see Mum's gesture. Slimy bastard. Why the fuck was he here?

Tariq dawdled, rocking back on one foot and patting his pockets as if he'd forgotten something. Kareem, seemingly unfazed, continued to wait. Jesus, he looked like one fit fucker under that suit. And with all his nodding and smiling, not moving an inch. Eventually Tariq admitted defeat and walked, stiff-backed, into the sitting room, far too aware of man and bird following close behind him.

Baby was already curled up next to Mum on the sofa, sniffling and sighing: milking the big reunion scene for everything it was worth, that was for sure. You'd have thought she was the one who'd been overseas for a year and a half, instead of in London and only three months since she'd last been home. She was sounding off to Mum about how they had ended up at the Abbey on the way, and met Henry and Thea Bourne, and were all great friends now. As if that was likely. Perhaps she'd leaned out of the car window and waved at them on the way past.

And who was this Kareem wide-boy Guri? Mum was crying again: Kareem was talking about the old country, beautiful bloody Bangladesh, the tailor's Dhaka shop, now taken over by some cousin apparently. Even Dad had tears in his eyes.

Tariq stalked to the wing-back chair opposite his father's and sat at an angle so as to keep an eye on everyone. No one had looked to him for guidance on how to treat this *gundah* muscle-builder, who seemed to have been accepted, even welcomed, without reservation. They were all in thrall to Kareem's novelty: his sharp suit and worldly smiles, his ability to spout sentimental Bangladesh bullshit.

When he, Tariq, had arrived last Saturday, turning up at dawn with Rohimun, their little Munni, white in the face and almost dead on her feet, he had been the man of the family then. No one had questioned his place to direct that she be put to bed with a hot-water bottle, nor his entitlement to sit up with Mum and Dad over chai and pakhoras to discuss the situation, decide what to do. Dad had deferred to his judgement about the danger of press interest, had acquiesced to all Tariq's statements about the future. Of course, Rohimun could not stay in the cottage: they all recognized that. And when Dad had made the suggestion of the Abbey as a temporary hiding place, he had done so tentatively, dependent on Tariq's approval.

Tariq noticed that everyone was looking his way and realized that he had lost the thread of the conversation. He was about to mouth a surly, teenage *What?* when something brushed against his hair, with the unmistakable scent of Giorgio for Men. Robbie's scent. His heart in his mouth, he turned his head toward the fireplace and almost into Kareem's rounded pin-striped bottom, inches away.

"Up, up, back," said Mrs. Begum. "Beautiful bird."

Kareem, standing between Tariq's chair and the fireplace, was arranging the stuffed peacock on the mantel at an angle so that its tail swept down behind Tariq's chair in a river of color. Tariq jerked his head back around, heart thumping, recrossed his legs and folded his arms.

A seemingly endless disjointed conversation ensued, all focused on the man behind him while he sat, trapped in his chair and surrounded by scented rustling, feeling every slight nudge to the back of his chair as Kareem adjusted the peacock's positioning under Mrs. Begum's pleased supervision. The rich scent, everyone's staring, Kareem's proximity were excruciating. How long was this going to take? *Robbie, why did I ever leave you?*

———————

TARIQ HAD KNOWN from that first evening in Tajura Barracks with Robbie that he, Tariq Choudhury, was what he was. Not a man who couldn't find love, or a straight man making use of what was available, but a poof, a faggot. And Islam couldn't change him, or save him.

From that night he'd felt liberated, enlightened, separate from the daily round of posturing and failure that barracks life had become. After that, it had only been a matter of time, stringing out his training at the barracks in Libya, stealing as much time with Robbie as he could until Robbie finished his three-month mercenary stint there and took off back to Jo'burg.

After that, it was suddenly easy to accept the humiliation of resigning, admitting that he wasn't up for it, was a failure as a soldier of God; the shame of his cell-leader's ready acceptance of this, and the Libyan officer's comment that Tariq was better suited to a *madrassa* than a military school. Easy to make vague promises to keep in touch, accept the hints of perhaps another role, later.

Then a roundabout route by light plane and private jeep back to South Africa and meeting up weeks later with Robbie in Jo'burg for a wild spree of partying, drinking and generally following him around like a Siamese twin. Desire did not fade in those early months, but, away from the petty desolation of Tajura Barracks, he began to see that his beautiful Robbie, as short and fair and free-spirited as he was not, was more of a temporary liberator than a lifelong companion: a fuck-buddy rather than the lover that he had originally thought, in the rush and high of feelings freed.

Tariq had truly begun to feel the void then: no lover to adore, no religion, no family, no politics. For Jamat-al-Islami and the cell he was a dropout, a failure. Who was he then? What was left? After three months Robbie had run out of money and was talking about another stint in Libya, or maybe something in Algeria or Darfur. Nowhere Tariq could follow: Tajura had proved that. Once Robbie went, what could he do? What would he be?

Chance connections at one of those endless Jo'burg parties had led to a job in a gallery, and then, once Tariq's Oxbridge background became known, an acting curatorship at the Goodman Gallery. The gallery, filled with moveable walls, natural light and risky installations, and basking in the kudos now given it as a supporter of black artists through the pre-Mandela years, was a breath of fresh air after his interrupted PhD studies. Tariq basked as well, in the joy of revisiting this side of himself, after so long without.

But the void was still there, and even before Robbie had left for a consultancy with a private security firm in Iraq, Tariq knew that, despite the gallery job, the all-embracing hedonism of the underground gay scene in Jo'burg was not enough. No one seemed to belong to anything larger than themselves, believe in anything greater than their own desires. He needed a community, and a system of belief. He was nothing, less than nothing, without that.

Over the next nine months, his career at the gallery had flourished, but his sense of aimlessness and homesickness grew. He carried it as a deserved burden and, he thought, a secret one, until one drizzly afternoon, his boss Linda's hand had landed gently on his shoulder.

"Go home," she'd said. "Fly to London for me, meet these people I want to exhibit, see their work, take some time with your family. You've earned it."

She moved away, then returned briefly to give his back a brisk, get-on-with-it smack, making him think of his father. Tears had sprung to his eyes.

"Then come back. You're the best bloody curator I've had."

---

KAREEM HAD AT last returned to the small occasional chair near to Dr. Choudhury, but Tariq's gut was painfully tight, and he tried to deepen his breathing, to relax the cramp, assuage the longing. *God, Robbie, where are you now?*

Dr. Choudhury laughed at something, and Kareem quickly laughed with him. Bastard. Tariq felt his hand clench in his lap as he glared at the visitor. Kareem, perhaps sensing the look, glanced at him.

He was a joke as a big brother, an eldest son. A *casra kusrah*, a dirty homo. Sex between men was pervasive in the traditional Muslim world, given the unavailability of its women. But a real homosexual: that was the unspeakable, the unclean thing. Even here, with his family, he was committing this sin . . .

A man without a wife was a boy, not a man. A man who had lost his wife was but half a man. A man who did not want to marry, to bring a wife into his family to care for his parents and to give them grandchildren, was no son, no man at all. He stole another look at Kareem, who, hands on knees, was listening with rapt attention to some Oxford gossip of Dad's. How could Dad even think that Kareem would be interested in college gossip? Then again, all he'd ever needed was an audience, and he certainly had that. Now Mum was trying to get in on the act as well, hovering, waiting for Dad to take a breath so that she could jump in.

Anyone would think that Kareem, not he, was the eldest son, the prodigal returned, the rescuer of sisters. Kareem sat and listened but at the same time seemed to be aware of everything else that was happening in the room, with an alert stillness that made him look ready for anything. This was the kind of man Jamat-al-Islami had wanted at Tajura, with the single-mindedness that Tariq had never had.

What had he taken away from that time in Libya, really? An efficiency in times of crisis, perhaps. Certainly he was physically tougher.

Kareem had that toughness too, Tariq could see that, despite the suit and the smiles, but with him it was a gift from the street.

What else? He could probably still strip and remount a Kalashnikov at speed, though he never would again. And the paramedic course had helped him out of a few tight spots.

A lull in the conversation brought him back to the present, in time to see Kareem head out of the room and come back with the gold-wrapped gifts. A Rolex for Dr. Choudhury and another for Tariq, both proffered apologetically, modestly. A box of mangoes ("Direct from Bangladesh yesterday, Khalama, Auntie,") for Mrs. Begum and a beauty box for "the other sister."

They all accepted their gifts and fell silent, his parents looking caught uncomfortably between sentimentality and suspicion. He could see it on their faces: the fellow Bangladeshi who could conjure up such memories of home, who had helped bury Mum's dearest uncle, who showed such respect, knew the old forms and traditions as if he were their generation, not Tariq's and Shunduri's. The unrelated male who had arrived without notice, ridden in a car with their unmarried daughter, known her in London.

---

MRS. BEGUM TOOK the box of mangoes into the kitchen, picked one out, put it to her nose and inhaled deeply. The sweet heavy perfume of this prince of fruits always took her back to eating them as a child in her village on special occasions, every last piece of flesh scraped off the skin with her teeth, the juice running down her chin. She bent to look through her cupboards, found her Royal Albert old-country-roses saucers and a sharp knife and proceeded to slice up three mangoes into six portions, neatly segmenting the flesh into squares. She bent the skins into convex arcs and placed one on each saucer, so the exposed cubes could be lifted off with a fork. Even the Windsors could not prefer cake to this.

What a good boy to bring gifts, touch their feet in the way he did, not like these modern boys with their Christian handshakes and phones always ringing. And he was in Mrs. Guri's household.

Mrs. Begum reserved the mango stones, with scraps of flesh still clinging to them, onto a separate, plain plate for kitchen-eating later. Was Kareem also the man in the car of whom Mrs. Guri had warned? Either way, Shunduri must be disposed of soon, before the scandal got worse. She frowned. Two could play at matchmaker.

If Mrs. Guri knew that Kareem was here, it meant that she wanted to marry him into the Choudhurys. Mrs. Begum loaded the saucers onto a metal tray and started to hunt for the small shiny forks that Mrs. Darby had given her. Fish-forks, her friend had called them. Who could eat fish with a tiny fork anyway? No wonder they had never been used.

If Mrs. Guri did not know that Kareem was here, then Mrs. Begum would make her own enquiries and would not be above moving events along. The love-match: so dreaded by all respectable parents, yet so common over here in UK, with boys and girls going to the same schools, driving cars, at college together. They happened often enough, hushed up, with everyone pretending that they were a quick-quick arranged marriage, in accord with the wishes of some family elder on their deathbed. She snorted. That family elder then being miraculously revived to attend the *nikkah*, of course. And the reception. And the *walima*. At least Kareem was not Hindu or Christian, *Inshallah*. In fact, the way things were going, he might be her only Bangladeshi son-in-law.

Kareem reminded her a bit of Prince Andrew, with his dark suit and jewelry. A good match for Baby, who, as far as her loud mouth and spending habits went, could have been Princess Fergie herself. But Baby could be managed. Even her worst behavior, her smiles-and-laughing one minute and tears-and-wailing the next, a gift she had had since childhood, was never known to operate against her own interests. And what could be more in Baby's interests than this?

Kareem looked like a good boy, with a good job. He would be a generous husband, give her lots of clothes, and be worldly enough to not be put off by news of a troubled sister-in-law. Just think of them in a big detached red-brick house close to her, just like Andrew and

Fergie used to have. Mrs. Guri was a good, practical sort of woman. Between the two of them, and the threat of scandal, there would be no need here for a *funchait* to force a reluctant suitor into marriage with slaps and beatings by a council of elders.

---

KAREEM KNEW HE was on a knife edge. The brother's glowering, he'd expected that. And he'd shown nuff respect to the elders, though he would have to watch his step: one car trip with their daughter he could get away with, and one only.

Not that there needed to be another: this should keep his princess happy for a while, show her he could be relied upon, keep everything sweet. While he nodded and smiled, he looked around uneasily. That castle, Bourne Abbey, which he could see out the window, like something out of Transylvania. In this room, books, magazines and newspapers everywhere, no television in sight. No community here to visit. What did they do in the evenings? This was not your usual Bangla family, with the father a professor, the whole family so wealthy with their own house, detached too, and removed from the community.

He tried to remember what Auntie had said about them. The father was involved with those people at the castle, with their dogs. And Auntie had thought that the brother had gone fundamental. He'd planned ahead: set all his mobs to vibrate, first time ever, and put Baby in the back seat once they'd left the motorway. He'd even been prepared to touch Tariq's feet if necessary.

It had been a surprise to find Tariq in jeans and t-shirt, clean-shaven. And there was something else about him, a familiarity, though he was sure they'd never met. He dressed like a clubber, but looked tougher: maybe he'd gotten into some trouble wherever he'd disappeared to in the last few years.

Mrs. Begum came back in with a trayful of mangoes, and as Kareem shifted small tables and pot plants to make room, he took the opportunity to have a good look at the wall above the mantelpiece, on which hung a gilt frame around a portrait of Dodi and Princess Di. A photo originally, or rather two formal shots put together so that they appeared to be gazing lovingly almost into each other's eyes, and covered by a thick layer of clear acrylic to give the illusion of paint strokes. Dodi was slightly out of focus, squinting into sunlight, while Diana, soulful and evenly lit, was a studio shot.

Mrs. Begum must have noticed his interest in the picture, for she smiled at him and shook her head, giving a sideways glance at it. "So sad!" she whispered under the flow of Dr. Choudhury's talking, then sprang up to pick another, smaller picture off the same wall and gave it to him.

This was no composite portrait but an ordinary Kodak shot blown up just beyond its limits, of a bearded Christian man and a blonde, toothy woman in a Chanel suit standing in front of a McDonald's.

From one side of the photo extended an arm and part of a plump shoulder partially draped in a bright yellow sari, the hand reaching toward the couple at the center of the photo, fingers stretched out, as if to hold the moment itself for posterity. The blonde woman also had her hand extended, but her expression was ambivalent, and it was not clear whether she was about to grasp the hand or fend it off.

Kareem watched as Mrs. Begum's fingers traced the outline of the yellow arm.

"Is *me*," she whispered. "I was *there*."

Kareem, in the dark but playing safe, gave an exaggerated start. "You were there?"

Mrs. Begum nodded. "The Prince and Princess Michael. Grand Opening of the McDonald's restaurant. By Special Invitation." She stretched out her arm and gestured to mimic the arm in the photo. "This, my arm, was in the newspaper."

He stared hard at the picture and nodded respectfully. Fucking hell, they did know royalty.

# Ten

KAREEM WAS JUST what Dr. Choudhury needed. A successful man-of-the-world, able to recognize and respect his position as both an elder of the community and as a man of learning. Kareem's sympathetic interest was slowly but surely drawing out of him (for he hated to talk about himself) the full story behind the inexplicable falling-off of student attendances at his Historical Architecture lectures and tutorials over the last few years. Not to mention the sad and disturbing changes that had overtaken so much that he had loved about Oxford since his first days there as a young man. As young as Kareem.

From here, and encouraged by Kareem's undivided attention, he segued into a brief outline of how a new wave of professors with a mania for publishing and self-promotion had washed into the university and suddenly placed him in the untenable position of having to justify his time, his publishing record and his falling enrolments.

Not also to mention (though he did: this Kareem was so *simpatico*) the disturbing rumors of Saudi funding, which had coincided with Professor Bertha Beeton's sudden enthusiasm for a Chair of Islamic Studies. And for the current departmental fashion in *soi-disant* authorities on Eastern culture such as Edward Said and Tariq Ali, and the need for what Professor Beeton, as faculty head, was calling "engagement" with Jamat-al-Islami and other, similar extremist religious groups that had somehow, while he wasn't looking, become key players around the university.

Dr. Choudhury had found himself isolated, he was not sure how, by this new talking, these new attitudes. His own philosophy, that of a Westernized, moderate Muslim, seemed to be no longer *comme il faut* and even seemed to irritate some parties, as indicated by a variety of hurtful and unexpected comments made in recent faculty meetings about Asian Anglophiles.

And all of it had been made worse by the loss, in quick succession, of a number of colleagues with whom he was familiar and comfortable, who had retired or moved on, and the fact that he and Professor Beeton were dons at the same college. The senior common room, his beloved SCR, in which he used to spend such a large part of his time, was no longer an oasis of pipe-smoke and newspapers and the odd fashion magazine. It was a tense, watchful place, with positions being taken and alliances forged and broken in a way that he seemed unable to keep track of.

To Kareem's attentive and understanding eyes, he explained himself further. No one appreciated his little *bons mots*, his classical allusions, his love of beauty and color. Nor his tales of life at the college when he was young and, if he may say so himself, its number-one student at that time. All they wanted to know was how he felt about the British imperialist hegemony that had alienated him from the workers of Dhaka. His Rhodes scholarship award, he told Kareem now just as he had said then, was one of the proudest achievements of his life. Kareem was nodding admiringly. How good-looking this young man was, how respectful.

---

DR. CHOUDHURY AND Kareem seemed happy enough downstairs; Tariq, unsociable boy, had left muttering something about someone he had to see, and Mrs. Begum needed, *needed* to know, so she followed her daughter, who was heading upstairs. She sat on Shunduri's bed and watched her tie and retie her headscarf in front of the mirror as an excuse to look at her reflected face and figure. How young and healthy she was, and in full possession of the powers that went with that.

And now coming home with a boy. There was only one way, the time-honored way, to deal with that, before there was any more talk. She squinted at her daughter's behind, which had developed a some-thing, a sideways shifting, in short a wiggle, since she had been up to London. It was definitely time.

"Your studies must be ending soon."

"Yaah, maybe . . ."

As far as her studies went, Shunduri had never shown the interest or ability that her siblings had. But then, she had always been so easy to manage. Mrs. Begum was able to dress her up like a little doll for visits and weddings. Tariq always had his head in a book the whole time and Munni had to be dragged out of the car, shedding bracelets with every step, then watched like a hawk so as not to draw on walls. She always had a felt-tip pen hidden somewhere.

"Your father and I have been thinking about your future." Shun-duri, in the act of reapplying her lipstick, locked eyes with her mother in the mirror.

"You know we want the best for you and want you to be settled. And you are of an age . . ."

Shunduri turned away, flounced to the wardrobe and pushed open its sliding door with unnecessary force.

Mrs. Begum decided to adopt a firmer tone. "You are now of an age where you should be getting married."

Silence. A coat hanger clicked into place on the rail amongst its fellows.

"We have a few boys in mind, but we are a modern family: you may also ask around." Shunduri's back was still turned toward her mother, her head bowed, and she appeared to be biting her nails. She hadn't seen her daughter do that since she was twelve. "Well, then."

Shunduri spoke into her nails. "Why are you pickin' on me? I'm the youngest, in case you'd forgotten. Why don't you marry off Baiyya or Affa. And where is Affa, anyway?"

Mrs. Begum kept her temper with difficulty. "We are not talking of Tariq or . . . anyone else."

"You always side with them. You just want to get me off your hands. I must be a problem to you or somefin'." Sniff. "All I want is to be happy. Is that too much to ask?"

Mrs. Begum swallowed her annoyance and tried to speak soothingly. "That is all we want, Baby. We want you to be happy, to find a good boy who'll take care of you . . . I have asked around. There is this boy, Hassan, he is a doctor-in-training. His sister is married, she is a teacher, and his brother is an accountant . . ."

Shunduri's hands flew out and she crashed the wardrobe door open so hard that it bounced shut again. "You're not listening to what I'm saying!"

"I have his ceevee—"

"You don't care! You don't know anything about me! You don't know who I want! You want to get rid of me!"

"Shunduri!" Mrs. Begum rose to her feet, and her daughter beat a strategic retreat out of the bedroom door, crying. "You want me to be happy, you marry off Affa then! See if you can!"

Shunduri disappeared from the bedroom doorway with some haste, and by the time Mrs. Begum reached it, she heard the slam of the bathroom door and the rattle of the bolt sliding home. She smacked the doorframe with her open palm: a poor substitute for her daughter's most deserving face. Now Baby would have a bath, as she always did when upset, and use up all the hot water.

Mrs. Begum walked back to Shunduri's bed and sat down to think. In all those words, Baby had never said no marriage, never-never, unlike her other children. She had just fussed about the choice. And about the need to marry off Rohimun first, as if her mother needed to be told. That was the problem then: she was afraid Munni's reputation was spoiling Baby's own chances. She would need to think on this slowly, then act quickly.

Time was running out, even for her beautiful Baby, what with being only a breath away from twenty-four and having a sister in disgrace. Families would start asking themselves what was wrong with her that she was not betrothed by now, would start to speculate. A modern girl, like her sister perhaps.

Her hand clutched the red satin bedspread. Shunduri must, and would, get the wedding her mother had never had, with every traditional trimming, every visit and gift and celebration that she was entitled to, as the youngest child of Dr. Babru Choudhury and Mrs. Syeda Begum.

She went to the bathroom and banged the flat of her hand against the door. "Stay then. Stay upstairs, I tell you. I do not wish to see you now. We, all of us, will talk downstairs and you will not be allowed."

An angry gasp could be heard, a sliding of locks and turning of handles, then the door opened, and Shunduri's pretty face appeared, as creased up with frowns and wantings as a sultana. "That's not fair! I want—"

"Wanting-wanting. You *stay*." She turned her back on her daughter's outraged face and started walking toward the stairs. As soon as she got to the kitchen, Baby would follow, quick as a chicken at feed-time.

But there was a creak on the stairs, a cautious and dignified creak, and Mrs. Begum huffed a sigh of annoyance: only her husband, of all husbands, could be in so many wrong places at wrong times. Dr. Choudhury's head rose from the stairwell, peering upward, and the bathroom door slammed shut again.

He coughed at her in his usual way. "That temper in your daughter."

She glowered at him and folded her arms. Now Shunduri would never come out, and there would be no chance for mother–daughter talking in the kitchen. She, Syeda Begum, was the only worldly passenger on this ship of fools.

He spoke again. "Has she decided on a boy?"

Did he think that such things were done in an instant? "No, no. Soon." Her tone did not invite the requesting of details.

"Ah."

Silence rose between them, along with all the thoughts and worries so familiar to them both that there was no naming them. They appeared before Mrs. Begum's eyes like phantoms: unmarriageable son and daughters, elopements, children born out of wedlock, disgrace upon disgrace. Soon, soon, marriage must be soon, or disaster, more disaster, would surely follow. She knew what was best for them.

"Kareem is outside. In the garden," Dr. Choudhury added, with a rising inflection as if he really could not understand why. "A cup of tea?" he asked tentatively.

Mrs. Begum could see steam escaping from under the bathroom door, and she could hear Shunduri humming. She was happy enough now, ungrateful girl, running a bath while they had visitors in the house. As she went downstairs, her husband's voice floated back up the stairwell, from where his bald patch was descending in front of her. "The way forward, Mrs. Begum, is to use tact and subtlety. I do appreciate that these skills do not come easily to one of your nature, so I draw your attention to the fable of the sun and the wind and their competing attempts to remove the overcoat of a man passing by. The wind blew with great force, which led the, ah, everyman to wrap it ever more closely around himself. The sun however, inclined its life-giving rays upon his back and shoulders and in no time at all . . ."

His voice faded around a corner, and by the time she caught up with him, the story had evidently ended.

She followed him into the kitchen. "Perhaps next, her father can talk to her. I am sure she will be happier," she said, as she handed her husband half-a-cup of tea, just the way he liked it. *You being so full of wind anyway, maybe you can blow her into a good temper and a betrothal with one big puff.*

---

WHEN DR. CHOUDHURY returned to the sitting room, Kareem was still outside. What a pleasant young man, and certainly more socially responsible than Tariq, just leaving like that. Not intellectual perhaps, but with an untutored quickness of understanding so lacking in his own nearest and dearest when it came to the exigencies of professional life.

Dr. Choudhury walked to the sitting room's front window.

Intermittent puffs of smoke were emanating from the roof of Kareem's car. A slave to the god tobacco, it seemed. Their cosy little coterie had scattered now: first Shunduri skipping upstairs to primp and preen (what an attachment to her mirror that girl had), closely followed by her mother, who, of course, could not leave her alone for an instant. No wonder they had had words and were now both sulking.

Kareem had not been able to offer any insights as to how to manage the bumptious rudeness of the head of department, who, it must be admitted, had become simply unbearable since her last visit to Riyadh, cutting him dead in corridors and lending out his rooms to postgraduate students to have coffee and drop biscuit crumbs in. But Kareem's undivided attention, the way he had leaned forward, his eyes fixed on Dr. Choudhury's, the hmms and ahhs of respectful empathy, had been a balm, a positive balm, to his troubled mind.

Truly, he felt now, as he moved further into a patch of sunshine in the window embrasure that, incidentally, also enabled a better view of the smoking SUV, Professor Beeton's dislike of him had grown into what could only be called outright aggression. Perhaps it was a result of those hormonal disruptions that some women seemed so prone to in their teens and then again in the autumn of their lives.

He was not certain of Mrs. Begum's status in that regard, but her sudden flarings of temper at unexpected times, her irritability, and at other times her strange absentmindedness—his cravats had been missing for days now—could well be put down to this. How prey to their bodily functions women were.

The smoke had ceased, but now Kareem could be seen talking to the Bourne children, Andrew and Jonathon. They must have walked over from the Lodge, hoping for more of Mrs. Begum's *ladhu* balls, most likely. A minute later both of the children were on Kareem's shoulders, laughing and screaming as he ran across the side lawn with them and pretended to fall, tipping them onto the grass. Really, Kareem had lost all notion of dignity. But Dr. Choudhury was in a mood to be indulgent and allowed himself to smile with theoretical understanding at the high spirits of youth.

Anyway, perhaps he was, as the elder statesman of the college and still, of course, a fine figure of a man, also a convenient authority figure for Professor Beeton to beat herself against. Ah, that sunshine was very pleasant. He laced his hands over his stomach and closed his eyes for a few seconds to enable himself to concentrate more fully. In short, her behavior could well be viewed as a cry for help from one of his sex, his age and his experience. His, shall we say, *savoir faire*.

Kareem was standing again, but now rotating with increasing speed while grasping a child's arm and leg. That child's mouth was open in a sort of continuous, happy wail, while the other child jumped up and down, shouting, "Me! Me next!" Surely Henry and Thea never did anything of the sort.

Bertha was indeed one of those women who, having sacrificed their childbearing years to academia and career, were perhaps, in the twilight of their lives, grappling with regret, nay, even remorse, that certain opportunities peculiar to the female sex had passed them by. The more Dr. Choudhury applied his mind, the clearer it seemed.

Yes, that was it. He nodded sagely and squeezed his tummy a little with his interlaced fingers. In short, Bertha had developed feelings for him, and was now exhibiting all of the behaviors of a woman scorned. Possibly that hope had been fanned by his sitting next to her at the last-but-one faculty meeting he had attended. And, how could he forget, later that same day he had also made her a coffee (a dreadful muddy concoction of decaffeination and soy) after dinner at High Table. Poor woman. Thrown together as they were: his distinguished features and intellect, her understandable susceptibility as a woman of a certain age, or, to put it more kindly, a *femme de trente ans* . . .

And his absence at the most recent faculty meetings, coupled with, he must admit, his failure to respond to her incessant emails about budgets and publication records and goodness knew what else (as he had only skimmed them), what a blow that must have been. In the circumstances. Although in the final analysis, his status as a married man, his personal unavailability to her, would have to be the real cause. She was a woman after all: it could only be personal.

Where was that young man? Dr. Choudhury could no longer see the smoking. Excellent. He left the sunshine, walked to the sitting-room doorway and back again, then sat at one end of the sofa, in pleasant expectation of the furtherance of their friendly chat. A faint sound reached him from upstairs: a slamming door, then a flurry of downstairs patterings and a moment later his youngest child flew into the sitting room, flapping and flouncing, hair damp, bosom heaving, eyes brimming, and flung herself down on the sofa next to him.

"Abbaaah!" she wailed, then wriggled even closer to him and tried to tuck her head under his arm, like a baby bird. "Why won't Amma tell me where she is? She's my sister!"

Why did no one in this family have any self-restraint? Even the bath had not calmed her. Dr. Choudhury stiffened, caught, he well knew, between the hard place of Baby's demands and the rock of something far worse, should he be so foolish as to divulge even a hint of Munni's present location.

Shunduri was sniffing miserably now, and her wail had been succeeded by a kind of invisible bouncing jiggling motion of the sofa springs, which made him feel most uncomfortable and tense in the calves. He tried to extricate his arm.

"Shush now, Baby. Go and help your mother in the kitchen."

"Abbaaah!"

"Baby, shush. You must . . ." He tried to think of a way to turn the conversation. "How are your studies? What are your grades?"

"Abbaaah!"

"I have a cramp." He stood and moved with alacrity to the mantel, leaned upon it and stretched out a leg and rubbed it with ostentatious concern. "Perhaps it is the blood supply . . ."

"I need my sister. I *miss* her." Shunduri stood up as well, and Dr. Choudhury shrank back. So much emotion, and her mascara was smeared.

"Baby, your face."

"I don't care . . ."

He looked at her more closely. She must be truly upset. What had

Mrs. Begum said to her? Perhaps her marks . . . no, Mrs. Begum had never been concerned with such things.

"Why won't anyone tell me where Affa is?"

"My leg . . ."

"My only sister!"

"Perhaps it is my heart . . . referred pain."

His daughter walked to the window and pressed her nose against it, but the sight of Kareem striding back toward the front door, running his index finger under his top lip as if he had a sore spot there, seemed only to ruffle her further.

"Abbaah!"

"Tariq! Tariq!" Mrs. Begum's call from upstairs, virtually a shout, ricocheted around the house. "Tariq! Are you home? You must come!"

No reply was heard, and he continued to clutch the mantel while he waited, with all the experience of so many years together, for his wife to scold the furniture in each room with her son's name, before finally resorting to her husband for assistance.

"Tariq!" was heard clearly through the sitting-room doorway now, but when Dr. Choudhury, with the feeling of Mafeking relieved, turned to look for his wife, Kareem was there as well, eyeing Baby's stormy state with no apparent surprise. Mrs. Begum's head was poking around the doorframe behind him, her hair disordered and a double crease between her eyebrows.

"What, what?" cried Dr. Choudhury, grateful for the distraction, though maintaining a wary grip on the mantel. He cast a quick eye at the mirror for reassurance, then turned to the new arrivals.

Kareem ducked his head toward him. "Can I help, Khalo? Can I do anything for you, Khalama? I'm at your service."

Mrs. Begum ignored him and looked at her husband. "It is . . . The time is one o'clock. I cannot find Tariq." Her right hand swung into visibility, carrying the brass tiffin holder.

He opened his mouth, then shut it again as Shunduri moved to his side and gave his arm a jealous squeeze.

"What, Abba? What is it?"

His wife cut in, glaring at him. "I promised . . . I promised Audrey Upwey I would send her my fish biryani to taste."

"Ah," he said, confused. Really, the convoluted mind of the female. "Now? Why now, of all times?"

"I will take it for you, Amma," said Shunduri.

His wife's telegraphing stare redirected to her youngest daughter and transformed into sweetness itself. "Nah, nah, nah, my Baby," she coaxed. "You will help me here."

Shunduri met her mother's gaze with a smile of steel. "I want to show Kareem the Abbey, Amma. Properly. He has come all this way, and we only saw it for a minute, just before. I will take the tiffin for you."

Mrs. Begum's face, though still wreathed in smiles, underwent a subtle change, hard to describe but somehow alarming.

Kareem shuffled his feet a little, seemed to be trying to catch Shunduri's eye. "Eh, no need to go back there, yeah?" No one responded, and he looked around the room, as if for help that was failing to arrive.

Mrs. Begum switched her gaze to Dr. Choudhury. Suddenly he realized, with one of those telepathic flashes that only happen between couples who have been married for such a long time: the tiffin was actually for Rohimun.

Ah, the instinctive cunning of Mrs. Begum. His stupid son had neglected to deliver his other daughter's food. Feeling both triumphant and aware that he had better set off before things got any more complicated, he cleared his throat and, by dint of turning to the mirror to adjust his shirt collar, liberated his arm from Shunduri's grip.

"Ahem. I have not yet had my, er, pre-prandial stroll. And in my state of health, with this cramp, I do feel that it would be most imprudent to depart from my routine at this juncture." As he spoke, he strode to the doorway and took hold of the tiffin container. "I will take this."

Shunduri squawked in protest. "Let me come with you."

Dr. Choudhury had a flash of inspiration of his own. "Your shoes are not suitable for outside-walking."

"But, Amma, Abba!" cried Shunduri, with escalating tragedy. "I'm only trying to help!"

Mrs. Begum shook her head in concert. "Nah, nah, Baby, we have a *guest*," she said, but was unwise enough to allow a victorious note to creep into her voice.

His wife should know better, that such a thing would be a red cloth to a bull for their youngest child.

Shunduri folded her arms, with an expression that said this was war. "I have to go, Amma."

"What, my Baby?"

"I have college tomorrow."

"*Now?*" Mrs. Begum gasped, gripping the doorframe with her free hand. "To London? You, you leave your mother and father here now, this afternoon, before eating with us?"

"Yes, Amma. I have to go. *Studyin'*." Shunduri fixed her eyes above her mother's head, arms still folded, and tapped her foot.

"You come to visit your father and mother, your only brother, and you do not even stay one night?"

"I can't, Amma. *I've* got college."

Mrs. Begum's shoulders drooped. "You do what you wish, then. Go, go. I do not mind. I am grateful that you remember us, visit us at all now. Now that you are so big-big at school in London and the bank. My pride in you is as high as the sky, with all your study and your big job."

Shunduri flushed then, her eyes filling with tears. Dr. Choudhury waited for a rapprochement between mother and daughter, but it was not to be. His wife's arms were folded as well, leaving Shunduri no choice but to press on, bending to touch her father's feet and then her mother's, in farewell. Mrs. Begum turned her head away.

After a brief hesitation, their daughter slipped between them both and ran outside, as his wife pulled her *pallu* over her head and walked toward the kitchen. There was a brush against his trouser leg: it was Kareem, touching his feet.

"Sorry, sorry. *Salaamalaikum*, sir, Khalo," Kareem muttered, straightening and bobbing his head at Dr. Choudhury, then in the direction of the kitchen. "My respects to Baiyya, to your family . . ."

"Yes, yes," he responded irritably. Kareem's attentions were noisome now that he was about to drive Shunduri, their youngest, home unchaperoned. What did they really know of this man anyway? He had smiled and smirked and made love to them all and now he was off again. Well, good riddance.

------------

As soon as they were both in the car, even before he'd started the engine, Kareem spoke, just like Shunduri knew he would.

"How could you treat your mother like that, Princess?" He looked sternly at her in the rear-view mirror, his tone very different to what it had been in the cottage. "That is disrespect."

She glared at him, but did not reply.

"What would your Affa and Bai think of you disrespectin' your mum like that?"

She leaned forward and hissed into the back of his neck, her voice quivering. "They don't care. And I don't care about them. At least I'm wantin' to end up in a *proper* marriage, yaah, like no one else in my family."

"Hey, what are you talkin' about? *Relax.*"

They were both silent then, Shunduri scrabbling in her bag for a tissue.

"You should go back and apologize. They're your parents."

"Never." She shook her head violently and looked out the window. They hadn't even come out to say goodbye. It was all his fault anyway, that she needed her sister so much. Her stomach was in a tight knot from the scene with her parents, and just when she needed Mum so much too. But she needed Rohimun more. Rohimun wouldn't, couldn't, judge her: how could she, given all the trouble she was in.

Kareem reached back and touched her knee. "You only have one mother, one father. I should know, yeah."

They drove away from the cottage slowly, and just up the road, out of sight, Kareem pulled the car over so that she could climb into the front passenger seat. He took her hand and squeezed it.

She gave a long shuddering sigh and held his hand with both of hers. "I miss my sister like you wouldn't believe, yaah."

"Course you do, Princess. What's all that about anyway?"

"She's . . . she's in trouble. She had a *gora* boyfriend, an' there was trouble, like, between 'em. Maybe he was giving her beats. But she wouldn't take my advice. So Tariq brought her home, but they won't tell me anyfing. And they won't let me see her."

"Hittin' your sister!"

"Yeah." She and Munni had never been close, but she appreciated Kareem's righteous anger almost as much as if he'd been defending her.

"So's Tariq going to sort him out? What's been done about him?"

"Nuffink. He's not a Desi boy, you know. You can't just have a *funchait* and break furniture over his head."

Kareem swore. "Want me to do somethin' about it?"

She considered. "No, I don't want you gettin' in any trouble. It's alright. We'll never see him again anyway."

"Are they sending her back to the old country, marrying her off then?"

She dabbed her eyes. "Dunno. Don't think so. I just don't know where she is right now and I haven't seen her in ages."

"Well, what else can they do with her? Eh, Princess, don't cry. I understand. And this was your day, yeah." Kareem kissed her nose. "Your day, Princess."

She felt better suddenly and pulled the sun visor down and started to repair her face. "That's what they say to the bride on the day she marries, yaah. It's *her* day."

He let go of her hand, started up the car and pulled out. "Plenty of time yet. You know I love you, Princess."

She cleaned away the mascara smudges under her eyes and re-powdered her nose and forehead, holding on to the dashboard with one hand. "Seein' as it's my day, take a right here. I want to go to Leicester and look at the shops, yaah." The sari and wedding-gold shops in Leicester were even better than in Brick Lane.

"*Leicester*? Princess, that's an hour away, in the wrong direction."

"We left Mum and Dad's early, innit?"

"Jesus Christ." He tapped the GPS as if hoping that it was still non-functional, but it sprang to life immediately.

*In three miles, turn right.*

"Look." She pointed to her side window. "There's Dad."

Her father was in the distance, upright and flat-footed, walking swiftly downhill from the cottage toward the Abbey ahead, the tiffin container jerking by his side.

Rohimun, her affa, would know how to speak to Dad. Or maybe Affa could get Tariq to lean on Kareem. Or something.

Kareem hunched over the steering wheel and stared at the building that loomed ahead of Dr. Choudhury, dark in the sunshine.

"Jesus Christ, we're not goin' there again. You can count me out. Leicester it is. Shoppin' in Leicester."

*Eleven*

DR. CHOUDHURY WAS striding with the tiffin container swinging at his side, his usual discomfort at plowing through all the ups and downs and unpleasant surprises of a grassland frequented by insects and other small wild creatures forgotten in his relief at escaping the marital home. Not that he was looking forward to seeing his eldest daughter, of course. She was a disgrace to the family.

Their old closeness over art and her painting and her doing so well at school was as nothing to him now. He would simply knock, then leave the tiffin container on the hallway floor. Or perhaps, if she was quick to open the door, he would inadvertently catch a glimpse of how she was looking, perhaps even see if she had done anything with that far-too-large stretched canvas that he had seen on the roof of Tariq's car the other day. Not that he would acknowledge her in any form: she was dead to him, a blot on the Choudhury escutcheon.

On his way up the hill, he could see that almost all of the scaffolding had been removed from one side of the Abbey, leaving it looking strangely crisp and clean. Not long now until everything would be finished. But this thought brought with it various difficult problems, so he resolved to think of nothing but the blueness of the sky and the greenness of the vegetation.

What a ridiculous size that canvas was, for someone who had only ever done life-size head-and-shoulder portraits. What was Tariq thinking? And also that she could have used those old paints that Tariq had dug up from the back of the shed, from her O-level days. His number-one-fool son should have known better than that, should have been well aware that such things degrade, as well as being of inferior quality compared to what she had probably been using in London.

Dr. Choudhury swung the tiffin pettishly at some intrusive long grasses. What indeed could he have done but to direct Tariq to Green & Stone in Chelsea and Cornelissen & Son on Great Russell Street, as far more appropriate purveyors of professional-quality oil paints and brushes? Not that he cared what she did anymore. He just didn't like to see his son so mistaken.

A disconnected whistling sound caught his ear, and he turned his head nervously from side to side, conscious of a most unpleasant occasion recently when he had been attacked by a nesting bird of some kind and had had to resort to an undignified jog back to the safety of Windsor Cottage, while waving his arms above his head in order to protect himself.

But no birds could be seen. After pausing to examine the summer sky for signs of enemy action, he had just adopted a brisker pace and a slightly more aggressive swinging action of the tiffin when there was a rustling of bushes and one of Henry's large yellow dogs bounded out of the undergrowth.

"Eh, eh!" cried Dr. Choudhury, advancing while holding the tiffin container protectively over his crotch. "Eh! Get out!"

But the dog seemed unperturbed by this show of courage, and Dr. Choudhury, despairing, increased his speed to a quick march and tried to ignore the dog's excited barks and intermittent forays into his private parts.

None too soon, he arrived at the open, lawned area that surrounded the Abbey itself, and the dog ran off ahead. Between him and the Abbey was a fair-haired figure in a hacking jacket and corduroys, performing a sort of slow extended spin with its arms stretched out, like a very tired dervish. Surely that was not Henry Bourne. But as he neared, he could hear Henry's voice, pitched to seriousness.

"*One*, two, three, *one*, two, three. Ah no, wrong foot."

He hurrumphed loudly to interrupt this private ritual. Everyone had them, after all. Henry stopped and, to Dr. Choudhury's horror, both dogs tore back down the slope toward him.

"Dr. Choudhury! Capital, excellent—I was hoping to catch up with you!"

"Eh, eh! Henry!" he said with a mixture of relief and irritation as he tried to fend off the dogs who were both evincing a single-minded fascination with his crotch and bottom. Really, there was no such thing as a truly domesticated animal.

"Darcy! Knightley! Come on now. Don't worry, Dr. Choudhury. I'll throw my stick. There they go. Look, I'm glad I saw you—you'll never guess."

"What, what is it that you think I will never guess?" He smiled broadly to ensure that Henry would recognize his question as rhetorical, and not an attempt to interrupt. "I *guess* that you were, er, dancing!"

"Oh, ah, that." Henry went a little pink. "Well, yes, you've sprung me there. I was having a bit of a practice, you know."

"Practice of what?"

"Oh, you know."

"No," said Dr. Choudhury, with all the geniality of a don trapping an unwary undergraduate into a sophistry. "I do not know."

"It's . . . the Hunt Ball's only five months away. Gay Gordons, Dr. Choudhury. It's fiendish. And waltzing. You don't know what it's like, having two left feet."

Having never danced a step in his life, Dr. Choudhury nodded sympathetically. "You will improve with practice. Though of course, we cannot all be Margot Fonteyn."

"Yes, practice, practice. That's the key. And this year's ball is at the Abbey. Thea's triumphed again, eh? Anyway, I wanted to tell you: here I was yesterday, just here, counting feet, stopped for a breather, glanced up, and there she was, sort of drifting across one of the second-storey windows."

"Mrs. Kiriakis?"

"No, the ghost. We've got a ghost."

"What?" Dr. Choudhury, still brushing himself down in order to remove an undesirable stickiness from the lickings and sniffings of the dogs, did not follow.

Henry went a little pinker, took a stick that one of the dogs had retrieved and began to bash the vegetation beside the path. "Well, ah, I was thinking, it could be someone that we could link to the history of that room."

"What room?"

"The green bedroom: that's where I saw her, you know. Yesterday."

Dr. Choudhury froze, and the returning dogs, sensing easy prey perhaps, moved in on him again.

"Come on, boys! Here!" Henry lofted the stick again. "So, what do you think?"

"The green bedroom," he managed to say.

"Yes. Not that I was actually there, you understand. I was down here with the dogs of course, and, ah, just happened to look up and there she was. At the window."

"The window." Dr. Choudhury was beginning to discern an unfortunate pattern in his own responses, but still felt that he was doing quite well in the circumstances.

Henry laughed and went even pinker. "Looking completely, ah, gorgeous and mysterious, you know, as all the best ghosts are. Hah, hah . . . It seemed to look at me, then just sort of wafted away."

"Wafted."

"Yes. Sort of. Exciting, really, don't you think?" said Henry.

"Indeed, most, er, exciting. Could you throw that stick again?"

"Oh, sorry, yes. There they go. Looks like you must have some food on you."

"Yes, yes," said Dr. Choudhury. "I was about to have a picnic you understand, but now I have to go. I have just remembered an urgent appointment and I must . . ."

"Not at all. Lovely day for it. I was just wondering, you know, whether you'd like to . . . perhaps we could have a look over the green bedroom together sometime. I asked Thea yesterday, but she wasn't—"

"Is that a breeze? Most terrible for my neuralgia. Henry, perhaps a shadow, yes, most likely a shadow brought on by the sunlight and, er, waving tree branches. And my easel is up there at the moment: perhaps you saw the top of that. But I must be off. Throw that stick again, please."

And with that request, Dr. Choudhury turned and hurried away from Henry in the direction of Windsor Cottage, shoulders hunched against discovery or challenge.

Henry's voice floated after him, growing progressively fainter. "I'm tied up with the Trust and, ah, church committee stuff, the next few days, but I thought I'd have a proper look around this Saturday night? You know, tap the paneling and all that. If you're free then? You'll let me know?"

"Perhaps. But it will be nothing. Nothing." Dr. Choudhury flapped a wrist in discouragement as he continued to walk away. Mrs. Begum would know what to do.

---

MRS. BEGUM, TROWEL in hand, scrambled from her knees in the front garden and rose on tiptoe to confirm her suspicions. There was no mistaking it. The white head of her number-one-fool husband could be clearly seen above the neatly trimmed privet proceeding toward the garden gate, far too soon to have delivered her carefully packed tiffin of fluffiest white rice, tender fish biryani, and some beautifully smooth and soothing dahl.

No one could make dahl like she could, and yet here it was, coming back again, having done no good at all. What had he done now? Dropped it in a cowpat?

All this upset today with its turvy-topsy visitings and leavings, and

Baby stabbing her in the heart like that, and Rohimun's father could not even get her fed now. Mrs. Begum pressed down the last transplanted dahlia and spared a hostile look for the tumbled foxgloves in the far corner of the front garden, innocent victims of a windy night, and they trembled for their fate with the breeze. Well that they should. As soon as she found out the name of those tidy little bushes in Mrs. Darby's front garden, the foxgloves would be dug out and chopped up, ready for the compost.

No one had compost like hers: she'd seen the smelly mess that passed for compost up at the Abbey, all those clippings on top, drying out instead of rotting in, and not enough kitchen waste in between. That man, Colin, called himself a gardener? More like a rubbish collector. She trotted along the wooden boards that crisscrossed her garden beds and, trowel held high, sped to welcome her husband at the gate.

Dr. Choudhury, only now appearing to notice his wife, hastily stepped back from the gate before it was flung open, and forestalled her challenge with a raised hand. "In the house, in the house," he whispered in Bangla, holding the tiffin before him like a shield.

She corrected him mechanically, "Cottage, cottage, not house," while she looked past her husband to the road. No cars parked and, more importantly, no dirty bastard reporters like Tariq had warned her of, standing around and spying, to their mothers' shame. She hesitated. Maybe a sneaky-sneaky one had followed her husband to the Abbey.

With that thought, she hustled Dr. Choudhury into the cottage, stood while he arranged himself in his wing-back chair in the sitting room, and waited for his explanation. A heavy sigh followed, so she flew into the kitchen and loaded up the pandan tray, and hauled it from kitchen to parlor, placing it close to him. She looked at him expectantly.

He still did not speak but rolled mournful brown eyes up at her, and with a huff of frustration, she squatted down by the tray. Pulling out the largest betel leaf, she lay a tobacco leaf inside it, then, one-handed, sprinkled it with betel nuts (finely chopped), one clove, cardamon, a hint of lime and a scattering of sugar balls. The entire package was quickly folded into an inch-long green envelope, which, succumbing to impatience, she turned and popped it into her husband's mouth.

She tossed a fragment of betel nut onto her own tongue, sat down on the edge of the chair opposite and glared at her husband. Either because of this special marital communication, or perhaps because now sufficiently fortified by the paan tucked into his cheek, Dr. Choudhury delayed no further.

"Ah, wife, it is good to be home."

"Yes, yes?"

"Something of, er, concern has . . . While walking, you understand, through the woodland that forms the most direct route between cottage and Abbey, I was hailed by Henry Bourne."

She leaned even further forward in her chair in consternation, dangerously close to the occasional table and, in her eagerness to speak, almost swallowing her paan before time. "It is a great thing that Henry does not suspect, unless in fact . . ."

But her husband raised his hand, and she stopped.

"As it was in fact I that spoke with Henry, others should desist from unnecessary interruptions and speculations, which would only impede them from being informed of the very things that they seek. And," he continued, "Henry of course wanted my opinion, my, well, views, about the historical provenance of certain, er, unearthly events that he believed he witnessed yesterday, in one of the upper windows of the Abbey, on the western side."

"Eh?"

"In short, wife"—and here Dr. Choudhury paused with a fine sense of drama—"Henry thought he saw someone, a woman, a ghost, in the green bedroom."

Mrs. Begum gasped and bit her fingertips, then tried to speak, but her husband's flow was unstoppable.

"Of course I informed him regretfully of my unavailability to explore the Abbey together today, due to my having just recalled a prior and pressing engagement. Several of them."

Dr. Choudhury's palm was slowly descending, but his voice rolled on. "Henry seemed to accept this blow with good grace, and even wished me a pleasant walk. However, he did mention he might investigate the matter further, on this Saturday evening."

Once Dr. Choudhury's palm came to rest upon his flannelled knee, Mrs. Begum erupted. "Has my husband forgotten that we have a child who needs to be fed, that he has just deprived her, yes, a bad girl, but still his daughter, of the food that is hers?" She jumped to her feet, almost upsetting the entire pandan tray. "And Henry will still go there on Saturday, I know it! Where does my daughter's father think she is going to sleep on Saturday night, and what does he think she is going to eat today? And tonight? Leaves from the trees perhaps? Or some of those builder-men's dirty pork pies? Perhaps he thinks that her so-skinny Londoni body is not skinny enough, or she is too comfortable in that big cold Abbey?"

She thumped her right hand, fingers curled into a fist, to her left breast. "Why doesn't my husband just go and stab the mother of his children in the heart, instead of making me watch them starve to death and be caught trespassing, all for nice-nice chats with Mr. Henry?"

Dr. Choudhury's palm rose again, belatedly. "My intention, Mrs. Begum," he said with dignity, "as I was trying to say, was to give this tiffin to Tariq and . . . and . . . to tell him to fetch the girl here for Saturday evening. She can stay here until the danger has passed. Tariq will then return her to the Abbey."

She felt her face soften.

"But know this, wife: I do not say that she deserves it, or that she is forgiven. That has not changed. It is, however, time that she benefited from traditional family values again. For one evening only."

---

"You really mean that?" Richard's tone was mild, even quizzical: guaranteed to wind Henry up even more.

"Yes, I *do* mean a ghost!" The line was so clear Henry could have been in the room, instead of eighty-odd miles from London, in the depths of Wiltshire. "I tell you, I saw it myself yesterday afternoon! All duskily Celtic, with long wavy hair, wearing some kind of smock. Quite medieval, which obviously supports my theory about the main house predating the outbuildings."

Richard reclined in his chair, uncharacteristically glad of the distraction, buoyed by Henry's enthusiasm. "So, now you're relying on the paranormal to date the main house?"

Henry rose to the bait, as Richard knew he would. "You're not in the courtroom now, Richard. I'm telling you, I *saw* it, no mistake."

"Alright, I'm listening."

"I saw her, clear as day. I was, ah, walking the dogs after lunch, bit of a constitutional, you know, thought I'd do a circuit of the Abbey. Anyway, there I was, stopped for a breather, looked up, and there she was, sort of drifting across one of the second-storey windows."

"Thea?"

"The ghost. The ghost, Richard. What a drawcard for tourists. We could have open evenings and take punters through the cellars."

Richard propped the receiver under his ear, unscrewed his fountain pen and started to doodle bedsheet ghosts on the blotter. "You said it was on the second storey."

"Cellars are spookier than bedrooms. And they'll be touring the whole upper storey already anyway, once we open the Abbey up again. It could be a whole separate tour, a twilight, ghost-hunting, sort of atmospheric thing . . ."

Richard grimaced. Another gimmick to market the Abbey to the weekend daytrippers, along with cream teas on Temple Lawn and Audrey Upwey's nieces in authentic medieval smocks selling authentic bloody medieval ale. So did Henry really believe that there was a ghost, or was it a wind-up?

"I've spoken to Dr. Choudhury, but he, ah, wasn't free to investigate."

"How about Thea? What does she think of all this?"

"She wasn't really interested in looking, but, you know, she's been researching the antecedents of the green room, where I saw it, to try to identify her—historically, that is, so we could put something in the new leaflets. And of course, the boys are over the moon! Talking of which, I thought I'd have a good look on Saturday night: there's a full moon then, you know."

"What difference does that make? The wiring's been fixed."

"Oh, you know, that's sort of supernatural prime time, isn't it? Midnight on a full moon. You remember that BBC series where they . . . or perhaps that's werewolves . . ."

Richard halted his doodling and glanced at the faded Persian opposite. Its central design was of an archway with an onion-shaped top, like a doorway into another world. He could not quite believe that Thea was taking Henry's ghost seriously enough to spend time on it. But then he well knew her weakness for that bloody Abbey.

"Look, how about I visit this weekend, have a read of those grant papers. I'll come down Friday after work, take the terrible two ghost-hunting on Saturday night, and you can take Thea to that new restaurant that's opened up in Swindon. Florian's." God knows what Henry had done with this latest round of Trust papers anyway.

"That's terrific, Richard. Terrific! And a child-free evening in the school holidays—Thee will love you forever!"

He smiled despite himself.

"How about, ah, Deirdre?" Henry added.

"No, just me."

"So, she's gone the way of all the others then, eh? Cast aside like so much . . ." Henry didn't finish his sentence, obviously at a loss as to how you cast aside anybody.

Richard took his opportunity. "See you Friday then."

"London must be quiet! See you then." The line clicked off.

Richard still held the receiver. It wasn't like Henry to be facetious. Or so quick with his comments about girlfriends. Time his big brother went down there to sort him out.

He was surprised at how much he was looking forward to it. He'd never have believed he'd feel like that about hitting the motorway at Friday rush hour to drive down to Bourne Abbey and sleep in the

Lodge's study. Shit, he'd forgotten about that sofa bed. Richard walked over to the Persian rug hanging on his wall and ran his hand across its soft, undulating surface, warm in the sun. What did it remind him of? He used to like to pull his fingers through its pile as a boy when it had lain on the floor of his bedroom in the Abbey, but that wasn't it. He was getting soft in his old age: stroking carpets, chasing ghosts.

# Twelve

MRS. BEGUM STOOD on the sitting-room Axminster, arms folded, and eyed the peacock on her mantelpiece. He was not what he had been when he'd arrived, just two days ago. The proud curve of his feathered chest had drooped and widened into what was almost a paunch, and his head had tilted, giving his features a leery, calculating expression. His stance, once aristocratic, had become something crooked and degenerate. An omen, perhaps.

His beak had begun to open, and she remembered something that Mrs. Darby had told her, about the danger of looking gifts in the mouth. Or was it to be recommended? She couldn't recall, but the thought would not leave her, so she pulled Dr. Choudhury's ottoman over to the hearth and climbed up. But the ottoman, old and soft like her husband, gave a dusty puff and sank in the middle with her weight. Left at eye-level with the peacock's neck, she reached forward and grasped the bird around his spreading tummy to lift him down.

Two things happened. Once she touched the bird, instead of the stiff dryness of old feathers, her hands encountered a damp, yielding stickiness, as if it had been incompletely preserved and was rotting from the inside out. And when she tried to lift the peacock, it refused to budge. Mrs. Begum grunted in disgust: this dirty-dirty thing in her sitting room had to go. She tightened her grip, her fingers sinking, and pulled upward fiercely.

It was then that one leg, apparently glued to the mantel by that same sticky substance, suddenly broke clean off. The peacock sprang into the air, Mrs. Begum's arms still attached, its tail feathers going every which way, and after a moment, in which Mrs. Begum saw herself in the mantel mirror, arms at full stretch with the peacock directly overhead, like Tariq's old picture of Magical Johnson catching the orange ball, she and the now one-legged peacock sailed backward onto the carpet.

She was unhurt and soon recovered herself sufficiently to look around. Peacock tail feathers were scattered over armchairs and occasional tables. One had landed across the top of a picture frame, looking like one of Mrs. Darby's Christmas decorations. The bird lay in the hearth, its remaining leg pointing up the chimney. Mrs. Begum grunted in disgust: cheap-and-nasty gifts shame the giver. Dr. Choudhury's so-shiny new watch had probably stopped by now as well.

When she returned from the kitchen with dustpan and brush and squatted to sweep up the remains, she saw that the peacock's body had pulled apart in a spill of old straw to reveal a dark object about the size of two fists pushed together. She poked it with the brush, and it rolled free of the straw, gleaming with cling wrap. She leaned closer to look and cautiously picked it up. This was not peacock.

It was as heavy as a stone from her rockery. It felt like the Plasticine that little Tariq would bring home from kindergarten, but a rich brown instead of the blues and yellows that had made her son's wobbly soldiers and serpents. Its substance came off on her hands in streaks with a distinctive, delicate perfume. She sat back on her haunches and lifted the object to her nose, sitting-room mess forgotten. Her head hurt.

She was little Syeda again, perched on her grandmother's lap in the dull heat of the late-afternoon harvest. Watching the silhouettes of the men and women from her village walking slowly backward through rows of nodding, bobbing poppy heads, armed with their *nushturs*, selecting and scoring the seed pods.

Then other memories, of herself older now, headachey and nause-ated and following her father with the small earthenware pot into which the poppy milk, now dried to a dark resinous gum, was placed after being scraped off the poppy heads by his curved iron *sittooha*. Between each pod he would lick the blade, and when she once com-plained of headache, he had taken a little of the gum off the blade with his thumb and wiped it on her bottom lip.

Opium, scourge of Bangladesh and its five neighbors and forbid-den by the Prophet (peace be upon him) as the most soul-destroying of the addictions. That number-one-dirty-bastard Kareem had brought opium, a cake of cooked opium paste, into her house. In a peacock, a creature so pure that its feather was permitted to touch the Qur'an. The essence of evil and death was here, in her home, her sit-ting room.

She stood up quickly, spilling the dustpan to the floor, her breath-ing tight, her headache growing, and looked for the solitary crooked shelf (put up with much difficulty by Dr. Choudhury) that held the holy book. It was still there: she could see its green and gold spine, high in the corner. She ducked her head, pulling a corner of sari over her hair, and looked up at the Qur'an then back at the hearth and at her stained hands. Too polluted to touch and take protection from the sacred words of Allah.

She remembered Uncle's son, his only living child, seen by her just once soon after she had arrived in Dhaka. Uncle had never spoken of him, but one of the market stallholders had pointed him out from a distance as her uncle's curse, a *casra charsi*, a dirty addict. He was filthy, painfully thin and swaying against a wall in one of the refuse alleys that led off the market. She had been standing perhaps twenty paces away, but could still smell the animal dung in which he must have been walking, lying. His *sherwani* was torn at the front and, between the flaps of fabric, his abdomen looked like knotted rope. One of his hands was curled like a claw under his chin, dark, almost black lips were drawn back from his teeth; and his cheeks and chin were glazed with saliva. His eyes were half closed, and even though he was upright, she had wondered if he was dead.

The words of the village mullah at Friday prayers, echoed at every *Jumma* she had been to in this country, came back to her then.

*Remember death . . . remember that you will stand before Allah to be accountable for your deeds on a day that no wealth or children will benefit you. Beware the seeking of mufattir, intoxication, for it is addiction and damnation. Die and meet Allah in this state and you will drink eternally, eternally, from the impure rivers of Hell.*

She'd had nightmares for days after seeing her cousin.

Dreams about her little sister, dead from the typhoid, and her parents as she had last seen them after the river, in the wet-season floods, had swept most of their village away. Drowned by Allah for harvesting the poppy. Dreams of herself rotting in that alley, a *casra charsi* for carrying the earthenware pot for her father, licking the gum from her lip.

A few months later, by which time she was over her big-city shock and navigating the laneways around her uncle's shop with impunity, she heard from the same stallholder that her cousin had been found dead in one of the ancient water cisterns that still existed beneath the city, and into which waste water now flowed. She never spoke to her uncle about what she had seen, or dreamt, but from then on had seen his quietness and removed life with different eyes.

———

Mrs. Begum shuddered. Averting her eyes from the hearth she retreated to the kitchen. The clock said three. Dr. Choudhury would be home in an hour from his healthy-walk, and she had a strong urge to make *salat*. And she could not pray if she was impure, unclean. That thing in her house, on her hands. She slipped the fingers of her right hand into her mouth and, biting their tips, muttered "*Il Allah, wah il Allahu,*" the old formula for passing graveyards, speaking or thinking of the dead. What could she do?

Fingers still in mouth, Mrs. Begum looked out the kitchen window to the back garden—vegetables in rows, tall and strong, her washing flapping behind them, the rabbit hutch flanked by the neat hessian-topped curve of the compost—and thought.

With sudden decision, and tucking her sari's *pallu*, peasant-style, into her waistband, she ran to open the front door, grabbed hold of the cast-iron shoe-scraper, a strange but practical present from Mrs. Darby, and dragged it into the hallway. She shut the door and pushed the shoe-scraper hard up against it. If Dr. Choudhury was to return early, he must not catch her unawares and perhaps stop her from taking the necessary steps.

This house, her sanctuary and her pride, had been polluted. Police would come, perhaps those reporters. The Women's Institute would hear about it, perhaps exclude her. And Mrs. Darby, her great friend, what would she say? Mrs. Begum knew what was necessary, what only she could do. She hurried out to the back garden.

With a trowel and fork from the miniature shed, she attacked the far side of her perfect, symmetrical compost mound, digging steadily until she had excavated a narrow cavity that ran into the steaming heart of the heap. She dropped her tools and hastened back to the sitting room, where she levered the opium cake off the floor and, holding it before her like a hot pan so as not to stain her sari, proceeded back outside.

Once she reached the heap, she peeled off the remnants of cling wrap, then squatted opposite the hole and carefully fed the opium in, only releasing it when her arms were at full stretch. The cake, hitting the warm interior of the mound, flooded the air with its perfume, and she felt her stomach contract. Swallowing a retch, she grabbed the trowel, rapidly filled the hole and patted it down. Done.

Mrs. Begum sat back on her heels and took a few deep breaths of the rich familiar smell of leaf-mould, mango skins and tea leaves. The tightness in her chest started to ease, though the headache, the old harvest headache she remembered, still pounded. In one month, maybe two, the evil thing would rot away into the soil from where it had come, and no one would be the wiser. Then she would spread it around the perimeter of the garden, under the privet hedge. Nothing could kill that.

She got to her feet, then hesitated. It had been a hot day and a hot night was coming. Normally she would have forked over the tightly compacted heap and taken away a little for her radishes, but there was no time left. What would they taste like after this anyway? She had to clear away the rest of that dirty bird, then do *wudu*, washing herself three times in the proper way so she could make *salat* and finish before her husband came home and wondered what had been broken, who had died, that she needed to pray. She threw the tools into the shed, lifted the skirt of her sari and ran inside the house.

By the time Dr. Choudhury's signature fumble at the front door was due, the peacock's tail feathers had been gathered, plopped into an ugly vase from Bora Khalo, her dirty father-in-law, and positioned on the mantel, not that her husband would ever notice. The hearth was swept and polished, and an elaborate and heartfelt *salat* had been performed. Dinner was not yet started. She flew into the kitchen, banged a saucepan into the sink and started to wash the rice.

---

DR. CHOUDHURY'S HEALTHY-WALK had not gone well. Halfway around the village he had become uncomfortably hot and sweaty, but had not been willing, in the muggy June heat, to remove his tweed jacket and be seen walking like some laborer in shirtsleeves. People expected more of him than that.

He'd developed a disagreeable dampness under his arms and across his upper back, and he suspected that his upper lip and forehead were shiny. This was confirmed by a glimpse of himself in the latticed display window of the new Ye Lydiard Style dress shop: a most unflattering representation in more ways than one, due to the convex nature of the glass.

Now, with two-thirds of the steady incline of High Street still to traverse, a small, sharp stone somehow crept into his shoe and under his right foot: the one with a particularly tender bunion and several significant corns that Mrs. Begum had neglected to completely remove. He arched his sole and wriggled his toes as he walked, but to no avail. With every step it embedded itself further into his sole.

There was no way he could stop, stand on one foot and be shoeless in the high street to remove a stone. He would look ridiculous. He was an academic, not an athlete. He would just have to soldier on until he found his home.

Finally his front gate came into view. Stoic, he struggled with the gatepost, which seemed to have developed an aggravating lean, catching his right thumb painfully in its latch before managing to swing it open. Mrs. Begum was often in the garden at this time of day, but now it was silent and empty. He struggled up the gravel path, the uneven surface a further refinement in pedal pain. Stones on the outside and the inside. He would far rather just have had one big one to deal with, like Sisyphus.

A dog barked, and he stopped abruptly to look around, nursing his sore thumb, but no one, animal or human, was to be seen. Odysseus returns, full of tales of heroic achievement, but no one recognizes him, no one cares. Nursing his digit, he limped up the path and slowly climbed the three steps to the front door. Why had Mrs. Begum never expressed concern about his pounding heart, his labored breathing? She should have made him see a doctor, have some tests.

He tried to turn the door handle without using his sore thumb, but could not get a sufficient grip. Other men, more traditional, less modest, would just have banged on the door, expected their wife to fly to greet them after such a trial. He leaned his left shoulder against the door and fumbled with his uninjured hand to twist the knob.

The catch gave suddenly, and he stumbled into the house, just missing the edge of the hall table, but temporarily tangling with some minor domestic item that Mrs. Begum had left lying about. He gave the item an impulsive shove with his foot, merely to move it out of the way for others, only then recalling that it was his sore foot, and discovering that the object was both hard and heavy. Pain shot up his leg. He rested against the wall and tears welled, mixing with droplets of sweat and stinging his eyes.

Still no one even knew he was there, what he had been through. He sniffed, straightened and for the first time ever avoided the hall mirror as he hobbled into the sitting room to divest himself of the instruments of his suffering and collapse into his wing-back armchair. Oh, the bliss of being finally shoe- and jacket-less, the comforts of home all around him, the pressures of his public persona left behind.

And where was his Penelope? He must not forget that her many trivial domestic tasks were all designed to contribute in some small way to his material comfort and happiness. Not that the physical comforts were ever paramount with him, given the vastly superior pleasures that the mind could bring. She must be cooking his favorite dish right now, or perhaps rolling a soft, fresh, green betel leaf around a mixture of paan, lime powder, scented sugar balls and cardamon, perfectly tailored to her husband's taste. He swallowed, and realized how dry his mouth was.

But he would leave her in peace for now. Her presence, though well-meaning, was full of hustle and bustle: the ceaseless, needless noise and activity so symptomatic of the shallow mind. Only true stillness, deep repose, was conducive to, nay, almost indistinguishable from, deep thought. His eyelids began to droop.

He reclined his head into the chair's soft tapestry, closed his eyes and let his legs rise from the floor to rest upon . . . nothing. They floated in midair, wavered from side to side, searching for their entitled resting place, then dropped, defeated. Where was his ottoman?

He opened his eyes, pained and annoyed. Had he been through so much, expected so little, for this? It seemed an intentional betrayal, a mockery of his pain, that the ottoman, always precisely placed for his shoeless feet, was sitting on the far side of the hearth, a good five feet away from its appointed spot.

This wifely dereliction must not be tolerated, for where would it end? How could Mrs. Begum respect herself if she did not know her failings as a wife? And if not a good wife, then not a good mother, for did not the two go together, hand in hand? For her own sake the rot must be stopped, before she could no longer look at herself in the mirror. He cleared his throat. That alone, she should be able to hear from the kitchen. Due warning.

"Paper, paper," he shouted, then sat back, feeling a little calmer.

She would come in with a collection of newspapers from the hall-stand and offer them to him. Once he had made his selection, he would clear his throat again, meaningfully, perhaps look at the otto-man sitting flagrantly by the hearth. She, comprehending, would rush to replace it under his feet. She would notice the odd way in which he positioned his injured foot and show wifely concern, offer to wash or massage it. She would perhaps ask him if he wanted some paan or a cup of tea to demonstrate her contrition, which of course he would accept. Domestic harmony, the natural order of things, would be restored, all would be forgiven and forgotten.

Something banged and hissed in the kitchen. There was a rushing and a rustling and his wife was suddenly in front of him, and a cas-cade of papers fell into his lap. Before he could speak she was gone again, back into the kitchen, to a flurry of cupboard doors opening and shutting, the clash of utensils and the rattle-crash of a pan land-ing hard on the stove. He sat perfectly still, a hurrumph dying in his throat. More banging from the kitchen, and now that he thought of it, dinner was usually almost ready when he returned from his walk.

He stood, pushing all the papers to the floor except for the fashion supplement, and limped on socked feet back down the hall and into his study. Sometimes, when dealing with the truly irrational aspects of womanhood, which Freud so well recognized, discretion was truly the better part of valor. Not to mention demonstrating a mature understanding of the frustrations and known moodiness of the inar-ticulate sex. He was not retreating, merely respecting, in the civilized give-and-take of the modern marriage, Mrs. Begum's need for space. He had read all about this in *Cosmopolitan*.

He shut and locked his study door. It had been a hot day, and it was going to be an even hotter night. The accoutrements of man were so constricting and unhealthy in this weather. He unbuttoned his shirt and turned to the cheval, breathing in and upward. The afternoon sun lit his skin to shades of golden brown, threw his stomach into shadow and made his chest gleam. Yul Brynner knew what he was doing when he wore those open waistcoats, so heavily embroidered, over his naked torso. Humming the theme to *King of Siam*, he considered his reflection further. What a fine figure of a man he was.

# Thirteen

THEY HAD ARRANGED to meet at Shilpi's house this time, rather than Aisha's dorm room where they usually went every Thursday. But while Shunduri was still with Kareem in his flat, Aisha had texted to say they were doing *mendhi*, henna designs, and could she bring her magazines for the patterns. So Kareem had done a detour and was now waiting in the Rover while she ran up to her dorm room to get them.

Despite having showered before she'd left Kareem's flat, she felt tired and somehow still dishevelled. She quickly changed into one of her college *salwars* and lower shoes, then freshened up her make-up with a nude lipstick and more kohl around the eyes. She wasn't going to have a repeat of last week, with Shilpi deciding to hold forth about Muslim modesty while she was in her leggings and backless *choli* with just a bit of chiffon around her.

Kareem was smiling and relaxed when she returned. He had three mobiles out and was finishing one call while he held another and texted on the third.

She got into the car, and he started the engine, leaned over and kissed her on the lips, then spoke again into the mobile against his ear. "Yeah, brother, I'll be there. Twenty minutes max—you can depend on me, man."

*I hope I can too.* The thought floated into her mind as they moved into the traffic, and would not leave until she had smoothed her eyebrows in the visor mirror.

Kareem sped down unknown side roads and up hidden back lanes on the way to Shilpi's house. "It'll be a busy night, Princess," he said.

"Don't forget to do it tonight, yaah."

"Eh?"

"You're going to speak to Auntie and Uncle. About us."

"Princess, how could I forget, yeah?"

"You'll text me tonight, when you've done it?"

"Yeah, of course."

Kareem dropped her a block from Shilpi's house, behind a parked van. She disembarked swiftly, anxious to avoid the sharp eyes of aunties or small children, and didn't turn to look as Kareem accelerated past her. This couldn't go on: they were going to be seen by someone soon. She unlooped the veil from around her neck, covered her head with it, crossed the front and threw the ends over her shoulders. Please God, don't let getting caught be necessary to get him over the line.

The last thing she wanted was some hole-in-the-corner wedding, all over in five minutes, with no visits and everyone talking about the *funchait* that had to be called to make Kareem marry that slut Shunduri, his girlfriend. And everyone watching her stomach and counting the months since she'd married. Her pace quickened, and she pulled the veil further forward over her hairline. She hated being late.

A quick knock on the door of the little two-up, two-down council house, and then the smiles and inquisitive eyes of Shilpi's mother and grandmother and some aunties. *Devdas* was on the TV; the scene where Madhuri Dixit, as the beautiful prostitute, acknowledges her love for the hero, whom she can never marry because of what she is. The sound was turned up so loud that it vibrated painfully in Shunduri's ears, and the aunties were all chewing paan and talking over it about some local scandal, oblivious to the tragedy unfolding in front of them. They were all headscarved up as well now, except for the grandmother, Shilpi's daddu, so it looked as if Shilpi's newly acquired ninja style was having a bit of an effect all round.

They waved her upstairs, and she gave her respects and left the room, but as she turned back into the hallway, she heard the name Guri. She stopped with one hand on the banister, her ears straining. Were they talking about her and Kareem already? There was a burst of conversation, but she could make out nothing further. Were they already discovered?

But then one woman's voice rose above the rest, speaking with the authority of an auntie who felt she had seen everything, as they always did. "Well, of course, it is only natural, with Mrs. Guri doing so much matchmaking and Mr. Guri a businessman that has done so well, that his opinion be asked about the marriage and the dowries."

Shunduri crept down a few steps to listen better, a sudden hope rising in her breast.

Shilpi's mother's voice cut in then, triumphant. "Mrs. Guri was not needed for my girl. Shilpi, when her studies were finished, she came to me and told me she was ready. Twenty-two: just right."

"Twenty-two," Daddu's voice rose querulously. "That is a very good age to be married. That is not too young. I was thirteen when I married, and fifteen when I had you."

"Yes, Daddu. Would you like more paan?"

"Nah, nah. They should do as their parents did, marry who their parents find for them, none of this quarrelling and delaying."

"But Daddu," said a younger, more tentative voice, "you know that for these modern Desi boys and girls, marriage is different for them now, with living apart, and jobs. You cannot just say they are a good family, have a good reputation, and finish it there."

"Love-match, is that what you say?"

"Nah, nah, nah, it is not just that. I don't say for love-match, Daddu, I don't. These girls that are brought over, they are not always looked after. We all know that. The family just wants the dowry, and a slave in the kitchen."

There was a pause, then bossy auntie responded. "Or she is not brought over at all. What does that do to a family? Look at Kareem Guri, you know, the boy that Mr. Guri brought over years ago for his restaurant. I was telling you about this before. He married a girl in Bangladesh last year that the Guris betrothed him to long-time ago, and filled in all the forms for the visa like Mohammed Guri wanted but then his son-in-law Ahmed told me that Kareem had said to Immigration he had been forced into it, and they said to him, don't worry, we will never grant her the visa and then in a few years, when your family has accepted the situation, you can divorce her, you know? And marry who you like."

A quiet *aaah* came out of Shunduri's throat, and she sank down to sit on the stairs, her hands flying up to cover her face, then dropping to make fists on the carpeted step where she sat. She could not bear to listen, or move.

"That Ahmed, always such a gossip. That should have stayed in the family. He could make much trouble, talking like that."

"The Guris kept that very quiet."

"I heard the Guris cancelled their trip home two months ago because they didn't want to run into the girl's family, in the marketplace."

Daddu's voice was audible then, rich with disapproval. "That is a bad, bad thing. That girl's village, that girl's family, will not forget. There will be a feud."

There was tsking and chewing, and bossy auntie spoke again. "Ah, men, they cause us a world of sorrow. And those immigration-wallahs, they have no idea about why men do these things, for the dowry, and that poor girl is left in her village unable to marry, for who would want her, and her family shamed and in debt."

Shilpi's mother recommended the story, as if hastening to finish. "They're saying, yeah, that the dowry money all went to Kareem's pocket, and the Guris, thinking they are so clever, saw none of it. And now they have been left with nothing but a bad reputation in Sylhet province for matchmaking. A good thing for them that both their daughters are already married."

"Help me up. My shawl. My glasses. Children—they are all the same," said Daddu.

Shunduri shot to her feet, trembling, then ran up the stairs. As she reached the landing, she looked down at the yellowish-white head of Shilpi's daddu, an auntie on either side of her, being walked with every appearance of reluctance, along the hallway to the downstairs toilet. The two aunties were still talking, about how the girl in Bangladesh was only fifteen, sixteen, with her parents so in favor of the visa, not thinking of what could go wrong.

Shunduri banged the knuckles of her clenched fists together. All this time, Kareem a married man. No one had told her, no one had said a word. All his talk of love, and plans for the future.

How stupid she was to have fallen for his words. To have become the foolish girl that everyone else jokes about, that mothers hold up as a warning to their daughters. Be careful, or you could end up like Shunduri.

She pushed on the door to Shilpi's bedroom, feeling lightheaded, as if she were floating between the two worlds: of the aunties and tradition and arranged marriages; and the Desi world of the girls she had come to visit here, with their talk of clothes and boys and jobs and Bollywood heroes.

Where did this leave her? She was lost somewhere in between, in that place that Aisha's mother spoke about. Purgatory.

She pushed Shilpi's bedroom door, and it swung open, onto a vision of pink. The walls and carpet were a matching pale pink and the bed, the curtains and the bottom part of her dresser were covered in white satin frills. Amina and Aisha were sitting with Shilpi on her bed, all three in pastel *salwars*, their hands covered with intricate henna designs and resting, palms upward, on their knees. There wasn't enough room on the bed for Shunduri, and despite the cries of welcome, no one seemed to be inclined to shift up for her. But that was alright because the last thing she felt like doing was lining up in a row with them and laughing and giggling when she had this painful lump in her throat, and her face could be showing anything, everything. She drifted toward the dresser, half tuned to their chat.

They were listening to Shilpi's tale of her recent betrothal to Shareef, a Desi boy from Manchester who was just finishing his optometry studies and was a big man in the University of Manchester branch of Jamat-al-Islami. They'd met on a Muslim matchmaking website and then for real through a Young Muslims Organisation rally, and she'd managed to steer her mum and dad in the right direction to find him, and he'd done the same with his family.

Shunduri looked at herself in the dressing-table mirror. It was her mouth that would betray what she had heard on the stairs, hanging in a long O of shock and fear beneath the gloss of lipstick. She pressed her lips closed and looked down, Shilpi's smug little voice going on and on behind her.

"As you know, I was all anti-marriage until I went on this *particulaar* Desi website, yaah. And saw dis *particulaar* bruvver. His bio data, I mean. But you know, it's a Muslim woman's duty, yaah . . ."

On Shilpi's dresser, amongst all the stuffed animals, spilt make-up and untidy piles of bangles, was a neat pile of shiny DVDs. *On Muslim Prayer*, *What It Means to Be a Muslim*, *The American Military-Industrial Hegemony*, *Jihad for Beginners*. They were all still shrink-wrapped, except for two: *Shakira* and *The 100 Best Songs of Rani Mukherjee*.

Coiled on the white fluffy seat of Shilpi's dresser stool was her discarded *abaya*, black as night and as full of presence in that room as a snake in a flower garden. Shunduri's eyes were drawn to it. It seemed to be the only thing amongst the frills and fluff that made any sense. While the girls talked on, she touched the *abaya* with her fingertips, then lifted it up to shake it out and refold it. The mass of beaded microfiber weighed as heavy as her heart. There was a green label on the neckline with black writing: *From Shukr's Sakina Prayer Collection. For those Intimate Moments with the Divine.*

"It's a prayer robe, yeah," she heard Shilpi's voice from somewhere behind her. "I got it on the Internet. Go on, try it on."

"Why not, yaah." She heard her own casual tone, as if from far away. She slid her arms into the wide sleeves, pulled the shoulder seams forward so that it hung straight down at the front, found and fastened the hidden ties and buttons at the front and sides, then looked around for the headscarf.

"Here." Shilpi tossed the smaller piece of black fabric toward her. "It's a *shayla hijab*, so it just wraps around, yeah. Much better than the *amira hijabs*, you know, wiv dere elastic."

"Oh that's so true, yeah," said Amina eagerly. "Those elasticated ones make you look like you've got no neck."

Shunduri caught it, found the ends and started to wrap it over her head, but it was slipping on her short haircut. Her usual sureness of touch seemed to have deserted her. Everyone was quiet now, watching.

"Sit down," said Shilpi, "and I'll put it on you. It goes on better wiv the underscarf."

She sat on the fluffy dresser stool, feeling as if their positions had been reversed, while Shilpi's small hands, rough with dried *mendhi*, wrapped and packed away strands of Shunduri's hair and smoothed the fabric across her forehead. "There!"

Shunduri stood, and Amina and Aisha slid off the bed, to examine and exclaim.

"Wow, Baby," said Amina. "You look so tall, really elegant." Shunduri took in her reflection in the mirror. She did look dignified, her eyes large and brilliant, and the *hijab* outlined the fine shape of her head. It shouldn't spoil her bob too much if she wrapped it carefully. She would have to practice.

"And here," said Shilpi, reluctant to abandon her creation, "you can just pull this bit across the face, and pin it, and now it's a *niqab*. That's how I wear it, anyway. Like in the Qur'an."

Mysterious, fascinating. Modest. She could go the whole way, cover her face as well. The *abaya*'s fabric hung in sculptural folds from her shoulders, as if she were a Greek goddess. Some long gloves like Shilpi's wouldn't go astray, either.

"Wow," said Aisha this time. "That looks so cool. Can I try it?"

She took the *abaya* off and passed it on with every appearance of nonchalance, but with possessiveness and reluctance in her heart. She could see herself so clearly, walking to the front row when *takbir*, spontaneous prayer, was called at college, the crowd at political rallies parting for her like the Red Sea.

And Kareem seeing her with new eyes, the eyes of a suitor and a husband. Aaah. Her eyes stung, and she turned her back on her friends, tugging fiercely at the *hijab*'s knot at the side of her neck. But she only seemed to be able to make it tighter, and as she tugged harder, the tears started to spill down her cheeks.

"Baby, are you all right? Baby!" First Aisha, then Amina were staring at her expression, her tears.

She tried to say of course she was fine, she was just trying to get this knot undone, but the words didn't come out properly, and she started to cough on choked tears, had to sit down on the bed while her coughing turned to a kind of gasping crying, and Shilpi ran to the bathroom for a glass of water and Amina tried to give her tissues and Aisha squeezed her shoulders.

Still no words would come out, and eventually her friends seemed to decide that she was sick, there was some sort of bug going around, and they should head back to the college dorm and put her to bed. They phoned for a taxi.

Shilpi walked her downstairs to the cab, the knot in the *niqab* undone, but Shunduri was holding it over her head with one hand as if her life depended on it, her left forearm hard across her midriff as if she had stomach ache. There was little conversation in the taxi on the way home, and once they were back in the dorm, she told them no, she didn't want any company, she didn't need a doctor, just wanted to sleep. She shut her bedroom door on their faces, locked it and climbed into bed still fully dressed, averting her eyes from her bedroom clock, which kept flashing the time, as insistent as her calendar with its missed due date. The tears started again as she pulled off the *niqab*, clutched it to her chest and curled up under her duvet. On Friday morning Shunduri woke late with the alarm already on snooze, her mouth foul-tasting and a headache well entrenched at the base of her skull. Squinting at her phone screen, she checked for texts from Kareem sent last night. Nothing.

It was past nine so she telephoned the bank to call in sick, dragged on her dressing-gown over her clothes and wandered down the corridor to Neena Varios's room to beg a couple of migraine tablets. Once in her own room, she washed them down with a cup of cold tea and climbed back into bed.

Only then did she text Kareem's number: *Don't bother 2nite. Or anytime u casra bastard*, turning off her phone straight after. The *niqab* was still there, crumpled up like a used handkerchief on her pillow, and she tucked it into her fist, lay down and waited for sleep.

## Fourteen

"Uncle Richard!" Two small boys in superhero pajamas cannoned into him at what was becoming a dangerous height, and were immediately campaigning for a wrestling match on the back lawn.

"Absolutely not, monsters. That's your father's job."

"Oh, but Daddy won't—he gets all puffy," said Jonathon, struggling to dislodge brother Andrew, who, hanging grimly on to Richard's belt, and not to be outdone, cried, "Yeah! And red!"

A smiling Thea was not far behind. "It's so good to see you, dearest Richard. Henry is, of course, just as pleased, simply a *little* caught up in some new primary sources we've just unearthed. He's on his way back from the Abbey now. It's all very exciting, but let's get your things out of that townie car and you into a dry martini."

"Nothing better, Thea. It's good to be off that motorway. Sorry I couldn't get here sooner."

Richard kissed his sister-in-law on both cheeks, remembering her preferred continental style, before maneuvering gingerly, boys still attached, through the door of the Lodge and dumping them unceremoniously on the sitting-room carpet. "Remember the mixer, please: I'm not a QC yet."

Thea, tilting her head, flicked at the tangle of gold at her neck. "Well, come and help me then. We can put your bag away later. Boys!

*Boys!* This may be your last chance to play on the trampoline before bedtime."

She turned, ignoring the stampede to the back door that passed her by inches, and Richard found himself following her sauntering walk down the passage with interest. Thea Kiriakis, former Chelsea fashionista, had lost her old angularity and was now affecting lady-of-the-manor cashmere and tweeds. Which actually suited her very well, perhaps because of the unexpected contrast with her dark coloring. The only jarring note in this new image was the familiar quantity of gold at neck and wrists.

And, of course, everything was a little too well cut for county. Images from their past assailed him suddenly, and he brought his train of thought up short. What else had he expected? Of course, they would be moving back into the Abbey any day now. She *was* the lady of the manor.

And he was a little too preoccupied with old times, perhaps? Those particular times in London nine or ten years ago, when he and Thea had played host and hostess, and Henry was the occasional visitor? Richard decided to take a kitchen stool this side of the breakfast bar, rather than go round and lean against the countertop and share the space with her. You could never be too careful. But of what? Surely not himself: he'd seen their break-up coming a mile off, in a sense had engineered it, and besides, it was ancient history, and he'd never been into that.

"I suppose Henry told you all about our ghost?" said Thea, as she moved toward the fridge. She took two martinis out, already garnished, and slid one across the counter, smiling. "And I suppose that's why you made this lightning decision to visit? Not that I'm not glad to see you."

Henry appeared through the scullery door, carrying a Tupperware container behind his back and making a beeline for the fridge. "Hey, Richard," he said indistinctly, one hand over his mouth. "Thee, I just need to . . ."

"What are you eating? Is that cake?"

Henry shook his head. "No, no, Thee. It's just one of Mrs. Choudhury's pakhoras. You know how she never lets me leave without food."

"How many have you eaten?"

"Well, ah . . ."

"I thought you were trying to lose weight."

"Oh, ah, just one while I was there, then one on the way back, and then, ah . . ."

"She thinks I never feed you."

"Richard, would you like one? They're delicious."

"Very fattening," said Thea. "You should see how much she feeds the children: no wonder they're over there all the time."

"Oh, I see you're onto the hard stuff already." Henry tried to steer the conversation elsewhere, as Thea pulled the Tupperware out of his hands. "It's great to see you here at last, by the way."

Richard sipped his drink cautiously: Thea's martinis were pretty near to pure gin, with olive. "It was good timing as far as work went. And of course I had real reason to be concerned about my brother's and sister-in-law's mental health. Seeing ghosts. Researching ghosts. Help was clearly needed . . ."

"Rubbish!" Thea reached out to snatch his martini back, and he swiftly lifted it into the air. Even sitting down, this was well out of Thea's reach, and Henry was happy just to laugh.

"Now, Thee, you must watch that excitable Greek temperament—superstitious too, by the looks of things. Oh, now, that was pure temper. Pass the tea towel, Henry. You two owe me another martini."

---

THAT EVENING, AFTER dinner, Richard, feeling uncharacteristically flat, stretched his legs out on the sofa in the sitting room. Ready for bed, and it was only nine-thirty. Must be his London hours catching up with him. Or more likely Thea's martinis. Henry, a sheaf of papers in his hand, was murmuring with Thea: something about the ghost, no doubt.

Backlit by a silk-shaded lamp, with Thea, immaculately groomed, sitting on the floor and leaning on Henry's knee to emphasize a point, and the boys for once not squabbling over their card game, they looked like a movie-screen family, too good to be true. He rested his head back against the cushions and watched them through half-closed eyes.

The image needed a title. *Country Life at Bourne Abbey Lodge*. Or maybe, *This Could Have Been You*. Well, there's a thought. The room felt too warm now, to the point of oppressiveness, and he had a sudden craving for the cool blue space of his Chambers. Or maybe he just needed a cigarette. He got to his feet, signalling a watchful Thea and an oblivious Henry with two fingers to his mouth, and found his way outside via the scullery door.

The grind and snap of his lighter in the quiet of the garden was obscurely comforting, although it was certainly no cooler out here. The lawn stretched before him. He breathed in slowly and deeply, savoring fresh air and acrid smoke in equal measure.

In the still, moonlit air, smoke from his neglected cigarette curled into a luminous, almost vertical, stranded spiral, a DNA helix. Inheritance. You could run, but never escape. Well, hadn't he proved that wrong? Henry was inheriting, and he, Richard Bourne, eldest son, was free of it forever, free to live his own life in London and pursue his chosen career. No crumbling wreck of an Abbey to blight his existence and tie him to the regions, none of the county social round to put up with come hell or high water.

He flicked the cigarette's long ash tail and frowned. But he was here, wasn't he? Back in, not quite the Abbey, but its Lodge. And in a month or two, he would be invited, knowing Thea, to a grand unveiling of the fully restored Abbey, now on the National Trust A-list, no less. He'd needed a break, but why hadn't he gone down to Cowes, or flown to Paris for the weekend? The paperwork for Bourne Abbey was not so pressing that he couldn't have dealt with it the next time Thea came down to London. So, why was he here, back on the family land, sorting out family problems again?

His sense of oppression was lifting with a little fresh air, and the unease that remained was probably just work-related. Yet he could think of nothing outstanding, nothing out of control. He prided himself, always had, on knowing exactly where he stood on all his current matters: no sprinting down from Chambers, gown flapping, for unprepared applications, or scrambling to hide sloppy preparation from his instructing solicitor and the Bench. No, it wasn't work. And it wasn't Thea, startling though her transformation was.

So why this discomfiting sense of something missing, or impending, that had been growing on him for the last few months? Something that he would have to rise to meet, or understand, that was outside of his experience. He squared his shoulders and glanced further, beyond the Lodge garden, toward the Abbey itself, invisible in the dark. But there was nothing untoward there: Henry's ridiculous money-making plans, his avoidance of paperwork, were an irritation, no more.

Perhaps his work was a problem in a different sense: was he entering into that no-man's-land of restless anxiety that so many senior juniors, waiting for the magical appointment to Queen's Counsel, were said to suffer? He blinked slowly, reluctant to close his eyes to the sting of the smoke. No, not yet anyway: two more years at the earliest at his own estimate, though Sternbridge, his Chambers' senior bencher, had hinted that a few more high-profile briefs from Her Majesty's Inland Revenue could accelerate things somewhat. And certainly, until recently, he'd been happy to do just that. The Reid brief, where he was instructed to preserve and protect a family Trust, make it work as it should, was not his usual style: he was more an anti-Trust man, as the Americans would say.

The scullery door creaked open, and Thea emerged, her pearls shining in the moonlight. She had discarded her tailored jacket and the shirt underneath was sleeveless.

"Company?"

"Always a pleasure, Thea. Light?"

"No, trying *very* hard to give it away. Just let me smell the air.

Aren't ex-smokers pathetic? Never thought I'd join their ranks till I caught Jonathon playing with my pack. No moral high ground to tell him off, you see. And he knew it."

"You'll have plenty of distraction soon enough."

Thea swung her arms out, then spun lazily, her heels scraping on the flagstones.

"I don't know what we're going to do with ourselves when we have all that space at the Abbey. It seems almost unbelievable that it's only a few months away now after—what? Five years of renovation and restoration. And no small thanks to your legal nous."

"Nothing could have replaced your hard work, Thea." Not to mention her family's money. He hesitated. "I'm just glad that Henry—both of you—were willing to take on what I was not."

"I've always wondered about that eldest-son thing, you know. If Henry hadn't been so passionate about the Abbey, or if you hadn't been able to break the Trust, would it *really* have been so awful for you to take it on?" She paused and, in the face of his silence, gave a husky little laugh.

Giving up hadn't changed that. How strange that now, after eleven years, or was it twelve, she was so direct on the subject. Or was this sudden need for forgiveness, or closure, some kind of recognition, actually very timely, with all the hard work done and all she had wanted for so long, now close enough to touch?

His coming down at this juncture had had repercussions, caused anxieties, that he hadn't fully appreciated. He squinted at the glowing end of his cigarette, taking in Thea's guarded gaze and stopped breath, and made a conscious effort to throw sufficient emphasis into his voice. "Not in a million years."

She gave a little jump, whether of unrelieved tension, or joy, or something else, he could not tell. But then her feet resumed their dance, and her voice thrummed lower and softer than before. "I'm not so sure I believe you. Oh, give me just one puff."

He smiled, shaking his head, and stepped out of her charmed circle to flick the remains of the cigarette into the garden before heading inside. "Absolutely not, Thea. Think of your moral ground."

After Thea made noises about turning in, Richard went upstairs with Henry to do a dutiful look-in on Andrew and Jonathon, to find them fast asleep on the bedroom carpet under a tangled mess of duvets, sheets, and Twix and Mars Bar wrappers. The boys' arms and legs were sticking out at odd enough angles to suggest a massacre. The video they'd been watching was long finished, and the battle scene from a re-colored *El Cid* was playing on the television.

While Henry pulled on duvets and unwound sheets, Richard scooped up the nearest body and tipped it into the top bunk, then stopped to watch the confrontation between a red-faced, red-crossed knight and a glamorous, dastardly infidel, speechifying with swords drawn under the green flag of Islam and Saladin.

"Great words. Henry, wasn't this one of your favorite movies?"

Henry straightened to look. "Oh yes, wonderful stuff."

"*Yonder lies the castle of my father*. Remember that line? Brought the house down."

Henry tugged on a sheet that seemed to have wrapped itself completely around both a boy leg and a bunk leg, and had formed a granny knot. "Tony Curtis. But that wasn't *El Cid*. It was *Son of Ali Baba* . . ."

"Who could have cast that pretty-boy Tony Curtis as a serious hero? Should have been Gregory Peck or this fellow with the beard."

"Charlton Heston. No one laughed at *him*," said Henry, sounding almost bitter.

"Here, I'll pick him up and see if you can slide his leg out of the sheet. Looks like his brother tied him to the furniture."

"Wouldn't be surprised," said Henry. "Big brothers for you."

Outside, a fitful moonlight shone down on the Abbey and its great estate, in darkness no longer shrunk by death duties and new roads to merely Park and Lodge. Night restored the ancient boundaries, when the Abbey lands encompassed Windsor Cottage, Lydiard village, Tregoze Church and the farmlands beyond, stretching to the gleaming line of the Stowe River on three sides and the first gigantic upward sweep of the Wiltshire Downs on the fourth.

In the back garden of Windsor Cottage, hutched rabbits slept, and snake bean and okra leaves drooped from the long summer's day. In the center sat the compost heap, its smooth, even darkness at odds with the soft-edged asymmetries of bush and plant. It had been steaming all afternoon and the nearby cucumber frames dripped with condensation.

Perhaps because of the long hot spell, or Mrs. Begum's failure to fork the heap over, or even possibly some process connected with the ancient, dense substance hidden within it, the heat of the pyramidal pile had climbed and continued to climb. There was enough heat radiating from it now to cause small rippling distortions in the single shaft of moonlight that fell on its peak.

Then a tiny wisp of smoke appeared at the topmost part of the heap's cone. It rose, hung in the humid air. Just as it seemed about to disperse, another, slightly more definite coil of white appeared, then several more. The rich rotting scent of the compost began to be superseded, then swamped, by another smell, a powerful sweet bitterness.

The wisps became larger, more frequent, and merged into a continuous flow of white that moved steadily from the peak and down the sides of the mound, spreading out over the grass and vegetable garden toward the patio doors and beyond.

Before an hour had passed, the smoke had formed a dense white duvet that covered the lawns and had begun to flow down the hill toward the river, and along the side lane toward the High Street. The sleeping village, the Lodge and the Abbey itself, all lay in its path. Inside the cottage, Dr. Choudhury was once again snoring in his study chair, legs apart and covered in swathes of a pink and gold sari, his right hand resting on its *pallu*. A bitter scent drifted through the open window. He dreamt of material beauty: silk georgettes softer than velvet, damasks revealing the subtlety of their designs in candlelight, wedding *lehengas* so thick with gold wire embroidery that they could stand up on their own.

And then there he was: standing at the lectern in the Sheldonian Theatre, giving the Chancellor's opening speech to two thousand students and wearing, with his professor's bonnet, a most outstanding silk chiffon sari, deepest pink over a matching blouse, both spangled with gold wire, iridescent sequins and glass beads. He could feel the swinging weight of the embroidery as it pulled on the chiffon. He gloried in how it must look under the lighting and knew that every videoing parent would preserve him for posterity.

His speech concluded, and the students stood and gave three cheers, throwing their mortarboards into the air. Bowing graciously, the cynosure of all eyes, he turned on his heels to sway gracefully offstage, anticipating the crowd's reaction when they saw the sari's magnificent *pallu*, encrusted with gold and precious stones, as it followed the sinuous curve of his back . . .

---

MRS. BEGUM, HEADACHEY even in her sleep and, despite the heat, cocooned in three-quarters of the marital duvet, also dreamt of beauty: the beauty of a perfect traditional wedding, with all the modern trimmings as well. At least twenty thousand pounds' worth. And she was somehow the perfect bride (young, beautiful, virginal, arranged, with lustrous hair and eyes so long and dark they hardly needed kohl) as well as being the bride's mother. She sailed triumphantly past envious aunties and neighbors in full knowledge of the perfection of the match, the super-abundance of the food, the enormousness of the dowry, the impressiveness of the in-laws, and the surpassing weight of the wedding gold (six kilos, nah) being heroically carried on head, neck, nose, ears, wrists and ankles by that perfect bride.

Mrs. Begum wriggled with pleasure at the sight, then moaned

quietly as the white stretch limousine drew into view, to take away the bride and groom. Off to Mustique for their honeymoon, like Princess Margaret.

———————

UP AT THE Lodge, Richard had delayed going to bed until Henry and Thea had settled in for the night, idling over the paper while goodnights were said and warnings were given, as always, about the dodgy downstairs loo. Then he went outside for one last cigarette in the certain, luxurious knowledge that he would not be interrupted. The usual evening breeze had failed to appear, leaving the garden still warm, although, strangely, he thought he could glimpse a bit of mist about. A hot day tomorrow then. He thought with resignation of the sofa bed and the single duvet, nylon-filled and covered by a pilling polyester Batman, that waited for him in the study. Christ knew how he was going to get to sleep at all.

But when he finally lay down in the Lodge's study, the masked avenger sitting clammily across his chest, and his own feet hanging over the bed end, he fell into sleep as suddenly and heavily as falling off a cliff. He occasionally came to, disturbed by cravings for nicotine and his king-sized mattress in Knightsbridge, breathed in the sweet, smoky atmosphere, then dozed and woke and slept again, returning each time to confused dreams of omission and failure.

In the Abbey Rohimun woke from a nightmare of fire and destruction to a painfully full bladder. She eyed the Tupperware container Tariq had given her for emergencies. No way.

The green velvet hangings were silver-grey in the moonlight, and a night breeze bellied them out as if the old house was breathing. Hundreds of men and women must have wakened like her, in this room in the night. Had any of them been exiled, she wondered, out of favor on some royal whim or error of judgement. Perhaps they spent their time here waiting on a message, not knowing whether to expect pardon or condemnation. Perhaps they were relieved to be exiled, free from all the pressure of having to keep other people happy. At least they had chamber pots, not bloody Tupperware.

She wriggled out of sleeping bag and camp bed, stood, then stretched her arms over her head and arched backward to get the kinks out. Oh, for a decent bed. She creaked open the door and trotted cautiously down the corridor to the bathroom.

But once she was back, she wasn't sleepy. She moved to the window and looked out. Moonlight, titanium white, flickered between bands of scudding summer cirrus, strobing the garden's topiary creatures into almost-life. The giant yew hedge, darker than the night, loomed like a wall between her and the rest of the world. A greyish-white mist had crept up from the river and over the lawn, spreading out as if to encircle the Abbey.

She needed some fresh air. Rohimun wiggled open the window and leaned out to take a deep breath. The air was smoky and bitter tonight, like wet leaves burning, and made her think of gardens, and gardeners. How satisfying to create a garden like that spread out below, to know that at least some of it would last for generations. How many paintings did that, out of all the dross that was produced. Nothing of hers, for sure. Not yet.

While she was still a student, and Dad had just started to get involved with Bourne Abbey, he had told her some of the stories of the Abbey and the people who had stayed in this room. The famous Victorian Islamic convert Lord Headley Al-Farooq. The colonial adventurer and translator Marmaduke Pickthall. Lady Evelyn Cobbold, who had been buried upright facing Mecca on her Scottish country estate. Poor artistic Edward Lear, so fat and lonely. And now her. Rohimun turned to look at the great bed. It was testered in a deep green velvet, which also covered the undulating down mattress, fifty years old at least. Her camp bed squatted next to it, runt-like, the repository of all the bad dreams that had followed her from London.

She shivered again and pulled her tracksuit top down over her tummy. It slid back up, exposing a roll of flesh to the cold. What was the difference between her and Lear anyway? She turned away from the window and aimed a vicious kick at the camp bed. Fucking hell that hurt. The camp bed took off like a rocket with the force of her kick, sliding over the floorboards until it had almost disappeared from view under the great bed's green coverings.

Rohimun limped over to the old bed and rested against it, then fished around and pulled her sleeping bag out from where it had hidden itself. The bed stood as high as her waist, so she hoicked herself awkwardly up over its side, taking the bag with her. She crawled across the velvet cover into the middle and, tracksuit top around her armpits, wormed into her sleeping bag in the soft sinking center of the mattress. The bed had probably last been slept in before central heating was installed. Rohimun sneezed, then yawned, her anger and her headache evaporating. She pulled her long rope of hair out from under her back, twisting it up above her head and throwing it over the top of the bolster. Then she moved further down, nestling in. Within minutes Rohimun had fallen asleep, dreaming only of swinging in a hammock under green trees.

## Fifteen

NOTHING, THOUGHT DR. Choudhury, could be more pleasant on a late Saturday afternoon than a happy wife and the eye-burning hiss of roasting spices in the kitchen. Especially after a morning where everyone seemed to have gotten out of bed on the wrong side. The kitchen window's curtains billowed, showing glimpses of green grass and sunshine. Tariq should be walking Rohimun over from the Abbey about now, and it would soon behoove Dr. Choudhury to prepare himself for this meeting.

Mrs. Begum, sari-end tucked into her waistband, was shallow-frying fish cutlets coated in coriander and turmeric for *mas biran*, and the stove was full of metalware. Looking over his wife's head he could see *muki*, taro, on a rolling boil in one pot, almost ready to be tipped into the rich brown sauce of *bamaloh*, what his damn stupid colleagues called Bombay duck. But this was set off in a way they would never see in a restaurant, by his wife's specialty: emerald green floating clusters of *lottha*, water-lily shoots, national flower of Bangladesh and staple of the villages. At the rear of the stove was Mrs. Begum's largest pot holding a whole chicken simmering in a turmeric-golden sauce, the glorious *muruk murgh moshla*, gubbing and bubbing in a slow bass-note to the scream of frying fish and his wife's flying hands.

He clasped his hands behind his back and considered the kitchen table. His favorite salad—green tomatoes, chilli, garlic, onion and coriander—already stood near to his placemat, and there was a bunch of rather raggedy pinkish flowers in a glass in the center of the table. Dr. Choudhury raised his eyebrows but refrained from comment. It had only ever been Rohimun who picked flowers for the house. Tables were for food.

On the placemat for their eldest daughter was a small gold-rimmed glass of sherbet milk. He bent down disbelievingly to smell the distinctive mixture of pistachio and rosewater, then straightened. This welcome drink for honored guests, new brides, was utterly unsuitable for a disgraced, unmarriageable runaway. This could not be allowed.

He turned to face Mrs. Begum's plump back and cleared his throat loudly for her full attention, but she did not seem to hear him over the frying and gub-bubbing. He cleared his throat again, and his wife whirled around but sank below his line of sight to the floor behind the kitchen table.

Was this an attempt to avoid him? It was not his place, as the husband and father, to chase his wife around the kitchen to get her attention, let alone to go onto hands and knees under a table to catch her eyes.

He leaned forward a little, careful not to move his feet from their dignified, magisterial position, and knocked sharply on the tabletop. Mrs. Begum's head bobbed up at the level of the table, and as she was now paying him the attention she should, he felt able to stroll to the sink, which brought him to her side of the table. Her eyes followed him silently.

Having reached his target (for he had required a small glass of water), he could see that Mrs. Begum was squatting on the ground, yellow and black sari folds tucked through under her bottom, and the long and deadly *dhaa* blade upright on the floor between her thighs as she slowly sliced into the firm flesh of a papaya.

She was still working as she watched him, and he could see her thigh muscles flex through the thin cotton as her right foot, placed firmly on the base of the *dhaa*, braced against the strain on that sharpest of edges. One gentle brush on the blade and deep gold gave way to a dark-seeded center, the fruit opening up again and again as she continued to work.

Dr. Choudhury opened his mouth, then shut it again. His wife, despite her position on the kitchen lino, was staring at him in such a disconcertingly direct manner that he felt as if his back was pinned to the kitchen sink. Without shifting her gaze, she put the papaya segments down on a piece of newspaper and rested the fingers of her right hand, glistening with juice, on the flat of the large blade. He felt the need for a small sip of the refreshing water, nature's champagne, and swallowed carefully.

"You have made sherbet milk."

Mrs. Begum's eyes narrowed. "*Jiioi.*"

Yes. What could he do with yes? This was not how conversations were supposed to flow between husband and wife. And why did she have to be using the *dhaa* at such a time? She showed no inclination to move, to approach him in an appropriately supplicating manner, as would befit the anxious mother of an exiled daughter. The sound of the frying fish, covered now, droned in an off-key, and the *muki* buzzed frantically against one another in their pot. She continued to stare, and he felt his back slip against the counter's edge.

He hurrumphed loudly. "Be sure that all this mess is cleared up soon, Mrs. Begum." He clicked his glass onto the draining board in a decisive manner, folded his hands behind his back and, still hurrumphing, retreated toward the sitting room. He would wait there for his children. At least he knew how to do things properly.

---

TARIQ WATCHED ROHIMUN fuss with her clothes. This meeting with Mum and Dad had come about sooner than he'd expected.

"It's no good," she said. "Nothing fits."

He couldn't believe Rohimun, of all people, was getting in a state about what to wear. She'd become plumper since he'd been away, and her old college *salwarkameez*, in fashionable-again pastels, strained across her chest and hips. Staring at the old cheval glass, she plucked vainly at the fabric, which had formed horizontal ripples over her breasts, and pulled down on the side seams.

"You'll rip it."

She glared at him through the cheval. "Who asked you? It's *fine*, yeah?"

"If you say so."

"Well, are we going or what?"

"Alright, alright." He picked up the matching scarf from the bed and handed it to her. "Don't forget your *chunna*. I'll go first," he said, pretending not to see her roll her eyes, and led their cautious procession along corridors and down stairwells until they were outside.

Halfway across the stretch of lawn that sloped from the Abbey's front, he turned to face his sister. "It's not going to be as bad as you're thinking, yeah? Mum and Dad have changed too."

Rohimun, rushing behind, promptly ran into him. She dragged a length of the *chunna* back around her neck and pulled at her *salwar*. "It's wrapping round me like a bloody bedspread."

"It must be a result of their moving here, out of the community," he continued. "Or maybe all of us leaving home. It's like they've gotten younger, more modern." He took Rohimun's hand to walk, automatically smoothing her wrist with his thumb to move non-existent bracelets out of the way. He felt it twitch with annoyance. "They've got new interests. New friends. Mum's joined the Women's Institute."

"I know. It *is* only a year since I was here. They're not that different. Bai!" One end of the *chunna* had fallen again, then caught on a bush. She tugged at it. "Can you help me out here?"

"You're making it worse. Why'd you wear it if—"

"You bloody gave it to me. And you know why," she retorted, wrenching on it now.

Since when did his own sister swear in front of him? Tariq started to speak, then reminded himself she was stressed, afraid, didn't know what she was saying. Everything hinged on this meeting: her whole future.

"Can you see me taking the beats in jeans?" Tiny silver beads sprayed onto the grass as she snapped threads and tore muslin to free herself.

He winced at the damage, so unnecessary, and broke off the offending twigs to forestall further destruction. "Look, there won't be any beats. All I'm saying is don't expect the worst. Dad took it pretty well, considering. And you know Mum. She's the one's been putting all the soft bones in your meat curry."

In fact, the long uncomfortable talk they'd had early that first Saturday morning, about Rohimun and her past, his mother standing while he and his father sat at the kitchen table, had for him marked that seminal point that most of his friends had experienced in their last years of school, where they suddenly found themselves with more presence and authority within the family than before.

He remembered Ali, whose father, like most of his friends' fathers, had kept the family in line with beatings, arriving for class in what was to be his last year of school, with a black eye and bruised chin, and announcing that he was head of the family now. There would be no more beats from his father. Ali had told them how he'd blocked his father's arm, preventing him from hitting his mother and sisters, and after a few blows, his father had suddenly folded, left the house for some hours and, on his return, asked him to pay the restaurant staff's wages.

Tariq's own father, his friends always joked, had always been more like the stereotypical henpecked Hindu father, with his easygoing attitude, white-collar job and managing, ambitious wife. But then he was a Dhaka man, from the capital, not the villages. He had always been legal, had never cleaned toilets or driven taxis, and they had been one of the first Bengali families in Oxford to get their children through A-levels.

So Tariq had stayed "the boy," and when he had occasionally fixed something around the house, or deputized for his father at a wedding or a funeral, Dr. Choudhury would say with stagey wonder, "Who would have thought he'd become so useful!"

He had resented this, but at the same time had been well aware that he did not want the situation to change anytime soon. That same year, Ali's parents had entered into marriage negotiations with a Brick Lane family of good standing in the community, and two months after Ali left school and joined the restaurant full-time, he was betrothed. Head of the family brought with it many responsibilities, in the community as well as the family, and a responsible man was a married man.

"I'll just be glad when it's over, you know," Rohimun muttered suddenly.

Tariq, startled, agreed without thinking, then swallowed a rising irritation. She must know herself that it was simply a matter of going through the motions. Kneel, touch Mum's and Dad's feet, a few slaps, a few tears, and it was all done. Wayward second-generation daughters weren't exactly unknown in the community. All he had to do was babysit her, keep his mouth shut. Not every problem had a formula like that.

With a breeze came a faint musical sound: some instrument being played. The notes rose, then faded. Tariq watched Rohimun stop to look around for their source, tugging down on her tunic again.

The player came into view: as Tariq suspected, it was Denny, leaning against a pine tree, a tin whistle in his mouth.

"Who's that, then?"

"Oh, no one," said Tariq. "I think he works here."

Denny grinned and waved at them, and went back to his playing— only the most ragged semblance of a tune.

"Do you know him?"

"Not really. We chat sometimes."

"He'd better not give up his day job, yeah. Whatever that is. He looks like a traveller."

"He's Colin the gardener's son. He helps out a bit, that's all. Come on, we're going to be late."

As they walked on, Tariq turned for a last glimpse of Denny. He'd slip out to meet him later, in their usual place near the river, after everyone was in bed.

Through the trees ahead, Tariq could see his mother's washing on the line: gold, purple, deep pink and turquoise. All madly flapping in the breeze, only a fence's breadth from Mrs. Darby's line, where a strict white-on-white policy seemed to be in operation. No wonder Mum never appreciated the washing-powder ads. "What's that whitey-white?" she would say to the television. "Plenty of time for whitey-white when I'm a widow, till then, browny-brown, bluey-blue, greeny-green . . ." And Dad would give his newspaper a tiny expert flick and remark to no one in particular, and in Bangla for maximum sarcasm, that Mrs. Begum should be consoled by the fact that she could avoid the whitey-white of widowhood altogether if she was to meet with Allah before him.

He felt a tug on his hand, and saw Rohimun's face tensed in profile.

"Look. There's Mum."

Just visible in the garden was a tiny yellow-and-black figure that stood in an attitude of frozen concentration, before abandoning a laundry basket on the grass near the washing line and scuttling inside the cottage. The tinny slam of the back door was just audible.

Rohimun groaned. "What does that mean? They've changed their minds?"

"You know Mum. They want to do the big forgiveness scene through the front door, yeah?" Tariq tried to make it a joke, but his voice came out harsh with tension. "At least you'll get to kneel on carpet, not lino."

She stared at the cottage, then tore off her *chunna* as if it was choking her, and dropped it. "Shit."

Disgusted, he let go of her hand and moved toward the trees. These were really old: oaks, probably planted by the monks of the original Abbey. Had they ever intervened in family quarrels, he wondered. Or had they kept to themselves, spiritual brotherhood being more important than blood. Or maybe they were only there because their families wanted nothing more to do with them.

He remembered how one endless, lonely Friday, in his second year at university, living in college and away from home and community, he'd found himself wandering only a street away from the central mosque when the *azan zuhur*, the call to midday prayer, sounded out. He felt transparent, ghost-like, as he drifted with the crowd of men making their way to the front entrance of the mosque.

When he'd reached the top of the first flight of steps, almost inside, he'd stopped. What was he doing there? He hadn't been to the *Jumma*, the special Friday prayers, for almost five years, and he had nothing to cover his head. But he could not bring himself to turn around and walk back into all the curious and condemnatory stares that such an act would attract. He felt so delicately poised, on the very edge of existence, that it would only take one more act of coldness or misunderstanding to tip him into extinction.

Then a warm hand had touched his shoulder and a friendly voice sounded in his ear. "Come, brother. Come on inside. Lost your topi?"

He turned to see a man his own age in full beard and the flowing robes of a *dishdasha*, and tried to conjure a sensible reply over the hollowness inside. Words would not come.

"I have some spare topis inside, brother. Come with me to wash."

Tariq tried again to speak. "I'm not . . ." but his throat had seized up. How long since he had spoken to a man like himself? He could not speak the words of denial.

Tariq's legs moved in spite of himself. Shame assailed him when he was led into the shoe room, and he stepped on his heels to remove his shoes like a boy unable to untie his laces. He felt a topi placed on his head from behind, and the words he should have uttered outside the mosque came to him unbidden. *Allah aftah li abwaba rahmatika.* O Allah, open Your gates of mercy for me.

He was steered into the washroom, crowded with other men stooped and crouching over taps and troughs. He bent down to strip off his socks and roll up his trousers. The old routine that he used to follow with his father at Ramadan and Eid reasserted itself. He began to wash hands, mouth, nose, face, forearms, head, ears, nape, feet and toes, all in the marvellous comfort of prescribed order. He had come home.

No guiding hand was necessary now as he walked into the open hall of the masjid and took his place on the jigsaw puzzle of carpets, the hundreds of men standing shoulder to shoulder. The *kutba* had just finished and the imam was descending the *minbar* to lead the congregation. Tariq's throat was still closed so he could not speak his *niyyah*, his intention, but he bowed his head in submission to the imam's "*Takbir!*" As the slow ballet of the *raka'ahts* began, his breaths deepened, and the multitude of voices around him resonated through his body: *Allahu Akbar.* God is great.

His throat opened and his voice flew out to join them. "*Assalaamu 'alayna wa'ala 'ibaadillahi-s-saalihin.*" May peace be upon us, the righteous servants of Allah.

Seated on his left calf with the toes of his right foot flexed forward for the *Tasha-hud*, he gloried in the peculiar, familiar muscular tension of the position, and extended his right forefinger toward the mihrab and Mecca. This is my destiny. His eyes had followed the line of his finger toward the short, broad back of the man in front of him. This is where I belong.

———

JUST LOOK WHERE all that had gotten him. Tariq felt the breeze strengthen and caught an oak leaf as it tumbled. He turned to see where his sister was. Who was he to tell Munni where she belonged?

"Hey," he said to her. "It's up to you, yeah?"

She was silent.

"I'm not going to make you do anything. We can go back to the Abbey, hide out in the stables till Henry's gone if you want. Go visit Mum and Dad another day. It doesn't matter."

"No." She dug a toe into the ground. "Let's get it over with." He returned to her and picked up her *chunna*, draping the muslin across her shoulders so that it hung behind her. The sky was darkening from pale blue to violet, making the silver embroidery on her top shimmer. "Come on then."

They skirted the garden hedge, around to the front door of the cottage. Tariq knocked, with Rohimun standing behind him. The door swung open with no one visible, like some B-grade horror film, and he repressed a groan of his own at his family's need to wring every drop of drama out of a situation, Asian-style.

He moved forward, but Rohimun did not. "Come *on*."

Her head was tucked down so he couldn't see her expression, and her arms were tightly folded. He grabbed her tunic, pulled hard to get her into the hallway, and nearly fell over Mum, who'd been hiding behind the door.

"Shush, shush!" she admonished before he'd said a word. "It is all fine, fine!" But she was clutching the talisman pinned to her blouse, like she always did when she was saying what she wanted the truth to be, rather than what it was.

Tariq looked toward the sitting-room doorway, and his mother nodded at him in vigorous confirmation.

"Go there. Go!" Then she threw an end of the *chunna* over Rohimun's hair and started to push her down the hall, walking behind her and telling her in a piercing whisper, "Kitchen now. Go, go. The men will talk first."

As Tariq walked through the open doorway into the sitting room, he could see his father standing at the room's far end, facing the fireplace, one hand on his chin and apparently deep in thought. Jesus. He'd seen this before. Dad was playing Amitabh Bachchan as the sorrowing tycoon disappointed by his children in the big reconciliation scene out of *Khabi Kushi Khabi Gum*. And milking it even more than Amitabh did. He walked to the center of the room.

"*Salaamalaikum*, Abba."

His dad was in a cravat for the occasion and wearing his gold rings. Mum had weaned him off these for work years ago, having been quick to realize that at Oxford, striped ties with a regimental feel were the thing, and that in some circles even a wedding band on a man was inappropriate. Trust him to go by the Bollywood book tonight.

Dad half turned, and Tariq bent and reached for his father's feet, but was gently prevented.

"My son, my son . . ."

He was drawn upward to be kissed on the forehead, twice. He'd seen his father just two hours ago. The perfume had been ladled on as well.

"Abba." Tariq reined in his temper, tried to match his father's tone. "Your eldest daughter Rohimun, your little Munni, she's here, to ask for your forgiveness."

Dr. Choudhury gave an exaggerated start and faced the fireplace, one palm raised in negation. "I have no daughter by that name."

Pompous bastard.

"*Dad*. Abba." Tariq took a steadying breath, alarmed at his own welling anger. "There's been enough sorrow already, yeah? She's suffered and she needs your help. Family help."

The palm did not move. "I have no—"

"Look, Dad." He could feel his neck and scalp filling with heat. Rohimun could probably hear everything, and the prick knew it. His father was enjoying himself. He'd already decided to accept her back but he wanted to enjoy his big scene first, really draw it out. Didn't matter that he was making her bleed.

"She's here, yeah, like you *asked* her to be. Last Tuesday."

Dad gave him a reproachful look, making it clear that Tariq wasn't playing his part properly. He gave an Amitabh-style sorrowful paternal sigh and reverted to the mantelpiece. The raised palm did not waver, and Tariq could see, reflected in the mantel mirror, his father's approximation of noble sorrow overlain by an expectant complacency. The urge Tariq felt to grab him by his stupid cravat and tell him everything, tell him how it really was, rose in him like a wave.

The back of his father's head showed the same thinning white hair and hint of scalp that he himself would have in twenty years. He had a dizzying sensation of blood draining away from his face, and drifted toward his father, his hands closed into fists. But as he moved, there was a sound from the hallway, a gasp, and he saw his mother's horrified face in the mantel mirror. He felt sick. Jesus Christ, what had he been about to do?

He whirled around and strode out of the sitting room into the hall. His mother was standing with her back to the closed front door, watching him, her lips pressed thin. Shame overwhelmed him, and he went to touch her feet, but she stepped aside, opening the door and whispering, "Your father, he must think you have left. Go, go. Munni is out back, on the patio. Go to her now, around from the front. Be quiet." She shoved him outside.

He looked back at her, his clever mother, then she slammed the door hard behind him, giving Dr. Choudhury the desired message that he had, to all appearances, lost both son and eldest daughter.

Tariq stood still, breathing fast, dazed. He'd never gotten so close to real violence before, with his own family. What was happening to him?

He walked blindly into the little front garden and turned to face the house. It was proper twilight now. He could hear floorboards creaking in the hallway, and the rise and fall of his father's voice, perhaps less pompous now, a little hesitant. Or maybe that was just his own wishful thinking. He started to make his way quietly around to the rear of the cottage. Would Mum do this for him as well, fight with cunning and flattery, treats and lies, to get him back, if she knew?

Around the back, he found Rohimun sitting on the stone flags of the patio, hugging her knees. Her head and neck were bare. He stood in front of her. "You alright?"

She gestured to a basket next to her, lined with paper towels and filled with samosas. "Have something to eat. Mum's made samosas."

Tariq thought he could see Rohimun's *chunna* in the darkened garden. It was quite a way away, a little bundle caught up in the shrubbery. "Did Mum put you out here?"

"Yeah. She took me into the kitchen first. Then of course she wanted to go back and listen, so she sent me out here with the basket. Look." She pointed toward the Abbey, only just visible against the last of the setting sun. Three small lights, torches probably, moved slowly back toward the Lodge. "My visitors are going home already."

Rohimun seemed relaxed, almost cheerful: very different to what he'd expected. Perhaps it hadn't all sunk in yet. Yet she'd been stressed enough before. He felt sick. Mum had seen something of his state, had acted to stop him going further.

"What did Mum say?"

"She wasn't too bad. She calls me her *naughty girl* now."

"What does that make coolie-girl Baby?"

"The good one, I guess."

He sat down and managed a tight smile. "She'd be pleased, yeah."

"Does Baby know what's going on?"

"No. She was down this week, though, and she knows I took you home, so you're around somewhere. But we'd be mad to tell her. She's not called Sky-News Shunduri for nothing."

"She'll be really pissed off then." Rohimun put on the rapid, high-pitched drawl of their Asian princess sister. "*No one* ever tells me *anything*, yaah."

He reached across his sister to choose a samosa, but once he had it in his hands, it no longer looked so good. "I can't take any more of this tonight."

"What do you mean? What happened, Bai?"

He let his head drop until it rested on his forearms, muffling his voice. "I almost lost it with Dad." They could've all been eating together now, if he'd handled it better, let Dad stretch it out, do all the posturing he wanted. If that had happened, if they had welcomed Munni back, it would have been a sign.

"Maybe it's for the best."

"What the hell do you mean by that?"

"I just mean, you've . . . we've . . . tried . . ." She looked embarrassed and uncomfortable.

He couldn't believe it. This was all wrong. Angry and resentful before, relieved now. It didn't make any sense. She should have been, should still be, crushed with anxiety about what Mum and Dad thought, what was to be done, whether she could ever be part of the family again. How could she not be when he was feeling all these things, for her as well as himself?

He stood up. "I'll get your *chunna*."

"I don't want it."

"Don't talk rubbish."

Rohimun scrambled up as well, her voice high and tight. "I don't *want* the stupid *chunna*. It's you that wants it. You're the one that keeps pushing all this, not me. I never wanted any of this."

Tariq, not trusting himself to speak, turned and strode into the shadowy garden. His whole family was fucking mad. Dad playing the Bollywood Abba, Mum maneuvering them all like fuckin' chess pieces, now Rohimun saying she didn't want to come home in the first place. After all he'd done. Not to mention that he was turning into some kind of *gundah* psychopath, wanting to beat his own father up. Why did he ever think he could just come back?

He stopped at the far edge of the lawn and gazed back. The mound of compost, backlit by the light from the house, seemed like a crouching, mourning woman. To never be allowed to return. What would that be like? To be treated by his family as if he'd already died?

Rohimun was cautiously picking her way down the garden toward him. With the house lights behind her and without her *chunna*, she looked like some *gora* girl in jeans and a shirt. When she reached him, she didn't gesture toward his feet, say *Sorry, Bai, sorry*. Her head was high, her eyes met his. He braced himself for more anger, but she took his hand without a word. They stood silently in the cool prickle of falling dew and crisp grass. He understood nothing anymore.

"What sort of Desi family are we?" Her voice was calm now. "Fucked up, I reckon, like all the Anglo-Desis."

His chest heaved in a half-laugh, half-sob. "Yeah."

So these were the new rules. No apologies for swearing in front of him, no *chunna*. No need for family ties, perhaps? He felt sick. But then she put her arms around him, and her soft plumpness, so like their mother's, leaned into his chest. He rested his chin on her head.

They stood like that for a time, until Tariq's breathing slowed and his nausea receded. Perhaps it didn't matter what his sister was, what she did, as long as she didn't abandon him, because he would fall, fail, without her. He could never do this on his own.

Eventually, quiet now, they drifted together back up the garden and sat down again on the patio's edge. And then they talked properly for the first time in years.

And it was here that Tariq learned that his sister was perhaps even more afraid of re-entering the family fold than of returning to London, friendless and free. And how she had always known that her brother's need for family, for belonging, was so much greater than her own. And for a time, at least, even the terrible secret that still lay between them—that he was not all that he appeared—seemed a little less insurmountable.

# Sixteen

WHEN DR. CHOUDHURY finally left the sitting room and walked into the cottage's hallway, there was no one to be seen. It was very quiet.

"Mrs. Begum?" he called out. "Where are your children?" He could hear her slow tread on the landing above, but there was no reply. Where were they all?

After a little while, he found himself standing irresolutely by the front door. He may as well open it: the house could do with a little freshening up. Cool air flowed in, but nothing else. Perhaps there was a full moon. Women were so prey to their natural cycles.

He teetered on the edge of the first step before retreating inside, shutting the door on nature with secret relief. Claude Levi-Strauss was a man of such insight when he divided the world between the natural and man-made forces. Like him, Dr. Choudhury was a man of civilization and culture, whereas Mrs. Begum, less developed, was all nature and impulse. Perhaps he could surprise her with a nice set of Wiltshire Staysharps in their own pine block: he had seen one on the shopping channel. And then she would relinquish that dangerous village-type *dhaa* for good.

The hallway was still dark, not an auspicious sign. After a consideration of the risky complexities of microwaves and how they had a tendency to ding in a way that could be heard all over the house, he decided to forgo the dangers of a wifeless meal for the pleasure of intellectual exercise in his study. And he was almost certain that there was a leftover *ladhu* ball, still edible in its foil, in his desk drawer.

Was that a noise? Maybe his wife was intending to come downstairs again. His stomach rumbled. Perhaps he would wait in his study until he was sure. On the way he passed the ornate hall mirror, almost full-length, and stopped to briefly examine his reflection in a manner that would be virtually imperceptible to others.

Yes, first-rate. A man of the intellect, but of compassion too, like Amitabh Bachchan in *Mohabbatein*. Or maybe *Ek Rishta*. The life of the mind was so preferable to these petty domestic matters that preoccupied the minds of women. Was that a hint of jowl? Of course not. He smoothed his hair, a distinguished white now, back from his high brow. Jowls were on Mrs. Begum's side, along with lack of height and incessant activity.

Beneath the hall mirror was a small telephone table on which Mrs. Begum had placed a stack of saris. The top one was the color of a ripe plum with a deep edging of antique gold, Mughal-style, on a black background. An excellent combination for the coloring of maturity. He slid his fingers underneath so as not to disturb the folds, and carried the stack into his study.

When they had moved to the cottage, just on three years ago, the lack of storage space in their bedroom had prompted him to suggest that Mrs. Begum's most elaborate and rarely worn saris would be best stored in the built-in cupboards of his study, and the arrangement had worked very well. They were not crammed upstairs, and he had the pleasure—the cultivated aesthetic pleasure of the well-educated man—in seeing the glow and sheen of these rich fabrics every time he opened his cupboard doors.

Viewing them, sometimes moving his hands over them in the quiet evenings, brought him a measure of comfort, of gratification impossible to explain, ridiculous to discuss. The three-dimensional roughness of the gold and silver embroidery, the slippery liquidity of modern silks and microfibers and, most precious of all, the stiff smoothness of the raw silk Benares saris, some of them three generations old (many his mother's and her mother's before her), were like a secret treasure trove all his own. Truth be told, he even found it hard to tolerate his wife's occasional forays into them on special occasions. He had arranged them by texture and color, in piles of three, with their matching petticoats, but without their fitted blouses. Those were still upstairs, in the top drawers of the tallboy.

His stomach rumbled again. He had not eaten, his wife was upstairs . . . how had this mess happened? He had prepared himself so well for the role of stern but ultimately compassionate father figure. He had been willing to give his son and daughter all the time in the world to bring him round, to soften his paternal heart with their pleading. But where was the younger generation's patience? Where was their respect? Did they not know that he was a man of many, many parts?

He had been a good father; no one could say otherwise. Dr. Choudhury thought of his own father, of all the changes after his mother's death. His father had started to lock him in the spare room after school to study until bedtime: the beginning of a relentless pressure toward the holy grail of a Rhodes scholarship to Oxford that ground on and on, through the end of primary school, secondary school and Dhaka University first-class honors degrees in History and Architecture.

How many tears had he shed there, just him and the books and the old wardrobe full of his mother's saris, forgotten since her death. He could still remember the scent of coconut oil that lingered on the material, which he always believed came from his mother's hair oil. And the tiny catches in the fabric that perhaps were from snagging on bracelets, or the necklace sets that she was never photographed without.

He had never pressured his own son like that. He had always been a first-rate modern father to all his children. Tariq had been free to choose his own path at university and his own friends. Even when Tariq joined Jamat-al-Islami and started dressing like some ignorant village elder, he had not interfered. And he had been right, right all along. Here was his boy, a grown man, broad-shouldered, no longer a fundamentalist, a number-one success *Inshallah*, with his Oxford master's and now home with his family. He was the perfect blend of East and West: comfortable in *sherwani* and dinner jacket, Bangla and English. Yes. Curry and pudding. Dr. Choudhury's stomach rumbled again. He would have the *ladhu* ball in peace and quiet, so rare in this house.

He opened the sari cupboard and carefully placed the three saris on the piles that were most complimentary to them, stood in contemplation, then moved away to lock the study door. It was, after all, his *sanctum sanctorum*.

As for his daughters, there was no escaping the fact that they were a great disappointment. Especially his eldest, so promising in her paintings, like his own mother, but with the chance to fulfil her promise that his mother had never had. And now where was Rohimun? Her picture in a magazine and now a newspaper, like some page-three slut.

Yet he would not think on such things. In fact, not the *ladhu* ball either. For now, the north of his internal compass was set once more for the sari cupboard.

And pretty little Shunduri, never should have called her that, it was asking for trouble to call a girl Beauty. Unmarriageable, both daughters, unless of course his own high-prestige reputation in the community . . . But that was the trouble, all these peasant-type matchmaking families were the same. They cared nothing for art galleries and master's degrees, just whether the girls could cook traditional-style and if Tariq had his own car.

He removed the plum sari and shook out its folds to see the embroidery on the *pallu*. This, the most elaborate end of the sari, designed to highlight the swing of fabric down the back or over the bent arm, was truly beautiful: a series of alternating black and plum squares, framed by dark gold *aari* cutwork.

Yes, this was the one he had chosen during their last trip to Leicester. Mrs. Begum must have just finished sewing the blouse. A beautiful choice, but a pity she was so short. And stout. A dramatic sari like this deserved a taller, slimmer figure. He looked up from the fabric to meet his own eyes in the cheval glass that stood in the corner. An essential piece of furniture, as he always told Mrs. Begum, for those occasions when he could not adjust his dress in the hallway mirror before leaving the house, that is, cottage. This color was perfect for him.

Keeping his eyes on the mirror, he drew the fabric up to his neckline. He was so right about the color. He started to rotate as he wrapped the fabric around his waist, his head swivelling back toward the mirror with each turn. Beautiful. He jiggled the folds of the *pallu* until it fell in one symmetrical sweep over his forearm, then stared at the cheval, *ladhu* ball forgotten.

---

MRS. SYEDA BEGUM sat in the dark watching her children from her bedroom window. She smiled and nodded to see them embrace, and resumed her own plotting for family unity, grandchildren and general advancement of the Choudhurys. The sooner her troubled son unburdened his heart to his favorite sister the better for everyone.

She reached out to the pile of old *Royalty* magazines tucked into her window recess and selected one, turning the pages reverently. Tariq still had time: Mrs. Darby had told her that Prince Charles had not married till he was thirty-two. Inside the magazine was a newspaper cutting: a double-page spread of photographs showing that good Muslim boy Dodi with poor Princess Diana before they died.

Mrs. Begum examined the photographs in the article. Laughing and smiling and enjoying themselves, like young people in love should. And why not. She was beautiful, and he was rich, and his family did not object. She would have converted, like Imran Khan's wife, and they would have lived happily ever after, with more sons, and everything she wanted from Harrods. A great pity that the Windsors were unable to accept love-matches or mixed marriages. Then again, honor killings were not unknown amongst Muslims either.

A wife for Tariq . . . She had a feeling in her stomach that she needed to look again at the ceevees of prospective brides that had been arriving since he graduated. First choice must now go to those girls who did not look too passionate: more study-types, or motherly, perhaps. Thin lips and big hips. And they could not have the parents and all the aunties living just around the corner, either. The parents, especially the mother, must be dead, invalid or distant, too distant to be always visiting and calling. She herself could give her daughter-in-law all the mothering she needed, and make sure that her attention was properly directed.

After all, that was where the Queen had gone wrong. If she had mothered that poor motherless Diana a bit more, kept her busy in the bosom of the family, then she would never have left. A strong, loving mother-in-law will always be more important to a marriage than a weak husband.

She thought back to the circumstances of her own marriage: she, a nobody, an uneducated village girl who had married up, up, into the dizzy heights of a Choudhury family in Dhaka. Their furious grudging acceptance, forced by a combination of her rounded belly and Babru Choudhury's passionate protestations. It had been the first and only time he had stood up against that dirty-bastard father of his.

Then after the marriage, no welcome, no celebration. She was hidden away in her father-in-law's house while her new husband left for UK to take up his Rhodes scholarship. But she hadn't cared. Even while she hauled her heavy body around working like a slave for that man, she had known it was only a matter of time.

And sure enough, within a few months, Babru's cousin had arrived one day while Bora Khalo, father-in-law (he had never asked her to call him Abba), was sleeping. He gave her the aeroplane ticket and one hundred British pounds. Twenty pounds plus two Benares saris from her uncle the tailor got her the Bangla passport. The remaining eighty pounds, hidden inside a cigarette packet that dropped discreetly onto a file-filled desk at the British High Commission, procured the precious spousal visa.

She had packed in secret, constructing a parcel of newspaper and string—just as she had done for her journey two years earlier, from the drowned paddies of Syhlet province to Uncle's shop in the great dusty capital of Dhaka. The parcel held all her clothes, along with a new shirt and perfume for Babru.

Mrs. Begum marvelled. She was so young then, and alone, yet she had been far more fearful of the train journey with Uncle to Dhaka at fourteen, than the prospect of flying, alone and pregnant and only sixteen, across the world in an aeroplane to a foreign country and her new husband. How much she had grown up in those two years.

Bora Khalo would never have consented to her going. Never. It was the first thing he had said to her after the *nikkah*: that Babru could only go to UK on his own, as a single man, otherwise the Rhodes would be lost, her dirty ways having almost ruined his career before it began.

She shivered and turned another page. Princes and princesses. Kings and queens. No different to anyone else: family troubles, wayward children, the difficult, bitter father-in-law. Look at Prince Charles, so lonely and awkward, just like Babru when she first met him. Long and skinny and shyer in the tailor's shop than a child on his first day of school, wordlessly handing Uncle a bundle of *sherwanis* and *kurtas* for alteration.

Standing at the other counter, shaking out a wedding sari for three anxious aunties, she had seen how his eyes were drawn to the flash and glitter of the embroidery as they fingered it. He had drifted toward her counter, coming to a standstill just behind the aunties with such an air of concentrated desire that the three women, until then arguing amongst themselves about the sari's merits, had moved as one to claim it as theirs.

She had pulled down a selection of the brighter saris from the high shelves behind her, putting them on the far edge of her counter for him to inspect. Then she was back in the whirlwind of bargaining with three determined aunties, and when she next looked up, he was gone.

But a week later he was there again, with his long fingers leaving damp marks on a shiny leather wallet. More saris were shaken out and stroked, and one was bought, for the first price Uncle named. Forced to reply to the tailor's cheery questions about the wellness of "your honored father, the judge," he dropped his parcel twice as he was bowed out of the shop.

Three months and ten saris he had taken before he was able to look her in the eye with his *salaamalaikums* and stumbling enquiries about her health. He would spend whole half-hours wandering around the shelves, or standing still in a corner like a dressmaker's mannequin, watching her. Her uncle would smile and roll his eyes when he spotted Babru gazing into the shop window, but rebuked Syeda when once she made fun of him.

"He has no one, that boy. His mother is dead a long time now, and his father has quarrelled with everyone, thinks they all want his money." Uncle tapped the back of her hand gravely.

"He and that boy are poorer than any of us."

She still ached for her own parents, killed by the typhoid that had come in with the monsoonal floods in the last wet season before Uncle had come to take her away. When the shop was quiet, she began to make a second cup of chai, so that Babru could sit with her uncle out the front. His gratitude for such a small thing both irritated and moved her. He desired so much, yet expected so little.

Then had come the crashing arrival of the monsoon rains, a full three weeks early. Uncle was at mosque, and the street flooded with rubbish. She closed the shop, barricading the entrance with rags stuffed under the door, before leading Babru upstairs into the sewing room to wait out the downpour.

The tin roof's drumming reverberations made it impossible to talk, so she waved him to sit while she made some chai. The room, as large as her own so-pretty wallpapered bedroom now, seemed small, being filled with hundreds of rolls and bolts of fabric for blouses, leggings and pants to coordinate with the multitude of saris, *salwars* and *sherwanis* downstairs. The little sewing machine was tucked into a corner, and the floor was covered in scraps of fabric too small to save, which she would periodically sweep up into a bag and sell as stuffing to an upholsterer in the next street. Her bedding roll was spread out in the opposite corner.

She remembered it all as if it had been yesterday.

Holding the chai, she had turned to find that he had sat himself down on her bed. Her bed. The little cup dropped from her hand. He stood at her expression, his arms reaching out, then she was against his chest and he held her. He dipped his head down past hers and rested his cheek against her neck. "Coconut oil," he murmured into her ear, too close now to be drowned out by the thunderous rain. "You smell so beautiful."

---

MRS. BEGUM CLOSED the magazine, trying to recall if she had anything sweet downstairs. The sherbet milk. Why not. After all these years, never having had her proper bride's welcome, she was entitled to it. When her children married, she would make sure that everything was done the proper way.

She walked quietly downstairs. The study door was closed, and light shone from under the door. Dr. Choudhury would be there for hours. She hoped that hunger was cramping his fat stomach. She took the jug of sherbet out of the fridge, poured some into a small cut-glass vase that Mrs. Darby had given her in exchange for the secret to number-one butter chicken, and carried it upstairs. She would have her bridal drink with the Windsors.

When she returned to the windowseat, her children could no longer be seen, and the samosa basket was empty. Well and good. Her fool of a husband needed time to reflect on his errors, and she needed to plan. Like all great strategists, she knew that victory would only be hers if she could keep one step ahead.

She raised her sherbet drink and spoke softly to her reflection in the darkened glass. "For you, daughter Syeda, beautiful bride who blesses our house."

## Seventeen

A SLEEP-IN ON that sofa bed had probably been a little optimistic, Richard reflected, taking the chair at the head of the breakfast table, shaking the Sunday paper straight, and wishing he could do the same with his back. A bleary-eyed Henry came in, resplendent in a pale blue dressing-gown that looked as if it belonged to Thea.

"Marvellous restaurant, Richard. Don't know how you hear about all these fantastic local places in London. Thee's sleeping in, but only because I made the ultimate sacrifice and got up to hear the boys' gory details of sinister shadows and strange eerie sounds. They've gone up to the stables to make a ghost trap, bloodthirsty little buggers. I take it you didn't see anything out of the ordinary?"

"That's right. And also no signs of any break-in, I'm glad to report."

Henry stopped, coffeepot in hand. "Good Lord. Hadn't even thought of that, so caught up in the, ah, historical aspect. Perhaps I'll have a word with our Dr. Choudhury and the builders about keeping a bit of a lookout. Awful Audrey hasn't started proper cleaning duties in the Abbey yet."

"Must say that dressing-gown's pretty fetching. Goes with your eyes."

Henry stretched out a sleeve and scrutinized it critically. "Suits me, does it? They're from the in-laws, a sort of cashmerey thing. I'll let Thea keep the red one. Much more her sort of color."

Richard raised his eyebrows but decided to forbear. Thea would hear and would not see the funny side. He put out his hand for the coffeepot. "I thought I saw Dr. Choudhury in the Park this morning, near the Abbey. I thought his role was over by now?"

"Well, actually, Dr. Choudhury's more likely than the builders to be around on the weekends: he's told me he's still got a few bits and pieces to finish off upstairs. His easel's up there, I believe." Henry waved the coffeepot around to emphasize his point, just out of reach. "So we often see him pottering around the Abbey when it suits him. Did you know, when he writes his papers on Bourne Abbey, he's going to give me a shared byline as well."

Richard grabbed the coffeepot from Henry and went over to the cups on the sideboard. "Not so surprising, really. You have turned yourself into a bit of an expert on the Abbey: wainscoting, priest's holes, that sort of thing." He turned just in time to see Henry squeeze past and slip himself into the vacated chair, ducking to avoid an anticipated but non-existent block.

Henry pulled the sports section out of the paper, messily refolded the rest, leaned back, and stretched his legs out luxuriously. "Well, then, Richard, perhaps you getting us stuck in one as children wasn't entirely wasted."

Richard snorted and kept pouring his coffee. "You're such a romantic, pretty-boy. I'd always thought that was more of a linen cupboard myself. Whoever heard of shelves in a priest's hidey-hole?"

Henry half rose, then remembered that ownership was nine-tenths possession and sat down again. "The shelves were a later addition, as you damn well should know if you'd read my last letter to the Trust!"

———

LEFT TO HIMSELF in the sitting room that afternoon, Richard found he was not quite as sanguine as he had led his brother to believe. His Saturday evening torchlight tour of the Abbey with the children had elicited the expected shrieks and giggles and, as anticipated, nothing of substance.

Yet, when touring the upper levels, one of the rooms, the green room, had had a different atmosphere. Over and above the smell of fresh paint and linseed oil from the sheeted painting equipment stored there, was something less tangible but, to him, distinct. He had felt a prickling awareness of a presence, a feminine one. And there'd been a single hair, dark and wavy and very long, lying across one of the windowsills. This was a room inhabited by a woman. And not a hundred years ago, either.

To mention it to Henry or Thea would merely add fuel to the fire without being helpful, and anyway, Richard felt more than a little silly coming up with something so airy-fairy. A smell. A hair. Then this morning a glimpse through the bathroom window: Dr. Choudhury hurrying to the Abbey, carrying something. Had he looked furtive, or was that just Richard's own, overactive imagination? He wanted to dismiss it, turn it into a joke about his susceptibility to Henry's imaginings. Yet when the opportunity had come up today, with all the references to the subject, he had not. And his conviction that there was something would not go away.

A little discreet questioning had established that Thea had had no involvement with the upstairs work and, besides, her hair had never been that long. And from Audrey Upwey's purplish perm, it was certainly not. The building crew downstairs were all men. A long-haired tradesman? It was a woman's hair, a woman's smell, he was sure of it. Ridiculous.

He only had this evening, before an early start tomorrow morning to get back to London and his Chambers. Perhaps he should revisit the green room to test his first impressions.

Richard moved irritably out of Thea's too-soft armchair. Everywhere he looked, photographs: the parents, Thea's multitude of Greek relatives, lots of the boys of course, and a few of Henry and Thea's various friends. Some of those faces he recognized from university years ago. Typical of Henry to have made the necessary effort to keep in touch, though Thea probably did her fair share in that regard as well.

From the window, he could just see Bourne Abbey on the upper slope of the hillside to his left. Henry had always been the one dazzled by the romance of the place, and from an early age had been determined, like their father, to dedicate himself to Bourne Abbey's resto-ration and a proper understanding of its history.

A proper understanding. On second thought, maybe some of the romance was flowing in his veins as well. He would head out later for a look around and be back in time for Thea's drinks do tonight. No one would be the wiser.

---

ROHIMUN SWORE AS half a tube's worth of cadmium yellow plopped onto her breast. She unzipped her tracksuit top, folding it in on the oily blob and using the top's fleecy lining to scrub the floor in case any paint had made it that far. The metal tube must have split along the seam. She would have to paint in one of Mum's old *salwarkameezes*: more comfortable anyway, since she had gotten so fat.

She grabbed the first one that came out of the kitbag and pulled it over her head, enjoying the susurration of the microfiber as it slid down her body. It was a dark cobalt blue, only relegated to the too-old pile by the turmeric stains on the cuffs and front. She took off her tracksuit pants as well and slipped on the soft *salwar* pants, tying them loosely at the waist.

Back at her easel the rose floated before her, taking up the entire top left-hand quarter of the canvas, luminous against the dark greens and lamp blacks of the yew hedge that she had started to block in. She was not painting this *alla prima*, *impasto*, like her Freud- and Bacon-inspired commission portraits, all speed and dash and texture. It was time for a different method, and for once, she was going to take as long as she wanted.

Discarding the palette knife in favor of soft brushes, she had taken days to build up layer after layer of pure unmixed colors, heavily diluted and the most transparent she could make them, to form a glaze that mimicked the translucent depths of the colors within the rose. That part of the canvas was virtually complete; the rest was primed and lightly blocked-in with sepia. Breaking the rules, but it had been too difficult to think about the figure on the canvas until now.

She turned to the cheval, using her forearm to push hair back from her face and squinting at the shapes that her figure formed. She really needed an SLR to take a few shots to help her out, for when the light was different or she was focusing on detail. And it was going to be tricky working on her own profile. If only there was a second cheval, or even a hand mirror . . . Perhaps Tariq could pick one up cheap in a local pawnshop. In the meantime, she needed a general idea of the shapes and proportions her body would create.

She rotated slowly before the looking glass, letting her eyes come back into focus. It had been so long since she had really looked at herself. For once, the dark bulk of hair didn't swamp the rest of her. She smoothed her hands up over rounded hips, inwards over the indentation of her waist and out over full breasts. The *salwar* fell as it should: the curves suggested but not outlined.

She'd felt fat before, wearing the tight jeans and sheaths Simon liked, then trying to squeeze into old school clothes when she first came here, but now she wasn't so sure. She looked . . . grown up. Not some skinny student anymore. And not a Bounty bar either. The *salwar* looked alright.

And her hair . . . She thought of what Munch had done with hair, how it would swirl around his paintings like a live thing, creeping into cloud formations, flowing water, transforming into spermatozoa and embryos. Hair was power, life, wild nature. She stared at the canvas, dipped her finger into the sepia mess on her palette and started to change the faintly outlined figure into something larger, bolder and fuller. And then the suggestion of a mass of hair flying upward against the hedge, to balance the rose, high in the opposite corner.

———

RICHARD STOOD IN the middle of Bourne Abbey's library. There were no books to be seen, having been packed away with all the moveable furniture. The massive outline of the stone fireplace, still under its protective coating of bubble wrap, was about the only thing he recognized. That and the dusty, thirty-foot-high mullioned windows that formed the room's southern wall. Light streamed through them in angled shafts that turned the drop sheets the same creamy gold as the walls, and gave mystery to the barren bookcases.

When he was little, family Christmases were held in here, with the pine tree's smell competing against his mother's cigarettes and the aroma of Bristol cream sherry that clung to her clothes and skin. He and Henry would compete to bring a smile to their parents' faces, try to stretch out the anticipation and the unwrapping, the brief moments of cuddles and jokes, and to delay sitting down to the family lunch and the inevitable bickering or worse.

Mother was long gone, some twenty years ago, and Father, nine years now. His father had spent his life struggling to make-and-mend, with mortgages on mortgages to line the roof, repair the plumbing, hold back the ever-present damp rot. While his wife and his marriage were falling apart in front of him. Maybe he'd thought that fixing one would fix the other. Or perhaps he had just decided to concentrate on the things that could be mended.

How many Christmases had there really been in this room, so long ago? Shortly after Mother died, chunks of masonry started crashing down from the front parapets, and they had moved to the Lodge. By then Richard was consumed with hatred for the monstrous building that just seemed to carry on what his mother's drinking had started: a perpetual problem with no solution, a cancer in their finances, a hole in his father's heart.

Oxford had been a fading hope until Richard had scraped into a scholarship for the fees, and a part-time-rounds clerk position in a local solicitor's offices had been enough for the rest. Anything to escape his decomposing family. Henry was bloody lucky to have ridden in on his coat-tails three years later, just when Father was ready to give up and sell out to developers and was finally willing to listen to Richard, freshly acquainted with the law of trusts and his idea of breaking the deed and ceding the Abbey to Henry. The back-breaking loan Richard had taken out, on the strength of certain objects now on perpetual loan to the Victoria & Albert and the Bodleian, to cover

Henry's university fees, buy out Father and get both of them free of the Abbey, had been a small price to pay.

And now the monster was tamed: shiny new in places, not a hint of mustiness, woodworm conquered and parapets safe again. For a few years anyway.

Perhaps Thea was the best person for the place. Her family were loaded enough to withstand the money-sink that the Abbey would always be. And she had no history with this house and was thus free of the gigantic burden of ancestral obligation that had distorted his parents' marriage and eventually destroyed them both. Nouveau riche gave her a protective coating of utilitarianism that had always been lacking in the Bournes.

How calm and quiet it was, in this late-afternoon light. He had seen Thea's decorating plans for this room: cream and gold with touches of mid-blue. He'd withstood her hints about returning the blue and gold Persian in his Chambers, but had been relieved at the projected color scheme, despite his pose of unconcern. It bore no relation to the dark red flock and black japanned side tables that he remembered from his childhood. And the bookshelves, cleaned of centuries of smoke stains much to the horror of the National Trust, were now closer to the honey shade of new oak than the blackish brown that he remembered. He smiled—he was fairly sure that Thea had hidden that particular series of indignant Trust letters from Henry, who was always such a slave to authenticity.

Richard strode out to the great hall. He and the boys had taken the main stairs last night, clomping up with flashing torches, plenty of ghost sounds and shrieks of anticipatory fear. This time he would take the servants' stairs and walk up quietly on green baize. He pushed open the swing door and paused to let his eyes adjust to the semi-dark. There was that smell again. No, it was a different one. Damned if it wasn't curry: the builders must have gotten in takeaway.

---

THE DEEP BLUE of the *salwar* Rohimun was wearing would do nicely against the equally deep green of the hedge. Harmonious colors. It would also ensure that the golden rose was the true center of the painting. Light shining out of darkness. Pagan nature worship. The hand of God in all things. Whatever. That stuff was for the dealers and, God forbid, the critics. What really mattered was the physical response, which bypassed the brain and went straight to the gut and the heart and the hairs on the skin. Like music. Critical analysis was just an attempt to understand those reactions. Or rationalize them.

Rohimun squinted again. For the *salwarkameez*, the darkest darks would be Egyptian violet and lamp black. Later, she would use the lighter darks: Prussian blue, with ultramarine and indigo, for the blocked-in highlights. The dusted gold of turmeric on cuffs and front she would paint as half-embroidery, half-reflection of the rose itself: alizarin orange-gold with Indian yellow, cobalt yellow, a touch of that almost edible Naples yellow, perhaps the odd flash of Courbet green. But no layering for a glaze effect here: using the very tips of her finest brushes, each color would be scattered individually onto the *salwar*'s blues, as if the rose's tints had fractured, pixilated, into their components. A sort of prismed reflection of the flower. But the glow of the rose itself eclipsing that effect. She sighed with pleasure and set to work.

---

RICHARD WALKED SLOWLY up the stairs, keeping his hand on the balustrade so as not to lose his footing. With the entry door shut, the darkness in this windowless space was almost total, and he was annoyed at himself for having forgotten this. As children, he and Henry had played in this network of narrow stairs and corridors that fed all the great rooms of the house and which were like a separate world, a cramped and distorted copy of the great staircases and spacious halls used by its official denizens. The great and the good. Who had said that? And who had ever believed it?

He remembered daring Henry to ride with him down these stairs on a sheet of cardboard. They had managed the same feat on the main stairs until caught and banned by Audrey, but to do it on the servants' stairs, with their much steeper gradient and smaller landings, looked

206 · Lesley Jørgensen

like suicide now. Plucky of Henry really, being that much younger and determined to follow where Richard led. A broken collarbone had been the result, along with Audrey's told-you-sos in the ambulance all the way to casualty because Father couldn't leave Mother.

Reaching the upper floor, Richard started to feel about for the door that would take him into the hallway near the green bedroom. It was quiet and close on the little landing, and an image came to him, unbidden, of the scullery maids, often no more than children, who would have had to feel their way as he was doing, probably carrying hot water or linen at the same time.

Why was he here again? What possible result was realistically to be expected? He would surprise some traveller or tramp camping for a day or two, then have to deal with the inevitable unpleasantness before the local magistrate, which Henry would expect him to handle as a matter of course. And what if it really was a woman: an addict or some broken homeless creature? What then?

---

Rohimun looked at the sky outside her window, gave a cursory rinse to her fingers in the turps jar, and moved to the door. This was exactly the image she wanted: a summer sunset partially overcast by piled-up clouds, with shafts of light coming through at a sharp angle. She must see what it did to the colors in the *salwar* first-hand, see how it looked against the yew. This light would only last half an hour.

She ran out the bedroom door, crossed the hall, grabbed hold of the handle to the servants' stairs, then hesitated. No time to waste stumbling down the back way in the dark: she would take a chance on a Sunday and head down the main stairs and out the back. She set off, running barefoot.

---

The door handle had moved, trembled in Richard's grasp like a live thing, and he gripped it harder, tensed for confrontation, all indecision gone. But when he turned the handle and pulled the door inwards, there was no one there. He stopped in the hallway, puzzled, feeling that it was he who was the intruder. No more delays. He strode to the green room and opened the door.

---

ROHIMUN RAN TOWARD the walled garden, relishing the grass under her feet and the freshening air. In the *salwar* instead of the constricting tracksuit, she felt like she was flying. It might rain tonight, and now that she was sleeping in the great bed, she would enjoy the sounds of a summer storm. The bad dreams had ceased since she had abandoned the camp bed.

On the eastern side of the garden, some remains of the original stonework still lay below the hedge, no more than waist high. The yew must have encroached, then been shaped to form a replacement wall. She stood against it and looked at her arms and torso. As she had hoped, the blue and the green were more intense together. Truly harmonious. And the difference in textures was also heightened: the sheen of the fabric's draped fall was almost liquid against the yew's dense confusion of miniature spikes. She closed her eyes and leaned back against the hedge's luxuriant growth.

---

RICHARD STOPPED IN a patch of sunlight on the floorboards, dazzled after the dark stairwell. He'd forgotten how much light this room caught, with its clerestory windows as well as the windows at the western end. When he could see again, he approached the jumble of furniture by the window, feeling more of an intruder with every step. Then he saw the rose.

It glowed from the canvas: golden, gigantic, three-dimensional, hovering above the figure like a tent of light. And the woman reaching for it, almost touching it, her breasts straining against fabric, her arms rounded in yearning, reminded him of someone. Who was she, and why was Dr. Choudhury painting her?

---

THE LIGHT BREEZE that had met Rohimun at the back door had strengthened, and with it came a few spots of rain, then a ripple of thunder. A sharp gust of wind blew roses apart in front of her eyes, the petals rising and catching on her hair and clothes. As she left the secret garden, a sudden eddy of wind lifted her hair in a mass and swirled it around her face, blinding her. She clawed at it as she walked toward the house, anxious to get back to the painting. The wind was behind her, blowing her hair forward, and she could see the open back door as though through a dark and twisting tunnel. Fleetingly she wished that the front entrance was closer so that she could run straight into the main hall, but thunder clapped again, the rain began in earnest and she skipped into a sprint for the doorway ahead.

---

A GUST OF rain lashed windowpanes, and Richard moved back from the painting and looked around him. He'd heard that Dr. Choudhury had some artistic leanings, but hadn't realized their extent. How must it have been, the professor standing in this room, the long-haired model posing before him? Were they lovers? The thought was loathsome. Wasn't he Muslim? And married? No wonder the secrecy, the smell of curry.

Lightning flickered, and he went to the great bed and fingered the velvet cover. Was this the green of the backdrop in the painting? He could not decide, and walked back to the windows. Dr. Choudhury would not be coming tonight: probably having a cosy dinner up at the cottage with his wife. Fucking hypocrite.

He'd thought that this visit would clarify things. In the dwindling light, he swivelled the easel toward him, then sat down on the edge of the bed to look at it, feeling old and tired. Prim and pompous Dr. Choudhury, with a double life. He lay back, turning his head so he could still see the woman and the rose. He would wait here until the storm had passed, then think about what to do.

---

ROHIMUN FOUGHT THE back door closed against the wind. The weather had changed her mood, sobered her, and she tried to ignore a small resurgence of old fears. Her hair was dripping down her back in rats' tails, and her feet were wet and covered in grass cuttings. She detoured to the builders' quarters: a temporary toilet and tearoom set up in the scullery, and found some clean drop cloths to dry herself and take some of the moisture out of her hair. In the fridge was a pint of milk, so she put the kettle on and raided the builders' biscuit supply while she waited for the water to boil. She felt like a worker again, entitled to the tea and digestives.

---

THERE WAS NO such thing as lying on the edge of this bed. Richard slid and kept sliding until he was fair in the middle. The hollow in which he came to rest curved his shoulders inwards and pressed his upper arms to his sides, so he laced his fingers together over his stomach and closed his eyes. Last time he believed that Posturepedic rubbish: this was the best mattress he'd ever lain on.

---

ROHIMUN RINSED OUT her tea cup and replaced it on the draining board. The rain had set in, and through the scullery window, her peaceful golden sky had turned vermilion and cadmium red and French ultramarine and cobalt violet, in rough and hectic streaks.

She set off up the main stairs and along the upper hall until she came to her room. The door was wide open; she was sure she'd shut it. Tariq had already come and gone, so it wasn't him. She edged cautiously in, looking for the easel. Still there, thank god. A snore came from the great bed, and she froze. Simon was here. He had come for her, had invaded her sanctuary, touched her painting. And now he was asleep on her bed. Well, he could just fuck off. She wasn't scared of him anymore.

She snatched up the palette knife, shiny from disuse, and walked softly to the edge of the bed, her heart pounding. This time, she would have the upper hand, and he would be the one running away.

But when she got a bit closer to the figure shadowed by the bed curtains, it wasn't Simon at all. She exhaled, trying not to make a sound. This man was tall, well over six foot, and thinner. His hair was dark, and stubble shadowed his jaw. She stood still and tried to think, thumbing her blade. Not a tramp. Some kind of burglar? Well, whoever he was, he could still just fuck off. This was her room.

She crept nearer, until she was next to the bed, carefully climbed onto the mattress and, on her knees, inched toward the figure, then paused. She looked at the length of his body, the symmetry of his stance, his clasped hands and the upward-pointing toes of large feet in some truly naff white trainers. She crept closer, leaned over his face. It was his position: just like the effigies on those crusader tombs in the old churches. All he needed was a sword to hold. Well, she had the sword.

# Eighteen

RICHARD WOKE TO find some creature leaning over his face. He tried to rise, but the bed defeated him and a hand reached out and pushed on his chest. He grabbed the hand to move it away and a mass of hair swung over his face in a wet clinging tangle of black. Jesus Christ, like some kind of gypsy succubus.

The bed sabotaged him again, sinking him further as she tilted forward, defeating his efforts to rise one-handed. Some shiny object in her other hand flashed. Without thinking, he grabbed that wrist as well and with a muffled "Shit!" she fell onto his stomach.

He had a firm hold on her but was unable to rise from the hollow in the mattress and she, smaller than he had first thought, and with both wrists held, was clearly in the same predicament. He lifted the wrist with the weapon and saw its blunt, rounded end. Not a knife at all, just some kind of spatula.

No. A palette knife. Her hair: was this the woman in the painting? What the hell was going on?

She must have sensed a slackening in his hold because she wrenched her arms hard, and he almost lost his grip. He pulled her right arm out over the side of the bed and twisted her wrist until he heard the implement hitting the floorboards.

"You can just *fuck off*!" she hissed.

Young enough to be Choudhury's daughter. Sick bastard. They were still stuck in the same ridiculous position, but without the threat of the improvised weapon, he managed to transfer both her wrists into one spread of fingers and used his free hand to push both of them into a sitting position.

He could hear the harsh sound of her breathing, and saw the roll of eye-whites through her hair. Masses of black hair curling and twisting all over the place—and were those yellow petals caught up in it? He looked to the painting, as if he expected to see torn canvas, bleeding paint, where she had stepped out of it. What was she doing here on her own? What sway did that old man have over her?

"Where's Choudhury?" He'd almost shouted the question, the first he could put into words. Her wrists jerked in his grip.

"I don't know what you're talking about."

To think of that old man doing his morning visits. Using the Abbey. Abusing Henry's trust in him.

She twisted sideways and started to slide her feet toward the edge of the bed but stopped short, her head awkwardly angled. At the same time he felt a tug on his shirt: a length of hair was caught on the topmost button.

"Wait," he said. "We're caught up."

Now she looked familiar. Had he seen her before?

"Not *my* fault," she snapped, but after a moment she grabbed the offending tress and pulled impatiently on it.

"That's hardly going to help. Let me try." He slid his hands under hers and felt for the point of connection between his shirt button and the lock of her hair. "It's quite a tangle." Surely he could've done better than that. He sounded like Colonel Blimp. Changing tack, he said, "What are you doing here?"

"What are *you* doing here?" She averted her head despite the fighting words, and her hands reached out over his fingers and pulled fiercely on the edge of his collar.

"No point in doing that."

She tugged again. "I don't have *time* for this."

As if it were his fault. Her hair seemed to have twisted right around the button's axis. They both shuffled closer as they worked on the tangle. He hoped she didn't have any other makeshift weapons on her person. A staple gun, or a jar of turps. A really sharp pencil.

"Look, it doesn't matter, yeah, just rip it. It's only hair. I . . . *you* have to go."

Was she expecting someone? Choudhury?

"There must be a way," he said, bracing against her pulling as he tried to puzzle it out. What right did she have to tell him to get out. Expecting him to apologize. *More front than Harrods*, as Audrey would say.

Her hands suddenly tugged at his, and he felt his shirt jump forward. Something fell to the floorboards, and she laughed abruptly, revealing twin dimples in her cheeks. They both bent down to pick up the shirt button, just avoiding cracking heads. In doing so, her hair, freed now, swung against his shoulder, its massy weight as different as it was possible to be from the light brush of a tossed bob.

As he put the button into his shirt pocket, she moved to the painting, touching it in several places with her fingertips as if to reassure herself, then folded her arms and glared at the mantelpiece to his right, as if waiting for him to leave. Some nerve. In profile, her lashes curled extravagantly, below a dark brow as thick as his finger.

"What are you doing here? Are you meeting Choudhury later tonight?"

She swung to face him, her mouth open for a moment as if searching for a riposte. "What do you care? Are you here with some fucking paper? Why am I so interesting anyway?"

As she spoke, Richard stared at her face. Jesus. Was she the girl from the V&A? "Who are you? And why are you here?"

"What's it to you?"

The question struck home. Who was he to judge how she had

arrived at this point in her life? He opened his mouth to rephrase, renew his questioning, but she turned away and swore again, her voice quavering now. Trying to get to the bottom of things at this stage seemed pointless: she was only getting more upset. He noticed the palette knife and kicked it under the bed for safety. It hit something with a metallic ring.

He pulled up the valance and saw a camp bed and a duffel bag. When he turned back to question her, she was fingering a jumble of brushes and paint tubes on a box, as if checking that they were all there. Facing away from him, her hair fell past her hips. He'd thought that the wild mass of hair in the painting was an exaggeration, artistic licence, but not now. Was this how Choudhury saw her hair, spread out in the wind against greenery? Or tangled across a green velvet bedspread? His stomach knotted.

He went over to her. "Look, you can't stay here, you know." She ignored him and walked to the window.

He tried again. "If you need somewhere to stay, there are shelters. I could make some enquiries." He felt like a complete bastard. Compared to him Choudhury must be looking pretty good right now. "Or perhaps a youth hostel. Until you can sort something out. But you can't stay here. You must know that."

She crossed her arms. Her feet were bare and grass-stained, and her fingernails were rimmed with black. How rough had she been living since she'd left the V&A?

"Is there someone I could call for you?" Don't say Choudhury.

"What paper is it then? Which one?" Her tone was calmer but still edgy, hostile. "What's your name?"

"Richard Bourne."

"Bourne." She was rattled now, clearly caught by surprise, recrossing her arms, hugging her elbows.

"This is my family home." He surprised himself, had not volunteered that information for years, and felt an odd kind of pride in saying those words.

"So, you live here," she said, in a couldn't-care-less tone. "I mean, you're moving back in when it's finished." She glanced at his trainers with contempt, and his feet twitched uneasily, despite himself.

"I live in London. My brother and his family, they're in the Lodge. They'll be living here."

The rain was still falling. He couldn't leave without some kind of agreement or understanding with her.

"What's your problem with papers?"

Perhaps there was a warrant out for her as an illegal alien. A forced marriage in the offing? Or a violent husband? That Asian man in the dinner suit? No ring. But that didn't mean anything. Didn't they wear crimson on their hairline, if they were married? Perhaps he could do something, if there were legal problems. The silence stretched on, and the room grew colder and darker. A change of subject perhaps.

"Is the painting of you?"

She looked at him oddly. "It's a rose."

"No, the figure beside it."

"Oh. Sort of." Her voice was flat and dismissive.

The silence returned, and he found himself casting around for something to say, as if he were at a cocktail party and she a difficult date. His watch alarm sounded tinnily. Shit. Thea must have set his watch alarm for her faux-casual pre-dinner drinks, and there were guests tonight, he'd completely forgotten. He couldn't tell them about this unwanted visitor when there was company: far too disruptive.

"Look, do you need to stay here for now?"

She appeared to hesitate, then nodded.

"Are you safe here? No one's bothering you or . . ."

She stared at him pointedly, but eventually shook her head.

"Alright. I have to be in London tomorrow but I'll be back at the end of the week to work out what's to be done. You can stay till then." She continued to stare, her expression disdainful, and he quashed a strange urge to apologize.

"Okay," she said, turning back toward the windows as if those black rectangles held more interest.

He left the room, stood in the darkened hallway, trying to collect his thoughts. What the hell was all that about? He remembered Thea's dinner party again. Maybe he'd just stay for drinks, skip the dinner and leave for London tonight, pleading pressure of work. No. Thea would have a fit and that would make coming back next weekend tricky. Thirty-five years old and still on Thea's social fucking leash.

## Nineteen

THEA SURVEYED THE Lodge's front drawing room. Everything was ready: fruit juice for the Choudhurys, martinis for the others, and Andrew and Jonathon in their room upstairs with a Disney classic on the DVD player. She was pleased that she'd managed the double feat of fulfilling their obligations to the Choudhurys and of not scaring Richard off to London early. Perhaps because she had been careful not to tell him too much too soon. Even he wouldn't dare to change his plans this late.

She drifted closer to the fire and tweaked into artful disarray the pile of *Paris Vogue*, *Wallpaper\** and *Architectural Digest*. Richard's allergy to social obligations was second nature to her by now, as were the endless cigarette breaks outside that he would resort to if trapped with company not to his liking, or if things went on too long.

Choudhury was always an attentive guest, even though his wife tried to reverse-engineer the recipes and was prone to suddenly developing passions for strange items like the pen-holding coronation mug by the telephone. Perhaps she was a collector. No, Thea couldn't see it. The son was coming tonight as well: an art curator from Johannesburg. He and Henry could discuss the Abbey collection, and Richard had an eye for paintings. Richard shouldn't be too burdened, not being the official host, and Henry, with the Abbey to talk about with Dr. Choudhury, would be in his element.

She drifted over to the gate-leg table where the Abbey decorator's latest proposals had been left as a talking point, but also because, although she would never admit it, Richard's interest and approval still counted. What little difference Richard's breaking of the family Trust all those years ago had made to this family. Henry had been the heir for longer than she'd known either of them, but he still deferred to Richard, and even the National Trust people wrote to him first. She tapped the papers with one perfectly polished scarlet nail. Once they were installed in the Abbey, everything would be different. She glanced at her watch: a favorite Tiffany in honor of the occasion. Seven-forty-five. The men should be down any minute now.

Perhaps she would sit Richard with Mrs. Begum, and if she became too much he could give her one of his put-downs. And tonight could act as thanks for all Mrs. Choudhury's babysitting. Andrew and Jonathon loved everything about her: her food, her rabbits and her garden. It was too easy sometimes, having her just across the way, and always happy to take them.

The gender balance was wrong—too many men—but county was difficult to combine with the Choudhurys and impossible to inflict upon Richard. Henry, on the other hand, usually seemed to find the Choudhurys quite amusing. She smiled at the thought of Richard's face and of the knowing looks he would give her once Dr. Choudhury got going.

The scullery door banged, and Thea scooped up Richard's martini to present to him, a quip about Dutch courage ready on her lips. But instead there were his footsteps on the stairs and a shout to Henry to hurry up in the shower. A pity: she'd been looking forward to a bit of their old acerbic pre-party banter, perhaps one of his perceptive comments on how she was looking, while Henry faffed about upstairs with his tie. Eight o'clock. Her watch gave a silvery chime, and she replaced the cocktail and started to light the reflectors on the mantelpiece. Such a flattering light, and somehow festive as well: perfect for one of their last cosy little evenings before the transition to the Abbey.

She turned her back on the mirror and took in the rest of the room. She had done her best with the Lodge but cute and cottagey it remained. She couldn't wait until people were visiting, seeing her, in the Abbey itself. Much more her style. Perhaps they could have a late-summer ball to celebrate the completion of restoration. Perhaps *Country Life* could send someone. Or even *Tatler*. How wonderful that would be. She sighed, feeling the soft roll of double-stranded pearls over her collarbones as she did so. No gold tonight: Mrs. Choudhury always had enough on for both of them, and she wasn't going to compete.

The doorbell rang, and Thea moved to the stairs to call Henry but was met by Richard, running down the stairs while adjusting his tie, his hair still wet. She stepped in front of him, holding out the martini glass, but he ignored it. His expression was alert, even predatory, but entirely focused on what was to come. Not on her. *This is how he looks when he's about to go into court*, part of her thought, while another part felt as if she'd been slapped. She searched his face and found an absence of their shared history in his eyes.

"It's the Choudhurys, isn't it?" There was a grim undertone to his voice, as if his worst fears about tonight had just been realized.

"Yes." Damned if she was going to justify her choice of guests to him. "Richard, darling, the door. *Could* you?"

There was no reply, but he strode down the hall, and she suddenly felt unaccountably weary, as if she'd just come home from standing at some all-day dressy event, like a polo match, or a society funeral. She turned away from the sight of Richard's back and entered the drawing room. Even though it was only the Choudhurys, she couldn't face them just then. She needed a moment.

Everything was in order, impressive to those in the know, but welcoming too. No one could say that she was a bad hostess, whoever the guests were. She stopped next to the Le Corbusier mirrored tray, one of her treasures, now holding the juices and cocktails. When she looked down onto its surface, her pearls, refracted through the various liquids, appeared impossibly lustrous and twice their size. Wasn't it Cleopatra who dropped pearls into her drink, to impress that successful young general Antony with her wealth, and her nerve? It worked too, for a while.

She leaned forward to see more clearly, the drinks sparkling and winking, lit from above and below. The vinegary scent of gin and dry vermouth was bracing, and on impulse she picked up one of the martinis, plucked out the olive and swallowed it whole. Imagine doing that with a pearl. For once she would break her rule of drinking last and least. Stuff the guests. She lifted the glass to her lips and sculled the lot. Hell, she hadn't done that since Oxford.

───────────

Mrs. Begum, slightly out of breath, was at the Lodge front door in her second-best non-wedding sari and minimal jewelry: only her usual gold bracelets that never came off, four extra colored glass ones on each wrist that Dr. Choudhury had forced on her at the last minute because they matched the sari, and her smallest gold set, earrings no bigger than her thumbnail and one little necklace almost entirely hidden by her blouse. They had headed off from Windsor Cottage the second the rain had stopped.

All the way, Tariq, stupid boy, was fiddling with his phone and wandering all over the place like a goat looking for the greenest grass, so she'd had to dodge around him, while her scuttling cockroach of a husband was trying to tell her that she was disrespecting these so-great-and-mighty Bournes by dressing as if she was off to the shops, showing him up as a lower-class man, a man who could not afford to buy his wife enough gold, or good saris. What number-one fools, both of them.

She had been to enough Oxford parties to know that the bigger the gold sets she wore, the more fancy-fancy her saris, the less people would expect her to speak English. But if her sari was plain, and she wore her sewing glasses and a friendly smile, talk-talking about weather or motorways or gardening was all that was needed. Sometimes they even asked her what college she was from.

When they were close to the Lodge's front gate, she'd picked up her sari pleats and put on a last burst of speed to beat Dr. Choudhury there: a maneuver that turned out to be unnecessary as at the same time her husband stopped completely. He seemed to have been distracted by the sight of wet grass cuttings sticking to his shoes and was lifting first one foot then the other into the air and waggling it, then tapping his soles on the gravel, muttering something about the virtues of pavements.

She'd slipped through the gate Tariq had just opened, bustled up the broad path, now clearly leading, and leaned on the doorbell, victorious. No long-winded greetings and introductions with them standing on the doorstep like beggars for minutes and minutes while Dr. Choudhury pretended he was Rabindranath Tagore getting the Nobel Prize. It would be just quick *salaams*, kisses between the women like Mrs. Darby did, then inside, as it should be.

---

THEA COULD HEAR everything from where she sat on the sofa, her eyes watering. The front door opening, then complete silence. What was Richard doing? She stood too fast and had to sit back down as the room shifted with her. There was a burst of talking: Mrs. Choudhury, then Dr. Choudhury's lower tones and, at last, the sounds of movement down the hall.

If, on top of everything else, Richard was going to be difficult . . . Thea got to her feet, more cautiously this time, grabbed Richard's cigarettes and lighter from the occasional table and stuffed them under a sofa cushion. And the scullery door was going to be bloody well locked.

Henry, fair hair sticking up and tie askew, shot into the drawing room a split second before their guests and propped when he saw her. Thea, concentrating on standing steadily, affected to ignore his anxious glance, and before he could speak, their visitors came clustering through the doorway.

Henry spun around to greet them. "Mrs. Choudhury, lovely to see you again."

"Begum, Begum."

"Oh, ah, you're welcome . . . Some juice, Mrs. Choudhury? Thee managed to source some mango nectar for you, I think. Dr. Choud-hury, good, good. And this must be Tariq, weather's a bit wetter than South Africa today, hey? Juice as well? How was your flight?"

Thea did a slow circuit of the room, smiling and nodding in the swirl of movement and chatter, then returned to where she had started, to pretend to listen and hand out drinks through Henry. The dizziness had eased and, conscious of a certain redundancy, she took another cocktail. She'd touched Richard's arm in passing and made some comment about Henry's recalcitrant cowlick, but his brief mechanical assent left her feeling marooned.

Richard stood on the far side of the guests from her, his dark still-ness rising above Henry's bustling geniality like a yew hedge behind a flowerbed. No glances of shared amusement, no watchful eye on those she spoke to.

Why did she feel so diminished this evening, so pointless? It was she who'd jilted him, then moved on, married happily, two boys, the Abbey. He was the one who hadn't progressed, living in a flat and still single . . .

She picked up another drink with her free hand and started to move around the edge of the group, back toward Richard. When she was almost there, she caught his eye and lifted the drink, forcing a wry smile and raising her eyebrows. Pax. Truce. Besties. Former Lov-ers. You Must Need A Drink With This Lot. He stared, as if puzzled by her presence, then waved away the proffered drink, her peace offer-ing, while that fat nobody Mrs. Choudhury burbled on into his inclined ear.

Thea felt the heat in her face, the weight of the drinks in her hands. Her smile, her eyebrows, were as tight and numb as if she'd just been botoxed. No one noticed her. Henry was by the window, chatting with Tariq. The Choudhurys were nodding eagerly at Richard, defer-ring to his comments, watching his expression.

Look how everyone always revolved around him. Richard said lit-tle, seemed to want none of it, but everyone focused on him, deferred to him as a matter of course. She was just a burden to him, as was

Henry and the Abbey and everything else that she held precious. He wanted none of it, none of them, but they couldn't do without him.

Including her. How she wanted him still. Nothing had changed: the disinheritance was a paper sham, for Henry would never be first-born or stronger because of it. He would never be Richard. She had lost something so precious, so . . . what was it? She finished her cocktail and started the martini meant for Richard. Was that her second drink, or her third? Her stomach burned, as did her heart.

Choudhury was talking now, and she saw Richard's expression change, his long fingers play with his cufflinks, his eyes glittering and sharp. He was angry. Like when she'd told him of Henry's proposal, of how they both wanted him to be at the engagement party. Richard's anger had been thrilling then, proof of her power, and somehow enabled her to make everything—the Abbey, the Kiriakis Trust, family relations—move forward and work out. This was different: she had no inkling at all of what had upset him, and all she knew was that it did not involve her.

Mrs. Choudhury touched his arm, and he shepherded her to the other couch and sat down with her. God, even this silly old woman could hold his interest more than she could.

Their heads were together now, and Mrs. Choudhury was ticking something off on her fingers. One, two, three. Thea could hear some of the words. Children. Mrs. Choudhury was talking about her children. One son, two daughters. How fascinating for him.

But he was watching Mrs. Choudhury intently, listening to every word. Thea sat down on the nearest chair to them, tried to formulate some light comment about how she'd met Shunduri just the other day, delightful girl, but the words stuck in her throat. How could she be in this position, trying to find an opening to talk to Richard of all people? She got up awkwardly, sat further away on the other sofa, on some uncomfortable lump . . . Richard's cigarettes. He hadn't even looked for them, hadn't left the room for a smoke once. What was it now? Eight-thirty?

She glanced at her watch, but its small face was blurred, unreadable. Audrey had not appeared, her watch had not chimed for nine, so dinner could not be ready yet. She got up, at a loss as to where to go, what to do, then realized that someone, Tariq, had silently joined her.

He smiled at her and said one for the hostess and pressed her fingers around a glass. His irises were so dark she couldn't distinguish his pupils; his skin, a darker gold than his father's, had the taut smoothness of youth. The mantel reflectors glittered behind him, as if wings of fire were sitting on his shoulders. She took the drink from his hand (her third? fourth?) and held it like a talisman as she tasted tears in the back of her throat.

Tariq was talking to her, something about paintings. She could get by with just nods and smiles as she continued to watch Richard on the couch. Then Henry was beside them, telling Tariq about the Kiriakis Trust and what central heating can do to oils and watercolors and somehow her glass was empty again, and Tariq, so attentive, was taking care of that while Henry went on and on . . .

---

THINGS WERE GOING very well, Mrs. Begum thought, as she chatted to this so-friendly Richard. Still single, just like Prince Charles's youngest boy, and she'd never believed for a minute that an eldest son would refuse his inheritance, especially something so important as Bourne Abbey, so famous that the government was helping to pay to fix it, paying her husband to supervise, it was of such greatness. Was he planning, now that all that hard work was done, to take it back from his brother and his wife and the two little boys, so lively, though not so handsome as Tariq at that age? Perhaps he was planning a marriage and wanted the Abbey so that he could pass it on to his own children?

But it didn't matter, she thought, patting his hand as he spoke. He had enough money even if he didn't take the Abbey as well, and so interested in her family, even asking if Tariq was married, which of course was halfway to asking about her daughters' status. No sense of humor, but his wife could give him that. Tall thin men were well balanced by short-and-round. He would do well for Rohimun. A good match for outside the community. No one could turn their noses up at that. And then Dr. Choudhury would be forced to bring her back into the bosom of the family.

How to do this? Mrs. Guri's matchmaking skills would be of no help here. Richard now knew that Tariq had two sisters, she had made sure of that, but how to introduce them when Shunduri was sulking in London and Rohimun was still forbidden to Windsor Cottage? Richard and Rohimun were so close to each other right now, but so far. The photos, she would show the photos to him. He was a man: all men lived through their eyes. That would be enough to start something.

She put her hand out, arresting his next question to her, something about bindis. "Not Choudhury, dear Richard. We do not change our names on marriage like Christians do. That is my husband, Dr. Choudhury. Begum. I am Mrs. Begum." She patted his hand. "You must come to us at Windsor Cottage, Richard. And I will feed you. You are too thin with your London living."

He looked pleased, if still solemn, and accepted for next weekend.

---

Dr. Choudhury was having a wonderful time. He kept catching his reflection in the mantel mirror, side-lit by the candles like that special make-up mirror Baby used to have, and his hair was a silver floating nimbus around distinguished, nay, noble features. Patrician, that was the word.

Perhaps not quite as tall as Richard but far better dressed: what had Richard been thinking of with his blue suit and green tie? Surely he had looked in the mirror before coming downstairs. And those lines in his skin. It was true, *gora* skin did wrinkle early, but didn't they have creams for that now? Even he, perhaps twenty years older and hardly a line, would occasionally make use of Mrs. Begum's Nivea pot. With which, really, she should have been a bit more liberal herself.

Everyone wanted to talk with him; he hadn't been left alone for a moment. One would almost think that this little gathering was in his honor. And perhaps it was in a way: the Abbey was almost completed and where would they have been without him? With his knowledge of historical architecture, not to mention his first-rate artistic sensibilities, the Abbey had been transformed. Richard Bourne, the eldest son, such a serious man, had distinguished him by his attentions at the door and had only just left him alone now. Henry treated him more like a baisahib, a big brother, than anything else, and of course he would be happy to continue to guide Henry and his family into the future.

He lifted a hand to his hair and could see out of the corner of his eye the reflected glint of gold on his little finger. He had secreted the signet ring in his pocket when Mrs. Begum, too anxious to be on time, was pushing him out of the house. When she had caught him slipping it onto his finger as they walked, he had pointed out that Prince Charles had one just like it. Pah. He knew her weakness for that family.

There she was now, sitting with Richard. Dr. Choudhury glided to their couch, a little two-seater, and perched himself graciously on an arm with an opening hurrumph to let Mrs. Begum know that he had arrived. What a picture he must look in his charcoal-grey flannels, navy blazer and white shirt. His deep burgundy tie with its gold Ottoman print was a sign of his taste triumphant over Mrs. Begum's predilection for stripes, and threw a little extra color onto his skin. What a splendid duo he and Richard would make against the pastels of the couch, if only Mrs. Begum would move.

But Mrs. Begum did not appear to hear him. He hurrumphed again, and this time detected a little twitch of her shoulder, almost as if she were intentionally ignoring him, though this was impossible. She knew what was due to him: it was just that strange intermittent deafness that had befallen her in her later years. His own hearing was excellent. He tapped her shoulder gently, repeatedly, until she stopped talking.

He immediately addressed Richard with the little aside that he had prepared for their introductions, but which, in the surprise of meeting him and not Henry at the front door, and waylaid, furthermore, by Mrs. Begum's chitter-chatter, he had been unable to bestow.

"My dear friend Richard, when will we meet again in the halls of civilization, by which of course I mean London: so different to the wilds of nature that lie between our two present abodes."

Richard gave him his fullest attention. "Indeed. And I think I saw you in the Park, heading toward the Abbey this morning. I spotted you from the Lodge. Were you carrying something?"

"Ah, a little *déjeuner sur l'herbe* . . ."

"A picnic, then. A bit early, wasn't it?"

Dr. Choudhury sat up a little straighter. His movements, his activities, were of such interest to Richard Bourne. Mrs. Begum seemed to have grown restless, and was beckoning to Tariq. Dr. Choudhury ignored her signs of feeling left out, enjoying this exchange between one man of the world and another.

"Even the most civilized amongst us need to ensure that they expose themselves to the natural beauties of the world. And on such a sunny day. As Khayyám himself did say, *Wilderness is Paradise enow if here with a loaf of bread beneath the bough, a flask of wine, a book of verse . . .*"

"*And thou.*" Richard finished the verse. "So where was Mrs. Begum on this beautiful day? And Tariq, for that matter."

Dr. Choudhury was still leaning back on the couch but for some reason he felt as if Richard was leaning over him, almost cornering him in some way.

Dr. Choudhury's hand stopped halfway down his tie, a feeling of unease, of positive discomfort building in him. Why didn't Mrs. Begum say something about why he'd been seen with a tiffin container, walking toward the Abbey? For someone who never shut up, she was choosing an odd time to be as lively as a radish.

Her attention seemed to be focused upon her son, who had also picked a fine moment to be deep in conversation with Thea, just when his mother needed him. His own memory for Omar's verses seemed to have deserted him, and he gave a little giggle of surprise and discomfort. Richard stared at him expectantly, and he had the oddest feeling that their little trio had stopped breathing.

"Tariq!" Mrs. Begum spoke with considerable force, not at all the tone that one should use as a guest in a drawing room. The silly boy turned and looked but did not move.

Dr. Choudhury, beginning to feel warm under Richard's gaze, opened his mouth to call the boy himself, but with much rustling and a thoughtless passing kick to his ankle, Mrs. Begum leaned forward on the sofa so far that she blocked Richard's view of him. She complained to the room at large of a pressing need for more mango juice, then told him *sotto voce* that he had something, some bit of fluff, stuck just below his nose.

While Richard set off in search of juice, Dr. Choudhury was forced to repair to the powder room, his hand hovering delicately before his face *en route*. But search though he did in the pitiful excuse for a mirror, he could find no sign of anything untoward.

———————

When Richard returned with Mrs. Begum's juice, she was standing and, instead of the drink, took the edge of his sleeve and pulled him into a corner between the couch and a table holding a stack of Thea's magazines. To hear her, he had to bend his head down to hers, and he realized that she had put them in this position so that Dr. Choudhury could not easily intrude. Not that it had stopped the old reprobate before.

"Dear Richard, you will come to us next weekend?"

"I may be down a bit earlier, on the Thursday," said Richard slowly. Thursday, for some reason, now seemed preferable than waiting till Friday. And it would certainly give him more time to sort things out, for Henry and Thea's sake.

"Thursday dinner then."

"I'll look forward to it."

She smiled and reached up to pat his shoulder. "You are a *good* man."

Oddly moved by her praise, he was lost for words.

She beckoned him even closer, then whispered into his ear. "Dear Richard, your brother went to look for ghosts, last night."

He shook his head. "No, I did. I took the boys with me."

"Ah. Ah." She nodded, waiting.

He hesitated, then continued. "I returned late this afternoon, on my own," he said, watching her. "I did see something then. Someone."

Mrs. Begum looked blank, but he suspected that this was a sign not of lack of understanding, but of rapid calculations going on beneath her smoothly coiled hair. She shook her finger at him, her eyes twinkling. "Do not question my husband, dear Richard. Do not question my son. Talk with *me*. Thursday, we have a nice-nice chat, talk properly. And you will understand. You will wait until then. Wait now."

At her words, Richard glanced involuntarily at Dr. Choudhury, then Tariq, then felt Mrs. Begum pat his arm again and saw that she was dismissing him. He stepped backward, still holding her drink, and watched her go to join her husband.

What was all that about? Was he now going to be privy to the Choudhurys' marital woes? Or was there some other kind of message being given? And where did Tariq fit in to all of this? He thought back to that Friday night at the Victoria & Albert Museum two weeks ago. What the hell was going on? Four more days.

He looked over at the occasional table, but his cigarettes were gone, and Thea and Tariq were nowhere to be seen. His skin prickled with craving for nicotine, but the thought of leaving Dr. Choudhury in happy command of the drawing room, perhaps missing something . . .

Richard took a swallow of the juice. He felt as edgy and pumped up with adrenaline as on the first day of a trial, but there was no one to fight. Not yet, anyway. And in a minute he would have to sit down and eat his way through each course of Thea's strategically planned menu.

———

TARIQ WAS ADMIRING the two sets of paired engravings in the Lodge's hallway when Henry's wife shot out of the kitchen and into him, her hands over her mouth, then almost fell backward, her heels skidding on the parquetry until he grabbed her arm. He could smell the alcohol on her breath, and beneath that, a sourness. This woman, whose elegant, tragic face had so drawn him, was about to be sick. She let out a yelp of distress and again covered her mouth. He couldn't leave her like this.

The toilet was close to them, under the stairs opposite the kitchen, and he hustled her in. Her skin was cold and damp beneath his hands. She dropped to her knees, and he only just got the lid up before her head was over the bowl, her long red nails gripping the rim as if she was going to pull it apart. And then, the growling scream of a whole-hearted vomit. He pushed the door shut behind them both and grabbed a handtowel, wet it and squeezed it out. When the first heave was over, he wiped the back of her neck with the cloth and, after she lifted her head, moaning and teary, her face. He'd never done this for a woman before.

After a few more dives for the toilet bowl, and a gradual subsidence into retching, then silence, she sat down on the floor and leaned, eyes closed and sweaty, against the tiled wall.

Shit. He'd been the one plying her with drinks for the last hour. And she'd hardly been sober when he'd arrived. Who knows what else was in the mix. Valium maybe: mother's little helper, wasn't it, for these women-who-lunched? Perhaps this was her regular Sunday night. Or equally, there could be some desperate family secret behind it all—he knew all about those.

He gave her the handtowel and left her to it. At least she'd lost the lot fairly early in the night. He found Henry in the kitchen. A large blousy woman, some kind of char, had him getting plates out of cupboards. What a fucked-up family. But even though they were *goras*, he was not going to tell any man that his wife drank too much.

Henry straightened up when he saw him. "Hey, ah, Tariq! Did you see Thee come past?"

"She's not well, man."

Henry froze, his mouth slightly open, looked at a platter on the kitchen table on which lay a pinkish terrine and then in the direction of the drawing room, telegraphing his concerns like a child.

Tariq put his hand on Henry's shoulder, ignoring the blousy woman's inimical look. You'd think she owned the place, that Henry was the servant. No respect. Well, fuck her.

"It's okay," Tariq said. "We'll handle it."

Henry didn't move. "I, ah . . ."

Clearly not good in a crisis.

"It's okay. We'll hold the fort together. I'll plate this up and take it out, you get your wife up to—"

The char pushed between them both, bent down to open the oven door and slammed it again. The smell of hot roasted meat rose up like a wave and filled the kitchen.

She straightened, folded her arms under her bosom and, staring over Tariq's left shoulder, said in a hard flat voice, "I'm not *racist* but . . ."

Henry dodged around the woman, took Tariq's arm and shuffled him out of the kitchen. "Thanks awfully, Tar. I'll, ah, I'll serve up and could you deal with . . ."

Behind them, and despite a sudden furious bout of coughing by Henry, the end of the char's sentence drifted out of the kitchen doorway.

". . . I'm not having *Pakis* in my kitchen!"

Henry gave an anguished glance behind him. "I'm *so* . . ."

"It's okay, man." Tariq headed back to the toilet and Thea. As the toilet door was shutting behind him, he heard the char's voice again, chastising Henry for putting his thumb on the plates.

Thea was sitting bent forward on the closed toilet seat, her white face streaked with mascara.

"Let me stay here," she said through clenched teeth.

He squatted down in front of her and held out his hand. She stared at it, then at him, and slowly placed her hand into his.

"I'll get you upstairs, yeah," Tariq said. "Henry can't leave the kitchen."

"I don't want Henry."

Tariq pulled her to her feet, opened the toilet door and peered out.

He felt like a teenager again, helping some pissed friend home through a back door, on the lookout for elders. And older sisters. They always blabbed.

Thea was fairly steady on her feet, though once they started climbing the stairs he had to put an arm around her waist to support her. Jesus, these *gora* families. There was a silvery chime, and she sighed, passed her wristwatch in front of her face and said something about dinner at nine. He could feel her looking at him as they climbed. She was managing better than he'd expected, would likely not be too bad in the morning, considering.

At the landing, she seemed with-it enough to lead the way, but when they reached the bedroom doorway and he tried to leave, she turned and sagged heavily against him. Her unexpected move made him rock backward against the doorframe, her breasts against his chest. His heart gave a thump of fright. How the hell was he going to get out of this?

He grabbed her forearms, propelled her toward the bed and pulled back the covers. She reached for his face, but he shoved a handful of bedding between them and used it to push her down.

"Go to sleep," he said, his voice cold. "No harm done." And he turned away.

As he left the room, her little watch chimed again, and he thought he heard her call out faintly, "Entree."

---

IT WAS HENRY who'd had to call the guests in to dinner. He'd explained that Thea was lying down upstairs after an unfortunate incident in the downstairs powder room, but not that it had been precipitated by Audrey summoning them both into the kitchen to inspect the salmon terrine.

"It's the last time I'm cooking this furrin' muck," Audrey had said, meaty forearms flexing as she pulled the dish out of the fridge. "Next time, ee'd be much better with a nice bit of bacon pudding. Or stewed kidneys. Something with suet in to stop this wibble-wabble." And she had thrust the terrine under Thea's nose and given it a good shake.

He'd had no time to ponder Thea's state: Audrey was only staying till the main course had been served and then she was off to her bingo night. Thank god for Tariq: he'd been a champ for ignoring Audrey's rudeness and then taking Thea upstairs.

Now Henry would have to hold the fort at the dinner table. One look from Audrey, and he decided to carry the terrine in himself, and Mrs. Choudhury kindly helped him distribute slices to the guests. Richard took on drinks and was up and down topping everyone up, and Dr. Choudhury told some stories about goings-on at college. Everyone pretty much sat where they wanted and chatted and said the terrine was just lovely, and the main, though the Choudhurys as usual refused the meat. And although he forgot the pudding and went straight to coffees and they had to balance pudding on their knees in the drawing room, it all seemed to turn out just fine in the end. In fact pretty jolly good, though perhaps not exactly how Thea would have run things.

Henry felt quite chuffed, waving the Choudhurys home at the end of the evening: no great disasters and everyone looked well fed and happy, which was really what it was all about anyway. Tariq had told him Thea was fine, just wanted to sleep, so Henry had run up just the once to see, and she was curled up under the covers. A stomach bug, Tariq had said, best to leave her alone for now. A good thing Richard was talking about coming down again next weekend: she would be over it by then and always perked up when he visited.

―――――――――

Mrs. Begum, towing Dr. Choudhury (blind as a bat at night) toward Windsor Cottage, with Tariq off up ahead somewhere as usual, had much to think about and much to do. Dr. Choudhury had to be stopped from hogging Richard when he came to visit. She would send Tariq to visit friends in Oxford that night. She needed to borrow some of Mrs. Darby's silver photo frames. She would put the best photo of Rohimun on the mantelpiece. And her college degree, even if it was just for painting. Dr. Choudhury would never notice this. But—and with this sudden thought she almost steered the short-sighted Dr. Choudhury into a shrub, causing much complaining and flapping of arms—he would never tolerate Mrs. Begum talking about Rohimun in front of him.

Ah. Richard could come early, while Dr. Choudhury was still on his healthy-walk. She would get Henry to call him for her and arrange the time. Then she would have small-talk with him in the kitchen as she cooked, just as Mrs. Darby did with her friends. A cup-of-tea. And he would see the photos of her beautiful older daughter lying on the kitchen table, no frames, just accidentally there.

He was a man, he would not be able to resist the photos, speculating about them, asking her, perhaps. And she had gauged what he knew of Rohimun already, and seen how he felt. He wanted, needed to know, more even than he realized. She was certain in her stomach that he had not yet told anyone else. It would have been all over Henry's face, if Richard had. It had been best, therefore, to let him know she knew this also. Shared secrets bind.

After his healthy-walk Dr. Choudhury could very naturally interrupt them, and Richard would be in a situation for the rest of the evening of curiosity unsatisfied. A very good thing for a man, a restless man in need of falling-in-love. He could talk with her husband in the sitting room, facing the picture of Dodi and Diana as a good example for him; that even a member of the royal family could marry into a Muslim one. Or they would have, if not for that number-one villain, Prince Philip.

Ahead of her, Tariq seemed to be on that phone that he loved as much as Baby did hers. Who at this time must he speak to so much? Dr. Choudhury was beginning to tire, and Mrs. Begum tightened her hold on his sleeve and pulled harder. Almost home. Richard looked like a man who didn't care much for food, which was a good thing if he was to contemplate betrothal to Rohimun, who could burn water. But he was not one of those *goras* who could not see beyond the traditional clothes. Tonight had proved that.

And Rohimun had made an impression on him, she could sense it. A man like that, meeting her Munni in circumstances so romantic. It was meant to be, and must happen, must involve family sanction and supervision as soon as possible. So the sooner he was brought on side, the better. Then he could help her with Dr. Choudhury. What a pity Richard was not living at the Lodge, and Munni in Windsor Cottage. Then she could have sent her daughter over almost every day with cuttings and recipes, and have let things happen almost naturally.

## Twenty

AFTER RICHARD BOURNE left on Sunday night, Rohimun had felt shaky and drained. She'd gone to bed early, craving the encircling comfort of the great bed. It had worked its magic, and she'd slept dreamlessly and well: the untroubled rest from having worked hard, of having painted all day for the first time in years. She felt less trapped, less frustrated than in a long time, despite Richard Bourne's evening intrusion and the disturbing wave of energy that had carried her through the whole episode.

But that Monday morning, as soon as it was light enough to see the canvas, anger filled her. The painting was ruined, now that he had seen it. The figure in the painting was supposed to be just a prop, a foil, to focus attention on the rose. Now when she looked at the canvas, she could only see herself, centerd in that world, and the rose, offset and almost peripheral in comparison, bowing to her, giving up its yellow light to her face and fingers. She had seen his reaction to her painting: as an object of power, not some art gallery product.

Why should his view of things, his reaction, affect her so much? As a painter, she meant. She shoved her paintbrush back into the jar and turned her back on it. God, she wanted to get out today, just leave everything behind. Whatever she'd had, it had been lost. She glimpsed herself in the cheval, and her reflection seemed different too.

She stared, trying to hold on to her anger but feeling it fade despite herself. Her eyes had a luster, her head a tilt that she hadn't noticed before. Prettier than Shunduri. It wasn't just the painting, then. Perhaps, before the portrait, she had never looked at herself like this. Either that or she couldn't even see herself straight now. She turned back to the easel. Jesus, it was hard painting yourself, trying to see yourself truthfully.

She thought of the great painters of self-portraits: Rembrandt, Freud, Kahlo. What did they tell her? That it was a process of self-discovery. And self-invention. But then look at Dürer: every self-portrait an exercise in ever more monstrous vanity, until the final painting, of himself as Christ. The more you painted yourself, the more what you saw changed. She shut her eyes, breathed deeply and opened them again, trying to look at it afresh, with less emotion: as a painting, not a portrait. Not herself.

It was obvious that in order to balance the massive bright presence of the rose, the darker, flatter colors of the figure needed the static charge of a rapt profile, dramatically swirling hair and raised, palm-outward hands. As if receiving something from the rose. Light? Blessing? What did the rose represent? Rohimun shrugged, muttered to herself. Love. Sex. Enlightenment. Allah. McDonald's. It didn't matter. She was just the painter. Let other people figure it out, analyze every brushstroke. Thinking only gets you so far. Thinking doesn't paint the picture. Hands do that.

More light from the rose needed to fall on her, pick out lashes, forehead, the upper slope of her breast. It needed to fill her hands and spill or leak out, like cupped water. A libation. Was she giving something back? Was the radiance coming from her? Let it be unclear.

She would use the layered glaze effect for the yellow light around the hands—like a halo—but for the face and breast she would stick with the scattering of separate yellows, keeping the pigments as pure as possible as they fell onto the skin. Rohimun felt around absently for her palette, then broke her gaze to shuffle through the tumbled paint tubes. Time to get going.

---

THAT MORNING, WALKING to work and still tired from the long drive back to London, Richard had been stopped in his tracks by the sight of a rug with rich, glowing colors: a deep blue covered by an intertwined pattern of crimson poppies and golden roses, repeated in larger version in the foot-deep border. Spotlit and framed by the dull grey stonework of the shop window, it seemed a ridiculously beautiful and exotic thing to come across here. He walked down this street almost every day on the way to the Inns of Court, and had barely registered the shop before. The dealer must have just hung it.

Inside, the shop was full of rugs, on walls and underfoot, giving a hushed quality to his discussions with the owner, who was a reserved and dignified elderly man. No, the rug had been in the window for a few weeks now. Yes, it was for sale: a Persian silk, not antique, from northern Iran. Four hundred knots per square inch. No, the price was not negotiable. When he'd tried to offer him less, the man turned his back. Richard had started again, apologized and introduced himself. Yusuf Ismail accepted the original price and Richard's handshake, and delivery was arranged for Wednesday.

Richard hurried the rest of the way through the warm, almost tropical drizzle to his Chambers, with his head full of roses and poppies. The Reids were coming with the redoubtable Felicity Harporth to discuss his advice in detail. He itched for a cigarette, but had lost track of his packet last night, and was running too late now to detour to a shop. He suddenly realized he'd not had a smoke since early Sunday. Perhaps he should make the most of the inadvertent break and go cold turkey.

When he arrived, Mr. and Mrs. Reid were already there. They had the tanned skins, crisp white pants and bright tops that spoke of life spent largely in the Bahamas, and greeted Richard with that urge to recognition that he loathed from his days with Thea's in-crowd. Felicity, however, seemed delighted to listen to and join in with all the oh-so-you-knows and so-you'd-be-related-tos and you-must-have-gone-to-Oxford-withs.

Louise Reid, perfectly blow-dried even at this hour, smiled and small-talked with an anxiety that spoke of not wanting to deal with what they had come here for. Martin Reid, slower and sadder, with peeling yachtie's lips, had a stagey, jokey manner that made Richard think of superannuated club comedians. And his own father.

Father had always played the fool on family birthdays and Christmases: funny faces and goon voices and slapstick falls, to try to make up for their mother's anaesthetized blankness in the face of festivities. What capacity some people had to jolly over things. He could see that in Henry too: his eagerness to avoid conflict or confrontation, his unwillingness, amounting to myopia, to see malice or deceit anywhere.

Felicity was hovering around the Reids, fussing them into their seats in a way that indicated that they must already have passed a sizeable chunk of their legal work on to her firm.

Richard tapped the papers sitting in front of him to alert them to the need for some formality, the seriousness of the matter. "Mr. and Mrs. Reid, I'm glad that you could join us. I'm pleased to say, as I mentioned in my letter to Felicity, that this is a well-drafted Trust document. As I would expect from the capable people at Greengrasses. It will certainly enable you to make any extra payments to your son conditional, along the lines that you have indicated to Felicity."

"Well, you get what you pay for, don't you?" said Martin, adopting a bluff businessman-to-businessman tone.

"That was done when Simon was born, you know," said Louise Reid, as if discussing a minor but necessary medical procedure. "Such a happy poppet, when he was little. Always smiling."

Her husband cut in. "We wanted him to be well set-up, the best of everything. You do what you can. Only child and all that."

Richard sat and waited.

"He's always been a bit wild," said Louise, clearly having decided that if anyone had to say it, she would prefer it were her.

"Oh, but a *lovely* boy really," edged in Felicity. "And you are doing *absolutely* the best thing for him."

Susan came in bearing coffees, and Louise, back on familiar ground, turned to her.

"You are a lifesaver—Susan, is it? Now do you think you could find me a glass of water as well. Evian, if you could. And while you're there, some napkins because I seem to have . . . Oh, you are a treasure. Isn't she a treasure, Felicity?"

His patience fading, Richard stood and shut the door behind Susan to prevent any more distractions. But before he could say anything, Louise excused herself to powder her nose, and left the room, taking Felicity with her. Christ, these people who don't want to know, don't want to hear the truth.

After the door had closed, Martin walked restlessly to the window and spoke as if to the traffic outside. "You have children?"

"No."

"He takes after me you know, the boy." He turned back and rubbed at his fleshy, vinous nose. "But a good sharp shock: that should do it."

There was a silence, and Richard realized that although Mr. Reid had spoken with all the loud assurance of a man used to being right, or at least never being disagreed with, he was waiting for, needing Richard's agreement.

But he could not give it. He could not let them tell themselves that it was that simple. "You do realize that in a lot of ways this is not a legal problem, with legal solutions, at all."

"We've had him lined up for the best rehab centers half-a-dozen times. Geoff, that's my brother with the brokerage firm, is saying he'll have to let him go soon, because he's not a good influence on the others. He's already on commission only." He ran his hands over the patchy tan of his scalp. "The best schools you know. Always only the best for him. Thailand for his gap year—"

The door opened, and the women were back, in the middle of a conversation about spa treatments, Felicity flushed and happy with the bonding experience. Louise seemed to pick up on what her husband had been saying and added dryly, "Yes, Thailand. That was a mistake, in retrospect." Then smiled at Felicity. "But the beaches are *marvellous*."

"Ooh, I know, *aren't* they."

"Just a good sharp shock," Martin said again.

Richard felt a stab of pity for him, asking in his way for reassurance: Your son will not destroy himself. It's just a phase. You did your best. You are a good father.

"Oh, absolutely, yes," said Felicity. "He'll be right as rain in *no* time."

What rubbish was going to come out of her mouth next?

"What does he use?" asked Richard.

Martin fidgeted uncomfortably, and his wife puffed out a small irritable sound that made it clear that the Evian was not up to standard.

It was the father who eventually grasped the nettle. "Just about everything. There's so much choice these days, hah hah. But he's young. It's just a pity that after uni he didn't—"

His wife cut in. "Geoff could have done so much more for him: he just threw him in the deep end with that job. And I think he should have stayed at university a bit longer: they're not such hardened users as those sharks in Geoff's—"

Martin spoke again, his voice hard and flat. "He failed his university course because he never went. And he's always out-used them all." So Martin was a truth-teller when it came down to it.

Richard focused on him. "Has Ms. Harporth spoken to you about what to expect? From taking these legal steps?"

"My son is . . . he won't just accept it. But as long as your advice is solid and we can rely on it . . ."

Richard made sure that both Reids were looking at him before he continued. "It is very important that everyone is cognizant of the consequences of a protracted legal battle. In circumstances such as these, you are aware that the Trust is obliged to fund the legal costs of all parties, and could be significantly depleted as a result."

"Oh," said Felicity. "There's plenty of fat in *this* Trust . . . Oh, excuse me. Please go on, Richard."

"Mr. and Mrs. Reid, forgive my asking, but have you thought much about the other consequences, the extra-legal consequences of going down this path?"

Felicity couldn't help herself. "I'm *sure* that Mr. and Mrs. Reid have thought long and hard."

"I'm pleased to hear it. I'm happy to advise you that you can rest with confidence upon the maintenance provisions of this document. But it is important that we are all aware that looking at the situation as a whole, this of course is not a purely legal problem. We are not able to present you with a legal solution to the entirety of the problem."

Louise's voice was airily confident. "Oh, yes, but once he's in rehab . . . He's waitlisted for the Priory, you know, and they have a very exclusive . . . Places like that can do wonders."

"They certainly can," said Richard, keeping his voice neutral. He was going, had already gone, well beyond the point where even thick-skinned, perpetually bouncy Felicity would be annoyed. He felt driven to show them the truth of the matter. They had to know, to see, what it was like. People like their son—drinkers, junkies—destroyed families.

He intended to speak about the statistical chances of relapse, but then he saw that Mr. Reid was glaring at him almost unnaturally, and realized the man's eyes were filled with tears. And his wife was not far behind. He could kick himself. He had underestimated them: they were already looking into the abyss.

A few words of conclusion, an indication of the quantum of living expenses that would seem reasonable to the court, and he was done. Felicity was none too impressed, by the way she was shooing them out, away from all his pessimism. But that was an improvement on her usual habit of hanging around and throwing out hints for coffee or lunch.

Richard mumbled farewells at the door, went back inside his Chambers and slumped into one of the conference-table chairs. He could have handled that better: there'd been no need to rub their noses in it. His own family history, his own views, had been allowed to cloud his judgement of what the Reids thought and where they stood. He thought he'd put it all behind him years ago.

―――――――

ROHIMUN STEPPED BACK from the canvas as the light started to fade and sighed with satisfaction. After that bad start, she seemed to have found fresh eyes and had painted on for the rest of the day, despite the muggy weather and a flurry of activity from the ground floor: out the window she'd seen men in suits with clipboards, cleaners and a decorator's van, all of which meant that she'd had to keep a chair jammed under the door as a precaution.

Interruptions like those would formerly have rattled her, had her sliding under the great bed or behind the long curtains every time she heard a noise, but not now. She hadn't the time. Besides, Richard Bourne already knew she was there. Tomorrow she could start experimenting with colors: adding Prussian blue cut with ultramarine for the base color of the *salwar*, flashes of Egyptian violet where the *salwar* met the skin, Courbet green and indigo where the yew shadowed the fabric.

Then, perhaps on Wednesday, she could start blocking in the hair: big free sweeps with the brush while she thought about cold and warm blacks, browns and bronzes. The hair needed to be a different texture to both hedge and *salwar*. Not prickly-detailed and not liquid-smooth. Perhaps Tariq could bring her some of those rough-ground mineral paints for a grainy texture that she could use to heighten the hair's darkness with fine sweeps in warm metallic shades of bronze and copper. Her feelings of irritation and doom, her fear that in coming to the Abbey she had only exchanged one form of confinement for another, had faded. If she could paint again, paint well, something she had believed was no longer possible, then not everything was wrong with the world, with her. Perhaps there was some other path than the dingy passive neediness of her life with Simon, or an arranged marriage and breeding for Britain.

## Twenty-one

SHUNDURI HAD SPENT the whole weekend in bed, and yesterday had called in sick for work again. Amina and Aisha had knocked on her door more than once, but she'd just said she wanted to sleep, had a migraine, a virus, her period. Anything not to have to leave her room and the constant comfort of the television, phone clasped in her hand.

She had not once answered any calls, but read Kareem's increasingly anxious and frequent text messages repeatedly, talking to the screen and telling him everything she wanted to say. That he was a two-timing bastard, a dirty dog, that he had to marry her now and didn't he realize what he had done to her.

And this Tuesday had been awful so far: she'd struggled to get up and dressed and onto the bus to the bank where she had to be brisk, efficient Shunduri, who everyone could rely on and who never had an off day. She'd made two errors on the foreign exchange counter already.

When lunchtime finally arrived, she shut herself in a toilet cubicle to check her text messages, but there were none from Kareem since the night before. She cried then, but silently because there were other people in the ladies', and it took her so long to repair her make-up that she was late back.

The rest of the afternoon crept by, with Shunduri avoiding eye contact with the customers as well as the other girls' curious stares.

When at last the day ended, and she had finished closing up her counter, she bolted for the door and was first out the staff entrance.

But almost as soon as she walked onto the pavement, her heel caught in a crack and snapped. The other bank staff, her friends, rushed past her, not one stopping to ask her what happened and if she was alright.

She'd just gotten up and taken a few tentative steps, balancing on the broken heel, when Kareem was in front of her, saying, "Princess, I'm worried about you."

He looked sharp and sleek next to the tired commuters rushing for the tube or the bus. She turned her head away and tried to move forward, but he would not budge, and she felt even more stupid and awkward. Why did he have to show up here, at her work, with her shoe broken and no messages from him all day?

"Princess, is it your sister? I know you're worried about her, yeah. What's wrong?" He reached for her sleeve, and she tried to dodge his hand, stumbled and almost fell.

"What do you care?" *That I might be pregnant, that people will be beginning to talk. That you can't marry me.* She pushed his hand away as her tears started to spill. "Simon's been giving her the beats, and Tariq took her away, but you don't care. You're just like him."

"How could you say that, Princess? I'd do anything for you. You know I love you. You know how I feel about you." He had his arms out, blocking her progress down the pavement, shepherding her into the laneway down the side of a shop. She was hot with embarrassment at his public declarations, her tears, the broken shoe.

"What's going on, Princess? Is your sister really hurt? Do you want me to do something about him? Is that it?"

"Yeah, if you were part of my family, if you weren't . . . you're part of someone else's though, aren't you? Tell me, do you have children already?"

"Eh? What are you talkin' about?"

"You're fuckin' *married*, you *casra* bastard. How could you do this to me?"

His mouth formed a comical O, and she spotted a mini-cab and ran for it, limping, her smart bank uniform bedraggled with mud and rain.

As soon as she was in the cab, he was ringing her. Once Shunduri was back in her little room, she picked up but would not respond to his apologies and excuses.

AT THREE IN the morning, Shunduri woke to the glare of the television's light and her phone's bleating. She answered the mobile and lay back on her pillows and listened.

"Princess, don't hang up. I'm outside. I love you. I was never going to bring her over. Auntie and Uncle organized it for the money. They were pressuring me bad, yeah? Uncle wanted me to put the dowry into the restaurant. It was all arranged when I first got to England—but I always knew it wasn't for me. I'll never bring her over. I was never going to, I promise. I can give you everything you deserve."

He paused, and her phone filled with silence and static.

"If you'll marry me. Please marry me. Marry me."

Shunduri wanted to talk then, but could make no sound apart from a hiccupped sob.

"Princess, Baby, you don't know how much I love you. I'll prove it to you. Simon will never bother your sister again. I'll sort him out this weekend, give him a talking-to and a bit of a slap. Let me drive you to your family so you can see them. Anytime you want, yeah? Anything you want. Please say yes, Princess. Please."

Her voice was strangled and harsh. "Divorce her, then."

"Eh?"

"Do it now. Text her. Text her and divorce her. Say it three times. There's a fatwa that says you can do it by text message. And send it to me too or you'll never see me again." By now she was sitting upright in the bed.

"Jesus Christ, Princess. You don't know what you're asking. I was never going to bring her over, make it legal, but to divorce her just like that—she's just a village girl, never done anyone any harm."

"Well, fuck off, then."

"You can't just—"

"I'm *pregnant*, yaah? *I'm* pregnant and *you're* married." She felt a rush of horror and euphoria at having finally said the words.

"Jesus fucking Christ."

He stopped talking then, but she could hear his heavy exhalations, a shifting of feet, the slapping sound of a hand on metal, perhaps the railing around the halls of residence.

Her phone crackled into life again. "Alright, Princess, alright. I'll do it. As soon as I hang up. Check your messages when I hang up. I'll see you tomorrow, yeah? On your lunch break."

He ended the call then, as if afraid of her reply, and she sat cradling the phone until it bleeped and she opened the message. *Juri Shah, I divorce you, I divorce you, I divorce you. Kareem Guri.* The bitch probably couldn't even read English, but there'd be someone in her village who could.

## Twenty-two

DR. CHOUDHURY WINCED. What a way to start a pleasant Wednesday morning. The not-so-dulcet sounds of his head of department's voice on his answering machine, insisting not only that he attend the monthly faculty meeting first thing tomorrow but also have an appointment with her afterward for "necessary discussions," were certainly calculated to ruin the entire day. Even if she hadn't then also hinted at her displeasure at his non-responses to her emails.

He gazed longingly through his study window at the Abbey on the hill, the multicolored brick quoins of its Elizabethan wing glowing in the sunshine. They had only just finished cleaning and repairing the tessellated tiles in the hall, and he had been looking forward to a stroll around the freshly unscaffolded western wall of the main building this afternoon. And then a wander inside to examine the tiles and renew an interesting discussion with the Trust stonemason about whether the carved florets at the top of the library windows were intended to be asymmetrical.

However, other duties called so he turned his back on the sunshine and the Abbey's siren song and braced himself to sift through his college emails. It was rather disturbing to see just how many unread inter- and intra-faculty memos had piled up in his inbox over the past few months, while he had been fingering textiles and pondering stained-glass for the approval of the two Trusts. And, increasingly, he had to admit, also to gratify his own sense of color and line.

But though he conscientiously sat in his chair and scrolled through his inbox, opened and closed memos and allocated them to folders and subfolders, read them he could not. His heart was not in it. After half an hour, he gave up and decided to call Marjorie, the head of faculty's much put-upon secretary, to see if there was anything he really needed to know.

A great deal, apparently. About three months ago, Marjorie told him, the faculty had been approached by a Wahhabi Islamist institute based in Dubai asking, virtually begging, Professor Bertha Beeton to fly to Dubai to do a series of lectures on whatever she wanted.

And, Marjorie whispered, clearly still reeling from the experience herself, they were not only greeted with undivided attention by room after room full of covered women, but had also delivered lectures, seminars and workshops in the most opulent conference-room settings, slept and eaten in the most luxurious hotels that she had ever seen: marble lobbies, Lacroix-decorated suites with 2000-thread-count sheets, daily fresh flowers and unlimited room service. And further first-class flights had followed, all expenses paid, to Riyadh and back to Dubai for more lectures and meetings.

By the time Dr. Choudhury hung up he was filled with annoyance. Surely this was self-promotion and puffery. Such time and attention given to those second-rate theories of hers; that Derrida'd new-feminist perspective of Herstory. And surely she could have seen through them, with their covered women and their stonings?

But, as Marjorie (with a kind of breathless fascination) told it, it did not stop there. Repeated requests from Dubai and Riyadh for return visits. Valuable presents: jewelry, carpets, electronic goods, unexpectedly given to her personally, on each occasion. Hah, thought Dr. Choudhury after he hung up. Unexpected the first time, perhaps.

He called a colleague, one of the few of his generation and values that were left in the faculty, and shook his head in disgust as Marjorie's stories were confirmed: the Arabs' wooing of Bertha; their inviting her to do a ridiculously overpaid series of lectures based on her latest publication, which harshly critiqued the most recent generation of feminists as inadequate and misled, and which his colleague hinted was merely a thinly disguised rehash of her PhD dissertation.

After the fifth visit, Bertha had apparently returned to Oxford the proud bearer of a joint offer by Dubai and Saudi Arabia for a superlatively well-funded statutory Professorship of Islamic Studies at her own college, together with a veritable bouquet of new and most generous research and study grants.

Bertha had apparently already met with Jamat-al-Islami and several other activist groups, and the word around college was that she had recently also approved several doctoral topics, including "The Necessary Role of Jihad in the Diaspora" and "The Fatwa as Qur'anic Exegesis." She had submitted an article to the *Times Literary Supplement* titled "The Burqa as an Expression of Feminist Solidarity"—and had had her teeth fixed.

Dr. Choudhury thanked his colleague, promised him some of Mrs. Begum's butter chicken the next time he visited, and hung up the phone, feeling as if he were living hundreds of miles from Oxford, rather than a simple one-hour drive on the motorway.

He was well aware of the amount of damage Bertha could do to the faculty, but even that could no longer galvanize him into action. As long as she left him alone, to go on working on Bourne Abbey or some similar project. He loathed the thought of being forced back to sit on funding subcommittees and drafting recommendations, just to watch Bertha play Lady Bountiful and dole out largesse to her favorites regardless.

He would go to Oxford tomorrow morning, would dutifully listen to Bertha drone on *ad nauseam* at the faculty meeting and their private one, and count the hours until he was back in Wiltshire, where he belonged.

In the meantime, he would make his healthy-walk a pre-prandial one, and to the Abbey rather than the village. He would see the tiles and the unscaffolded walls and perhaps even deliver tiffin to the green

room, while he was there. An image of his second child came unbidden to his mind, siding with him against Tariq over some issue of
color and line, years ago. She must have been just fifteen or sixteen,
but already had an artist's judgement, an artist's sensitivity to such
things, that others—academics and experts—never would.

———————

RICHARD WAS WORKING hard on the Reid brief from home. After
Monday's discussions with the Reids, he'd drafted a Counsel's opinion setting out, in appropriately pessimistic terms, what the clients
should expect next. Formal notice had been given to the Reid son that
all extra payments were conditional upon his entering the Priory in
two weeks' time. Then Felicity had called, sounding rather subdued,
to say that his predictions had been correct and the Reid son had
moved quickly, already instructing solicitors to apply to dissolve the
Trust, so there would be cross-applications coming his way soon. But
not before the weekend.

It was about ten when the rug arrived, carried in by a man in his
twenties who turned out to be Yusuf's son. Ibrahim laid the carpet on the
sitting-room floor and together they slowly rolled it out over the floorboards, between couches and fireplace. When this was done, Ibrahim sat
down on it cross-legged and gestured for him to do the same. While he
explained to Richard how it should be cared for, he showed him the rug's
nap, stroking it back and forth with the edge of his hand, the colors deepening, then fading, then deepening again as his hand changed direction.
It was the most beautiful thing Richard had ever owned.

At the front door, they shook hands and parted. Richard drifted
back into the sitting room and toed off his shoes. Under his socked
feet, the pile quivered like a live thing, and he squatted down to look
more closely at the design. Roses and poppies. The design even varied
between the intertwining stems: some had thorns on them, and some
not. The leaves were different from each other too; he recognized the
familiar onion-shape of the rose leaves. The other ones, smaller and
formed into fern-like clusters, must be poppy leaves. Poppies were from
Turkey, weren't they? And roses, such an English flower, were origi-

nally from elsewhere, somewhere in the East. Was the design symbolic? Roses for beauty, opium poppies for pleasure. Love and forgetting, maybe. Or, given the rug's modernity, perhaps East and West.

---

THE PAINTING HAD been going so well, all through the previous day, but last night Rohimun had slept badly and was still lying in bed late this Wednesday morning, restless and enervated by the hot spell that had stretched on for six days now.

Finally, close to eleven, she dragged herself out of bed to dress, avoiding any glimpse of herself in the mirror. The euphoria of painting again, and painting well, was no longer enough. Doubts struck at her anew: that the last two days were merely a freakish exception rather than the beginning of something. That she would look in the mirror again and no longer see what she had started to.

Sneaking back from washing her face awake in the nearest bathroom, Rohimun opened her door to see a man standing before her easel. She was conscious of a frisson of fear, then disappointment. Dad. He didn't visit often—it was generally Tariq's job to bring her meals and check on her—and he had never come right into the room before. He was holding her lunchtime tiffin and peering at the rose. As she watched, he walked slowly backward then stopped about five feet away, still staring at the image, seemingly unaware of her presence.

"Abba," she said, going toward him, her towel and toiletry bag awkwardly tucked under one arm. She wondered if Richard had spoken to him, imagined the scene if he had, what Dad would do to her then. She'd be straight on the plane to Bangladesh for sure. She bent to touch her father's shoes with her free hand, warily.

"You have been painting."

"Yes, Abba." He had spoken to her, the first time since she'd come back, although it had not escaped her notice that he was not using her name. She walked to the duffel bag to pack away her stuff. One thing about squatting here in so much secrecy: it'd sure made her tidy.

"This, this is beautiful," he said, waving two fingers at the painting. "The depth of color, the translucency of this flower, is number-one."

He stretched an arm out in her direction, his hand beckoned, and she scuffed over in her flip-flops and stood next to him, pretending to look, hardly daring to hope. He picked up one of her brushes and used it like a pointer to follow the dark lines of the hair as it spread over a third of the canvas.

"This is lovely, very lovely indeed," he said. "Alive, like in Edvard Munch. Better, because he needed to put a river behind the figure: remember *The Scream*? But you have the river in the hair already."

He pointed at the female figure. "She is a holy figure, like the great Renaissance Madonnas. You have spoken to Rossetti here: his *Proserpine* you have conflated with a Renaissance Mary—when she turns in profile, and looks, to see the Angel of the Immaculate Conception. One might well say, an Adoration of the Rose."

She nodded; her throat had tightened up.

"There are echoes of Millais here, his drowned *Ophelia*, with her outward-facing palms as well as the floating hair, the room made for her presence by nature. There is the surrender and the gift inherent in such a gesture, you know?"

She nodded again, swallowed tears. This was better than forgiveness. She felt like a favorite student, a star pupil. She had only seen him like this at art gallery exhibitions and, occasionally, when she'd sat in on his university lectures and he'd go off on a riff about Early English and the Perpendicular style. Now it was about her, her painting.

He sighed. "You have truly excelled yourself with these colors: the glaze of such depth, the richness of that fabric." He turned to look at her. "This painting of yours, not even finished yet, it is the best you have done. Truly number-one."

She cleared her throat, finally got the words out. "You've seen my portrait work, Abba?"

"Yes, yes, very competent, very good. You always were a good student. But this, this." He swung the paintbrush in an elegant arc that encompassed the painting as a whole. "You have matured as an artist, I can see that."

There was a pause between them then, a little space to allow for the great adjustment that had taken place. And then her father hurrumphed, put down the brush, folded his arms and moved further back, still regarding the painting.

Rohimun, following his cue, went to her palette and started to talk, in fits and starts, about the halo she wanted to create around the hands, how it needed to fall onto the ground, like a blessing, but also radiate back toward the giant rose.

Dad stood and watched as she worked, and occasionally he spoke: something about yellow, its universal reputation as a holy or spiritual color. And Kandinsky's singular refutation of this, asserting yellow's essential earthiness.

Her lunchtime tiffin went cold as she painted, sitting unheeded on the floor where her father had left it, and while she painted, he continued to talk, telling her stories about possible alchemical influences upon the old painters' recipes for mosaic gold and lead-tin yellow, the Romans' use of slave labor to mine the poisonous, gold-like orpiment, the ancient Egyptians' preference for yellow lead antimonite.

She had forgotten about his knowledgeable, intellectual side, and had rarely glimpsed his aesthetic sensibilities in a positive light. So much of his behavior at home, with all of them, had been about appearance and prestige: like a fat peacock, all noise and show.

By the time she started to think of a break, half the afternoon had passed, and the two of them sat down on the floor in a patch of sunlight near the window. They opened up the tiffin lids and shared Mum's cold chicken curry and rice.

Then her father left, with some return of his distant manner but promising to send Tariq at eight with her evening meal, and she walked back to the magical painting that sat at the center of the room. She could do no more with the late-afternoon light until the latest layer of glaze had dried out some more, but the figure, she could work on. She washed out her brushes and placed them in the drying jar on the windowsill, then took a close look at the image.

Those important hands were almost complete, with the beginning of the yellow glaze around them. The logical next step was the neck and face. What a pleasure it was to mix in burnt umber for skin color. To place faint shadows under the eyes to show maturity, rather than crow's-feet.

The painting's transformative effects on her father, herself . . . She had to be true to it, not fall back into the populist, Freud- and Bacon-imitating portraits of her London years that had, along with Simon, eventually dried up her creativity.

When things had been at their height, and she'd had a waiting list of sitters and her agent chasing her for more canvases, the sight of the flashing light on her answering machine or the stack of invitations on her mantelpiece was enough to make her feel physically sick. Then at that first and only solo exhibition, she'd overheard one of the top-flight dealers, Deirdre somebody, say how of the zeitgeist her paintings were, perfect for gen Y. That said it all really.

Now she was with her father, and she had painted, was painting, something extraordinary, beyond her known capacities. And he was placing this painting into history, into the canon of those objects of irrefutable, inherent value that would outlast them all.

## Twenty-three

On Thursday morning, Dr. Choudhury's colleagues greeted his arrival at the monthly faculty meeting with rather more surprise and spontaneous enquiries about his health than he was completely comfortable with. Surely he had not been away that long.

He took his seat and picked up a copy of the agenda, but once again found himself in the position of being utterly unable to read the document. The long drive, combined with the prospect of this meeting, in this stuffy, ugly room with nothing but urn-stewed tea and stale digestives to sustain him, had reduced his motivation to virtually nil. The lone fly crawling on the windowpane behind Bertha seemed to have more purpose and meaning than the papers in front of him and the murmuring and asides of his peers.

As item one, the minutes of the last meeting, was announced, Dr. Choudhury picked up a pen and started to doodle pilasters and pediments on the margins of one of the subcommittee reports. Soon he had turned it over to make room for a classically inspired folly, which would look very well situated at the bend in the river that marked the halfway point between Abbey and cottage. At length, some time after he had detailed the moulding of the cornices, the decoration of the entablature and the form of capitals of the columns, and decided, after debate, upon a frieze with an idyllic theme of cavorting maenads and satyrs, Bertha came, with much important hemming and shuffling of papers, to the final item on the agenda: *Special Business*.

His doodling, which had now progressed to the interior of the folly, slowed and stopped. Certain words and phrases were percolating through to his conscious mind. Professor Beeton had moved on from speaking in general terms of the tidal wave of Arab funding that was about to hit the faculty, to an attempt to provide intellectual, even moral legitimacy for it.

". . . and of course, historically speaking, the Wahhabi, that is the desert sect of Islam that dominates the most forward-looking nations of the Middle East, is, arguably, Islam in its purest form. I understand that the Wahhabi movement can be traced back to . . ."

"I object." Dr. Choudhury found himself standing, his drawings disregarded, leaning forward with his hands splayed on the table for support. "These people of whom you speak, with more wealth than they know what to do with. They are not educated people, for all their universities of marble and ivory."

Bertha's chair scraped back abruptly. "Dr. Choudhury, do you mind!"

He hurrumphed and raised a palm. "I am obliged to object, Professor Beeton. You know not what you do."

A gasp ran around the table; all eyes were upon him. "These people, whom you should call Saudis not Wahhabis, they are intellectually dishonest, number-one politicians, every last one of them. And their intention, Professor Beeton, their only intention, is to purchase power and influence with their thirty pieces of gold."

Bertha clutched her new and quite heavy-looking necklaces to her bosom and again attempted to speak, but he would not yield the floor.

"To borrow the prestige of this institution to further entrench their right-wing influence in fair Albion, to cause students in our care and protection to view Saudi social and political values, and Wahhabi practices, as legitimate alternatives to democracy, moderation in religion, cultural inclusiveness, toleration. You do not understand what you do. These, these men and women are number-one villains for what they do, and want to do. Do not be fooled by their compliments, their flattery, their gifts."

He forgot himself so much as to point his finger at his head of faculty at this juncture, and he could not help noticing that she flushed an unpleasant shade of red. Brickish: dreadful with that pink top.

"This, this is the thin end of the wedge: a wedge of gold. They will start pressing for an end to Oxford's Christian traditions, push non-Muslim students out of the prayer rooms, object to the drinking traditions and to figurative paintings in the Ashmolean. You do not know it, but I have already seen this, this Wahhabism."

Silence greeted his words, until Bertha, her voice shaking a little, told him that his interjection had been out of order and, with a warning look to Marjorie, would not be minuted. Still standing and breathing fast with emotion and the unexpected excitement of it all, Dr. Choudhury wondered if this was how Richard Bourne felt in court.

His colleagues had all heard him: that was what mattered. And it might even save him from a few of those irritating subcommittee duties. And Bertha from attaching herself to him any more than she had done already. Perhaps he should make the effort to come to future faculty meetings—they had no idea of what they were dealing with, of the motives behind those Saudis throwing their money around. How true the proverb of the ivory tower.

Bertha broke up the meeting and bustled out before him. He would soon, no doubt, have to endure a haranguing in her office over points of order and probably something in his behavior that she identified as patriarchal, but what was that to him. He would be away from these internecine, infantile politics by twelve o'clock at the latest. And, being tenured, he was secure from whatever machinations she might engage in.

He would give Bertha a minute or two to compose herself, and so took the opportunity to repair to the men's room and check that his outburst had not ruffled his appearance. Satisfied by what he saw, he set off for her office and knocked on the door.

"Come in."

He opened the door and stepped onto a fine Persian rug that covered most of the floor. Other things had changed too. On the rug was an elaborate octagonal coffee table inlaid with brass and mother-of-pearl, and Bertha's mismatched collection of chairs had been replaced with a set of upholstered leather couches that looked Italian. Bertha seemed unchanged, however: in those ill-fitting jeans and the long pink tunic striped with silver that he now recognized as a Baladi dress, for performing the northern African peasant dances.

As she stood up from her desk, Dr. Choudhury realized two black-robed figures were seated before her, and they rose now too. He started with surprise and an instinctive repulsion. They were women, covered from head to foot in the Arabic way. They were also gloved, and with fine black gauze where their eyes should be.

Bertha introduced them to him as a visiting Wahhabi scholar and her postgraduate student, from Dubai. The *salaamalaikums* were cursory on both sides. Like most of his Desi generation, he abhorred the covering of women. And he knew what many Arabs thought of, and how they treated, their Bangladeshi guest-workers. Bertha ushered the women out with a promise to catch up with them later on.

"Sit down, Dr. Choudhury. It is so long since I've seen you. Properly. I'm afraid, as you seem to have been ignoring my emails, there is much to tell. In your absence, Humanities has undergone a significant restructuring."

Dr. Choudhury cleared his throat. "Due to the extra funding, I assume?"

"A little more than *extra funding*, Dr. Choudhury. Marvellous avenues have been opened to us, vistas of opportunity that are contingent upon, I mean, concomitant with, a fresh look at every aspect of the Humanities . . ."

He began to realize that this meeting was not about the Bourne Abbey secondment coming to a close. She was not going to be increasing his lecture and tutorial load, pressuring him into subcommittee memberships, or even picking on his publication record. This was something else.

She steepled her fingers and spoke down to her nails which were, as always, grubby and unmanicured. "As a result of this university-wide reassessment, Dr. Choudhury, to which, I may add, you were asked on several occasions to contribute, it became apparent that there was a certain duplication in the services offered by Architecture and History."

She seemed to have the bit between her teeth now.

"In short, Dr. Choudhury, a rationalization has necessarily had to occur, for the sake of the students, of course. And the faculty."

"But I am *tenured*, Professor Beeton." His voice sounded like a tentative bleat even to him, and he leaned forward, trying to force some eye contact. "I am a tenured Fellow of this establishment. There are rules."

Bertha avoided his eyes. "Of course there are rules, Dr. Choudhury, and we would have been most remiss if we had not consulted with all the appropriate authorities: the Pro-Vice-Chancellors of Planning and Resources and Personnel have been consulted, even the Proctors." She spoke hurriedly, as if the end of this conversation was in sight, to her at least. "Your tenure is not being tampered with, you see. That"—and here a shade of regret seemed to cross her face—"cannot of course be tampered with. Your salary will continue. It is Historical Architecture as a separate, ah, subject that is otiose, and on that basis you may wish to consider an extended, ah, sabbatical. From all active duties."

"But my students . . ."

"Such as they are, Dr. Choudhury. There are not many any longer. Most of the undergraduates are now sitting much more comfortably within Architecture, under the guidance of Dr. Felmstedt. The post-grads and a few strays more suited to History have been taken by Ellen—you remember Dr. Ellen Haversack, over from Stanford?"

"So . . . so you are taking away my lectureship, my students, my office as well, I suppose . . ."

She stood and began to clash papers noisily together. "Well, of course, why have an office when no work is done, you are never here."

"My secondment was approved."

"I must be off, Dr. Choudhury. You would have been aware of these changes weeks ago if you had been keeping abreast of college affairs, and now I have a meeting that I really must attend to."

Their eyes met for a second, her expression a strange mixture of triumph and embarrassment. "I have meetings for the rest of the day. Marjorie has cleaned out your office and everything is boxed up."

He stood as she hurried past him, then sat down again, found his handkerchief and blew his nose. His legs hurt, as if he'd been standing all day.

After a little while he walked down to his old office, treading quietly. The thought of running into one of his colleagues filled him with horror. His room seemed large and light with all the books and pictures packed away, and archive boxes were stacked in the middle of the room.

Marjorie materialized beside him. "I'm so sorry, Dr. Choudhury," she said softly, as if she too did not want to be overheard. "I've organized for everything to be delivered to Windsor Cottage this afternoon."

He tried to speak but failed.

"I do hope that's alright, Dr. Choudhury."

He nodded, defeated.

With relief in her voice and a certain forced cheer, she adjusted one of the boxes to line up perfectly with its base. "It's such a pity it's all happened just before the Long Break. But we'll give you a proper send-off when Michaelmas starts. For your sabbatical, I mean."

"Yes, of course, of course . . ." he said, backing out of the room and looking down the corridor. If he could just get out of this building and to his car without bumping into anybody. He could be home before midday. Tariq should be there. He already felt like a ghost of his former self, the one that had been a part of these buildings, this university, for almost thirty years.

----

RICHARD SPENT THURSDAY morning in Chambers, irritable without a smoke, trying to clear the decks for the anticipated cross-application by the Reid son next week. Meetings with instructing solicitors and anxious juniors about a number of briefs consumed much of his morning, leaving him concerned that the Reid matter would eat into his planned long weekend. It was going to be a demanding brief, as well as one that was increasingly feeling too close to home, though it somehow seemed timely as well: acting not for Her Majesty's Inland Revenue for a change; arguing for the preservation and proper use of a family Trust, rather than its destruction. There was certainly more merit in the supporting authorities than he'd first thought.

With his morning appointments finished, Richard returned to his flat at lunchtime to work. But once there, he decided to telephone a friend of a friend, a community legal aid solicitor, about likely scenarios. For a case. A young woman, English-born, possibly a runaway, in hiding, worried about papers. An older man.

He was walking into a minefield, she warned him. The things she'd come across with runaways were often extreme. The young woman could be avoiding abuse at home, or family pressure to return to the country of origin, escaping a prospective marriage, or fleeing one that she had already been forced into, which had hostile, demanding in-laws or a violent husband. And whatever it was, it was likely to be further complicated by the cultural differences, the presence of Sharia law in these communities. Those were the kinds of things she dealt with on a daily basis in her job, she reminded him.

If he was involving himself in a case like this, he must not let himself be fooled by English accents and Western clothes. "And remember, whatever you do, the Muslim sensitivities. Don't blaspheme, and never touch the women: not a handshake, not a polite touch to the back or the upper arm, or you risk losing all the trust and respect that you have worked to establish. And never, never, underestimate the pressure these young women are under."

The few that broke away for a while almost always returned, just so as not to be exiled from family and community any longer. She told him about *funchaits*, where the elders of the community met to enforce a marriage or preside over inter- or intra-family disputes. In the end, they would almost always take the rulings of the *funchait*, the family beatings, the arranged husband, in order to belong again.

Richard thanked her, scribbling down notes from force of habit. *Funchaits*. Forced marriages. Touching. Exile. Jesus Christ. He went outside, smoked two cigarettes, one straight after the other, without enjoyment, cursing his lack of willpower. What was he getting himself into?

Tomorrow was Friday. He still hadn't said anything to Henry or Thea. Henry would follow his lead, let the girl stay for now. Something would be possible. But Thea would be the difficult one over this: she would hate having a stranger squatting in her Abbey, amongst her antique furniture. Well, fuck it, he thought, with a sudden wave of irritation. The Abbey was his home too, and it was time she realized that.

Could he spirit her to London, to some women's shelter? Would she wither and die without her community? Prefer to return to whatever awful situation she had left, rather than be alone? Visions of her in his flat intruded—digging her toes into his new rug. Sitting on his balcony, the sunshine on her hair.

This was ridiculous: he was getting way ahead of himself, and time was running out. She deserved help to get away in any event, to have a safe place to stay, whatever did or didn't happen between them. God forbid that she could love that old man. Or was it the son?

And Mrs. Begum knew something, he was just not sure what. Presumably she would never accept Dr. Choudhury having an affair. But perhaps Richard was wrong there too. He stretched, took in the view, and with a further effort of will turned his mind from cigarettes to dinner with the Choudhurys. There were too many variables, too much that he just didn't know. Anything might happen. He went back inside.

His sitting room was lit up by the afternoon sun: the rug glowing blue and gold and green. The chimney breast seemed bare now. He had always preferred it like that, had always made a point of asserting the fact, to avoid the risk of something being foisted on him by one of

Deirdre's designer friends. But now the room was different: it did need something.

He walked over his beautiful rug to the mantelpiece, surveyed the pale space above it and the cavity below which housed the gas fire. Wasn't the hearth supposed to be the heart of the home? Where the Romans housed their *Lares*, hunters mounted their trophies, Deirdre and Thea propped their most prestigious invitations. He looked again at the roses on the rug, the chimney breast. The painting of the rose and the girl with the wild and waving hair would fit well here now.

Perhaps that was the solution. He could offer to buy Choudhury's painting to gain his cooperation, then fund her out of her situation. Although it would never be that simple, at least this was something he could put to her: something to talk about, without having to launch into more personal things like her history, her relationship with Choudhury. Make it evident that he wasn't her enemy.

So was that what was happening? Was he trying to make a home out of this flat, this sensible investment property, neutrally furnished, that he'd always intended to sell when he took silk? He paced the room, suddenly restless, the craving for nicotine making itself known again. His priorities seemed clearer now. He would let someone else in Chambers have first choice of new briefs from the clerks for the next few weeks, to give himself a bit more breathing space in case she needed his legal help. Perhaps even spend a bit more time in Wiltshire. God knows how the whole thing was going to work out. Dinner with the Choudhurys tonight, and perhaps the answers to a few questions, then tomorrow morning he could check that the girl was still there, was alright. Not scared away by last week. Or spirited away somewhere else by Choudhury, or the son.

He settled himself on the couch with a new brief, but, distracted, only read it intermittently. At three-thirty p.m. he realized that he'd forgotten all about Deirdre: she'd be expecting him tomorrow for their usual Friday. He called to let her know that he couldn't make it. The implication was obvious, they knew each other well enough for that. He'd expected calm acceptance, but the way she said, "Anyone

I know?" threw him. Then she laughed and said, "She *must* be special," and smoothly segued into, "Oh, don't worry about it, darling: you're still on my party list . . ." And, knowing Deirdre, he really was, and would still be invited to her perpetual rounds of drinks, parties and openings.

After he'd hung up, he had a strange sense of shame. His relationship with Deirdre, so dependent upon a concurrence of geography and working hours and a shared lack of interest in commitment, had ended in a way that was disturbingly bloodless.

---

HE SHOULD SET off. It would be so much easier to forget the whole thing, just stay in London and keep working at his flat, rather than head to Wiltshire, but there was no point thinking that now. He left a message on Henry and Thea's phone to say that he wouldn't be arriving until late, after dinner with the Choudhurys, would use his key, and that he planned to go out early Friday—to the Abbey, though he didn't say as much—and so would see them whenever. Running down the steps to his car, he felt tired and strung out. Jesus, why had he committed to these things?

As soon as Richard hit the M4, despite beating the rush hour, it was virtual gridlock. The traffic travelled at a crawl for about three miles then stopped completely. He felt edgy and headachey. When the driver in front of him lit up a cigarette and rolled down his window, Richard reflexively patted the central console where his lighter and smokes used to be, tried the pockets of the jacket hanging behind him, then stared grimly ahead. He could taste it. This trip was turning into a penance, and for what?

Looking for distraction from the driver ahead, who was positively luxuriating in his cigarette, he watched a bee brush against the outside of the car's windscreen, not quite landing, then slowly continue, flying parallel to the glass in wobbly zigzags, like a miniature helicopter on reconnaissance.

Perhaps traces of pollen were there from last weekend's visit, from other places too. Like a history of his movements around England, if one had the ability to read it: journeys measured not in clock-time, destinations and deadlines, but in the countryside he moved through, the nature of the weather, where he stopped on impulse for coffee. The importance of the journey itself. Like the old idea of a pilgrimage, where it was the commitment to travel, and the act of travelling itself, moment by moment of it, that changed everything. Not the end point, the arrival.

## Twenty-four

THE FRONT DOOR of Windsor Cottage was open, propped wide by a monstrous cast-iron doorstop. Down one side of the hallway, archive boxes were stacked three high. When Richard pressed the doorbell, Mrs. Begum's head appeared out of a doorway at the far end of the hall.

She walked toward him, her hands held out. "*Salaam*, dear Richard, come in, come in."

"Good afternoon, Mrs. Begum. Doing some packing?"

"No. They are from the college."

"Is Dr. Choudhury here?"

"No, no, not yet. He is still on his healthy-walk. Come with me, Richard. I am cooking."

He followed her into an airy kitchen painted in brilliant yellow and blue, its open window crowded with herbs in pots. Above them was a cafe curtain in a sheer fabric, almost completely covered by pieces of paper that were flapping in the breeze. Richard walked over to get a closer look.

Attached to the curtain with colored pins were newspaper and magazine cuttings of various members of the royal family, a glossy brochure with a white stretch limousine on the cover, a cruise ship advertisement showing a tropical island, and some brightly colored cards with gold writing in Arabic and English: *Eid Mubarak*.

Mrs. Begum, filling a kettle, nodded at the cards. "They are last year's Eid—my favorites. Happy Eid cards, Richard. Like your Christmas." She smiled. "But no Santa."

"You don't believe in Santa?"

She laughed. "No, we don't believe. I make you a cup-of-tea. Sit down."

He pulled out a chair and did as he was told. The smell of curry was pervasive, and a wok and two pots were on the stove bubbling away. His stomach growled. Ages since he'd had a curry. On the chopping board were neat piles of ginger, garlic, green onions, and some fine-cut coriander. On a shelf above the counter were two large tomes, in faded reddish binding with embossed lettering. *Home County Recipes. Traditional Cotswold Cooking.* His heart sank. Surely not. Growing up with Audrey's cooking, having to wade through it again whenever he stayed at the Lodge, was bad enough.

"Are they your books?"

"No, no. They are Mrs. Darby's, next-door. We look at the pictures, talk about recipes, ingredients." Mrs. Begum tapped a wooden spoon on the edge of the biggest pot, then lifted the spoon up and gave it a little twirl. "My friend."

Mrs. Begum carried a mug of tea to the table, white with milk. *World's Greatest Dad*, it read, in red lettering on blue. She placed it on the tabletop in front of him and, with a corner of the tea towel that was tucked into the waist of her sari, removed a drop of milk that balanced on its rim.

He wondered for a second if she was going to wipe the tea towel across his face as well, ruffle his hair, ask him if he'd washed his hands. How would he have turned out, with a mother like this? Perhaps he'd never have left home. Until he married.

His usual sense of containment, of knowing where he ended and other people began, had gone missing. He felt frayed at the edges, weakened by the cosiness, Mrs. Begum's matter-of-fact care. He patted his pockets for smokes and lighter before he remembered, yet again, that he was giving up. What had possessed him to try to do that? He sipped his tea, and its extreme sweetness brought tears to his eyes: she must have put in about six spoonfuls of sugar.

On the table was a scattering of photographs. The young man in a blue tunic was clearly Tariq, the V&A action man, and there was another of him in a master's bonnet and graduation robes, with Oxford spires in the background.

"What did Tariq get his degree in?"

"History-of-Art. Paintings," Mrs. Begum said, with an undertone of incredulity in her voice. "For learning about paintings."

"He must have been only a few years behind me. At Oxford."

"Yes." She pointed her spoon at him, her arm at full stretch. He froze. The spoon dripped onto the table. "But why did he need to go to South Africa? *Plenty* of jobs here. *Plenty* of study here." Before he could think of a reply, she turned away and brought the spoon down hard on the edge of the wok. Bang, rattle. "My pride is as high as the *sky*"—another bang, rattle—"that my son has to go so far away to work. To study."

He relaxed, sipped his tea.

"But now Tariq is home." She stuck her spoon into the other pot and stirred vigorously, did the same to the third impartially. "Home now."

Richard wondered how long that would last. The other night Tariq had looked as if he had well and truly outgrown home life with his parents. But in thinking this, was he just falling into the trap the solicitor had warned him about: mistaking city clothes, urbane manners, for Western views? Whatever they were. And besides, this looked like a pretty pleasant family life: very different to what his own had been.

Under Tariq's photos there were some others, and as he fanned them out over the tabletop, he saw the girl. Jesus Christ. A few years ago perhaps, less voluptuous and wearing full traditional dress: something pink, with lots of spangles, for a studio shot. It didn't suit her, and she seemed to know it, with those full lips pressed together, and the suggestion of a frown.

Her hair was down and had been flattened into even waves that caught the light, unlike the wild curls he had seen, but there was no mistaking her. There were long chain-like pieces of jewelry hooked into it and linked to her earrings. A diamante glittered between her brows: a bindi, he'd looked it up. Her forearms were hidden under pink and gold bracelets. She looked faintly ridiculous, as if in fancy dress that she had not chosen.

His hands trembled with the effort of not picking it up, not exclaiming. He considered ducking out the back for a smoke, wondered if he'd been mistaken and there was still an emergency pack in the glovebox. He hadn't checked that.

Mrs. Begum spoke from just behind him, making him jump. "Ah. My eldest daughter. My Rohimun."

He did not trust himself to speak. He grasped for his mug like a man in the desert. Mrs. Begum reached over his shoulder and flicked the photo to one side, revealing an old black-and-white photo of three children in school uniform. The boy in the middle was Tariq, probably about nine or ten, his shirt hanging out, flanked by two girls. One was clearly Rohimun: she and Tariq were grinning straight at the camera, hair awry and arms akimbo, as if they had just been up to some mischief. The other girl, more neatly dressed, held on to the railing that ran behind them, her other hand tugging on Tariq's shirt.

Richard thought of how he and Henry used to be at that age, when they were outdoors, away from family dramas. Building forts in the woodpile, rolling chickens down hills in milk churns to watch them climb out and stagger in drunken circles, sword fighting with the broad-bean stakes. All for one, and one for all.

Mrs. Begum's index finger, her nail stained with a dark reddish substance, tapped on the terrible two. "Tariq. Rohimun." Then she drew the tip of her finger gently down the image of the sulky girl. "Shunduri, Baby."

Mrs. Begum showed him a full-blown studio shot of Shunduri in a tight, pale blue sari, frosted lips pushed out, blue eyelids drooping, breasts cantilevered upward.

"Fifteen," she said.

"Ah," said Richard. Fifteen going on thirty-five more like. Something about her reminded him of Deirdre. And Thea, though Thea would never have posed like that. It was more the sense of a manufactured image. What was it in him that attracted such women? And why was it only now that he realized what poor measure his own feelings had been? He took a long swallow of tea and felt surreptitiously for the non-existent cigarette pack that might somehow have materialized in his jacket pocket. God.

He picked up the studio shot of Rohimun, careful of his tone. "So?"

Mrs. Begum edged around the table and sat down opposite him. She took a sip from her cup of tea, grimaced and added two more spoonfuls of sugar from a little cream-colored china beehive with a replica bee on its side. Then she clasped her hands and met his eyes.

"So," she said. "You have seen her. My daughter."

He nodded slowly, bracing himself for he knew not what. He felt responsible for the mess somehow, whatever it was, but also like a supplicant, waiting on her decision, her judgement.

"She has had trouble," Mrs. Begum said quietly. "We cannot have her here. My husband . . ."

Richard nodded again, his teeth on edge from the sugar and the need for a smoke.

Mrs. Begum stood to give a quick stir to the various pots, which all seemed to be doing very well without her. She banged the edge of the wok once, with decision, then turned down its flame and dropped in a handful of coriander. Its aroma filled the room.

"She is a good girl," said Mrs. Begum, with her back to him. "A *good* girl. She paints pictures."

"She's a painter." Of course she was. The painting was hers. Why hadn't he realized that before?

"Yes, yes. Always the painting, from when she was small. And then, everyone wanted her paintings, in London. Always in London, never home. And then . . ." She sniffed and wiped her eyes with the end of her sari.

"She can't be at home?"

"No . . . her father . . ." Mrs. Begum turned toward him, her voice high and strained, the steaming pots behind her rumbling away in counterpoint. "It was in a magazine, that she had a boyfriend. They say she is not a good girl, but she is. She *is*."

Mrs. Begum was crying properly now, her hands over her face, and Richard stood, wondered if he could touch her shoulder, then pulled out his handkerchief and brushed it on her hands. She took it and sat down, still crying, but slower now. He leaned back against the countertop, folded his arms and thought. Rohimun. Rohimun's mother. And Dr. Choudhury was her father, Tariq her brother. It *had* been her at the exhibition. And was that other man her boyfriend? He felt some of the tension leaving his shoulders and reflexively patted his jacket pocket.

"Ah, the rice."

"Allow me." He turned off the gas, found a handtowel, picked up the biggest saucepan and shook its contents into a colander standing in the sink. The scent and sight of the steaming rice started his stomach growling again.

Mrs. Begum bustled over, seemingly recovered, and took the empty saucepan out of his hands.

Perhaps now he could duck out, check the glovebox. He was really beginning to feel it. His skin crawling and clammy, his vision starting to blur, the beginnings of a headache. Day four: the doctor had warned him. His symptoms would peak, then subside. He just had to soldier on. Why hadn't he filled the script for nicotine patches? He felt like eating one. Why hadn't he considered the gum at least, kept some as backup?

Footsteps sounded in the hall, along with Dr. Choudhury's voice, raised and plaintive. "Tea, tea now."

Mrs. Begum took hold of Richard's upper arm and pushed him out the kitchen door into the hallway. "All done, all ready now," she said. "Go to Dr. Choudhury. I will bring the tray."

He hesitated, looking at the front door. Perhaps he could quickly duck out to the car, just on the off chance. But halfway down the hall, Dr. Choudhury's head had poked out of the sitting-room doorway in an odd echo of his wife's earlier.

"Ah, Richard Bourne. Hail fellow, well met. Come in, come in, sit down. Yes, there. No, I won't hear of it, sit down. I will pour you a drink. As you know, I do not, but I can manage a whiskey for my friend Richard."

After giving him his drink, Dr. Choudhury started to waffle on about some university politics, which Richard, headachey and distracted, could only partially follow, but felt obliged to try, given what he'd been assuming about the man until only minutes before. There was a certain subdued quality in his manner tonight, but what the Saudis had to do with Oxford, Richard could not say, so larded had the story been with complicated self-justifications and assertions of some kind of conspiracy to remove him. Apparently because he was a symbol of all that was civilized and moderate within the department's staff. And why would they bother with him anyway? Historical Architecture was hardly their beef. So to speak.

At least Tariq was nowhere to be seen, Richard thought, which took some of the pressure off having to socialize.

When they sat down to eat, it was a no-nonsense meal in the kitchen, as if he were family. He watched Mrs. Begum's quick but gentle placement of the various saucepans straight onto cork mats on the scrubbed pine. He could recall Audrey with the silver chafing dishes his mother insisted on, banging them down on the table so hard that their contents sometimes erupted onto the tablecloth.

Mrs. Begum served her husband first, then him, with a generous mound of rice and curry, just as he'd hoped. Once he began to eat he discovered that it helped with the cravings, and the headache. So he kept on eating, and Mrs. Begum, pleased, kept on serving him, until, looking at his plate which was as full as when he'd started, he felt as if he were going to slip into a coma.

When she saw that he had stopped, finally defeated by the never-ending food mountain before him, she sent him back to the sitting room along with her husband, flapping a dismissive hand at his token attempts to help clear the table.

Richard's head was pounding, and his stomach was uncomfortably full. Dr. Choudhury, who did in fact look older than he'd ever seen him, was now expanding upon his poor health and the stresses of fatherhood.

Mrs. Begum joined them, and though her hands were constantly occupied with the contents of her large silver tray and its leaves and powders, she chatted away, persuading him to try some paan. He refused the sweetened packages that she was making for her husband but did accept a few fragments of betel nut and chewed them diligently. They were almost tasteless, and hard work initially, but less than a minute later, he felt a pleasant buzz in his limbs and, for a blessed half-hour after, a measure of relief from his headache. Good stuff, although having seen Mrs. Begum's reddish teeth and maroon gums, he had refused a second helping. About the only thing he had refused, though.

It was late enough for him to make his excuses, but he kept sitting there, accepting cups of tea and mangoes—hoping for some word, some sign from Dr. Choudhury or his wife, that one or the other was going to resume the conversation about Rohimun. Or some kind of hint, at least, of current troubles, future plans.

He even followed Mrs. Begum out to the kitchen at one point, on the pretext of helping her to carry out the heavy tray, in the hope that something more would be said, even a passing comment. But nothing. The photos had been cleared away from the kitchen table as if they had never been.

## Twenty-five

ONLY AN HOUR after going to bed early, Rohimun awoke, a pulse beating heavily between her legs. The sixth hot night in a row. She slid out of her sleeping bag and off the great bed, pushing her hair back from her face, but it still lay along her back like a wool blanket; she wanted a glass of refrigerated water, a cool shower. But the builders had turned off the water and power yesterday for some reason. She couldn't wash, couldn't have a cold drink, was too hot and wakeful to go back to sleep.

A breeze stirred through the open window, balmy and warm. The river. She'd been in the gardens at night: surely walking down the front lawn to the river was not that different.

She pulled her duffel bag out from under the bed and found a towel, her flip-flops, the toiletry bag, and the thinnest *salwar* Mum had packed—a double layer of creamy muslin. Why shouldn't she get out? Four days solid she'd been cooped up inside. At first, because she'd been so rattled by Richard Bourne's visit, she'd really tried to keep a low profile. But then, because of the increase in her productivity, she'd been painting from dawn to dusk and hadn't cared where she was.

But now she'd started to recall being back in Simon's flat: the endless weekends where they never went outside, their dirty clothes piled in a corner of the bedroom, the depression in the plasterboard near the front door where he'd punched the wall. What would Richard Bourne think of someone like Simon? Probably be great mates, with their posh accents. Probably went to school together or something, maybe with Richard a few years ahead.

He had looked so peaceful sleeping, and when he'd first woken, his eyes had opened wide, staring into hers as if in surprised recognition. His pupils, clearly visible in the dim light against light-colored irises (blue? green?) had expanded rapidly, as if he'd been dreaming of some bright sunlit place, and woken into darkness.

Oh, for Chrissake. She bundled up her things and shuffled into the hallway. All was quiet: the hot spell seemed to have reduced the usual creaks and sighs of the Abbey's night-time cooling. She walked down the front stairs, the flip-flops clapping at her heels and her fingertips skimming the smooth banister rail—more like satin than wood.

Outside it was warm but without the stuffiness of the Abbey. Rohimun started over the clipped lawn for the river, stopping at irregular intervals to hop about in search of an errant flip-flop. She would feel better after a dip, and she could wash her hair.

---

AFTER ANOTHER HOUR of desultory post-dinner conversation and even more tea and some snacks, Richard was a man in pain. The betel nut had worn off, and the headache had returned worse than before and was making his vision shimmer so that Dodi and Diana above the mantel seemed to be following him with their mournful dead eyes: watching, waiting, for him to do something.

It was almost midnight when he left Windsor Cottage, feeling as if he had been run over by a steamroller and then somehow overinflated, with lamb ghosh and rice and dahl and rice and chicken korma and rice and green onion salad and pakhoras and onion bahjees. And mango. And more sweet milky tea. God, he couldn't bear to think about it.

His skin crawled with nicotine cravings, and he had to stop himself from breaking into a jog as he walked down the front path and closed the garden gate. At the car, he wrenched open the glovebox and pulled out its contents looking for cigarettes, hoping without hope that some long-forgotten second pack was hiding in there.

---

ROHIMUN ONLY RELUCTANTLY decided to get out when her shivering had become continuous: she must have been in the water half an hour at least. She scrambled onto the stone steps and stood awkwardly to towel and dress, her body leaden and cold, missing the river's buoyancy. But she felt fresh and clean, and not at all tired.

Without the restriction of underwear, the muslin top and pants were cool and airy against her skin. She wrapped the towel around her head, and her hair hung heavily down her back, its dripping ends brushing against her bottom as she walked up the slope to the Abbey. Her restlessness and claustrophobia were gone, and her fingers itched for dawn, to hold the paintbrush, to start mixing white spirit into the yellows so they would go on as a thin, watery wash, like a beam of morning sunlight.

By the time Rohimun had paced up to the Abbey's great main door, she was warm again. She stopped there, reluctant to go straight into the black, airless interior, but also wanting to clarify her thoughts about the painting before she headed upstairs.

She unwound the towel from her hair. In the toiletry bag somewhere was an elastic. She wove her hair into a loose plait, swinging her hair to her side to continue plaiting when she could no longer reach behind. She hadn't done this in months, except for that last night in London: Simon had hated her plait, called it low-rent ethnic, to go with a sari and cardigan in the high street.

In the painting, the figure and its landscape were static and the rose hovered stilly. It was only the hair that was active, powerful, dynamic. A force of nature? Of womanhood or sexuality? Or maybe it was freedom. Her scalp crawled at the memory of the weighty chignon that was Simon's preferred dress-up style for her, so tight it was an effort to blink. And then there'd been the patronizing advice of the women in his clubby London crowd, to get her hair straightened or to crop it, telling her she was too short to carry that much hair, that it made her look like Cousin Itt.

She remembered Mum plaiting her hair, could almost feel her fingers, her voice telling her to stop wriggling, that it was her one beauty. And Bai pulling on it at school, saying she didn't need to get a paintbrush, she had one already. When she reached the ends, she slipped the elastic over the plait then squeezed it out so that it left a pattern of drops on the moonlit flagstones. Plaiting it wet like this, it would take two days to dry, but it would be a cool line down the middle of her back while she painted, and a connection to the past that, for once, she was happy to have.

She would paint the hair wilder, she thought, as she ran up the stairs: each flying lock thick and solid, but also more snaky and sinuous. Hair with muscle and movement, rather than shine: Medusa, rather than a shampoo commercial.

---

BY THE TIME Richard pulled up in front of the Lodge, the clock read a quarter past midnight. The options, of a half-hour drive to the nearest motorway service station to buy some smokes, or letting himself into the Lodge and trying to sleep in that bloody Batman sofa bed, were equally unattractive. There was no way he could sleep feeling like this. He couldn't even sit comfortably in the car. A small, painful burp escaped. He was Monty Python's Mr. Creosote after that last fatal wafer. He had to get out, get some fresh air.

Outside the car, the air was pleasantly warm, and there was a soft homogeneity about the country darkness, entirely different from London's busy evenings, where the night was continually displaced by streetlights, car lights, shop windows.

He put his keys in his pocket and started to walk, moving off the gravel and away from the house as soon as he could so he wouldn't disturb anyone, breathing deeply in an effort to clear his head. After the low-ceilinged clutter of the Choudhurys' cottage, the flat silent fields, punctuated by mature oaks, seemed gigantic and simple and dignified, like Norman churches or concrete sports stadiums. His eyes adjusted to the dark, and even the headache seemed to lift a little. Jesus, he hoped that was the worst of it. He had given up before, but never cold turkey from the pack a day that he had crept up to over the last twelve months. The thought of another day like this gave him the horrors.

Going this way, there was only one field between him and the Park proper, and he began to walk diagonally across it, long grass swishing noisily against his legs, punctuated by the intermittent scutter of a rabbit or rat in the hedgerows, disturbed by his regular strides. He should be heading directly for the Abbey. What was to be done about the girl, Rohimun Choudhury? Or was it Begum? He'd assumed too much already. She couldn't stay at the Abbey indefinitely: that much was clear. Dr. Choudhury of all people must be aware that it was only a matter of weeks now before Henry and Thea moved back in. And the disappearance of the photos once Choudhury came home, the absence of discussion of their middle child, did not bode well for her father allowing her home anytime soon. Surely there was some way he could help, a reason for her to need him.

The idea of pilgrimage came back to him: how it was seen as more pious to journey by foot, and to travel lightly as a sign of one's detachment from material things; how the most zealous, or perhaps those most in need of redemption, would go great distances barefoot, or even on their knees. Giving up smoking was certainly a penance. But where was he travelling to?

A dark presence loomed ahead: the Abbey. He paused, trying to orient himself. It must be the western wall. The rose garden should be close by. When he thought of her, he had several images now. There were the photos taken before he knew her: a cheeky, happy schoolgirl with her brother, a resentful overdressed teenager. And then his own memories: her flying run as she left the exhibition with her brother, the fierceness of her expression as she half lay on him with the palette knife, her hair falling over his face and chest. And the woman in the painting, communing with the gigantic rose as it shed golden light over her visage.

He followed the yew hedge that marked one side of the sunken rose garden, one of his favorite places. He stepped through the Romanesque archway and stood amongst the bushes. He could just make out the garden's four quarters, separated by little clay channels and a central, circular depression, recently excavated: a Celtic cross design, he recalled Henry saying. Henry and his ghosts. Was Henry's ghost sleeping? He thought of the ghost stories they used to scare each other with as children, while their mother wandered, alone and lonely, through the galleries and halls.

Had Mother left an impression here, her misery a vibration that had sunk into stone and wood, flags and threadbare carpets? Or had all trace of her disappeared when she'd been taken to London for treatment, a wraith even before she'd departed. He'd tried to hold on to her the morning she'd left in the car. Her sickly nicotinic sherry-sweetness had been almost tangible in the air, but her thin, narrow palms, the soft pebbled tweed of her skirt, had slipped through his fingers, impossible to grasp. Even now he could see the flash of her pale nape, between coiffed hair and collar, as she turned into the interior of the taxi. His father's hearty falseness. "Mummy'll be back soon. When she's well. Who's for a game of checkers?"

He'd run up to her room then and seen her hairbrushes and scent bottles gone from the dressing table, with only circles of dust to mark their passing. The wardrobe half empty, her best coat gone from its special hanger, and the empty sherry bottles cleared away. That afternoon he and Henry had fought hard and bloodily in the stable yard. Henry still had the scar from that fight: a small chunk taken out from between his eyebrows, courtesy of one of the garden stakes they had been lunging with. But Richard carried no mark from that day. Nothing at all.

As he left the rose garden, the wall of the Abbey was before him, and he rested his hand on the stonework. He was near enough to see the green room's windows now, glassily blank, dark as any of the others. Was Rohimun asleep? Here he was, under her window like some minstrel lover. All he needed was some particolored tights and a lute.

He felt no closer to knowing what to say to her, despite so much having changed since last week, at least from his perspective. And this business of the media.

He froze as a window squeaked open above him. There was a clatter, then something hit his shoulder, fell to his feet, and he heard her voice, low and clear, "Shit."

He touched his shirt and his fingers came away wet; crouched down and found a paintbrush. He shook it a couple of times over the grass and set off for the main entrance, making no effort to tread softly on the gravel. He wasn't sneaking up back stairs anymore.

He was halfway up the main stairs when he heard her coming, saw her flying down the treads in loose white pants and a tunic of some fabric so light that it caught the air and floated around her as she moved. She hadn't seen him though, so he cleared his throat in warning, and she gave a small cry and stopped, gripping the balustrade.

"Who's there?"

"It's me, Richard Bourne," he said, some of the old Blimp awkwardness creeping back. "You dropped your brush." He held it out to her.

"Oh." After a small hesitation, she came forward and snatched it out of his fingers. "Jesus Christ."

"Sorry. I didn't mean to frighten you." He leaned toward her a little, although he didn't intend to. "Rohimun Choudhury. Ah, Begum."

She stared back at him levelly, beginning to catch her breath. "Choudhury."

He fought down the urge to apologize again. "I just wanted you to know I didn't realize you were Dr. Choudhury's daughter. I've just been at your parents' for dinner."

Rohimun blinked and broke her gaze. When she spoke again, she seemed less certain. "Who told you?"

Was she curious, or angry? "Mrs.—your mother. She wants you home, I think."

"It's Dad that's not so keen, yeah. But things are getting better." She seemed to be trying for a matter-of-factness that didn't quite come off. "They just don't know what to do with me."

"How can you paint at this hour?"

"I wasn't. I had some brushes on my windowsill to dry. I knocked them over, opening the window wider for more air. So, don't worry, no oil paint on your tiles."

"Henry'll be relieved." He almost felt like the intruder once more. "Though he would've been even happier if he'd been able to find his ghost."

"Is that what he thinks I am?" she said, watching her fingers bounce off the brush's bristles, then painting her out-turned palm.

"He was very excited: wanted to call the BBC, conduct midnight tours."

She half smiled, thank god. He should leave while she felt at ease.

"I'll head off now." He hesitated, not wanting to imply lack of faith in her family. "If you need anything, if things change and you need to get away, or get back to London, you can call me." He dug in his wallet for a business card, and held it out, but she didn't take it. "The phone in the main hall: it's working."

"I think it'll be alright now, yeah."

He started to walk downstairs, then turned. She hadn't moved, a pale wraith with the dark line of her plait over one shoulder. "I'm here all weekend, in the Lodge. And I'll be back next weekend as well."

She was silent, and he cursed the many possibilities for misunderstanding.

"Perhaps it will all be sorted out soon."

"I wouldn't count on it."

"Well, goodnight then. Sleep well."

"Yeah."

## Twenty-six

TARIQ WOKE ON Friday morning, headachey after a late night doing duty visits for Mum and Dad in the Oxford community, thinking that he was back in Libya, in the Tajura barracks. Perhaps it was the narrowness of his single bed, or the unusual warmth of the morning sun. He'd left the curtains open on the little dormer window last night, and now a hot square of sunlight fell across the red and white of his duvet cover.

The sunlit square lay centerd over his chest, with the shadow of the window's lattice forming a plus-sign directly over his heart, like the cross-hairs on a rifle. Or the old cross of Saint George that the Crusaders used to wear. He frowned. As an Islamist he should have thought Invaders, not Crusaders. But all that seemed so distant now. What difference did it really make? Was he a traitor or a martyr? Anglo or Desi? He stretched his arms above his head and grasped the vertical bars of the bed head. Gay or a criminal pervert? Tomayto, tomarto.

He tried to feel relief that he was not in Libya anymore, that those days were over forever. But the sick Tajura feeling, of being trapped, of living a lie, persisted. He got up, looked out the window. Blue sky, rolling green hills, no one in sight. A good day to get out of the house, get some fresh air, do a bit of exercise, think coolly and rationally, make some plans. Put his life in order. The chaos of uncontrolled feelings and impulsive acts must be avoided at all costs. How he would love to grab some of Mum's samosas and stay out till evening.

Things had been building up in the last few days, ever since the dinner party at the Lodge. Mum had been perky and busy, no longer so preoccupied with Munni's marital future and how to talk Dad around. It could only mean one thing: that that problem was on the way to being solved. And there was only ever one Desi solution for a daughter in trouble.

He drummed his fingers on the windowpane. Who on earth could Mum have fixed on? No one within the community would have Munni now. Surely not some opportunist from the old country, ready to marry anyone for a visa? If that was the case he would stop it. Take her away, back to South Africa, as he had promised. He was never going to let her down, not be there for her, again.

Stair treads creaked, followed by the tink and clink of crockery carried, and he froze. If Mum thought Munni was sorted, that meant she would now have the time and energy to devote to him. He threw on some clothes, padded quickly to the bathroom and slid the bolt across, just in time to hear her voice on the landing, using his pet name.

"Abu, are you awake? I have chai for you. Your father is in his study. I am on my own downstairs."

Tariq made a non-committal noise and splashed water vigorously.

"Abu-u-u." Mum's voice was at the bathroom door, as soft and sweet as sugar. "When you are ready. I will wait for you-u-u. I do not mind."

He was trapped. If she'd been head of Jamat-al-Islami, the US would be under Sharia law by now. Not to mention every American adult married off. He stared grimly into the mirror, then unlocked the door and stuck his head out.

"I will just wait here with your chai. It is no trouble . . . Oh, Abu, I did not mean to interrupt your washings. And you have not shaved."

"Alright Amma, just give me a minute, yeah? I'll shave and then I'll have a cup in the kitchen with you. Alright?" He could see it now: cup after cup, lots of arm pats and allusions to his single state, segue-ing into whatever secret stash she had of matchmaking CVs and photos of Desi girls in saris. "Then I've got to go out, yeah. I'm meeting someone."

She patted his arm with her free hand, and smiled up at him. "My handsome son."

Jesus Christ. He'd forgo the shave and the samosas and head straight out after the chai, one cup only. Perhaps he'd see Denny down by the river.

It took half an hour for Tariq to escape to the Park. Losing the samosas was a small sacrifice in the circumstances, and he appreciated Mum's strategic vision: he would have to come back to eat. She'd never needed Napoleon to tell her that her family marched on their stomachs.

Treetops tossed messily and wisps of cloud morphed as quickly as smoke, in a strong and noisy breeze that it tired him to walk against. *Fitna*, chaos, his cell leader had called a state of mind like this: roiling in confusion, pushed in every direction, prey to every desire, and a sin in itself, as the Qur'an makes clear. He let the wind push him downhill through the Park until he found himself in a sheltered spot near a bend in the river: a miniature oasis of quiet and calm.

The water was shallow here, and so clear that he could see the flicker of small fishes, throwing their shadows onto the pale sand beneath them. The shadows were easier to see than the fish themselves, which were almost transparent, less than half an inch long and seemed to be in constant, frantic motion. His own shadow above them caused a sudden flurry into hiding, and it was some time after he'd sat down, peeled off shoes and socks and started to think seriously about taking off his t-shirt, before they returned.

The drowsy heat of this sheltered spot, the glare of sunlight, took him back to Libya. Long days in the desert on some pointless sentry or picket duty where, squatting hard up against a boulder or wall for its sliver of shadow, he had spent minutes, maybe hours, watching the comings and goings of the ants at his feet, rather than the middle and far distance of those sweeping rocky vistas. The sun there had been so bright that the ants' shadows were easier to spot than the light grey of their segmented bodies and almost invisible legs. Sometimes, back then, full of the *shaitan* doubt, he had felt that their busy forays along established paths contained the answer to all his questions. Such purpose and unity. The ants never faltered, never departed from their own highways except to rush blindly and furiously to attack his idly stirring foot, with no thought for themselves. Why couldn't he surrender, submit to the will of Allah, the call of Jihad that seemed to have galvanized and fulfilled everyone around him?

As his training continued, week after week, he developed a flinching distaste for the perpetual shouting of orders and replies, and the webbing for his ammo-pack and radio that had rubbed a painful blister between his right shoulder and collarbone. Most of all, he hated the heavy, awkward Kalashnikov that he was expected to take everywhere, on every trip, every exercise. It burnt his hands if he handled it unwarily on picket and seemed to need as much carrying and cleaning and changing as a newborn.

He became known for volunteering for the solitary boredom of picket: anything to get out of barracks, away from the tasks at which he never did well, and his fellow trainees, whom he had come to loathe. Though it was also true that this gigantic, mutable desert sky, the scurrying ants, made more sense than anything that happened on Tajura's parade ground. What was wrong with him? Where was the sense of ecstatic purpose, of coming home, that had filled him at the Oxford mosque less than a year ago?

Then Robbie had arrived: a professional soldier, with all the no-bullshit, take-the-piss humor of a Special Forces NCO turned mercenary to help train Quaddafi's foreign guests. The other men hated Robbie on sight. He was an infidel, of course, but also a professional who made no secret of his opinions of the college dropouts, taxi drivers and mobile-phone salesmen that he'd been given to train.

In those first few days after Robbie's arrival Tariq felt, in his presence, as self-conscious and awkward as a teenager. Even more disturbingly, he began to see their group with Robbie's eyes: not as the Mujahedeen they wanted to be, but as the men they were—the

G.I. Joe fantasies of short-man Shahin, the pretension of Jamal's ostentatiously extended *salat*, and the bullying clinginess of Ali and Mohammed's "voluntary" scripture study group.

Through Robbie's occasional sharp exchanges with their Libyan superior officers, Tariq recognized the contempt they had for their group: men from the West who were so materially fortunate but so ignorant, not even speaking the language of the Prophet, and so ready to betray their own country. So much for the *ummah*, the international brotherhood of Islam. Here, Tariq and the other trainees were more foreign, more outsiders, than they had ever been in England.

One day soon after Robbie had arrived, they were sent out at dawn on a desert training exercise. This kind of thing had already happened often enough to feel drearily familiar: struggling to understand the orders given in Italian or Arabic; the feelings of failure, thirst and bone-aching tiredness; and the petty sniping between members of the group trying to recover their dignity.

When they were finally allowed to return to camp, Tariq and the others piled into a jeep driven by Robbie, with Tariq scoring the front passenger seat. "Fucking towel-heads," someone in the back muttered, but no one responded. Tariq jammed his cap down over his face and shut his eyes against a headache that seemed to be trying to escape the confines of his skull.

About halfway back to the barracks, Robbie pulled over at an ancient stone reservoir that Tariq had seen before. A perfect square of semi-dressed, mortared stone, filled almost to the brim with water, its palmetto corners dated it back to the Fatimids. Dad would have been pleased that he'd remembered that. An old shepherd and a teenage conscript were crouching in its shadow, next to a large bundle of bloodstained hessian, covered in flies. Robbie jumped out of the jeep, tossed a folded tarp from the back toward the boy, and told everyone to get out and cool off in the water.

Tariq had climbed out gingerly, his head feeling like it was splitting. Some argument seemed to have started in the back of the jeep. Something about the exact protocol for *wudu*, washing: the whole complex of rules and injunctions and *fatwas* laid down by the Prophet and the centuries of scholars who came after him, about the great importance of proper, godly cleanliness and how it was achieved.

Ali and Mohammed, speaking with the dropped eyes and half-smiles of the morally superior, seemed to have reached a consensus that *wudu* was not possible in standing water used by animals. Tariq glanced at the water, dark and sparkling in the midday sun. Its beauty hurt his eyes, and he closed them for a second. What a joke. Nitpicking dogma even in the desert.

"Come on, lads, it's not an order," Robbie said, seeming to recognize the inevitable. "Swimming's optional, orright?" He pointed at the bloodstained pile. "Make yourselves useful: that's our dinner there!"

Only then did the men slowly begin to unfold themselves from the various tortured positions they had taken to fit onto the vehicle, and climb down. The old shepherd and the boy started to drag the hessian bundles toward the jeep. They turned out to be goat carcasses, and Tariq began to heft the first blood-soaked bundle to throw it into the back of the jeep. But the fizzing flies, the smell and limp weight of the meat made him gag almost immediately. This place was even hotter than where they had been, the glare off the tarmac unbearable. He just made the jeep and, after dropping the carcass, staggered away, feeling cold sweat prickle his forehead and back. The ground swung beneath his feet, and he fell to his knees, the sand moving to meet him. But a steadying hand grasped his shoulder.

"Come on then, mate." Robbie hooked a hard hand under his right armpit, lifted him onto his feet and propelled him into a staggering run toward the reservoir. "Got a bit of heatstroke there. In you hop."

Tariq crashed into the hot stone of the reservoir wall, but could do no more. As he started to slide downward, hands hoicked him up and over the side and into the water. It burnt like ice. He sank, gasped, swallowed water, could not rise, and a moment later felt the explosion of another body entering the water, a forearm across his chest and under his chin, pulling him onto his back, and then his own face clearing the water.

His eyes shut reflexively as he faced up into the burn of the sun, Robbie's voice coming to him as if from miles away.

"Be the first fucking time I've lost a soldier in the desert from drowning, mate!"

Robbie helped him get out, took off his own wet shirt and draped it over Tariq's head and shoulders, and walked him to the jeep. The others, covered in flies, were sitting in two drooping rows on top of the tarped, stinking meat. They reminded Tariq of some old newsreel footage of German POWs, waiting to be moved on. Or was it French resistance fighters, or Jewish partisans? He couldn't remember.

All the way to the cookhouse, then the barracks, Robbie's naked torso was in Tariq's peripheral vision, the spray of blue tattoos across his chest and shoulders heightening the freckled silver of his skin.

After lights out, Tariq went to Robbie in the transport yard, and Robbie ran his hands across his shoulders and back and down his buttocks, and pulled him close to kiss deeply, his erection pressing against Tariq's thighs. No pretence that this was accidental touching or some kind of furtive shower-room fuck due to circumstances, necessity. No muttering of *Al-darurat tubih al-mahzurat*: necessity overrides the prohibition. Full eye contact, pleasure and desire openly expressed. No shame, no excuses.

The little fishes were bolder now: coming right up to the margins of the water, only inches from where Tariq's bare toes rested on the sand. What did he look like to them, refracted through the water and their fishy eyes? Something beyond their imaginings. Or perhaps not so unfamiliar in their collective memory: some presence, alien and unknowable that appeared on the margins of their world, invading then retreating at unpredictable intervals.

So, where to from here? He was home again, Munni was safe for now, and perhaps one day he would be able to tell her the truth. But Mum would not be put off forever: he had seen his own CV, the studio shots she'd dug out from years ago, heard the allusions to how nice it was to have her son home to look after them in their old age. And to look after his sisters. A low blow.

Marriage, even the kind he had envisaged in the past as tolerable—a traditional wife kept at his parents' to look after them as they aged, and whom he would visit occasionally—seemed unbearable, impossible, now. He thought of that woman, Henry's wife, whom he'd met at that *gora* dinner party last Sunday. Look what happened when a wife wasn't satisfied by her husband. And Henry wasn't even gay.

He would go for a wander, see if he could find Denny. The woody area just upriver was where Denny liked to chill out, or hide from Colin. Before setting off he shaded his eyes and scanned the area around and behind him, looking for anything unusual, any activity, then realized what he'd been doing and smiled wryly. Soldier Tariq. Just went to show, some things did sink in.

As soon as he was within the first group of pines, he saw Denny lying in a clearing, messing with his penny whistle, a joint drooping from his lip. He was wearing grubby Indian pants and a leopard-print T-shirt that had seen better days.

Denny raised a lazy arm in greeting. "Hey, man. Hot, innit?"

"Yeah." Tariq squatted next to him, picked up a twig with a pine cone attached and rolled it between his fingers.

"How about a dip? Me dad's asleep in the greenhouse."

Tariq glanced at the water, cool and dark under the pines. Why not.

## Twenty-seven

THEA STARED INTO the mirror in her ensuite, searching for what was still desirable. Or at least fixable. She avoided the softness at her jawline, the beginnings of pigmentation under her eyes, and focused instead on dark eyebrows winging back to smooth temples. But there the grey was just beginning to show—she must make an appointment.

Her hair was wound and pinned into a tight shiny knot at her nape, controlled with a mist of spray. Her lips, primed and glossed, gleamed symmetrically—mustn't overdo it, we're not in London. Thea didn't look into her eyes, tried to concentrate on detail: mascara, eyeliner, eyeshadow. Did her eyelids look crêpey, overdone? Perhaps . . . no. It would take too long to go back to scratch, deal with her naked face again.

Pip had had her face done already, at only forty, and her breasts. But she was divorced, children off her hands, making a fresh start. Thea slid on her wedding band. So plain: it had been Henry's mother's, and she'd never liked it. It almost disappeared when she put on the emerald-cut engagement diamond that she'd chosen, its surrounding brilliants sparkling under the bathroom's halogen. The Cartier ring, from her family, so classic with its three bands of silver, gold and rose gold, went onto the first finger of her other hand. Then a single strand of pearls, to throw light onto the face, give textural contrast with her cream linen sheath, and hide loose skin at the neck.

She rolled one fat sphere between finger and thumb. But then she saw the back of her hand in the mirror, its greyish web of veins and scattering of age spots (*fleurs de la mort*, her half-French nonna used to call them) and the bones of her wrist, all highlighted by the necklace's silky, nacreous glow.

Thea met her reflected eyes, filled with dread. She flicked off the overhead halogens, but now, underlit by the sidebar fluorescents, her head looked hollowed and empty. She mustn't be late for her brunch date: so late already, so much time wasted. With an effort she shifted her gaze to the mirror's edge. Her favorite photo of Jackie was there, a black-and-white two-inch square tucked into a corner of the mirror's bevelled frame as if casually, so that anyone coming in would see it as a temporary and unimportant thing. Jackie O, Jacqueline Onassis, formerly Kennedy, nee Bouvier. Guinevere to Jack's Arthur, the perfect fairytale, then disaster and death and finally betrayal with the ugly, successful foreigner, the Greek Lancelot. Onassis's Beast to her Beauty.

Thea picked up the photo and brought it close, tilting the image into and out of the fluorescents' glare. It was a candid head-and-shoulders shot, the background blurred, as if the photographer had been running to keep pace with Jacqueline Kennedy's rapid shining star. She was gazing beyond the camera, her hair blown about and her collar slightly awry, but her expression was serene, unmoved. Carefree, in Givenchy, Chanel, Cassini. Unworldly, despite the worldliness, the infidelity and publicity. Centered calmly in the storm's eye. Immortal, eternal.

Thea's eyes flicked back to her own reflection: the constructed, expensive, temporary perfection of her hair and face, tissue-thin over the deterioration beneath—lines pouching, darkening. And the wreckage within.

Right now she couldn't bear to leave this room. Henry used the family bathroom, thank god. Resolutely avoiding her reflection, she turned toward the glass shelving that bisected one wall and ran a fingertip over its precious bottles, casks and jars. The best of everything was in here: La Mer for smooth skin, Visine for clear eye-whites, Chanel primer and lipstick for the full, unlined mouth of the twenty-year-old. Forever young, if she stayed in here.

If she stepped out she would see her bedroom, where last Sunday night, stinking of alcohol and vomit, she had fallen into Tariq's arms, thought that he was falling into hers. She shuddered, remembering her hungry grasping, his detachment and disgust. How could she leave? Where could she go?

She realized that she was gripping Jackie's photo with both hands, and made herself put it down before it creased or tore. Why hadn't she arranged to go to the beautician instead of brunch with the girls? She just wanted to be out of the house before Richard got up. She'd claimed a headache last night, gone to bed early to avoid the pain of his arrival, but then could not sleep. He'd let himself in late, must have been after one a.m, fresh evidence of his lack of interest in her, and had apparently declined Henry's scheme of shopping with the boys, in favor of a lie-in. But he would be up soon.

Hiding behind Elizabeth Arden's Red Door Spa, face masked, eyes closed, seemed infinitely more appealing than faux jollity with her friends. Too late now, she just had to make the best of it. Get out of here. She smoothed her hair, smoothed it again. Now it looked too smooth. She glanced down at the little photo, thought about wearing dark glasses. But she would feel more naked when she had to take them off. If only she had chosen Red Door. If only Richard hadn't come to visit again so soon—had cancelled like he always used to, given her time to adjust. To heal.

She picked up her handbag, a baby-soft calfskin Hermès, and pulled out the contents, lining them up on the countertop one by one. She must be sure, be prepared. Eyedrops. Tissues, change purse, card holder, keys, blue-eye talisman, photos of the children, perfume (Yves Saint Laurent Rive Gauche, the fragrance of youth), panty liner (couldn't remember when her period was due, all over the place lately), headache pills (mustn't take too many), phone (what if Richard called), make-up bag: Chanel Rouge Noir lipstick, pressed powder (pure tinted cornstarch from Guerlain), Chanel Morning Dew nail polish, YSL Touche Éclat concealer, so good for older skin. Everyone said so. She zipped up the little make-up bag, stroked its plastic exterior. Eyedrops. Tissues. Change purse. A ticking started in her temples. Time was passing. She had to go.

Her chest hurt; she tried to breathe more slowly. How could she escape without being seen? Jackie's image lay on the countertop, youthfully serene. For a moment their eyes met. Thea snatched it up and reached awkwardly, inside and down her own neckline, to tuck the photo into her left bra cup. A talisman, stuffed into her underwear like Zia used to do with tissues, god help her.

Thea packed the countertop items back into the bag and shuffled quickly out of the bathroom, eyes averted from the bed, and into the passage, down the stairs, out the front door, to the garage, find the car keys. Keys. She felt sick at the thought of having forgotten her keys, and tried to remember to breathe out. There they were, in the bottom of the bag. She fumbled and almost dropped them. What if Richard got up now and saw her like this?

The Mercedes flashed its lights, making her jump, then flashed again. Damn, she'd re-locked it. Her hands shook, and she kept missing the button. In the cement-floored quiet of the garage, she could hear her heart pounding like a warning, counting down, faster and faster. The keys fell to the floor, and she cried out in fright, looking furtively at the garage door, open to anyone. She would never escape, never get out. She bent to grab the keys, but bile rose into her throat, and she hesitated, dropped the Hermès on the floor next to the keys and stumbled outside.

She leaned over, hands on knees, and retched once, one useless violent heave with no result, sweat prickling her back and upper lip, eyes closed against the sun's public glare. Anybody could see her. She couldn't stay here, had to find shelter, privacy.

What was that sound? Was that Henry's car coming back early?

God. She took off in a clumsy run around the side of the house, toward the back garden, her heels twisting in the gravel. Her eyes had filled with the effort of trying to vomit, and her vision blurred and stung. No tissues, no bag.

The garden sloped down away from the Lodge, and Thea followed it, weaving sharply between a series of prickly bushes. Hot tears were sliding down her cheeks now, and she placed a hand over her pearls, with some vague recollection that salt water was bad for them.

If Richard got up and found no one at home, he would probably just go down to the pub for lunch. But what if, before he left, he looked out of one of the Lodge's back windows? She must get out of sight. She kept moving, her heels sinking into the turf, following the downhill gradient as the vegetation around her became larger and less cultivated, and weeds whipped and caught at her stockings.

One heel sank deeply, and she tripped forward and almost fell. Her right shoe, handmade, handstitched, a present from Henry, was buried in mud. She bent, breathing hard, and tried to wriggle it out with her fingers. It would not budge. When she looked up, the noisy glitter of the river was right before her, inches from her toes, and she stared uncomprehendingly. She'd never been down this far before, hadn't realized it ran so close. Her way was barred.

But she couldn't stay here. She pulled her foot out of the shoe, which remained staunchly upright in the mire. Stupid fucking shoe, she'd get it later. She turned to her left, took a few more crooked steps along the bank, lost the other shoe, staggered forward, then continued more sedately, her stockinged feet sliding a little in the cool mud and cooler water. Fuck the shoes. The pull of her Achilles tendons from walking flat-footed, and the mud's soft, spreading pressure between her toes, became oddly comforting, as if she had come down here just for this: to get dirty, make mud pies or something. Had there been a river near where she grew up? She couldn't remember.

Thea was still hot and sweaty, but a little calmer and, squinting ahead, could see a patch of dark vegetation. She made her way along the river's edge, feeling like someone marooned, or maybe an explorer.

Her legs were beginning to ache, her stomach too, and when she came to one of the larger trees, with a mess of roots forming a natural seat, she squatted awkwardly, sat down and leaned back. She could feel the roughness of the bark through the linen of her dress, but it wasn't really unpleasant, rather like sitting on wickerwork. She stretched her legs out in front of her and saw without surprise that her silk stockings were shredded and filled with grass seeds. Her feet, still heavy with mud, flopped outwards, making a V through which she could see a sunlit patch of river below. She let her hands rest on the ground at her sides.

It was so quiet she could hear her own breathing, rapid and harsh against the shushing of the river. All that time in the gym: she'd thought she'd been keeping up with the twenty-somethings. That dull, tight pain was back. She bent her head, tried to ignore it. She would just focus on the grass seeds, pick out each one.

Soft murmurs came from the river. She looked past her muddy feet to see Tariq's golden body float into view on the surface of the water. He was on his back, eyes closed, and his palms floated with fingers cupped and pointing upward. The bloom of his sex was visible, against a cushion of black hair just below the surface. She gasped. Magical, supernatural. She instinctively gestured with her fist, index and little fingers extended, against the evil eye. But he did not disappear. Or transform.

He had come for her. Thea stumbled to her feet. The power of her desires had brought him into being. But before Tariq reached the bank, there was a splash as another body dived in and surfaced near him. Thea froze. This man was white-skinned but covered in dark body hair. His face was obscured by long, hippyish locks, with a separate stream of water running off each. He tossed his head to free his face, and she saw with shock that it was Denny Upwey, Audrey and Colin's son.

The men reached for each other in the water. Embraced. Kissed. Tariq's fine fingers in Denny's hair. Thea stood still now, like Lot's wife, unable to look away. They broke apart and swam for the far bank. Denny, broader of build, climbed out first, and turned to give Tariq an arm to pull him up. Thea dodged behind the tree and crouched down, feeling such shame and sorrow that it was a relief to bite her tongue and taste the rusted blood, which had surely come straight from her heart.

They were talking now, in low voices. She couldn't make out the words but she could hear the relaxed tone, the staccato breaks of soft laughter. The smell of cigarettes. How fiercely she suddenly longed for one.

Silence fell across the water. She inched forward on all fours, holding her breath, until she could just see round. There, on the opposite side, above the riverbank, was a figure walking stiffly downhill from the cottage, toward them all, carrying what looked like a shiny metal thermos. Dr. Choudhury? She had a desperate urge to pee.

Were they gone? She looked down to the river itself, her vision blurred with sweat and tears. On the far bank, dappled shadows shifted under the trees. Amongst them, shining against the dull earth, she could just make out two bodies mingling. A few small stones and pieces of leaf rubbish rolled down the slope and into the water, and she crept back around her tree, alone again in this hostile natural world.

------

THEY HAD LEFT eventually, laughing and talking quietly, as relaxed as when they had arrived. It was only she that was different. Stiff with fatigue and filthy, Thea crawled out of her hiding place, but her legs were too cramped to stay upright, so she slid on her bottom down the leaf-mould to the edge of the bank, just stopping in time. She grabbed hold of an overhanging branch and edged first her feet, then her legs, into the river. She could smell herself, sweat and urine and mud, and the shock of the cold water made her wet herself again. Her feet found the bottom, oily and soft, and she knew then that she would sink no further. She let go of the branch and stepped away from the bank, hip-deep, trailing her hands. She was suffused with weariness, cried out, completely empty. Nothing mattered anymore.

Thea cupped her hands and brought water up to her face, ran her hands over her hair, let it trickle down the nape of her neck. She bent her knees and dipped down into the water, up to her neck, and pushed off in a cautious, old-lady breaststroke, toward the center of the river.

She closed her eyes and bobbed under the water for a couple of strokes, enjoying the sensation of holding her breath, moving her face against the water's soft resistance. Then she came up, reached with her feet for the bottom, couldn't feel it and, after a moment of panic, slipped into an awkward sidestroke that by degrees became elongated, leisurely. She hadn't swum like this since she was at school.

When she started to feel cold, she let herself drift back to the bank, to a shell-shaped outcrop a little further down, and climbed out. She pulled the remaining pins out of her bun, and stood enjoying the sensation of looseness and movement on her scalp.

Her dress clung to her, dripping down her legs. When she looked down, it was sheer and she could see, over her heart, Jackie's outward stare. Thea's underwear, a flesh-colored set from La Perla, was not only outlined by the dress but was see-through as well. For a second her hands went to pubis and breasts, then she dropped her arms. Who was she covering for? She strode up the bank and started to walk home.

The sun warmed her back, and she swung her arms, letting their momentum carry her up the hill. When she reached the back garden, she could hear the dogs barking inside, and a man's voice, happily chastising their noise. Feeling as if it were someone else's house, she walked softly to the sitting room's back window and peered in.

Henry was on the floor wrestling with the two Retrievers, brandishing a slipper and yelling over their barks. One of the dogs had hold of his shirttail and was growling and shaking its head, and Henry, in twisting away, had his shirt pulled up to his shoulderblades. How like his sons he was right then, writhing and quick, white skin gleaming against the dim carpet. The two dogs were tumbling on top of him and each other in an effort to take the slipper, and while she watched, they knocked into the Pembroke table and her carefully *dérangé* Abbey drawings fell onto the floor.

From the outside the sitting room looked dark and static, as oppressively full of meaningless objects as a Victorian parlor. Her precious cluster of silver-framed photos, her row of Meissen figurines on the mantelpiece, the stack of fashionable magazines looked like nothing more than pointless obstacles to be negotiated by eager dogs and men. Was it just a trick of the sun blazing on the glass, or was what she was now seeing more real, closer to the true nature of things, than she had seen before? She gripped the windowsill, staring at the puzzle of her own life before her.

The slipper went flying, followed by the yelping dogs, and an occasional table tilted under the onslaught. The china bowl on top slid and fell onto the stone hearth with an audible crack and a waterfall of potpourri. Dogs and man parted, temporarily silenced. With a sudden sadness, Thea realized that the real tragedy of the shattered bowl, her prized Moorcroft ware, was that the rhythm of the joyous game had been broken.

"Shit! *Scheisse!*"

Henry looked worriedly to the far end of the room, where the double doors opened onto the hallway, as if anticipating a judgemental visitor, who, she then realized, was herself.

He had the dogs by the collars now. "Out, maties, out you go before we get caught!" He was running them forward out of the room, almost catching their tails in the slamming door.

Henry came back into the center of the sitting room, but he was different now. He was her familiar Henry, slightly stooped and staring a little absently at nothing in particular, before squatting to replace spilt papers and fallen cushions with much unnecessary patting and shuffling. She felt bereft. Where was that quick, laughing man?

Henry left again and returned carrying a cloth, which he laid on the hearth next to the shattered bowl. He knelt down with his back to her. She guessed that he was picking up the china pieces, but still resented being shut out by the gentle curve of his back. She wanted to see everything. She wanted to see the dogs again, the wrestling, how they brought the room alive and sparked off her husband's bright vitality, unfettered by domestic constraints.

But that was all gone now. She was expected home. The breeze had cooled, and her dress and underwear felt gritty against her skin. She walked around the side of the house, avoiding the gravel of the center path. The water pipes that ran down this side and into the scullery started to vibrate: Henry must be washing his hands downstairs. The television blared faintly from the boys' bedroom, and she thought she could hear Richard's voice in there too. Henry still had the potpourri to sweep up: if she moved now she could avoid explanations and get upstairs. She trotted quickly around the corner to the front of the house, and straight into the dogs.

For once they did not stand off and bark, instead surrounding her and nosing her with quiet intent, as if she were some large but not unfriendly creature that had wandered into their garden from the woodland. Perhaps she smelled different now. Feeling strangely tender, even regretful, she ruffled their ears, getting a lick on the hand in return, then slipped through the front door.

As she tiptoed past the sitting-room doors, she caught a glimpse of her husband, kneeling by the hearth. There was the scrape of a brush and pan. She crept by and sped upstairs.

## Twenty-eight

TARIQ RETURNED HOME before eleven, hair wet and his appetite sharp, in time to placate—and distract—Mum with an offer to drive her to the shops. But he had barely sat down at the kitchen table when his mother's hand smacked him hard across the back of the head.

"Amma! What?"

She slapped him again, so hard that it echoed around the kitchen. "You think your mother is so, so stupid? That I can carry you in my womb for ten months, ten months, and not know what you are thinking, what you are doing, every minute of your life?"

"But what did I—"

His head jarred with the force of another slap, this time on the right side. He felt his eyes begin to water. Her nail-tips had caught on the edge of his ear: Jesus Christ that hurt. He should have known not to interrupt.

"You think, after I gave birth to you, almost dying with the agony, you can stab me in the heart like this?"

He kept his eyes on the scrubbed pine of the kitchen table, resisting the urge to put a protective hand over his ear. Mum sure hadn't lost her touch. And she'd been wearing her rings too. His right ear and the back of his head burnt and prickled. He had a vivid mental picture of a few strips of his skin sitting curled around the raised stones of the eternity ring Dad had bought her when he'd seen Mrs. Darby's.

"You think you are so modern, with your dirty habits? You think I know nothing of what used to happen between the men, out in the fields in my village? You, you *Anglo-Desi* to think that all such things are only invented by you!"

Jesus Christ. Had she seen him with Denny? His stomach dropped.

She started to cry, big gulping sobs, but when he turned his head toward her, she screamed something unintelligible and reached out to slap him again. He fell onto his knees and tried to touch her feet, but she backed away.

"I'm sorry, Amma. I'm sorry, I'm sorry."

She bent to push his shoulder, hard, as if he repulsed her. He felt his face twisting into a grimace, like a child with a skinned knee, his eyes welling up. Anything but this. Not Mum. She walked to the kitchen window, then turned back. He sat on the linoleum, his tears falling now, and stared at the red hem of her sari, at her feet in worn leather sandals, too far away to reach.

"Please forgive me, Amma. Please. I can't bear this." His throat felt like it was closing up, and he choked out the last words. "You know I'm nothing without family."

"Your father, your poor father . . ." Mum took a deep gulping breath, blew it all out and spoke in a tone that was lower but still dripped with anger. "You know nothing of married life, what it is to see all sides of a person. That person is you, their faults are your faults. His sorrows, his pain, are mine also. I know him like I know myself. I know him in all his ways."

She lifted her sari hem to her eyes and wiped them hard. "Your father, you have broken his heart."

It was so quiet in the kitchen now. Tariq could hear the kitchen clock's regular tick, and beneath that the dull accelerating beat of his own heart.

"Your father, you do not understand . . . He came home from the university yesterday. They took his job, you know."

"What?"

"They will pay him still, but that is not . . ." She picked up a large saucepan from the draining board, and Tariq flinched. "He did not even eat his lunch, all his food that I had ready. All this time, when you are out so much, always with your *friend*, he is needing to be with his son, to talk with him. But, no, you have more important things to do. So now, this morning, he goes through the Park to give Munni her tiffin, as his son is out, *again*." She walked to the counter, banged the saucepan into the sink as if she were hammering a nail, and turned on the tap. "He *sees* you." The water roared in, splashing the floor. "He *finds* you . . . with that boy."

Tariq rocked forward and bowed his head to the linoleum. "Oh god."

"He came back, he could not talk, not at first. He could not even eat his food. He said, 'I have nothing now, nothing.'" She gave a series of hiccupping sobs and started to swirl the rice in the saucepan, around and around.

He slowly got to his feet and backed away from her toward the table, feeling old and tired. "Where's Abba now?"

"And Richard Bourne came to dinner last night, while you were in visiting Oxford. For Munni. I am the only one trying to fix this family—I am the only one. You, bloody idiot, you just break it more."

He reached for a chair and sat down at the kitchen table, put his head in his hands. He had ruined everything. He should have just stayed on in South Africa, accepted his exile.

Dad's cup of tea was sitting on the table in front of him. Mum must have made it just before Tariq came back, not put the milk in yet. He pulled it closer and wrapped his hands around its warmth, the way his father would have done. Mum was still at the counter, half turned away, peeling a clove of garlic with her thumbnails. All the comfortable kitchen sounds were there: the hiss of the gas flame under the rice, the fizz and plop of boiling water, the rustle of Mum's sari as she shuffled between sink and stove. Only he was different. Everything had fallen apart, not because he was absent, but because he was here. Here and being himself.

He wished that he was seven again and his biggest worries were the kids at school, or homework neglected. That he could bury his face in Mum's sari, or cuddle up next to Dad on the couch. How had things gotten to this, despite all his efforts to plan and control things? What did that say about his fate, the trajectory of his own life?

He looked down into the cup. Some fine golden specks rested on top of the tea: pollen from the jar of flowers in the middle of the table. He brought his head closer. Although the tea had settled, the fine golden specks continued to move: a quivering, seemingly random dance across the liquid's surface. Brownian motion, he remembered it from school. The pollen's movement was the result of the accumulation of multiple blows from forces too minute to detect, from objects too microscopic to see.

He'd been so careful, until today, only seeing Denny at night or when his parents were busy. Tariq considered the accumulated effect of all the different forces that had led him to the Park, then the river, then Denny. Of being seen at that particular moment, and by his father. Yet that dirty episode last Sunday with a drunken *gora* wife, only meters away from her husband, his parents and a whole roomful of people, had been suspected by no one, spawned no consequences for anyone concerned.

"Amma . . ."

Her wooden spoon smacked down on the table next to his hand, sprinkling rice water onto the tabletop. He jumped and almost spilt the tea.

"*Don't* you think that this stops you from being part of this family, of being a man for this family, for your sisters!" She hissed into his sore ear, her betel-breath hot on his skin. "You *will* marry. You will marry a good girl, if it kills me. If it kills *you*. If you do not, you are no son of mine."

He clutched his cup and stared into its depths. What she wanted was action, not remorse. Mum moved away, and he could hear the rice being stirred vigorously. Even now that they all knew, there was no escape.

"Where's Abba?" He had spoken more loudly than he intended, the sudden clarity of his next step lending strength to his voice.

She stopped stirring, and he realized that she had been expecting him to beg her for more time, or to intercede for him. The realization made him repeat his question.

"Sitting room," she said eventually, then held up her hand, her voice almost soft. "Wait. I will make more tea."

She whisked about and presented him with a small silver tray holding a cup of fresh tea and a roll of paan. He took the tray, and she held the kitchen door open for him to walk through, but he did not hear it close behind him. Of course: Mum would be down the corridor to listen as soon as he was in the sitting room.

When he entered, he could see the top of Dad's head in the wing-back chair that had been swivelled to face the view of the Abbey. He advanced cautiously, put the tray down on the ottoman and went to shut the door. He thought he heard a small, stifled gasp of annoyance from the hallway as he closed it, but could not be sure.

"Abba." He walked to his father's chair, knelt and embraced his ankles, putting his head on his father's feet.

His father said, did, nothing.

"Please forgive me." He kept his head down, felt his father try to pull his feet away, and held on more firmly. "Please, Abba. Please."

There was a silence that stretched on for some time. His father hurrumphed.

"Please, Abba, I know I was wrong. I'm sorry. Please forgive me."

Dad cleared his throat again, blew his nose. He spoke quickly, as if rushing through a prepared speech. "You have cast great shame on this family, great shame: you, the eldest son, the protector of your sisters. And caused great shock and sorrow to your mother. Your devoted mother."

"Please, Abba. Forgive me. I know I am not worthy, as your son, but please . . ." He held on desperately to his father's feet. Tears rose, his voice cracked, but no more words came out.

After some minutes his father spoke. "We are men, made in Allah's image, made to . . . to procreate, to take a wife . . . We have duties . . .

so that we are cared for in our turn . . ." His voice faded to nothing, and he stared out the window again.

Tariq felt adrift. Where was the shouting and beating? Had what Dad saw earlier broken him, on top of what had happened at Oxford? Had he done that to his own father? He sounded so distressed and confused, so lacking in anger. Or direction. Tariq couldn't bear the silence, the sense of multiple sorrows. He opened his mouth to beg for forgiveness again, say something to bring on the necessary beating.

But his father forestalled him with a hand raised, palm upward. "To be a man . . ." he began, but stopped on a slight quaver. "When I was younger than you, I came here, to this country. I was on my own. I knew no one. There was no community in those days. You know the Rhodes then: no one could be married. I had to live in single-men's digs. No one visited me."

His father tucked in his outstretched feet and picked up a silver-framed photo from the side table. Tariq recognized it. It held an old black-and-white photograph of Dad in his then brand-new doctoral robes, arm-in-arm with Clyde Royston, his doctoral supervisor, taken outside the Sheldonian Theatre. It usually sat in pride of place in Dad's study. In the photo, the two men were laughing, heads tilted back, eyes half shut against the sunshine. Clyde had a bottle of champagne tucked under one arm.

"I had no friends. For days I would speak to no one. Your mother did not join me for almost six months. Clyde was like a brother to me, when I had no one else." He rested the photo face-down on his chest and sighed deeply. Then he seemed to recollect himself and jabbed his finger at Tariq.

"*You* were never so alone, never so lonely. *You* have no such excuse."

Tariq stared at his father, wondering when the world had been turned on its head.

"Marriage is a duty, my son. The Qur'an makes that clear. I, er . . . When you are away from home, many things are different. Islam is a compassionate faith, hence the doctrine of necessity. Now, but now, you must do as we all must do."

Tariq swallowed, tried in his surprise to halt himself, but the words and the tears came out in a flood, a rush of feeling and truth as he bent to touch his right cheek to his father's slipper. "I can't, Abba, I just can't. I thought for a long time that I could—it's why I came home—but please forgive me, I can't. I'll never leave you again, I'll be a good son to you, I'll do anything you ask, but please don't ask that of me. Please, I beg you, I can't."

He looked up to see his father staring at him, right hand splayed over the picture's back as it lay across his heart, and there was nothing but truth in both their gazes.

With a rattle of the door handle, Mum swept into the room and fetched up against the ottoman. She stretched her right arm toward her husband and spoke in a strangled voice, part rage, part desperation. "Make him, make him. You *must* make him."

She stepped backward then, as if suddenly horrified by her own temerity.

Keeping a protective hand over the photo, Dad cleared his throat again, in an extended kind of way. "This catarrh, so troublesome. Always when I least expect it."

"As I am the mother of your children, he must, he *must* be made to."

His father gave an excellent imitation of puzzlement, with a slightly defensive edge. "What, what?"

"Your son. He must marry. I have the ceevees. If he does not, he is no longer my son, I am no longer his . . ."

Dad's hand rose up, and Mum stopped with a kind of gasp. Tariq realized that he had been holding his breath and tried to exhale in complete silence. Dad, very deliberately, brought the photo frame to arm's length, looked at it, and placed it onto the occasional table so that it faced out to them all.

The silence continued. Mum did not move a muscle.

"So, you say he must marry?" his father said musingly, as if this was an interesting academic point raised by an undergraduate. "Or, if not, he must leave your home?"

Tariq had a sudden sense of how his father's tutorials must have been conducted, with the leisurely teasing out of arguments and drawing together of threads of reasoning. Plenty of pauses for thinking time. How pleasant to have been in one of his classes. Not that he'd ever wanted to back then.

Dad steepled his fingers and looked pensively at them. No one spoke. Tariq considered breathing, but it seemed like bad luck. Not that there could be anything but one outcome to such a conversation. Asian men married, or they were not men. Asian men married, otherwise their families could not advance in the community, their future was not secure. Everyone had to marry.

His father spoke at last. "Well, that then is a sad conundrum; a number-one Gordian knot that cannot be untied. For you see, Mrs. Begum, whichever way he turns, the boy stands to lose one of his parents forever."

Dad stared at her with such directness that she dropped her eyes and pulled her *pallu* across the top of her head, as if meeting him for the first time.

"For I say to you, wife and mother of my children, that if the boy does marry, then he will no longer be my son." He gave a little dry cough, the lecturer's modest epilogue to an outrageous, revolutionary analysis, and Tariq half expected him to say *quod erat demonstrandum.* Perhaps he had, for Tariq could not quite believe his ears. He looked at his parents for guidance, but their faces were blank, neutral, as if they were now dealing with a situation, with emotions, that had no precedent.

Then his mother raised her head and, almost as soon as she had, she was a whirling dervish of rage and scorn. No man, no head of a family would behave this way, no son would be so ungrateful. No one knew what she went through. This family was a sinking boat, and she was the only one trying to save it. How could they behave as they had? But at the same time, she seemed to know that she had already lost, and why. Something had wakened between her husband and her son that had not been there before, and she knew she could not win against this new alliance.

She disappeared out the sitting-room door. Perfect quiet reigned, although Tariq was still having trouble with his breathing. What force had accomplished this impossible thing, that his parents now knew his true self? That he was not doomed to fight a losing battle against wife and children and be trapped forever?

"Abba?" Tariq whispered, still kneeling.

"Hmm?"

"I was thinking of going to mosque today, in Swindon. For *Jumma*, Friday prayers."

Dad gave no sign of hearing him. Pots banged in the kitchen, louder than usual, and he wondered if he could smell burning, or whether that was his imagination.

His father spoke as if to himself. "Hmm . . . perhaps it would be politic to be *in absentia* for a while." He stood, glanced in the mantel mirror, smoothed his hair, and only then seemed to notice that Tariq was still on the floor. "Get up, get up. Perhaps we will eat in Swindon as well. Make a day of it, as it were."

---

IT WAS MOST soothing for Dr. Choudhury, as a man doubly heartsore, to proceed through the solemn rituals of *wudu* and *salat* in the old Broad Street mosque. He felt as if he had regained a little of the dignity lost in Oxford yesterday. He could see clearly now: to keep clinging on to tenure alone would be unworthy of him, like scrabbling for a toehold in the face of an avalanche.

The head imam came to him afterward, wreathed in smiles, and grasped his hand and elbow in greeting, clearly grateful that, after the unfortunate radical connections of recent years, this mosque was again to be patronized by the community's intellectual elite, its forces for moderation. Dr. Choudhury gave a dignified nod and introduced his son and graciously acknowledged the imam's admiration (partly concealed but obvious enough) of such a fine young man, and an Oxford graduate too. So wonderful to have your son back now. For good? Of course, of course.

A late lunch in one of Swindon's finer Bangladeshi establishments, with a son as tall and good-looking as Tariq, was similarly punctuated by the smiles and greetings and respectful questions of other members of the community. Dr. Choudhury's son has come home. A good boy, going to *Jumma* with his father. What a distinguished pair. He knew how these people thought.

After lunch, they strolled down Cricklade Street to ponder an interesting renovation being carried out on the Gilbert Scott–designed Christ Church, then drifted toward the shops. Dr. Choudhury could not remember a more pleasant afternoon. The slight excess of emotion that he intermittently detected in his son, he put down to similar feelings. What a relief it was to speak what was in one's heart, however obliquely. And that meal had been excellent. He could not recall Tariq wanting to spend so much time with him since he was a teenager.

Relief and pain were enthroned together in his heart. What Clyde had meant, still meant, to him, he had never thought he would be able to say to anyone. And now he saw that same secret pain in his son.

He gave a contented sigh. "To think that I am now a man without a profession. Life is full of surprises." He snuck a glance at his son's face and was pleased to see his remorse.

"I'm sorry, Abba," said Tariq, as he should. "I didn't know. I didn't know that you had enemies there. At the university."

Ah, the love of a son for his father. My enemies are his enemies. That is how it should be.

"My son, there are always enemies. Wherever there is real achievement, there will be those who wish to destroy you."

*Real* achievement. Giving his views on period architecture and interiors for the two Trusts had been no novelty, was simply a continuation of what he had done at Oxford for decades. But at the Abbey, for the first time, he had seen his views translated into reality by workmen using the same labor-intensive, highly skilled techniques that were used four hundred years ago. That had been a revelation. He found himself moved by the immediate beauty of freshly carved wood and cut stone, the fine modest focus of master tradesmen, in a way that publications and higher degrees never had.

It put him in mind of many things. His daughter coming to life again with the brush in her hand. His mother's pleasure in painting and embroidery, which he could only just remember. And the knowledge of his father's increasing bitterness and isolation in his life as a circuit judge, fulfilling his own parents' wishes.

He pulled out his pocket handkerchief to wipe his eyes. "These are number-one villains, you know, these Saudis. Ignorant people, thinking that they can buy anyone and anything with their dirty money. Thinking that their Wahhabis, because they control Mecca and Arafat and the other holy sites, are more truly Islamic than Sunnis in Indonesia or Shiites in Iran or Sufis in India." He flapped his handkerchief in emphasis. "Thinking, as bad as those American Protestants, those Pamelas of the New World, that their wealth itself is virtue rewarded."

Tariq spoke with strong feeling. "They're Muslims, but that's about it, yeah."

"Yes, yes, no better, no worse than any other."

"So, you've left Oxford now, Abba?"

"Yes." He was surprised at how easily he said it. He seemed to have found a measure of philosophy, just forty-eight hours after his exclusion. But the boy could not be expected to take it all in quite so quickly. "There are other things in this life. Art, beauty . . ."

"Those dirty sons of dogs," his son muttered.

Dr. Choudhury coughed in a manner that was only mildly reproving. It was so warming to the muscles of his heart to feel his son's anger on his behalf. "Well, the head of faculty, she is very much under their influence. A clique of Islamist radicals and Saudi hangers-on, and of course, large amounts of money, very large, being offered to the department, the college. And I of course am well-known as a moderate." He turned to his son.

"But what about you? Are you still a member of Jamat-al-Islami?"

His son flushed deeply, then shook his head. "No, Abba. I mean, I never broke with them. But I'm not really involved anymore. I promise you."

He had thought as much, but sometimes it pays to let your children know that you are not stupid. "Angry young men, eh."

Tariq laughed. "Yeah."

They walked on, Tariq speaking in short, broken sentences.

"It was more the spiritual side, Abba. I thought that they had that; I felt it, with them, at uni, but not later. When I was away, I realized it wasn't for me."

"Are you under any obligations, my son: any bond that you cannot break?"

"No, no. I don't think so." Tariq kept his eyes down. "They didn't have much use for me, in the end."

"A good thing, then."

"Yeah."

"Sometimes, my boy, in such instances as these . . ." For the second time that day, Dr. Choudhury felt uncharacteristically hesitant. "Sometimes the ways marked out for us by those who have come before us are . . . wrong." He paused again, gave a light cough. "But sometimes those ways, some of them, can be of help to this next generation."

They had reached the shops and stopped where the pavement took a sharp turn to the left, wrapping around the plate-glass frontage of a travel agency. Opposite them, across the intersection, was a multistorey shopping center, plastered with red-and-white sale posters: *Because you're worth it.* Beneath that a second, larger poster stated: *You can't go home without me*, the last two words, torn and flapping.

Dr. Choudhury slapped his hand against the travel-agency window. "This is our world; more than the past, much more than where we came from. We cannot pretend that it is not." Under the glass were posters of happy, semi-naked *gora* families throwing beachballs in Dubai, a woman in a bikini and a lotus pose gazing at the pyramids, floats and fireworks at the Sydney Mardi Gras. He lifted his hand off the glass. Beneath it was a small triangular green sticker poster.

Tariq was staring at it, fascinated. "Haj," he said.

"Eh?" He followed his son's gaze and read the sign: *Haj Tours.*

Haj. The unimpeachable decision. Honor of honors. To be a Hajiri, see the great sights and monuments of Islam as Dr. Choudhury's father never had, and return home to the glory and respect of his community, the wary awe of his secular colleagues. Former colleagues.

The humiliation of the impending announcement of his early retirement—everyone knowing what it really meant. And Bourne Abbey, his second home, soon to be no longer in need of him. There was an emptiness within himself and he had a sense of something similar in Tariq: it had always been all or nothing with that boy. It was obvious that Tariq could not live with the compromises that Dr. Choudhury and so many of his generation had made.

And why should he? Was this not one of the reasons Dr. Choudhury and his wife had striven so hard in this new country? Perhaps there was a way forward, for both of them. He slapped Tariq's shoulder. "We will go, you and I."

"Jesus Christ," said Tariq, wide-eyed. "You mean it."

Dr. Choudhury raised his eyebrows reproachfully and turned his back on the shop window to face the street. He placed his right hand over his heart and spoke loudly and sonorously, in his lecturer's voice. "I have come to that age where I am impelled to consider my own mortality. No, no." He raised his hand, pre-empting his son's inevitable expressions of concern for his health and well-being. "I know that I could pass for a man ten years younger, and in his prime at that. But in my heart of hearts, I know, as Tennyson says, that *Death closes all.* This era, this stage of my life of academic eminence, and material success, is finished with. Phut." He snapped his fingers. "Phut," he said again.

But enough of lightness. These were serious times, serious matters. He thrust out his other hand and went on. "*But something ere the end, some work of noble note, may yet be done.*"

Someone across the road clapped sarcastically, and he gave them a carefree wave. A woman with a stroller started to edge around him on the pavement as he spoke a few words further, about honor and toil. He nodded benignly at her as she struggled past, two wheels in the gutter and her toddler, in a Disney Piglet suit, hanging on grimly to the stroller's sides, but she was unresponsive. So few people had a spiritual dimension.

"A new age, my son. A new age. We will welcome it in by doing the great duty of all Muslims." With his head high, and in doubt no longer, Dr. Choudhury walked into the travel agency.

## Twenty-nine

As it turned out, Kareem did not have far to look that Friday night to find Simon, the dirty *gora* who had beaten Shunduri's affa. His relationship with a Muslim girl was known about by some bouncer friends, who said he often tried to score at the clubs. Kareem went to Jerusalem first, the newest Soho club (formerly Mecca but just now renamed after one too many firebomb threats), which had queues round the corner, even though it was only eleven. He'd been meaning to go there for a while, to give respect and some gifts to Jerome and Sujad, the two bouncers at the front door, and also wanted to see if the name change had affected business any. It hadn't, but the threats had stopped, so the owners were happy.

They'd been chatting for about twenty minutes when a taxi drew up and a whooping posse of Hooray Henrys tumbled out, bypassed the line and sailed right up to them. Suj did his job well, giving Kareem the nod to confirm that the first one was Simon, right there in front of him, as if he'd been delivered, *Inshallah*. Too easy, man. Suj doubled the door price with a straight face and walked them to the bar to ensure that they all bought early. Kareem bumped fists with Jerome and followed them inside.

The dance floor was full of bodies with their hands in the air, and the explosive drumbeats of Bhangara trance thudded through

Kareem's belly as he moved into position near Simon and his friends. They were already well-oiled, and he guessed that they had already been to some kind of work function and were probably here just to kill some time, perhaps score early in the night before moving on to some other party: a private affair, probably back in Knightsbridge or Notting Hill, where e's and cocaine would be in demand.

Another time he would have ensured that his face and his number were known to each of them—they were clearly Trust-fund boys with more money than they knew what to do with—but not tonight. He genially rebuffed them, pleading no gear, no stuff, he was cleaned out for now, maybe in a few hours, then headed to the toilets. He pissed into the urinal with exaggerated care, trying to slow down his breathing, and retreated to a cubicle to do a couple of fat lines. Afterward, his eyes shining, he stood in front of the full-length mirror behind the door and checked his nose and lips for residue. He smoothed his shirt-front and shrugged his suit jacket forward to test the shoulder room.

He tried a few moves, still watching himself: a quick one-two rabbit-punch down low, a sharp uppercut to the jaw. Man, that looked mean. Or maybe even a Thai-streetfighter-style high-kick, to thigh, buttock or stomach. Nah, pants definitely too tight for that.

He readjusted his trousers, then dampened some toilet paper and wiped it across the toes of his shoes. Presentation Is the Key to Success, he'd seen it on *Oprah*, and that woman knew what she was talking about. Believe in Your Own Powers, that's The Secret. He knew what he had to say to Simon. He just had to get him on his own, away from his friends. He had no wish to be the first Desi dealer to be given the beats by a group of nancy boys. He straightened and drew his brows together, staring intently at his reflection. Yul Brynner in *The Magnificent Seven*.

Yeah. He maintained the glare but sneered, like Gulshan Grover in *Ram Lakhan*. That always looked better wiv a moustache though. And everyone was scared of dealers: he'd seen it in the eyes of these Trust-fund Henrys; that mixture of fear and contempt, that he had his own sources, could survive on the street. Yeah, that was him, alright. Like Al Pacino in *Scarface*: ruthless, will stop at nuffink, yeah. He glared at the mirror again, shook his wrist so that the joint cracked and his rings glittered menacingly.

Hard man Kareem. Those boys probably thought he was carrying a piece on him right now, had backup waiting just around the corner. Simon was probably one of those pub-men that had never been to the gym in their lives, had no street nous, never been in a fight.

Man, it'd be good when Simon was sorted: it'd put a smile back on his princess's face and enhance relations in that direction, not to mention his rep on the street generally. He took his rings off and put them all on the right hand, doubling up. Time to get out there before Simon and his mates took off for another club and some other dealer.

The heat and noise of the dance floor hit him like getting off the plane in the old country, straight into the humid chaos of Dhaka airport: the same disorientation, of being a stranger in a strange place. What was he here for again?

But even as he turned toward the bar to look for Simon, there he was, grabbing Kareem's sleeve and leaving a damp imprint.

"Hey, Mohammed, I need you to fix me *up*, man."

Kareem smiled, making his voice, his expression, soft, intimate. "Hey, man, chill. Seein' as you're such a good friend of my friends, a valued friend, I might be able to make an exception. Just for you."

He put an arm around Simon's back, hot under the lights, and squeezed his shoulder, keeping him close and turning him away from his friends at the bar. He felt the confidence he always had when making a sale flood back. Believe in Yourself and the Customer Will Believe in You.

"But, you gotta understand, supply's tight, yeah?" The words were rolling off his tongue now. He knew these people. "Dere's not enough for everyone. Quality stuff, man, the best, but not enough ovvit for your friends."

"Fuck *them*, man. They c'n look after themselves. Where is it then?"

"I'll need to go outside. I'm meetin' someone there."

Simon clutched onto him again as he headed for the exit sign. "I'll come too, man, see how much he's got."

Kareem pretended to hesitate, then gestured for Simon to precede him through the rear exit. *After you, casra khota, dirty dog.*

In the alleyway, Gibran was minding the back door, his dark mass balanced on a minuscule folding stool. A lit match against a cigarette was angled into his huge palms, turning them into a bowl of light. Kareem bumped fists with him. "*Salaamalaikum*, brother."

Gibran nodded to him, his eyes sliding over Simon as if he wasn't there. "Eh, brother, *Alaikumsalaam*."

Simon laughed edgily and reached to punch Gibran's shoulder. "Yeah, man, Kumbaya to you too," he said, but Gibran ignored him.

While Simon strolled ahead, Kareem slid the Omega off his wrist and into his palm and then into the bouncer's free hand. Gibran closed his hand over it and moved back into the recess of the doorway with deliberation, making it impassable. Kareem felt impregnable with Gibran behind him. It was time. He looked down the alley at his mark with a feeling of revulsion and a reluctance that he would not name. But time alone with this dirty *gora* would not come again, and he needed a result for his princess.

Simon came back, an unlit cigarette dangling from his mouth, head down as he patted his pockets and executed some kind of complicated dance move.

"Hey, Mohammed, got a light?"

Kareem took a step closer.

"Where's your man then? He late or what?"

He moved forward quickly and swung the full length of his arm, hitting Simon hard and open-handed across the left cheek with a satisfying crack. "*Casra khota*," he said softly.

"Fuck!" Simon stumbled sideways, cigarette gone and cheek already blooming, then turned to face Kareem, his lips pulling back from his teeth. "You fucking cunt!"

Kareem was bouncing a little now, despite his heavy shoes and the cobbles, and reached out and pushed into Simon's neck while he was still off balance. His head hit the brickwork of the opposite wall.

Simon's hands came up instinctively. Kareem rabbit-punched him in the groin, and Simon, gasping and coughing, slid down and doubled onto his side.

Kareem leaned a hand against the wall, careful not to drag his jacket cuff against the bricks, and watched. All was quiet except for the sound of Simon retching. Things were going quite well, considering. There was a pale spill of something on the lapel of Simon's bespoke suit, and his pants were covered in alley filth. One cufflink was almost off, a Tag Heuer design. Or was it Dunhill.

Simon, panting with a little high cry on each exhalation, started to struggle with an inner jacket pocket. "You fucking want my cash, fucking Paki—"

"Nah, pig-dog." Kareem spoke slowly and clearly, imparting the lesson. "That's not what we're here for, yeah. We're here for a little chat. 'Bout you disrespectin' one of my sisters."

"Sisters? What the fuck are you fucking talking about?" Simon, amazingly, was starting to sit up. His face was as white as the moon, apart from the scarlet hand print, and his eyes were glassy.

"I mean the sisterhood, man. The Muslim sisterhood. You need to keep your dirty hands off our sisters."

He was on something, Kareem hadn't expected that. He must have taken something, speed maybe, just before he hit the club. *Gora* courage. A dirty drug, good for National Front–types and pub-men, anyone that wanted a fight. And nancy boys going into clubs where they didn't belong.

There was a creak behind him, and Kareem turned just in time to see Gibran's ham-sized hand, and a glint of the Omega, as the back door swung closed, shutting off the club music like a power cut. Jesus Christ, so much for the Muslim brotherhood.

Kareem didn't have a piece with him or even a knife, hadn't thought there was a need. And Gibran wouldn't be opening the back door anytime soon. Simon was lighter but taller, and buzzing, vibrating with the drug, first resort of soldiers, cons and *gundahs* to ramp up aggression and pain thresholds.

Simon was standing now, as if he'd never been jobbed in the nuts, not saying a word. Kareem had seen a speeder hit by a car and get up and keep going, running like a maniac. This was a serious situation, and no backup. He would have to rethink his strategy, improvise, use what was around him, like Bruce Lee. Kareem glanced down the alleyway. No one to be seen.

Simon's eyes were fixed on him and his hands were twitching and picking at his tie, his breaths coming faster and faster, as he began to move toward him.

Kareem smiled, spoke to him, his tone warm, conversational, as if they had just got chatting, while waiting for a bus, or a haircut. "We're very protective of our sisters, man. We treat them with the highest of respect, yeah? It's *izzat*, yeah. That's our sisters' honor and dignity."

Simon seemed to hesitate, then muttered something inaudible, his face blank and rigid. Kareem stepped back to widen the space between them, and his casting hand found Ali's little folding stool. He put a foot on it and started to fiddle with his laces.

He continued hastily, "We Muslim boys, we don't take kindly to people beating them up, dishonoring our sisters, yeah? You see, ignorant pig-dogs like you, no respect for *izzat*. No respect for family."

The socked foot finally slipped out of the shoe. Kareem rested a forearm on his bent knee to distract from his other hand picking up the shoe by its toe: Simon was close, but he was ready for him now.

Simon's forehead loomed, and his voice suddenly became audible: fast and monotonous, as if he was stuck on repeat. "You think you're so fuckin' cool so fuckin' cool you fuckin' Paki nigger loser cunt fuckin' go back where you fuckin' came from Paki I'll fuck all your sisters I'll fuck them up the arse I'll fuckin' fuck your mother, I'll—"

Kareem swung the shoe hard into Simon's face. *Allahu Akbar.*

The side of the shoe just caught his mouth, splitting his lip in the center, like a burst tomato. A tea-kettle scream started, and Kareem felt a surge of disgust: where were his balls? Simon rocked back, and in the slo-mo feel that Kareem knew from the ring, he noted the contrast between the spray of blood droplets over one side of Simon's suit jacket and the solid line running down his chin toward his shirt. His mouth was open, looking like a letter Q with its tail made of blood.

But Simon seemed to regain his balance and came for him, hands clawed like a woman's, no style, no strategy, still squealing like a pig. Kareem, his socked foot still on the stool, hopped backward to give himself room, take his time, and swung the shoe again, more comfortable with it now, a real roundhouse backhander, with all his muscle behind it.

Simon, his eyes still fixed on Kareem's like the amateur he was, didn't dodge, the heel angled into his nose with the unmistakable crunch of bone. The screaming stopped abruptly, as Simon, after an interminable second, dropped to his knees and smacked forward onto his face.

Kareem watched him for a moment, then bent down and wiped the heel of the shoe across Simon's jacket, back and forth until it was completely clean, then eased it back onto his foot, his hands only trembling slightly. You certainly couldn't do as much damage with just some cheap Kays shoe. And forget trainers. These handmades had real weight in them. Beautiful craftsmanship. Investment dressing was what it was all about.

He retied the laces, adjusted the waistband of his pants and prodded Simon with his toe. No movement. He sucked his teeth, hitched up his trouser legs and squatted to roll him onto his back.

Simon flopped over heavily and, to Kareem's relief, took a deep, snoring breath. His nose was mashed and bloody and some clear fluid—snot or tears—was bubbling out onto his mouth and chin, displacing the blood. He looked like he'd pissed his pants as well. *Casra charsi*, dirty addict. Kareem sighed. There was always this sour, gone-bad feeling afterward, Kareem reminded himself, it's only the winners who have the time to think about such things.

Nuff damage control: it was time he was off. Jerusalem's back door was still shut tight—Gibran had more nous than Jerome and Suj put together, as well as no fuckin' loyalty. He would phone once he was clear, and Gibran would make sure Simon was taken care of: that his friends found him or, if they were like him and had left without looking for their friend, an ambulance called.

Kareem straightened and patted the mobile in his other pocket. "This one's for you, Princess."

He glanced at his wrist before remembering and cursing Gibran again, then pulled out a mobile to check the time. After he got up, he would speak to Auntie and Uncle, tell them about the divorce before they heard it from someone in the old country. Then he'd call Shunduri and tell her he'd sorted Simon and that he'd never bother her affa again. He smoothed his lapels and smiled at the thought of her sullen, needy gratitude: only *mardy* on the outside, that was his princess.

She should be with her family now, so that they would be comfortable with an approach by the Guris. Perhaps he could drive her down to her family this weekend. He'd tell her to stay with her parents for a bit, take the week off work, so her family wouldn't be wondering what the two of them were up to in London in the meanwhile. He knew how these people thought. He wouldn't drive her up on Saturday, his best business day of the week, but Sunday. Yeah, he could pick up some gifts Sunday morning, then take Princess home, which would give him another chance to get the Rover on the motorway and show its style.

On Monday or Tuesday, he would talk to Auntie and Uncle about marrying again, so that when they were ready they could. No rush, but he felt comfortable with it all now. He was doing well: it was time for him to settle down, live like the successful businessman he was. As for the events of this night, maybe it was time he went more legit: the mobile-phone business was taking more of his energy and making more money for him than the dealing now. He'd proven himself. It was time to move on.

The girl in Bangladesh came into his mind's eye. Even in heels, she had only come up to his shoulder. While sitting in the palanquin in all her finery for her *haldi-mendhi mela*, someone had spoken of

England, and she had covered her eyes with schoolgirl-bitten nails and sobbed with her mouth open like a child. He would send her family something to ease the pain and make sure that she was provided for and was found a good husband. Someone from another village perhaps. None of this was her fault.

He shook the image away. He was a man with responsibilities now: here and in the old country, and he was doing well enough to carry them and more. Everything was working out fine. But as he jogged to the alley's only entrance, then looked back at the shadows where Simon's body lay, his usual sense of purpose was missing.

"Stick to your own kind, pub-man," he muttered and turned away, toward the street, to check out the crowd. Flickering lights traced the passage of cars moving down the congested street, its pavements packed with the night-time crowd of rich and poor, young and old, Christians, Asians and blacks, all looking for reprieve from sorrow or loneliness or the pressures of family or work. That was it: he was the man for all of them: the fixer-upper. He strode away from the alley toward the Rover, smiling brightly over his unease, wanting the immersion of his usual circuit. The night was still young, and it was time he showed his face elsewhere.

# *Thirty*

Mrs. Begum was in the garden on Saturday morning, digging furiously. The compost heap had broken apart down one side, like a volcano that had blown up its own crater, and a sickly scent filled the air. A small wheelbarrow stood nearby, and she was filling it from the heart of the mound.

The best humus, almost completely black with its wealth of organic matter as well as the thing that she would not name, would be trundled to Mrs. Darby, from back garden to back garden, for her herbaceous border and her roses. A true friend she was, unlike the snakes in her own family.

*Furu shaitan*, little devil, that her son was, defying her like that, when all she wanted for him was what every mother wants. She turned the spade over and patted smooth the mounded earth in the wheelbarrow. Look at Edward-and-Sophie. Look at Dr. Choudhury and herself. It was possible for everyone to marry: the Qur'an made that clear.

All beings need bodily pleasure and if the natural way is unavailable, then to take another path is understandable and allowed for by Allah, peace be upon Him. But marriage is what makes a man, as motherhood is what fulfils a woman. Marriage is the truest and best path to pleasure and happiness, as well as maturity and security. Tariq must marry: what otherwise to do with this boy? She knew what he needed, despite everything being as it was between himself and Dr. Choudhury.

With men, family only truly tied them when they had a wife, and children. If Tariq, with his father's blessing, did not marry, he would become an old maid of a man in his prime. She thrust the spade into the soil, stood on the edge and jiggled it deeper. And, in time, he would leave them again: she could feel it in her bones. Even more than Rohimun, he was liable to disappear on her if he was not safely betrothed.

She thought of how angry he'd been once he became religious, angry all the time: with Rohimun for her blue-jeans, and Dr. Choudhury for keeping whiskey in the sitting room for guests. That anger was still there, she could feel it, had seen it on his face that night he'd returned two weeks ago, but it was against himself now, for some personal failing. Well, they all knew what that was now. Far better that he married and could direct all this anger against the EU and the French, like Mrs. Darby and everyone else in this village.

But first she must deal with her daughters. She leaned on the spade's handle until the blade bent upward with a fresh load. Dr. Choudhury would be a sadder and lonelier man now without his Oxford, disloyal cockroach that he was, and she must trust that to turn his mind to thoughts of family unity, forgiveness and acceptance. Shunduri was not helping matters by bringing up her sister's failings at every opportunity either, although if she pushed that cart too hard, she could well find her father pulling in the opposite direction. And Tariq, well, Tariq was too busy getting into his own kind of trouble.

She stopped and wiped her brow with a forearm. Even now, digging here tended to bring on her headaches though, as Allah knew, she had enough reasons for headaches already. She looked across her garden, its neat rows of tomatoes and coriander, the English-style mint that Mrs. Darby had given her for cooking with lamb but which went so much better with yoghurt, the shiny white glass covering her cucumbers and radishes. No one ever need go hungry in this land, with a garden. All so ordered, tidy and flourishing. Why couldn't her family all settle nearby and marry and have children, the way nature intended?

She stooped to pull out a rogue weed from the bottom of the compost heap, then realized that it was a freesia. She scooped out the bulb with her fingers and carried it to the little patch of flowers that sat in one corner of the herb garden. She was still not entirely comfortable growing something that could not be eaten, but this little patch was Rohimun's.

Since Munni stopped visiting, she had found herself maintaining it, making sure that it stayed weed-free and had its share of compost. Once Mrs. Darby had brought over some bulbs for her and planted them herself, and had refused to say what they were. "A surprise," she'd said, and when they had bloomed—tall, stately cup-shaped flowers, red striped with white—she had fetched Mrs. Darby and they stood and looked at them. "Tulips," Mrs. Darby told her. "From Holland. And growing so fine and strong: better than mine."

After she had dug some more and filled the barrow and taken it over to Mrs. Darby's garden and heaped it around her roses, Mrs. Begum started to feel a bit better.

It was true that she had feared Tariq being driven away by an ultimatum. Children in UK had too many places to run to, to escape their responsibilities. She hefted the arms of the empty wheelbarrow and started to wheel it home. A son about the house, as a visible presence, was an important sign to possible or actual sons-in-law that her daughters were not without protection. And besides, she still had certain other hopes for his future. She parked the barrow in her shed, changed out of her gardening clogs from the catalogue and back into her sandals. She had lost the battle, but not the war, *Inshallah*.

A tinny trumpeting caught her ear, and she straightened to attention. It was the phone, and if she did not hurry, it could stop and she would never know who it was. She ran for the scullery door, flew down the hall, and snatched up the receiver.

Before she could even speak, her youngest child's voice came on the line. "Amma, *Salaamalaikum*."

"Baby!"

"How is everybody? I . . . I got a week off, so I'll be home on Sunday, yaah."

"Tomorrow? Oh, Baby, that is so wonderful. I miss you so-so much, you know. Yes, yes, everybody is fine. Your father, Tariq, they are themselves. Maybe, you could stay two-three weeks?"

There was a surprising pause, as if Shunduri really was considering her mother's routine request for longer, longer.

"Maybe, Amma. I . . . I'm a bit tired, you know? I'll be on the train: the twelve-oh-five is when it gets into Swindon, yaah?"

"Yes, yes. Twelve-oh-five. We will all be there for you. Are you alright, my Baby? Are you well?"

Her daughter's voice faded, then almost broke. "Fine, fine. Amma, I'm sorry, I've got to go now . . . er, studyin'. I can't talk now but I'll see you all on Sunday, yaah?"

"Yes, yes. Sunday, twelve-oh-five."

"*Salaamalaikum*, Amma. I'll see you soon."

"*Alaikumsalaam*, my Baby. That is wonderful, wonderful."

Mrs. Begum hung up with triumph in her heart. If one door shuts, many windows will open, as Mrs. Darby would say. Her daughter was coming home and, after her behavior last week, this visit, this phone call, were as good as an admission that she was ready to marry, ready for her family to make the arrangements, as one would ever get from these modern girls. Obedient, nervous and in need of her mother. Completely ready. As for her bank-job that she loved so much, there were many banks in Swindon. All the banks were there.

And as for that Kareem, she would ensure that he did his duty, or else. She remembered the recently arrived knife set her husband had ordered on shopping-channel, to be given to Mrs. Darby once he had forgotten. She could already think of one good use for them.

———

"HENRY," SAID THEA. "I was thinking about a picnic. Where the Park flattens out just near the river, so the children can do some fishing if they get bored with cricket."

Henry looked at his wife, startled. "For lunch, you mean? You don't want to, ah, go to Florian's again, or . . ."

"No, let's go outside, it's a lovely day. The blankets for the jumble sale are in the back of the garage. If we spread those out, then put my picnic blanket on top, that should do."

"What picnic blanket? We've never—"

"I bought it this morning. There's a Burberry shop in Bath now."

"Don't you have a hair appointment?" Henry said weakly.

"Cancelled it," said Thea, pushing up her sleeves. "It's too nice a day to waste."

Good Lord. She was wearing jeans too, and flat slip-ons . . .

"Come on then. Don't you want to?"

"Ah, yes, of course, it's a wonderful idea, I'll just change, I'm a bit—"

"You're fine as you are, just wash your hands and I'll call the boys."

"Rightio, lead on, MacDuff . . . Ah, do you know where my hat is?"

"Packed," Thea threw over her shoulder as she headed out to the side. "The picnic basket's ready on the kitchen bench and there's a wine cooler next to it. And the boys' cricket and fishing things are there too."

Henry trailed through the scullery and into the back garden after his wife. "What about Richard?"

"Gone to the pub to catch up with a friend, or so he said. Andrew, Jonathon! Lunchtime!"

Well, whatever was going on, Thea's organizational abilities hadn't changed. Henry headed back to the kitchen, washed and loaded up, then remembered the blankets and put everything down again as the boys came in, went to the sink and started splashing each other.

"Andrew, Jonathon, you know those blankets in the back of the shed?"

"Mum's already told us," said Jonathon, with a don't-bother-me-now air that reminded Henry of Richard. "One blanket each." He marched past his father, wiping his wet hands on Andrew's shirt and saying to his brother, "*You* can have the blanket at the bottom, wiv all the *spiders*."

"Nooo! That's not fair . . ."

"Cockroaches! Giant ones! *Moths!*"

"Daaad!"

Henry shook his head as he loaded up again. "Life never is, little man. Ah, can someone open the door?"

---

THE BOYS WHOOPED and screamed as they rolled down the hill toward the river, and Thea hadn't shouted at them once, about being sick after baguettes and pork pies and halva and cake, or dirtying their clothes. Henry sat cross-legged as he munched his pie and then, with no one to stop him, started on a baguette, covertly watching his surprising wife as she lay on her back on the blanket, seemingly relaxed after her usual birdlike meal of a single mini-quiche and, more surprises, no wine at all.

One arm was across her eyes and she could easily have been asleep. She seemed softer around the edges somehow, as if she'd put on some weight. If so, it suited her, though Henry knew better than to mention it. The slightest of sounds escaped her opened lips, and Henry, his mouth full of cheese and lettuce, grinned at the sight of perfect Thea snoring.

"Daaad! Come and play!"

He finished his mouthful, then rose and dusted off his pants. A clod of earth attached to some long grass hit his hip and he staggered backward and away from the picnic blanket.

"Aaaargh!"

Shrieks and giggles as both children ran and jumped on him, and were then joined by the dogs. "Aaagh! Not fair! Four against one!"

And in between flailing arms and kicking legs and tickled tummies and waving tails and wet excited noses, Henry caught glimpses of Thea, one hand on her stomach now, breathing as deeply and peacefully as if she was at home in the very middle of their queen-sized bed.

---

RICHARD HAD HOPED to see Rohimun that Saturday, not having seen her since Thursday night, and thought he'd try to catch her in between the two daily tiffin-visits she seemed to be receiving. With that in mind he'd wandered to the kitchen at midday to let Thea know that he wouldn't be around for lunch because he was going to walk through the Park, and would then head to the pub for lunch with a friend. His excuse sounded threadbare even to himself, and he half expected to have to put her off coming with him, but Thea, unpacking from a morning's shopping in Bath, had nodded with a preoccupied air and asked him to get the cricket set down from the top of the scullery cupboard. He did so, placing bats and sticks with unnecessary neatness against the kitchen wall next to some fishing gear, and feeling definitely superfluous.

Then, halfway to the Abbey, Richard spotted Tariq, walking quickly uphill toward the Abbey, the tiffin carrier in his hand flashing sunshine. It was too late not to be seen himself, so he sat down under a large oak to wait until Tariq returned. However, when he did, over an hour later, it was not to climb the opposing hill to the cottage, but to sit on the riverbank facing the Abbey with Colin's son and share what looked suspiciously like a joint. And outside the back of Windsor Cottage, Richard could see Mrs. Begum hanging out washing, giving her what was probably a bird's-eye view of everything else. Impossible.

He decided to walk back toward the Lodge and see if he could spot Henry and Thea's picnic on the way, and join in the family cricket, but instead found his brother and his wife canoodling on a picnic blanket. He veered sharply away, then spotted the boys fishing nearby, with an intensity that indicated high expectations: a whale or a shark at least. When he greeted them, he was unceremoniously shooshed, and waved off. He called out a cheery goodbye that they ignored, and headed for the village, swearing grumpily to himself: an old gooseberry, intruding wherever he went. He would have no choice but to do what he'd been pretending to do, and actually go to the pub for a solitary counter lunch with his imaginary friend.

―――――

WASHING DONE, MRS. Begum boiled and steamed and strained in the kitchen, far too busy this afternoon to think about those two snakes who had gone all the way to Swindon without her yesterday, and ever since they'd returned, looked like two conspirators, full of conspicuous silences and mutual glances.

Not to mention that now Tariq was floating about with his head in the clouds as if he hadn't a care in the world, and Dr. Choudhury seemed to have been lifted from the devastation of Friday morning to his usual self-satisfied comfort in a remarkably short time, even for a man. The worst of it was not that he was keeping something from her, or even that she could not yet discover it, but that he was so pleased about it. Fat cockroach that he was.

There would be no warm salad for him tonight, no fresh-chopped chilli for his son. She slapped the cork mats onto the table. She would heat up the leftover dahl and make rice and nothing else. If they wanted to behave as if they were two unmarried men digging together in Oxford, with no wife or mother to care for them and be told what was going on, she would feed them like they were too. Hah. She was not going to cook for them, only in readiness for Shunduri tomorrow and in case of visitors; not that anyone ever visited her unexpectedly, with three unmarried children and no prospect of change in that corner of the sky.

Perhaps Tariq had told Dr. Choudhury of a job somewhere—she hoped it was not Cambridge. She remembered Mrs. Darby reporting what Prince Charles had said, about Cambridge being in the fens. Swamps were dangerous places, prone to flood and disease, which she well knew could destroy families, even whole villages.

And there was no need for such a job. There were no money worries, she was sure of that. They had no debts and money in the bank, thanks to Mr. Kiriakis's generosity over the last three years. They had everything they needed. Except for children that did what they should. They could live here in comfort without Dr. Choudhury working for the rest of their days, even if they paid for three weddings. She took up her tea towel and rubbed the sink so hard that it squeaked. Not that *that* was so likely anymore, in this family born to bad luck.

———

DR. CHOUDHURY, ENSCONCED in his wing-back chair in order to await the Saturday evening meal, looked at his wife as she dusted around him in the sitting room. Mrs. Begum, it was true, though incessantly active and occasionally silly, was still his other half, his helpmeet, and the thought of leaving her for such a period of time, even for the holiest of purposes, was a difficult one. How would she cope without him, the wellspring of her life?

He allowed her to straighten his pile of newspapers and magazines and watched tolerantly as she slapped the ottoman back into shape, lifting his feet at the correct time so that she could ease it back under his slippers without inconvenience. Anything he could do to make her life easier. She truly was his other half. Since she had joined him in the UK so many years ago, they had never been separated for more than a couple of days, and even that only the once. And a great stress and strain and inconvenience to himself it had been.

The 1994 Manchester conference on Historical Architecture (the host city finally chosen by a despairing committee under severe but equal pressure from London and Edinburgh) had taken him away from hearth and home for only forty-eight hours, but in that time, smallish items such as socks, ties and underwear had unaccountably gone missing, the room telephone had proven to be a nightmare of unpredictability, he had repeatedly found himself locked out of his hotel room and, on one occasion, had the disturbing experience of his room disappearing completely.

He was not a man who could be expected to keep such minor things as underpants, the exact location of his room and the right way to use a key-card to the forefront of his mind, and he had found the whole episode most distracting, even distressing. It had certainly been a lesson to him: no life without wife, as they say, and he hated to think about how bereft Mrs. Begum had been for those two days, sitting at home without him. Pining.

But he would never expose his wife to the dangers and inconveniences of travel unnecessarily, so separated they must be. He had heard that the shopping was very good in Mecca and Medina, and he would bring her back some gold, and some nice saris. And besides, she had shown no sign of having developed a spiritual side, so she was not, to all appearances, ready for this experience.

Haj, or perhaps just Umrah Haj, Lady-Haj, would be best for her when she was old and sick and brooding on her own mortality; in short, had done some more thinking on serious things, as opposed to just dusting and cooking. And plotting marriages. *That* seemed indeed to be all she could think about now. He would not be so selfish as to rush her into such an experience before she was ready.

And with Tariq to travel with him, any such domestic problems, as he had suffered previously when travelling on his own, should be to some extent ameliorated, *Inshallah.* Though of course there was no comparison to the way that a wife would look after one's small needs, like socks warmed on the radiator, and paan mixed just the way it should be. Dr. Choudhury stretched and yawned. He and Tariq would have to rough it, iron their own shirts, et cetera . . .

But then he realized that for the five days of the pilgrimage he would be required to wear nothing but the ihram, which was no more than two lengths of white cotton around his waist and shoulders. He brightened. White had always flattered him, and there would be no ironing. He had many memories of bachelor disasters with laundromat and iron, until he had discovered the shirt washing and ironing services in Oxford's township. Not as cheap as in Dhaka, of course, but well worth the expense until his bride had arrived and had been able to take over such duties. If anything needed washing, he thought vaguely, Tariq would sort it out. He yawned again. The sitting room was quiet now that his wife's fussing had stopped, and she'd closed the door on leaving, so she must be intending to hoover.

He laced his hands over his stomach (hardly a stomach at all really, just a certain softness and fullness around the midriff entirely appropriate for his age and status) and allowed his eyes to close while he contemplated the changes that he would be bringing to their little household. The time was right to inform his family, and to prepare his wife the best he could, that they would be without his care and protection for the best part of three weeks. Mrs. Begum would not be completely alone: Shunduri would have a break from studies soon and she could keep her mother company, help her with the household, while he was gone.

Not that there would be much for them to do with their head-of-family gone. But he would not begrudge them some idleness while he followed his star. His mouth opened just a fraction and a tiny, contented rumble escaped, what some could almost have called a snore.

---

Dr. Choudhury snorted himself awake to the smells of onion and garlic cooking, and the sound of his stomach rumbling. By the time he had wandered into the kitchen, the onion-garlic smell had matured to sweetness as the onions had begun to caramelize. The stove was full of pots; he lifted lids and peered in. Rice of course, chicken, egg . . . How many mouths was Mrs. Begum preparing to feed? But she was chopping up a goat haunch with a cleaver, and his mouth was full of saliva, so he kept the question to himself.

He did feel a little irritated that she was so preoccupied. What had happened to all her curious hovering earlier, so desperate to learn his secret? In the sitting room, she had dusted the occasional table next to his chair for a good minute. He cleared his throat and moved away from the stove. Mrs. Begum dropped the cleaver on the countertop, darted in front of him and gave a rapid stir to the onions. He cleared his throat again, and his wife met his eye.

"Tomorrow, Sunday, Baby is coming." She turned back to the stove and messed again with the onions.

"Ah, yes. It will be good to see her at this juncture," Dr. Choudhury said, placing a weighty emphasis on the last two words.

Mrs. Begum gave the onions one last stir, then uncovered the spice tray and started to launch teaspoonfuls of powdered color into the wok: the warm gold, khaki and mid-brown of turmeric, cumin and coriander.

"*Haldi, Jeera, Dunya* . . . Baby might stay for a week. Maybe more," she said in an airy tone, without turning, and started to stir each pot, banging the respective spoons on the pan sides before moving on.

"Ah," he said, flinching at the next round of pot-banging and water-splashing. "That is good." He needed to make his announcement now, before it was lost in the hurly-burly of kitchen preparations. He wondered, not for the first time, if it was really necessary to make such a noise when cooking. But how to start? "A cup-of-tea," he said firmly.

Mrs. Begum gestured at the stove, upon which every hotplate was flaming and full.

"Where is that electric kettle I bought you? Have you returned it?"

His wife's expression made it clear that she would have if he had not hidden the receipt, and she nodded toward the cupboard-of-useless things, as she called it.

With a great show of self-restraint, he opened the cupboard and peered inside. Boxes. After some seconds of suspense, Mrs. Begum's arm dodged in front of him to remove a cardboard box with, he now noticed, a picture of a kettle on it. She thumped the box onto the kitchen table and started to undo the flaps, but he waved her away, delved into the styrofoam and pulled out a collection of papers. He sat down to read them.

"Warranty. Hmmm. Guarantee. Ah, Instructions. Electrical Safeguards . . . Wash first. This kettle must be washed before use."

Dr. Choudhury watched as his wife pulled the kettle out of the packing foam and gave it a lightning-fast rinse before filling it and plonking it on the kitchen counter. She grabbed a wooden spoon and gave the curry base in the wok a quick stir, throwing in aniseed and cloves. Then she sped back to the kitchen table, reached into the box and pulled out a disc-like object attached to a power cord, jammed the cord into an outlet near the stove and plonked the kettle onto the disc with an audible click. It started to hiss almost immediately.

Dr. Choudhury tapped the table and looked at his wife over his glasses. "Mrs. Begum. I have not yet read the Instructions."

She rushed back to the stove and started to pick up pieces of goat and drop them into the curry. "Mrs. Darby has one. I have seen it," she said, her eyes on the stove.

His annoyance deepened further. He dropped the papers on the table. "There was no need, Mrs. Begum . . ." But he was drowned out by the combined efforts of hissing kettle, whooshing flames, bubbling rice, sizzling meat and an energetically wielded wooden spoon. Mrs. Darby this, Mrs. Darby that: he was sick of hearing about Mrs. Darby.

These days their life on the outskirts of Oxford had a reminiscent glow. Until they had come here, they had been of one mind, one mind only. His. Such misunderstandings as had existed previously (he now had trouble recalling anything of significance) had been nothing, nothing, compared to this ongoing tension, this feeling of hidden, unspoken conflict and struggle for supremacy that had arisen ever since Mrs. Begum, at Mrs. Darby's instigation, had joined that Institute for Women.

She had her own ambitions now: this "fund-raising" lark. *Zakat*, charitable giving, was the fourth pillar of Islam. He could afford to give alms: why this need for sewing and cooking of cakes and painting of plates and selling these items to each other at market stalls as if they were hawkers on the street? Where was her dignity and sense of position? She should be tied to him, not some Mrs. Darby, with her electric kettles and her recipes.

Dr. Choudhury would have waited for a better time, would have built up to his important news with more tactful circumlocution, in short, broken it to her more gently, but there were limits to the disrespect that a *paterfamilias* could tolerate.

He raised his voice. "Mrs. Begum," he said. "*Mrs. Begum.*"

His wife turned to face him, spoon in hand.

"As you know it is exactly two weeks before *Dhu al-Hijjah* begins." She looked at him expectantly. "For a man such as myself, of, ah, a certain age, where one becomes more aware of one's own mortality, particularly when one's health is not number-one . . ." He patted his chest significantly.

Mrs. Begum was watching him now, listening, but again with that guarded blankness that he had observed on previous occasions when he had alluded to his own poor health. But no mind.

"The time has come for me to fulfil the fifth pillar and, some would say, the most important duty of Islam: to travel to Mecca and Medina and . . . the other places, to perform the holy duty, the great pilgrimage of Haj."

He had the gratification of seeing his wife actually jump at the last word. He had her attention now, one hundred percent. Full of the nobility of his cause, he lifted his head, splayed the fingers of his right hand across his chest and continued.

"Circumstances, recent circumstances, have conspired to free my time sufficiently, to undertake this great duty, *Inshallah.* And Tariq: while it is true he is young, he has recently reached a *crise religieuse* in his own development and would thus also benefit from performing his greatest duty. Particularly in the company of his own father. It will be, therefore, not only the fulfilment of an important religious duty, but also of great benefit to the, ahem, filial–paternal bond."

"Eh?" she said. "*Haj?*"

There was a short silence. Just as he was about to further enlarge upon his aims and goals and justifications for this decision, Mrs. Begum startled into action.

"I need my Munni back. She can help me while I am alone and be a big sister to Baby."

"Eh? What has that got to do with . . ."

"How, and what, would I do here, while my husband and my son are there? With one daughter in London doing only Allah knows what and one abandoned by her family . . ." She swung her arm, still holding a wooden spoon, toward the kitchen window, splattering the curtain and its contents with rich brown sauce.

"You just told me, wife, that Baby is coming home."

She dashed a hand across her eyes and dropped the spoon into the sink, her voice high and strained. "Only a week. What is a week? Nothing, nothing. I have lost one of my children, and you take another away with you. Only Baby is left for me now. This is the worst time for a father and a brother to leave her without care and protection." She clutched the talisman pinned to her blouse. "Aah, my god.

Munni in the Abbey and Baby almost betrothed and then my husband goes away and takes my only son."

"What, what? Baby betrothed?" He felt a little unsteady and sat down again.

"She had better be, very soon. What will become of us all? No father, no brother . . ."

"To, er, Kareem?"

"Of course to Kareem! We have no other boy. It has to be Kareem, and very soon too it must be. Baby is almost twenty-four now. She has been seen with him, more than once. She has to marry: him, or someone else, soon. Or they will think, the community will think, that she is a modern girl with no morals."

How could this have happened? Dr. Choudhury pulled out his handkerchief and wiped his brow. "What do you know about him? Who are his family?"

"The Guris. The Guris are his family. He has a good job, a nice car. He loves Shunduri, I am sure of it."

He clasped his hands, rested them on the table and stared vacantly at the ruined kitchen curtains. She was like her sister, then. They had both been such happy, pretty little girls. He wanted to ask when all this had happened, but had a sinking suspicion that Mrs. Begum would tell him that it had all been discussed and agreed to by him on some previous day.

"When will . . ."

"Soon, soon. The Guris will visit us soon." She spoke quickly, fingering the talisman pinned to her blouse. "Kareem will bring them, maybe next week."

It was all too much. "Cup-of-tea," he said faintly.

He knew that in saying this and nothing else, he had waved the white flag of surrender. He had been ambushed by a force that, while not of course actually superior in strength and intelligence, had all the advantages of better information and a willingness to use sneaky timing. He did, it was true, feel a slight discomfort at having temporarily forgotten about his daughters in his excitement for Haj, but that would pass. Surely he had enough to deal with. Other members of this family had to pull their weight as well.

In no time at all, Mrs. Begum put half a cup of steaming, milky, sugared tea in front of him, pulled out a chair and sat down to his right.

"We can give a good dowry, I think," she said, her voice soothing as honey now.

He said nothing, mainly because this was something else that he hadn't thought about. Mrs. Begum reached over to the paan tray, placed a green betel leaf across her palm, sprinkled it with betel and only the tiniest amount of lime powder, and added a generous scattering of sugar balls, just the way he liked it.

"Shunduri will be happy." She added more sugar balls, folded it into a tight little parcel and passed it to him.

He fiddled with it, then put it down. "Would we be even considering Kareem for Baby, if not for her sister's behavior? I think not."

Mrs. Begum put her hand on her husband's wrist, startling him. She was behaving like a *gora* wife now. "I want Baby to have the wedding she always dreamt of. The wedding we could not have."

She looked at him significantly, keeping her hand on his wrist, and then he understood, with a sick feeling in his stomach. It would be best for Shunduri to marry as soon as possible, before a *funchait* was needed, or worse.

"There is no time," he said. "There are two weeks, two-and-a-half weeks only, until Haj."

"We can do betrothal and registry office before you go, agree dowry and the gold and saris. Shunduri will stay here and Kareem can telephone her every night, send her flowers, until you are back. Then we will have the *nikkah* and reception and *rukhsati* after you get back. Mrs. Guri will know how to manage it. She will know all the best places, maybe even get a discount." She paused and, in a moment of seeming absentmindedness, squeezed his wrist. "This will be a very difficult time for Shunduri, for our Baby. She will need her mother, and with her father and brother gone, she will need, even more, her sister."

Dr. Choudhury shook his head. "She is not welcome . . ." His voice faded as he realized that he was in a corner indeed. Rohimun could not stay in the Abbey much longer anyway, and she would be needed at home. Back home once again, and her painting was so beautiful, like a golden thread linking him to his mother.

He picked up his tea. "I will be in my study, wife. I wash my hands of these machinations. I do not approve."

He stood and left her in the kitchen, walked down the hallway to his *sanctum sanctorum* with a feeling of great flatness and entanglement, and locked his study door behind him with pettish exactitude. So much for his Haj. Mrs. Begum would have her way, they all would, but he was not going to stand there like a puppet and endorse this railroading of his position. He was the head of this family.

# Thirty-one

TODAY WAS GOING to be different, Richard would make sure of it. He left his brother and Thea discussing the dreaded packing up of the mess that was Henry's study, settled himself on the garden seat just near the Lodge's garage, and opened his paper to wait for the first tiffin delivery, and any other movements in the Park. Rohimun's father came into view at nine, much sooner than Richard expected, stiff-armed and staggering slightly on the downhill stretches. He seemed to be in a bit of a hurry, and Richard hoped that Dr. Choudhury's impatience would return him home again as quickly.

It was only ten minutes before Dr. Choudhury reappeared, looked at his watch with a self-important air and began to beat his way back through the ankle-high undergrowth, stopping intermittently to whisk and pat at his trousers and shoes.

Right. Richard went to his car, pulled out a half-full duffel bag and began walking to the Abbey, oddly self-conscious as it swung, and pushing away the unpleasant thought that from a distance he could be mistaken for that old fusspot Dr. Choudhury.

*I've brought a few things. A couple of extra jars for your brushes. And I came across this in the attic: an old SLR of mine, hasn't been used in years. I thought it might be useful for the figure in profile. If it works.* No need to mention he'd had the SLR cleaned and serviced in Cirencester the day before, along with picking up some extra rolls of film, after some time spent debating what he could get away with giving her that would look sufficiently casual to be accepted without offence. He would put the first roll of film in while he was there, spend his time checking it to give him something to do, and maybe if he seemed preoccupied, Rohimun would relax sufficiently to go back to her painting and perhaps they could begin to talk.

---

THAT SUNDAY MORNING, Kareem picked his princess up, on time and everything. She was dressed in full ninja-chick gear just like Shilpi, but given recent events, he wasn't saying nothing, and was tender in his silence as he did up her seatbelt. Then he had to divert back to Brick Lane, having just received an urgent call from Suj the bouncer saying that he had to speak to him, couldn't put it in a text, man. Kareem parked up as discreetly as he could, and Shunduri, still not saying a word, just lay back on the headrest, her head tilted away and her hand shading her face from nosy aunties.

Suj sent his family out to the kitchen and, after they'd had a smoke together, told Kareem that the police had been around at Jerusalem last night looking for him, talking about an assault on a patron. Jesus Christ. After a moment Kareem laughed and patted Suj's knee. "I never touched him, man. But perhaps I won't be around for a bit, till things settle down. I got some business up north anyway. It's all good, I got it in hand, yeah."

Suj nodded and accepted Kareem's small, foil-wrapped thank-you, but didn't see him to the front door. Kareem, feeling a different man and as subdued as his *lalmunni*, shut it behind him and hurried back to his princess. He'd only slapped the dirty dog to teach him a lesson. What justice was this when all he'd done was defend the virtue of one of his Muslim sisters. Jesus, just when things were going so well, with Shunduri, with the car, and those new contacts for the phone business that were so promising.

When he got in, Shunduri jumped, and he realized that she'd been sleeping. He picked up her hand and kissed it, knowing that her smooth, perfumed skin would calm him. She needed looking after, in her condition. Kareem steered the car through the familiar tangle of Brick Lane streets—with men in lungis spitting in the gutters, women in saris and cardigans, little girls in frilly dresses and boys in homeboy jeans and long shirts—and tried to think of what to do, where he could go and how he could stop or at least get out of the way of this thing that seemed to be bearing down on him.

He did a quick stop at his council flat to pick up supplies: the gifts he'd organized yesterday, and a few other things in view of Suj's news, and then they were on the motorway, and Shunduri had still not spoken to him. He glanced at her. She was awake, looking thoughtful.

"Eh, Princess, you alright dere? Want a drink or a snack?"

She sighed. "Yaah. Nah."

"Listen, Princess, your dad," he said tentatively. "Does he know any judges? Or lawyers maybe?"

"What are you talkin' about?"

"Look, just chill, Princess. It's all good. I've got some shi—some stuff happening in London I need to sort out, that's all." There was a blare of horns from a lorry he'd drifted in front of. Fuckin' hell, since when did he drive like some yardie just off the plane? He had to cool it, find a place to think this all through before he was touching her parents' feet in the family home. Or being scraped off the road. He stole a look at Shunduri to see that her eyes were shut again, and he resolved to keep his mouth that way too, till he'd sorted out this mess. Jesus Christ, keep your eyes on the road.

---

Once Kareem had installed his princess in state in the Swindon Railway Cafe, bags all around her, he drove sedately back onto the high street, his hands damp on the wheel, watching the station's tiled roof recede in his rear-view mirror and counting the minutes until he would be on the A road again.

He felt under the front of his seat, his fingers brushing over the fine margins of his personal supply, taped into place this morning. He would pull off on some laneway, have a smoke, do a line, have a think. Could they lift fingerprints off skin, or suit material? He could lie low at some local pub for a few weeks, then make some calls and see what was happening before he made any more decisions. Perhaps Suj had been exaggerating.

The GPS beeped: *Change of route, recalculating*, and Kareem swore, realizing that he'd just missed the turnoff to Lydiard village. Still, he was prepared. He reached over to the left and opened the glovebox to do a visual on the maroon and gold of his EU passport, the blue of his Bangladeshi one, and the fat bundles of cash that he'd collected from the flat.

If things didn't work out with Baby's family, or if things got too hot here, he'd go to Pakistan maybe: those Mirpuris owed him some big favors, and they didn't give a shit about Interpol. And there were always business opportunities there, at the supply end of things. Six months away, up to a year would do it for sure. Next to the cash was a red velvet box holding the ring: two carats of brilliant-cut diamond set in soft Asian gold, that a supplier had had a mate drive down to him last night as a favor. A little surprise for his princess, providing all went well. *Turn left in two hundred meters for the A3102.*

———

LATE ON SUNDAY morning, Mrs. Begum stirred the dishwater with her hands, lifted them out, pressed them together and parted them gently. An iridescent film appeared between her palms and she blew on it and watched it tremble, then jump into a bubble, before floating up and away to the kitchen curtains, where it landed on the picture of Mustique.

She drew in her breath. An omen. Little Shunduri, her Baby, arriving on the London train soon now, would be married in the proper way, to a Bangla boy and with all the trappings that Mrs. Begum had dreamt of, ever since her youngest was born. She had always known that Shunduri had not been born so beautiful for nothing.

The oven alarm shrilled out, and Mrs. Begum jumped.

"Tariq! Tariq! It is time to get your sister!"

She ran to the hall, drying her hands, back and front, against the fabric on her hips. In the sitting room, Dr. Choudhury was already out of his chair and smoothing his hair in the mantel mirror. Tariq was there as well and moving toward the brass dish holding the keys, but Mrs. Begum was too quick and snatched them up. Dr. Choudhury, with genial authority, pulled the keys out of Mrs. Begum's hands and tossed them to his son.

"What are you doing?" he said to his wife. "Driving now?"

She gave him a speaking look, then snatched them back off her son and flew to put them in the front door, giving the two men barely enough time to squeeze past her and outside before she locked it. Number-one fools, both of them.

By the time they were all in the car and heading down the lane, she had planned the special meal to welcome Baby home: butter chicken, dahl of course, aloo ghobi and mango rice. Who cared if it was nursery food: those were still Baby's favorites. Ah, how long would it be, how many minutes, until she could hold her youngest child in her arms again?

From the back seat she watched Tariq driving, noting all the differences: the confidence with which he drove, so unlike Dr. Choudhury who sat so close he could rest his chin on the steering wheel, and who also had a tendency, on long drives, to drift across the road unless she said "Eh! Eh!" to return him to proper wakingness. Tariq could drive them both from now on: take Dr. Choudhury to his Leicester-shopping, take her to Cirencester and Swindon. He would be free for these things, seeing as he was going to be an unmarried man until roosters laid eggs.

---

IT WAS A pretty drive, through a landscape that still looked over-colored and miniature to his desert eyes, but Tariq had to concentrate on the road. What with Mum behind him and Dad next to him, he was surrounded by their desire for haste. He normally enjoyed driving them, especially Mum: her unexpected asides, her interest in all the sights and events of the journey, even her irrepressible urge to fiddle with the radio and any other knob or button within her reach.

But today their urgency weighed on him, and he had to keep watching the speedometer to make sure he stayed within limits. At least Baby was coming without that wide-boy boyfriend: it would make it easier for them to catch up a bit more. He always felt a twinge of guilt at how he and Rohimun never had much time for her when they were growing up.

Shunduri was alright in small doses, but she just seemed to have an uncanny bloody instinct for asking the wrong question at the wrong time, landing everyone in it, and then behaving as if she had no idea what she'd done. She'd been such a tale-teller when she was little. If Mum put the pressure on her to marry, nothing was more certain than that she would ask why Tariq wasn't, and bring up the whole thing again. She could make big trouble for Munni too, and god knows what they were going to do there, with the Bournes looking ready to start moving back in soon.

Ahead, the tarmac was covered in lumps and clods of earth thrown up from a dirt laneway that ran into it, and he slowed the car and automatically turned his head to look down the lane through the break in the hedgerows. He caught a glimpse of a large dark car and a man in a suit leaning against it, cupping his hands around a cigarette.

And then they were past. It was only a moment, but the image of the polished, gleaming car, the black suit and white shirt vivid against the soft greens of leaves and grasses, stayed with him through the rest of the drive.

Soon they were in the station car park and he was searching for a space. When they got to the railway cafe, it was crowded with disgruntled travellers, milling and chaotic, and the announcements of train cancellations and delays were almost continuous.

*Leaves on the line*, the PA system kept saying. *British Rail apologizes. Leaves on the line.*

Tariq found chairs for Mum and Dad, but they wouldn't sit so, parents in tow, he forged through the crowd, looking over people's heads for his tall sister. She was nowhere to be seen. He started to edge his way back, and it was then that he saw a covered woman sitting at one of the cafe tables. Although the place was packed, with at least four people to a table, each pretending in their *gora* way that they were there on their own, she had a table to herself. The woman picked up a coffee cup, showing long, fiery red nails, and he realized: that was Shunduri. What had happened to her? Was this some kind of payback for his fundamentalist years?

He moved toward her, acutely aware of Mum behind him, oblivious as yet and holding on to the flap of his jacket, Dad following, both of whom would spot her any minute.

"Baby? Jesus Christ, is that you? What's all this for?"

Shunduri stood up with a certain dignity. She looked even taller in the full-length black robes, and her eyes were heavily, even theatrically, made up. Seeing that, he felt a measure of relief: it was all just another pose, then. Or maybe also taking the piss out of him as a former Islamist. But Baby wasn't a great one for irony: the simplest explanation was the most likely. She was just trying it out for the reaction, the attention. He had a vision of what it must have been like on the train, with everyone trying not to sit too near her, trying to guess which of her bags was the bomb.

Shunduri dipped down to touch Dad's feet and, appearing to be struck dumb himself, he let her for once. Mum gave a short wail that seemed to be pitched halfway between surprise and anger, then darted forward to embrace her daughter and was almost swallowed up in the black robes. Tariq, disgusted, turned away and started to pick up her bags. She'd brought enough with her for someone who was going to be wearing the same thing every day.

Baby's bags filled the boot, and one had to be wedged into the middle of the back seat between her and Mum. Even Dad was doing his bit, with Baby's beauty case on his lap and the seat so far forward that his knees hit the dashboard. Shunduri was laughing and talking as they set off, saying how comfy and snug it was. He could see Mum smile and nod in the rear-view, considerably more squashed on her side by the suitcase, which seemed to have inched toward her.

Listening to his sister as he drove, he could not help feeling that Shunduri's natural self-importance, evident ever since the growth spurt she'd had in her teens, had been increased by London life into assurance.

"What's happening wiv Affa?" she said. "I haven't heard nuffink, *as usual*."

She sounded like a coolie-girl. He saw Dad raise his eyebrows, and even Mum was briefly silenced before asking her if she had any new favorite dishes.

As they drove home, Tariq found himself looking, with a lurking suspicion, for the man with the car he'd seen in the break in the hedgerows, but the narrow laneway was now deserted.

But when they arrived at Windsor Cottage, the same black car was already there, on the verge, and someone was pacing next to it. Kareem fucking Guri. Tariq met his deceitful sister's eyes in the rear-view mirror and watched her poor attempt at surprise and puzzlement over Mum and Dad's questions. No wonder she'd been able to travel with so much luggage, hadn't been affected by all the train cancellations.

Tariq parked up in the drive. Kareem turned toward the car and waved hello, but Tariq ignored him and walked to the boot and started lifting bags out.

Shunduri joined him there. "It's so nice to be home, Baiyya," she said, using her little-girl voice.

He dropped the last suitcase on the gravel and slammed the boot shut. "Drove up here with your boyfriend, then?" he said, but quietly so Mum and Dad wouldn't hear.

Shunduri brought her face close to his, and hissed at him through the fabric. "I caught the train! I didn't . . ."

Tariq picked up the two heaviest cases. "Leaves on the line, yeah. Save it, Baby."

She flounced off, leaving him with the bags. He took two steps with them, but then Kareem was blocking his path saying *Salaam-alaikum, Baiyya* and trying to touch his feet. Tariq suppressed an urge to kick him and walked around him. He wasn't greeting no boyfriend.

He stopped at the front door and looked back to see his father at a loose end, and Kareem half inside one of the rear car doors, wrestling with the last suitcase, which appeared to have become stuck between the front and back seats. Even Mum seemed a bit lost for words: torn between pleasure at having her daughter home and irritation at the timing of Kareem's arrival. Did Mum and Dad suspect anything? Surely Mum would.

---

MRS. BEGUM EYED her youngest daughter, her black robes billowing out around her on the lino as she squatted on the kitchen floor to pull out the largest silver tray. All sorts of thoughts were going through Mrs. Begum's head. She had a clear picture in her mind of Tariq's final visit home from university in full beard, Punjabi-pyjamas and topi, shouting at Munni for her Western clothes. And an older memory, of how she, Syeda Begum, had dressed to hide her stomach in the weeks of argument and shame that had led to her own marriage.

"Take that off, Baby," she said. "We are home now."

Shunduri looked up at her. "Kareem's still here, innit?"

"Take-it-off. We are not Arabs."

Shunduri placed the tray on the table and, in slow motion, started to undo the front buttons of the enveloping drapery, her veil still in place. Mrs. Begum folded her arms to stop them from slapping her into speediness.

Tariq's voice, then Kareem's, could be heard in the passage.

She laid a hand on her daughter's arm. "Stay here and get the tray ready. And mangoes."

When Mrs. Begum stepped into the hall, she saw Kareem at the front doorway, loaded down with boxes, much as he was the first time he'd visited. He genuflected awkwardly in a sort of half-bow. She felt a wave of heat, of hot rage, move through her body at the thought of the opium that he had brought into their house.

Had he known? No matter: even if he had, she had no choice; they had to be brought together, for everyone's sake. All must be forgotten, for the sake of their family's future. No one could know but her. She swallowed her anger and gave him a false smile and a look as sharp and cold as the blade of her *dhaa*. Take that and beware. We will love you like a son if you marry her, and kill you like a dog if you do not.

Dr. Choudhury appeared from the sitting room, which allowed Kareem to make his *salaams*. Mrs. Begum popped back into the kitchen to remind Baby not to come out until she collected her, as there was no need for Kareem to think that they were eager. When she walked in, Shunduri, headscarf still in place, was in the middle of doing the buttons of her *abaya* back up. *Furu shaitan*, little devil that she was. "Stay," Mrs. Begum hissed and returned to the sitting room.

There, Kareem was distributing his gifts: a whole durian for her in all its stinking, prickly glory; a GPS each for Dr. Choudhury and Tariq; and a large, brightly colored book, for the "other" daughter. Her husband read out the book's title in a neutral voice, *The World's Greatest Artists*, and put it to one side without comment. No present for Shunduri: Kareem had come with a purpose then.

Mrs. Begum relaxed a little and asked him did he know how Mrs. Guri was, and he bobbed his head and passed on Mrs. Guri's respects and all the news of Brick Lane with as much deference as the touchiest elder could have wanted. Did they realize, he added, he had a particular reason to know the Guris and be grateful to them: they had made him their son for the visa, and had been as good to him as his own parents?

Mrs. Begum listened to Kareem's proffered history and again reviewed her memory of her last conversation with that snake Mrs. Guri. She had never said that she knew Kareem so well, that he was her adopted son. So Mrs. Guri had warned her, but not promoted the match. Why not? Did she not think they were good enough for the Guris, with their big restaurant and their daughter married to an accountant? She realized she was staring at their visitor so hard that he paused, swallowed and seemed to lose the thread of what he was saying. Well, she would see about that. She would call Shunduri in soon then, no more delays, and she would see how they were together, and get to all the bottoms of their lies and disrespectings, this day today.

## Thirty-two

DR. CHOUDHURY WOULD want to know at once. Henry Bourne took the shortcut to Windsor Cottage from the Abbey: downhill to where the river turned and almost doubled back on itself, then straight uphill, using Mrs. Choudhury's colorful washing flapping on the line at the top of the hill as a guide.

Henry looked up every so often as he toiled uphill, to make sure he had not veered off course. He really should consider doing some sort of fitness thing: he and Richard used to run up here without thinking about it. Most unfair that Richard never seemed to put on any weight, even though it was Henry who walked the dogs twice a day. And he knew for a fact his brother did nothing but paperwork.

By the time he reached the cottage, he was sweating in the afternoon sun, and there was a big black car that looked familiar parked in the lane out the front. He hesitated: he hadn't considered they'd have visitors. But the thought of delaying his news and having to immediately retrace his steps up the even steeper rise to the Abbey, decided him. He would only stop in for a minute, perhaps have a glass of water from Mrs. Choudhury and, hopefully, persuade Dr. Choudhury to drop by later this afternoon.

He halted at the front door and flapped his arms about a bit to air his armpits. His shirt felt too tight and his hair was sticking to his forehead. Oh well, nothing ventured.

He knocked on the door. "Hello! Helloo!"

Curtains twitched at a front window, and he averted his eyes. But the next instant there was Dr. Choudhury, opening the door and smiling.

"Well, hello," he said again, relieved and pleased. Good old Choudhury.

"Henry . . ."

"So pleased I could catch you. I've, ah, got some . . ." Only then did he notice Tariq, standing behind Dr. Choudhury. "Oh, hello there! Beautiful weather, isn't it! Just going on and on!"

There was a pause, and Henry tried not to squirm on the outside.

Tariq pushed the front door wider. "Come on in, Henry. Good to see you."

Henry entered the hall and stopped. "I'm so sorry, you've got visitors. I should have called . . ."

"No, no," said Tariq, his hand on Henry's shoulder pushing him forward to follow Dr. Choudhury into the sitting room. "This is Kareem Guri, up from London."

"Ah, yes. We've met, haven't we. Good to see you again. Lovely day, isn't it?"

"Yeah, man." Kareem grinned and pumped his hand hard, several times. "You've been keepin' fit then?"

Henry, disconcerted, eyed Kareem's breadth of shoulder and bulging pectorals. "Oh, ah, yes. Just walking, you know. Lots of walking."

"And you know my sister, Shunduri." Tariq gestured toward a tall black-robed figure sitting next to Mrs. Choudhury.

Henry stepped forward, his hand out. "Good Lord. Ah, hello again, Shunduri, nice weather . . ." He dropped his untouched hand, feeling he'd done something wrong but unable to work out what.

"So, ah, Shunduri," he said, trying to make up for his involuntary exclamation, "how was the drive down from London?"

There was silence, and he had the definite impression that, yet again, he'd done the wrong thing. Perhaps they'd had an accident? But that car didn't have a scratch on it. A speeding fine?

Kareem's hand hit Henry's shoulderblade with a gentle smack. "The drive was good, man. All good. Shunduri came by train."

"Oh. Well, that's nice too."

Another pause: perhaps they'd had a tiff. Or something. He couldn't think of a thing to say. He stood on one leg, then the other.

Mrs. Choudhury appeared at his elbow. "Cup-of-tea?"

"Oh, ah, I would love to, Mrs. Choudhury, but perhaps a glass of water, if it's not too much trouble. Just a flying visit really. Dr. Choudhury, I was actually hoping I could have a word? About the Abbey."

Dr. Choudhury, sitting in a wing-back chair near the window, gestured to the seat next to his. "Please. Make yourself comfortable. Tell us all. My son would like to hear as well."

Henry sat down in the proffered chair with a small sigh of relief. "It's all the upshot of a last-minute decision really, that I, ah, took a bit of a punt on, earlier this week." He glanced anxiously at Dr. Choudhury. "I hadn't been able to get hold of you, Dr. Choudhury, on the Thursday, or after, you understand . . ."

"Yes, yes."

"Well, ah, a couple of archaeology students from Swindon Tech called me Monday morning and asked if I had anywhere in the grounds that they could excavate. Frightfully keen they were: said they'd be properly supervised and all that, by their Honors supervisor. At first, you know, I couldn't think of anywhere, but at the last minute I remembered the filled-in area in the eastern wall of the long gallery. You know, the one we originally thought was a walled-up window? Well, the next thing I knew they had drop cloths on the floor and rope around the perimeter and had dug out this niche. And it's *tiled.*"

Dr. Choudhury leaned forward in his chair. "Tiled?"

"Yes. I just had a look at it now. Rows and rows of tiles in a sort of flattish semicircle. They haven't excavated all of it yet, but it looks as if the whole niche is tiled. I've never seen anything like it before. All I can think is that the Reverend Bourne was behind it all. Ah, sorry, everyone: he was the first Bourne to own the Abbey, about a century and a half ago. So, I thought that the reverend might have tiled the niche in order to put a stove in there to warm the gallery in winter."

Dr. Choudhury stood and started to pace. "Any sign of a stove, or a flue?"

"No, that's just it. None at all. Though we haven't gone all the way up to the top of the niche yet. Those students are at it right now. Pretty keen they are too. I remember when I was young—"

Tariq interrupted. "What sort of tiles?"

"They're not really like anything I've seen before. I can't guess at the era, to tell you the truth. They're mainly a blue glaze, then some green with raised gold marks, sort of swirls."

"Art Nouveau, Arts and Crafts maybe?"

"I suppose. That would date it to around the Reverend Bourne's time. And he was happy enough to put heaters and running water into the family wing, and tack on the conservatory. But all my research says that as far as the Abbey itself went, he was a stickler for restoring its original features and stopping there."

"Well," said Dr. Choudhury, his tone brisk and happy. "It looks as if my duties here are not yet completed."

"I didn't mean to . . ."

"Not at all: I'm very glad that you came here, Henry. This could be an important find. It brooks no delay. No delay at all."

Dr. Choudhury looked expectantly at Tariq, who stood up from his chair and smiled at his father and then at Henry. "Nice day for a walk, yeah."

Kareem followed. "Yeah, it's nice weather, innit? I'd be honored to come along as well, Uncle, Baiyya."

"Yes, wonderful, the more the merrier," said Henry. "Is, ah, Richard around? I haven't seen him all morning and I thought he . . ."

Mrs. Choudhury reappeared just then, carrying a large silver tray heaped with samosas, diced mango and glasses of water. "Richard is not here."

"Oh. He's been out all morning, so I thought he might be . . ."

Mrs. Choudhury gave Henry a look that seemed to push him toward the door. "Go, go now," she said. "All of you. Stop. Take one," and she shoved the tray toward Henry and Tariq. "Take a samosa. You can eat them on the way. Tariq."

"Yes, Amma?"

"Take that too." She nodded toward a shiny metal container that was sitting on the hall floor, and Tariq scooped it up without a murmur and headed out.

Kareem set off after Tariq, and Shunduri started to do the same, but quick as a flash Mrs. Choudhury stepped in front of her with the tray.

"Take this, Baby. Into the kitchen. *Take it.*"

Shunduri made an odd little noise that sounded to Henry almost like a growl, but she took the tray.

Mrs. Choudhury, her hands freed, made a shooing motion at Henry. "Go. I will talk with my daughter now. Go."

Henry, pleased at so much general interest, hurried to catch up with Dr. Choudhury, who was at the front door. "I bet there'll be a few people at the university who'll want to hear about this," he said. Dr. Choudhury grunted in a non-committal way, and Henry added, "You might get another paper out of the Abbey yet, all to the academic good, eh!"

Dr. Choudhury still did not reply, and as his walking speed continued to increase and Henry was feeling the beginning of a stitch, he let himself fall behind. Perhaps Dr. Choudhury was being careful to reserve judgement until after he'd seen the niche himself—the most sensible thing to do, of course.

Excited though Henry was, it was also rather galling for him to find, on the return journey, Dr. Choudhury as well as the others moving inexorably ahead of him as he struggled up the hill, samosa in hand, to the Abbey's main entrance. Twice in quick succession was too much. He put his head down and did his best, but he was puffed before he reached the top. It was awfully decent of Kareem to come back and wait with him while he recovered.

Henry looked up at him. "I don't suppose you could eat another samosa?"

"No problems, man, not wiv Auntie's homemades. Give it here. So how old is this building, anyway?"

"Oh, ah, its oldest part dates back to the twelfth century and then, ah, various bits were added after. It came into my family about a hundred and fifty years ago. That's when the Reverend Bourne got hold of it. He's my, ah, great-great-great-uncle. Phew." He straightened up.

Kareem's hand squeezed his shoulder lightly. "Alright now, man?"

"Oh, yes, never better."

They walked together through the Abbey's front entrance, and Henry eyed the main staircase with aversion. He decided to take every opportunity to stop and explain the provenance of the various paintings that they passed on the way up. Kareem's favorite, the executioner, still glowered at the stairway's lowest point, but there were three other Orientalist beauties to give him a bit of a rest before they got to the first landing.

---

WHEN TARIQ AND his father reached the long gallery, Thea was there, in jeans and a t-shirt, working next to the archaeology students at the niche. She was squatting and seemed to be collecting some small items from the surface of the drop cloths. One student was on a stepladder, gently scraping at the ceiling of the niche, while the other brushed at its tiled wall. Even through the dust, the rich deep blue of the tiles was striking.

Thea must have heard them approaching across the floorboards, because she turned and held something out for them to look at. In her palm were some tile fragments, in the same deep blue as the rest.

"Look." She licked her finger and rubbed the glaze, and on the dark blue a small gold star appeared, then another.

Tariq spoke impulsively. "There's no way that's Art Nouveau."

Thea didn't look at him. "I'd agree there. Not even English, I think."

His father hurrumphed. "French, perhaps? Puts me in mind of those ceilings of stars in Sainte-Chapelle. And the Hampton Court chapel. But they were painted on the plasterwork between the vaulting, Tudor fashion."

Thea shook her head doubtfully. "It looks familiar to me somehow, from something I saw growing up, in Patmos. I can't think what though. There's nothing like this around here, in the original Abbey, or any of the Bourne additions."

Tariq and his father ducked under the rope and stepped onto the drop cloths. There was limited room and so the students retreated, heading straight for their water bottles and drinking thirstily. A haze of cement dust filled the air.

They moved in further still, into the niche itself, hard up against the stepladder. This close, the niche had an exotic quality: it felt both ancient and otherworldly, and Tariq saw his father shut his eyes, as if he also was trying to absorb, and understand, the unique, unnameable quality of this space.

Tariq copied Thea, licking his finger and running it down one of the tiles on the dadoed portion. Its green became a brilliant emerald, with embossed loops and swirls of glittering yellow. He drew in his breath. "That's real gold in the underglaze, isn't it?" he whispered to his father.

"Quite likely." Dad bent down until his nose was almost on the tile. "Handmade," he said. "And very old."

"How old can tiles be?"

"Well, I do believe the Assyrians provided the earliest, ah, non-Chinese examples. Glazed bricks, using an alkaline glaze colored by copper."

"That's old."

"I hasten to add, these are not likely to be that old. They are true tiles, not glazed bricks . . . The oldest European tiles would be fifteenth-century—Gothic, in other words. But I think, I cannot be certain, these tiles may be older than that. As old perhaps as the Abbey itself."

---

BY THE TIME they reached the long gallery, Henry was exhausted.

"Jesus Christ," said Kareem. "You could play football in here."

"Well," said Henry, leaning against the doorframe for just a moment, "we did, as children. And cricket, I think. No room for boundary fielders though."

At the far end of the gallery, Dr. Choudhury and Tariq could be seen standing in the niche, with Thea on the edge of the roped-off area, examining something in her hand. Henry pushed himself upright and pointed at the niche.

"There it is, Kareem. The cause of all our excitement."

They started to walk down the gallery, and he waved at the two students, grey with dust, who were sitting slumped on the floor with their legs out, holding water bottles and looking like survivors of a desert sandstorm.

"Well done. I can see you've progressed a lot in the last hour."

One lifted his hand briefly, before letting it flop back to the floorboards. "Yeah, thanks, mate. Any ideas?"

Henry waved toward Dr. Choudhury. "We've got the experts here now, so let's see what they have to say." He turned to Kareem. "This end wall, you see, is one of the original outer walls of the Abbey: local Cotswold stone and nearly four feet thick. But here, in the middle, the plaster covering the stonework was clearly deteriorating. When our National Trust boffins had a closer look, it turned out to be a different quality: a different ratio of lime, or, ah, gypsum, to sand and water, you understand. So it had probably been done later. And when our hardworking students took it back, we found this niche."

Henry pointed at the dressed stone quoins and central keystone that edged the niche. "So we thought, it's some kind of filled-in window because of this framing stonework; it's as old as the Abbey. But then, as you can see, once we cleared out the brickwork behind the plaster, and the rubble behind that, we not only find no sign of a filled-in window, but we find this."

Kareem stayed back from the ropes and brushed fastidiously at his suit jacket. "How about a builder's mistake then? Got the plans the wrong way round, thought they were doin' a door?"

Henry shook his head. "Unlikely. It's just too finely crafted. And look how the wall inside the niche is one smooth curve. And the top of the framing stonework sort of swells out then comes to a point. No, it's definitely both original and intentional. But what for?"

"Didn't they wall up nuns that had boyfriends 'n' that?" Kareem's voice tailed off a little, and Henry noticed him looking uneasily at the Choudhurys, as if regretting what he'd said.

"Well, technically, nuns were punished for adultery, because they were married to the Church. And, of course, for breaking their holy vows."

Thea, also in earshot, dropped something on the ground, but wouldn't meet his eye. He called out to her. "Hey, Thee, I'm back at last. You remember Kareem?"

Thea nodded in acknowledgement.

He continued his history lesson. "But no, ah, there never were any nuns here. It was a monastery only."

Kareem walked on to the far end of the gallery, and Thea started to leave, muttering something about needing to wash. Henry lifted a hand to hold her back, but then thought better of it. She did look upset, and now she was folding her arms: always a bad sign. Perhaps she'd been feeling left out of the conversation.

"Thee," he said tentatively. "What do you think of it all then?"

"No idea, I'm sure," she said, but when she was almost past him, she reached out a hand and splayed it against his chest. He froze in surprise. She kissed him on the mouth, dust and all, then quickly withdrew and walked away, toward the door, as if nothing had happened.

Henry blinked. Thee wasn't normally one for spontaneous gestures. But she had been different the last couple of days. More relaxed, until just now. Not even dressing for dinner. Perhaps the warm weather.

"I'm going to have a word with the movers" she called over her shoulder. "They're bringing back the books for the library today."

"Rightio, Thee. See you later."

Dr. Choudhury called him over, and he ducked under the ropes and walked gingerly across the drop cloths, anxious not to step on tile fragments like the ones Thea seemed to have been collecting. She seemed so fragile sometimes.

As he approached the niche, Dr. Choudhury beckoned him closer. "I do think that these tiles were made with this or an identical niche in mind." He pointed at the margin where tiles met the dressed stone-work of the architraves seamlessly. "Beautiful craftsmanship. See here? These tiles were not cut to fit: they were made with a curve to measure."

Tariq spoke up. "Or the niche was."

"No matter, no matter," said Dr. Choudhury, flipping his wrist dismissively. "What matters is that they were made for each other."

"You know," Henry said thoughtfully, sliding one finger down the cool gloss of a tile, "this is like heaven: the night sky and stars. Could we have had a Mary cult here? Like Robert Graves wrote about: Mary, Queen of Heaven, and all that."

Dr. Choudhury stared at the tiles. "Up here, in the gallery?"

"Yes," Henry continued, surprised at not having been shot down immediately, "worshipped in secret, by a chosen few—the abbot and his acolytes, *Da Vinci Code* and all that . . ."

Dr. Choudhury *pah*'d with disgust.

Tariq laughed at his father's face. "Good one, Henry. But it doesn't explain the tiles. And why have a statue of Mary in a niche at all? Until the Reformation, she was perfectly welcome downstairs in the nave, next to the altar."

Henry felt his face grow hot. "I know it's not my area, but I still think that this niche was used for something special. Look at where it is." He waved an arm at the long gallery. "Largest room in the build-ing: larger, even, than the nave and apse combined. Big window set high at the far end, the western end, throwing light onto this end. Door set way down there, as if they didn't want to interfere with some kind of gathering closer to the niche." The other two were silent, and he dropped his hand, feeling foolish. "I just think . . ."

"It comes back to the tiles," said Dr. Choudhury. "Perhaps if we could date them."

Henry sighed. "We should probably let the National Trust know about this. Their archaeological division will most likely take it over."

"Oh no. Oh, man," said one of the sandstormed students. "After all our work?"

Henry and Tariq looked at Dr. Choudhury. He hesitated, then smiled. "I do not consider that the niche is going anywhere. The excavation has been most carefully done." He nodded at the students, who cheered and lay back on the floorboards. "And besides, I am effectively the Trust's representative, in any event."

"How about, ah, Theo Kiriakis?" Henry said reluctantly.

Dr. Choudhury seemed almost carefree. "All in good time. When Mr. Kiriakis is told, he will want more information than we are currently able to give him, so, in all, I do consider that completion of these excavations would be prudent. And perhaps a little work on the, er, dating side of things."

The students sat up and began to put their face masks back on. Kareem strolled toward them from the far end of the gallery and ducked under the ropes. He picked up a cloth and, before Henry or anyone could warn him about the tiles' fragility, ran it along the dado in one horizontal sweep. The swirls and curlicues of gold on green stood out vividly, but without the regularity of a pattern.

"Holy shit," Kareem said. "Sorry, Uncle, sorry, Baiyya. What's that doing here?"

"*Arabic,*" said Dr. Choudhury. "Arabic writing, in a twelfth-century English monastery."

Henry bent down to look for himself. "Good Lord. Perhaps the Reverend Bourne brought these back from his travels."

"No," said Dr. Choudhury. "This is much older. I am certain of it now. And think of the stonework around it."

Kareem stepped backward to view the niche as a whole, then gave a shout of laughter, making Henry jump. "It's a mihrab, man! What's a mihrab doing in a monastery?"

Henry looked at Kareem. "What's a mihrab?"

"It's for the *qibla* wall—the direction for Mecca. Where you face to pray, in a mosque."

"Good Lord," said Henry again. "So, ah, you're saying that they must have brought this back from the Crusades. Heavens. I mean, brought the tiles back, and the idea, and maybe the artisans too."

A long *aah* sound came from Dr. Choudhury, who nodded at Henry's disbelieving face. "Good heavens. Yes. Of course. Well done, Kareem. In the great mosques they were often very elaborately decorated, often with glazed and marble tiles, glass mosaic . . . But here . . . Surely . . ."

"It does face east, doesn't it?" said Tariq.

Henry nodded.

"Jesus Christ. Abba, was the first abbot a Crusades knight?"

Dr. Choudhury coughed delicately. "That is correct, Tariq. He went on the Crusades, and he was knighted. But there are indications from the records extant, which Henry has been working on, that he was not knighted for valor on the battlefield. His specialty seemed to be more along the lines of, ah, gathering information."

"You mean, he was a spy?" said Kareem. "Deep cover, eh?"

Henry answered. After all, it was his family, in a way. "Not really. Some of the surviving documents, including a frieze in Tregoze Church, describe his services as, ah, in the line of obtaining information by force."

"Like torture, you mean," said Tariq.

There was an uncomfortable pause, and Henry realized that Dr. Choudhury was again waiting on him. "Ah, yes. Yes."

Kareem slapped his hands against his thighs so hard that the sound echoed through the gallery like a gunshot. "Extraordinary rendition! That's what all dis came from. Torturing Muslims!" He laughed and turned to Tariq. "We better watch out here, man! Nuttin' new in the world is dere!"

Tariq snorted with laughter, but Henry was mortified. How on earth could they find it funny?

"Why is the niche here then?" he asked Dr. Choudhury. "If it was the first abbot who built this—"

"Had it built, Henry. Had it built."

"Had it built. Why would he make his fortune from torturing the enemy and then have this built? Go to all this effort? I can understand bringing home rugs and scimitars and, er, ah, concubines—spoils of war and all that. But this, this is different."

By the time he had finished speaking, Kareem and Tariq appeared to have calmed down, but he still felt an obscure sense of hurt at their levity, as if they'd been making fun of him by laughing at his Abbey's history. And surely torture and war were nothing to joke about. And in front of the students too, who had drifted up, still masked, and were listening to the exchange.

Dr. Choudhury addressed them all. "When two cultures clash like this, invade each other's lands, settle and are reconquered again and again over the centuries, cultural cross-fertilization is inevitable. Look at Cordoba in Spain, the Hagia Sophia in Istanbul."

"Yeah," said Tariq. "But this, this isn't just a bit of Romanesque architecture. It's religion."

"Yes," said Dr. Choudhury thoughtfully. "I am wondering if our first abbot came back a convert."

No one said a word.

Then Kareem chuckled. "A convert. To Islam." He seemed to be enjoying himself hugely. "And so he sets up the monastery, and then what?"

"Well . . ." Dr. Choudhury appeared to ponder. "He worships here in secret. Comes up here to pray, perhaps with some other secret converts within the Abbey, maybe some other ex-Crusader knights."

Tariq nodded. "Yeah. Soldiers do stick together, especially if they've seen action together."

Dr. Choudhury stared at his son a little strangely, and Henry found himself wondering about Tariq's background.

"But, as I was saying," Dr. Choudhury continued, "there is every indication that the first abbot ordered the religious life—the religious Christian life, of the Abbey—in the usual way. It's quite possible to have, ah, a secret or double life, you know." He paused for a moment. "Otherwise he could never have survived, let alone flourished and acquired more land, the way that we know he did. This Abbey was one of the great pre-Reformation monasteries, known for its learning as well as its wealth, until Henry VIII decided to close it down and redistribute its lands."

Dr. Choudhury moved closer to the niche. The students, and everyone else, watched him.

"That, I think, is when this Abbey caught fire. You can see here, and here, some of these tiles showing signs of having been scorched and blackened, some cracked by the great heat of the fire. So, that tells us that this niche may have been open, perhaps even still in use, some three hundred years after it was built."

Tariq looked shocked. "You mean, in use as a mihrab, for all that time?"

"Well, that we do not know. In those days, tradition was everything. So *salat*, that's Muslim prayer, may well have been carried on in front of the mihrab by successive generations of abbots, or knights, though perhaps without a full understanding of what it meant. Many traditions are like that. Look at morris dancing. And maypoles."

Henry's mouth opened, and he gave a little start of excitement. "Come to think of it, the Reverend Bourne had all his Orientalist prayer and pilgrimage paintings up here. You haven't seen those, Kareem—they're still in storage. But they're all North African images: dawn prayer on a rooftop, pilgrims on camels, praying at the tomb of Ali . . . Good Lord. I'd never thought."

Dr. Choudhury stroked his chin thoughtfully. "Indeed, Henry. And I seem to recall, from early photographs, that the pictures were hung so that images in the paintings, the, er, dawn worshippers for example, faced east. Maybe he was a convert as well. The Algerian boys that he used to bring back from his travels would certainly have been Muslim."

Tariq stared at him. "Eh?"

Dr. Choudhury looked at a point just above his son's head. "The Victorian grand tour was not only, er, educational but, shall we say, for some of the gentlemen, a broadening experience, amongst what were, in some ways, the less repressed cultures of the Near and Middle East. Similar to the ancient Greeks. Perhaps the Reverend let them pray up here, put the paintings up to keep them company, thought it was appropriate. They would have needed to face east, toward Mecca, so it is possible that they unknowingly continued the Abbey's tradition."

Henry thought Tariq seemed pleased, even moved, but as for himself, now that he'd gotten it, he was bouncing on the balls of his feet with enthusiasm. "Never mind about that. Just think: those Templar knights coming back from Cordoba or Morocco or Tunis, with the tiles and the plans for the niche and goodness knows what else. Such a secretive order, you know. The rosy cross and all that."

Tariq and Dr. Choudhury snorted at the same time, and Tariq patted Henry's shoulder. "Forget about Dan Brown, man. Or our credibility's down the toilet, yeah?"

He ignored them. This niche, this mihrab, was so wonderful and exciting, and he wasn't going to let tasteless jokes about bestsellers or politics spoil it. He would find Thea and tell her the news, if she wasn't too busy with the movers.

## Thirty-three

MRS. BEGUM KNEW that where Baby was concerned she was standing on eggshells on her Axminster, and all her natural shrewdness and intimate knowledge of her youngest child rose up in her to meet the challenge. Baby was so liable to dramatics—tears and door-slammings and no-one-understands-mes and it's-not-fairs and I-wish-I-was-deads—that she would need all this time that they would have alone together, to soothe and stroke her into revealing what she really felt, really wanted.

She was sure now that they both desired the same thing. And there was no longer any time left to make mistakes. She would rather die than let Baby marry in the same circumstances that she had, shamed and disgraced by her own body.

Her daughter shifted restlessly in front of the sitting-room's side window, looking, looking at that Abbey into which the men had disappeared about twenty minutes before. Her face was thin and hungry, but not for food. She had that look, the one that she used to discuss with Mrs. Darby, as they sat over tea and pound cake, and leafed through some of the older *Majesty* magazines together, examining the pictures of Prince William and his then-girlfriend.

Waity-Kaity, Mrs. Darby had called her, with that smooth hair and so-fashionable clothes, but in those pretty eyes, a look of hunger and patience tested. Because he hadn't proposed yet and everyone was asking, or maybe he had said secret engagement (always such a mistake, Mrs. Darby said, and Mrs. Begum agreed wholeheartedly), or maybe he never would propose since she was no longer a good girl, or perhaps he had seen too much of the tragedy of his own parents' marriage to trust in his own future. Too thin, too hungry by half, Mrs. Begum had thought: such a contrast with the smiling relaxation of just-married William-and-Kate, happy with their new place in the world.

She took her daughter's arm, stiff but unresisting, and sat her down on the couch, nice-and-close. Shunduri sat upright, staring straight ahead, her profile made even more striking by its black frame.

"I remember so well, the day you were born. I knew you would be my last, my little baby, and all through the labor I suffered. Oh, how I suffered! But knowing, knowing all the time, that it would be worth the pain." She slid even closer to her daughter, tenderly fiddled the veil's knot undone, and took out the hairpins holding it flat to her hairline, one by one. "And you were so beautiful, even then. Even then, I knew."

She unwrapped the fabric from around Shunduri's head as if uncovering a rare and precious jewel, took the hated veil into her lap and slowly folded it. Her daughter did not move, but she could see from her tense and upright pose that she was like a little *Doel* bird, half ready to take wing. She would just have to keep talking, not give her daughter too much time to think.

"I *knew*," she said, with loving emphasis. She placed the folded fabric on the couch behind them, and took her daughter's face between her palms, turning it toward her. "I knew."

Shunduri's posture softened a little. "What, Amma?"

"I knew, Baby, that you would be beautiful." She rose up off her bottom for a moment to kiss her daughter on the forehead, then sat back down and let her hands return to her lap. "So beautiful. Tall and slim like your father, but with my skin and eyes. And chin. You remember how I had to put the dark spot on you whenever we went out, to protect you from the envy of other mothers? Ahh. I used to love taking you shopping. Munni and Abu would fight for turns to push your stroller. I miss those days. But I am so proud of you now." She gave a sigh. "Especially now, with so many other troubles in my life. My other children . . . It is a great comfort to my mother's heart to see how well *you* have turned out." She was startled by a look of need, even desperation, in her daughter's eyes.

"I can't be doin' any more study, Amma. I, I don't care that I haven't finished."

"Of course, my Baby."

"I don't care that I have to come home."

"Of course, of course."

Baby was ready, then, and even she knew it, suddenly so willing to give up London, even the bank. Mrs. Begum reached for the bottle of hair oil that she'd taken down from the mantel, and Shunduri lay down on her side, putting her head in her mother's lap. Mrs. Begum pooled a little of the liquid in one hand, rubbed it between her palms, then stroked it through her daughter's hair in a long, unhurried caress, and then another and another.

Shunduri wriggled into a more comfortable position, tucked her feet up onto the couch. She gave a heavy, little-girl sigh, and Mrs. Begum nodded tenderly, careful not to smile. My Baby is home, and ready to marry.

There was a watery sniff. She stroked the hair back from her daughter's face and leaned over her. A tear had snaked down Shunduri's cheek, leaving a trail of black.

"Ahh, Baby, you are sad?"

A violent headshake was her only answer, and another sniff.

"You know, your father and I, all we want, all we dream of, is for you to be happy."

Another sniff. A listening sniff.

"I would be so-so happy to see you married to a good boy who will take care of you." She jiggled her knees a little and allowed herself a small smile. "A *handsome* boy."

Shunduri semi-snorted.

Mrs. Begum, encouraged by this sign of a returning sense of humor (never her youngest's strong point), moved on. "We only want the very best for you, precious Baby. To see you settled in a good marriage, to a good boy . . . We have a few boys in mind: but you just tell me what you want. It is up to *you*, my Baby."

Shunduri rolled onto her back, and she saw her daughter's eyes full of tears. Shunduri pulled a tissue out of her robe pocket, dabbed at her eyes, then balled it up between her hands.

"Ahh, my Baby," said Mrs. Begum. "We only want you to be happy."

"I'm not . . . He's not . . . I'm not going to get married off to some Bangla peasant who won't let me work . . . I'm doin' so well at the bank . . . I'm not going to marry some taxi driver or kitchen hand just because he has some stupid degree from Dhaka University . . ." She went into a series of hiccupping sobs and sat up.

Mrs. Begum patted her daughter's back and made soothing noises. "There, there. Baby, we would not do that to you. I know you want a modern boy. I know what you want. A handsome Desi boy, with a good job, nah?"

"Have you an' Abba got someone lined up, then?"

Mrs. Begum gave a quick fingertip touch to the talisman at her neck and ventured on, her tone as bland as if she was Mrs. Darby discussing the weather. "The Guris are a very good family. The same caste as my mother's family. Hardworking, respectable . . ." She had the pleasure of seeing her daughter's cheeks flush darkly.

She took Shunduri's face between her hands again and bent it down to kiss her forehead. "You think your own mother does not guess what is in your heart? I will speak to Mrs. Guri then, and we will arrange a meeting." She hesitated for a fraction of a second, then continued. "He looks like a nice boy. A good boy."

She let the silence linger, to make it clear that this was a question, and her daughter answered with more tears and, eventually, the slightest of nods.

"You want this?" said Mrs. Begum, certain of the answer now.

Shunduri wiped her face with the wadded tissue. "If you an' Abba do . . ."

Mrs. Begum nodded, pleased and happy to show it, though hiding in her heart her concerns. Why had Kareem not initiated an approach from Mrs. Guri? He was clearly worldly enough to know that much. Perhaps they had fallen out. Had Baby compromised herself in some way already? Never: she could not bear to think of it, she must stop thinking that way, except to hurry up her husband. Was Mrs. Guri's last visit supposed to test them, to see if they had someone else in mind? Or was she warning her off? No matter, Kareem would be managed: the mere fact that he was here, and behaving as if he'd been caught halfway up someone else's mango tree, was indication enough that this marriage had to happen.

"Amma?"

"Yes, Baby."

"Could we do the *rukhsati*, the reception, at Oxford Town Hall?"

"Anything for my Baby. Ah, what a lot to do, a lot to look forward to." She embraced her daughter with a mixture of relief that it had all been agreed to so easily, and fear in her heart that Baby was not as innocent as the day she'd first left for London.

"Come, come, let us take this off. Ah, as slim as ever," she said, relieved, as Shunduri removed her *abaya*. "Come into the kitchen and I will make mango rice for you."

As Mrs. Begum pureed fragrant mangoes in Mrs. Darby's second-best food processor and mixed them with white rice, slightly over-cooked, Shunduri sat at the table, as chatty now as she had been silent before, talking about A1 WeddingWalla Wedding Planners, the best Brick Lane shops for wedding *lehengas* and the great need for a pre-wedding *haldi mendhi* that was bigger and better than all her friends' *mendhis* combined. Mrs. Begum nodded and smiled and every so often glanced at her speckled kitchen curtains, where Mustique and the white limousine shifted as the curtains swayed in the afternoon breeze.

Mrs. Begum sat down next to her daughter and fed her the gold rice with her right hand, smiling and cajoling her for each mouthful as if she was an invalid or an infant. This was always such a difficult time for girls, and it was clear that Shunduri had been thinking too hard, wanting too much.

While Baby's mouth was still full, she asked her, "Has Kareem spoken with the Guris?"

Shunduri stopped chewing, swallowed with effort. "He told me he was goin' to speak to them this week." But then the tears welled again, and her voice shook. "I don't know, I don't know what they . . . Amma, it's just a matter of time, innit? He, he said he wanted to see you an' Abba first . . ."

Mrs. Begum took her daughter's hand. "Don't cry, Baby. We will arrange it, we will fix it. If this is what you really want."

Shunduri stared at her mother and nodded, wordless. No pretence now.

"Then I will invite Mrs. Guri to come here. And we will talk." Really talk. If that dirty dog Kareem was not willing to marry Baby, she would force a *funchait*. They were in no position to find another boy. Not after Rohimun had gone off the railways—and when that had happened, Mrs. Begum had received enough sympathy visits from the community to last a lifetime. No more. Shunduri would be married in the proper way, with everything she wanted, as soon as possible.

"This Kareem. He has a good job?"

"He's a businessman. Import-export. Mobiles and stuff."

Stuff, thought Mrs. Begum. He had better not bring any more of his stuff into my house. The durian sat on the kitchen table, and she placed her index finger on it and rolled the fruit suspiciously, back and forth. It looked real enough.

"Eeuw, that stinks, Amma."

"Of course. As it should, it is a durian." She moved to the kitchen window, peering at an awkward angle so as to catch a glimpse of the Abbey hillside. No sign of the men returning yet.

"Amma."

"Yes, my Baby."

"What are you going to do about Affa?"

So Baby was still afraid that Rohimun would spoil her marriage chances. She went back to stand behind her daughter and ran her fingers through Shunduri's wispy straight hair, now shiny with oil: so like her father's, unfortunately. How lucky that the fashion in this country was for short and straight, like Princess Diana and Edward's Sophie.

She looked down at her daughter's bowed head. I, Syeda Begum, uneducated village girl born and bred in Bangladesh, am more modern at heart than my youngest child, so preoccupied with what people will think of her sister and with beating her friends to the *nikkah*. And my so-so clever husband with his Rhodes, and his cannot-forgives.

"We will not talk of your affa today, Baby. Come, your father and I will speak to Kareem, and he will bring Mr. and Mrs. Guri to us. Maybe even tomorrow."

# Thirty-four

KAREEM DIDN'T SEEM to fully understand the significance of the discovery, thought Dr. Choudhury. But his gut instinct, as they say, had been good, and Dr. Choudhury felt a warm flush of pride—it must be pride—that such a man, so young and confident and handsome and broad-shouldered and so much in the physical prime of his life, was his *brother* in the Muslim sense. Right then, he was able to look upon that word as a pleasant reference to the Muslim brotherhood in its historical meaning, as the *ummah*, rather than the *bruvver* of vulgar street slang and source of unwanted familiarity from taxi drivers and suchlike.

Henry had gone off somewhere, perhaps to supervise the movers, and so had Tariq, presumably to check on his sister and give her the tiffin. Kareem was laughing and joking with the two students; as he watched, Kareem slapped the back of one of them, raising a little puff of dust. How did he manage this? To be so at ease wherever he went, to get along with and know how to talk to anyone? Such a charming boy but, now he thought about it, surely such a universal facility indicated a certain lack of discrimination. Kareem was being as charming to those dishevelled students as he had been to him.

Dr. Choudhury looked longingly at the trio of young men but could not bring himself to approach them. If only they would join him. He pretended an interest in the long flattened arch of the ceiling, finding himself reminded too much of the outsider that he had been, at their age.

Kareem moved into view again, away from the two students and, arms folded, surveyed the rest of the long gallery as if, to Dr. Choudhury's dazzled eyes, he owned it. He reminded him of the Franz Ernst painting of an arrogant Ethiopian prince in full regalia, standing on the front steps of his mansion, that hung halfway up the main stairs. Kareem could have posed for it, to the life.

Dr. Choudhury felt old and pedestrian. He cleared his throat. "You know, my boy, I shall be in the land of our spiritual forefathers soon, *Inshallah*."

Kareem was immediately attentive. "Bangladesh?"

"No, no. I speak of our spiritual home. I do hope shortly to be seeing the minarets of Masjid al-Haram. As well as diverse other great sights."

Kareem gave a single anxious glance at his watch, as if suddenly recalling a pressing appointment. "Are you travelling then, sir?"

"The greatest journey of all," Dr. Choudhury said, with a faraway look in his eye, turning his left profile (his best side) toward Kareem.

"Some kind of world trip soon?" Kareem, seeming now both anxious and downcast, walked over to join him.

Dr. Choudhury felt a jolt of pity. The transparent impressionability of youth: so easily excited, so easily cast down. Kareem was obviously hurting at the thought of losing him. And perhaps, Dr. Choudhury thought generously, there was also some truth in Mrs. Begum's plotting and fantasizing: if so, this would be a bad time for a nervous suitor to lose contact with his prospective father-in-law. He really should put him out of his misery.

"Haj, boy. I am speaking of Haj."

Kareem's eyes opened wide. "Man." He paused, then seemed to recover himself. "Sorry, Uncle, I see what you mean about it being the greatest trip."

"The pilgrimage must be begun and accomplished within the

eighth and twelfth days of the twelfth lunar month, *Dhu al-Hijjah*, which commences in a little over a fortnight. Although, of course, as a pilgrim travelling from the UK, we shall commence our actual journey a little earlier than that. So very soon indeed."

"Oh, sir," said Kareem, now in accents of surprise and sorrow. "That is so soon. I had not expected . . . How long will you be gone?"

"Perhaps weeks, perhaps longer. I cannot be certain, given the testing and spiritual nature of such a journey. We may well stay a little longer. The shopping is apparently first-rate. And perhaps visit some additional holy sites."

"You certainly have taken me by surprise, Khalo." Kareem drew closer and his voice became pensive and confiding. "To tell you the truth, sir, I have been thinking for some time of my duties as a Muslim. I would be very grateful, very grateful indeed, if you, with your wisdom and experience, could advise me."

There was indeed nothing Dr. Choudhury liked doing more, particularly since losing access to Oxford's undergraduate student body. He hemmed in a professorial way and gave a fatherly pat to Kareem's shoulder. The boy was solid muscle. "Let us walk, my boy. Let us walk-and-talk, as they say."

They strolled down the main staircase and did a slow circuit of the principal rooms on the ground floor, as Kareem outlined the urges that he had been feeling, to fulfil his own duties as a Muslim. But not only this: the additional and increasingly pressing need that he had become aware of, please excuse his frankness, as a man contemplating marriage—Dr. Choudhury felt himself almost stumble at this point—who felt that, for him, Haj for him would be an important and necessary, almost cleansing, step before embarking upon matrimony.

Recovering his poise, Dr. Choudhury hemmed and hawed to draw the boy out a little more, watching his eager, almost worshipful expression. Ah, the crushes of youth. What a charming age. And the more that they discussed the great benefits of Haj, the more Dr. Choudhury was impressed with Kareem's hitherto unsuspected spiritual depths.

He, of course, counselled Kareem to follow his heart. What else? As soon as these words were out of his mouth, he could see Kareem's visage clearing and brightening to a remarkable degree.

They started to discuss the details of Dr. Choudhury and Tariq's trip, and Kareem suddenly remembered that he had a cousin in Swindon who could get them a discount on the Haj tickets, and furthermore that this cousin could arrange the Haj visas very quickly, organize a first-class trip.

"Khalo," Kareem said, "you may not have realized just how many crooks there are in the business of ripping off pilgrims, tainting the holy journey with their greed and usury."

Kareem went on to provide many instances of corruption and depravity, lost tickets and stranded pilgrims. Not to mention the reputation of the Wahhabi officials for bullying those pilgrims with an inclination to prostrate themselves before certain tombs and other holy sites.

Dr. Choudhury hemmed and hawed at the stories, and started to wonder whether Tariq's presence alone would be sufficient to protect them both from the shysters, robbers and officialdom awaiting them at every step of the journey. It all sounded so much more fraught with danger and difficulty than he had realized.

But then, almost as if he'd been reading his mind, Kareem turned toward Dr. Choudhury, ducking his head respectfully. "Sir, I would be most, most honored to escort you and Baiyya on Haj, sir." He was about to respond, but Kareem hurried on, his face clearly anxious now. "I would be honored to be of service to you in that way. The journey would be even more meaningful in your presence, yeah. *Inshallah*."

Dr. Choudhury patted Kareem's arm again. What a handsome offer. "My boy, my boy. That would be splendid. The more the merrier. Splendid."

All signs of concern left Kareem's face, to be replaced by joy and gratitude. Truly, Dr. Choudhury had not lost his touch with students, as evinced by the reputation he had always felt he had, of being one of his college's best-loved professors. Kareem had clearly recognized these qualities in him, despite his own lack of formal education. And who was he to criticize as failings those very qualities, those untu-tored, instinctive virtues of respect, strength and courage that made Rousseau's savage noble.

As they continued to stroll and to discuss related matters of the journey, Dr. Choudhury began to wonder if perhaps it was Shunduri who would be fortunate in acquiring such a husband, and himself in obtaining such a man as a son-in-law.

Just then Tariq reappeared, and Dr. Choudhury relayed the good news. He could not ignore the fact that Tariq seemed rather subdued by it. But this was understandable: after all, Tariq had expected to have his father to himself for three whole weeks, and was now having to share. But the more the merrier, Dr. Choudhury liked to think. He would be leading quite the little band of travellers. His mind briefly encompassed the telling of Mrs. Begum, then shied away. He was a busy man, what with mihrabs, and Kareem's need for guidance, and his son and daughter here to stay. Perhaps Tariq could do it for him.

# Thirty-five

MRS. BEGUM CLENCHED her right hand into a fist and used it to hit herself over the left breast. "Why, why do you tell me such things, Tariq, if not to stab me in the heart all over again? Just when I fix this family . . ."

Tariq flinched, as well he should. "Amma, please."

Good, she thought, you have not forgotten what you did to your own mother, and your father, just this past Friday. Though *he* seems to have recovered quickly enough. She could not believe what Tariq was telling her. How Dr. Choudhury, that old fool, stupid cockroach, number-one idiot could have thought that taking Kareem to Mecca was a good idea was completely beyond her. Was the deadline on their betrothal and marriage not tight enough already, without Kareem packing his bags the moment *Dhu al-Hijjah* began? And that cowardly snake had just sat here and eaten the meal she had prepared with her own hands, and not said a word.

"Amma, I'm sorry. I'm not that keen on that dirty dog coming along either. But you know Abba."

"Ohh!" She sat down at the kitchen table, then picked up a betel leaf from the pile she had washed that morning. Her husband seemed completely oblivious to the consequences of his actions, as usual, and while Mrs. Begum's fingers began to race, creating a multitude of paan packages in record time, she carried evil thoughts in her heart of lacing his share with poison. Or perhaps with some of those chocolate-covered laxatives that Mrs. Darby always said she could not do without. Only *goras* could talk of such things. Death, or perhaps never leaving the toilet, were surely the only impediments to her husband's ability to make such stupid decisions as this.

"What if he does not come back? What then?"

"Kareem? From Haj, you mean?"

"It happens, it happens. From there, he could go anywhere."

"Well, who cares. Baby could do better than that barrow-boy anytime."

She pressed her lips together and bent over her work. Tariq could not, must not, know her worst fears, the great importance of moving quickly, quickly, to secure this man, and this marriage.

"It'll be alright, Amma. You'll see. Abba might not even go in the end." Tariq checked his watch. "I've got to head off for a couple of hours. Do you want anything from the shops?"

She shook her head, looking at him until he flushed and turned away. She knew where he was going, and he should know that she knew, *furu shaitan* that he was.

The paan tray heaped high, she tucked a package in her mouth, squatted on the floor with her *dhaa*, sliced mangoes like a woman possessed, then stood, kicking the *dhaa* recklessly under the kitchen table.

No time, no time. If she could hold her breath until the two *nik-kahs* were over, she would, but as this was not possible she would have to do her very best to keep the waters smooth and good feelings growing nicely. She arranged mango segments, paan and a small pile of dates on her middle-sized silver tray.

What was of even more importance was that things had to be very clear to Kareem. He must not be allowed to think that he could just run off out of this country without doing what was necessary and right for Shunduri and for all of them. With that thought in her mind, she gave one last nudge to the silver tray and went in search of her son-in-law-to-be. No one would eat anything until this was sorted out.

Mrs. Begum found Kareem in the sitting room fiddling with an earring as Dr. Choudhury questioned Baby about her studies. She needed to get Shunduri out of the room, and Shunduri, good girl, turned toward her with something that looked like relief.

"Amma, do you want help wiv somefin' in the kitchen?"

Mrs. Begum beamed. Shunduri had never willingly helped before. "Baby, I need salt, the soft salt, not the rocks. And tea, from the corner shop." This village was good for little else, and if she asked for anything more, Swindon would be needed, and there would be the problem of who would drive her.

As she hustled her daughter out the door, she could hear that number-one fool of a husband start to hold forth on the different aspects of Haj. Mrs. Begum could restrain herself no longer and moved to stand by Dr. Choudhury. "What is it you are doing down here, Kareem? Why have you come all this way to visit us and now you are deciding to go away on Haj?"

He goggled, glanced at the images of royalty on the mantel wall and fell to his knees.

But she gave him no opportunity to speak. "Your elders, Mr. and Mrs. Guri, who stand in the place of your parents in this country, have not called us, or visited, and Dr. Choudhury would like an answer to these questions."

Dr. Choudhury, who looked dangerously close to goggling as well, recovered himself sufficiently to say, "Yes, yes. We would like an answer to these things, boy."

With a convincing air of spontaneous confession, Kareem spread his hands wide. "I'm so sorry, Khalo, Khalama. Please forgive me. I saw your youngest daughter from afar . . . at a Brick Lane wedding, er, a month ago, and the sight of her struck my heart like a bolt of lightning."

He paused and let his eyes fill with tears. "I have come here because I am a man *in love*." He brought his hands in and placed them, one over the other on the left side of his chest, and spoke quietly. "I hoped and I still hope to prove myself to you as worthy of being a suitor for your daughter. I know, I know that I have done the wrong thing by not speaking first with Mr. and Mrs. Guri, but I had hoped that by rendering some small services to your family that, when you were approached in the proper way, you would be more willing to consider me for the honor of becoming your son-in-law."

Mrs. Begum saw that Kareem's shoulders were bowed, his eyes were overflowing and that his hands had fallen palms upward onto the carpet, so that he was the very picture of abject misery. Most appropriate.

Well pleased with this but careful not to show it, she kept her voice high and angry. "What are you, a boy with no family, no money, no visa! You think you are good enough for a daughter from this family, a good girl, from a respectable family within the community and without?"

Kareem clasped his hands together, begging. "Nah, nah, nah, I am a British citizen now, I have a good job and plenty of money, plenty to support a family. The Guris have been like family to me, and I have been like a son to them. They will stand for my parents in this. I beg you."

"And who," said Dr. Choudhury, getting into the spirit of things now, "who will pay for this big wedding? Who will pay the bride's portion and for the betrothal and the *walima*? Who will support you both after you are married? Are you telling me the Guris will pay for a boy who was not born to them?"

Kareem, still on his knees, wrung his hands again. "No, no, I will pay. I will pay for everything! Please, I am begging you! I am on my knees!"

"And how will we do this?" said Mrs. Begum. "With you disappearing off on Haj and maybe not even coming back?"

"I swear, I will come back. I will do *nikkah* and registry office before I go, I vow."

"Oh, you vow now," she said, leaning forward from the waist, fists clenched. "Let us see you book the registry office and speak to the mullah and tell the Guris of this!"

"I will. I swear that I will. I vow on my mother's grave."

She sniffed in a *well, prove it then k*ind of way, and her husband, clearly feeling at this point that he should be more involved, took her cue.

"When, boy?"

"This week, I swear."

"Tomorrow. First thing tomorrow, Monday morning. When the registry office opens, you will be there."

"I will, Uncle, I will."

"Then, boy, straight to London to bring the Guris to visit us."

For the first time, Kareem seemed almost to hesitate. "Of course, of course. I will speak to my brother-in-law."

Suspicions rose in Mrs. Begum's breast. Why was he talking of his brother-in-law? Why wasn't he himself going back to London and driving Mr. and Mrs. Guri to visit them? She opened her mouth to frame the question, but Dr. Choudhury was already, with an almost royal flick of his wrist, dismissing Kareem from his sight and warning him to keep clear of Shunduri in the meantime.

---

KAREEM WALKED OUT of the house with his legs trembling, fighting a strong urge to loosen his tie and undo the top button of his shirt which, in a man as unfailingly sharply dressed as he, spoke volumes. He didn't want to think too much about what had just happened, given the Choudhurys' sudden transformation from smiling hosts to hostile and disapproving elders, but had a sneaking feeling that he had only just avoided a full family scandal and that disapproving baisahib of Shunduri's throwing him out of the house.

He glanced at his wrist where his watch should be and swore as he remembered again. Blipping the door of the Rover open, he climbed in and closed the door, suddenly desperate for that new-car smell. When he had calmed a little, he accelerated away from the verge and drove until he found the first lay-by. Once parked up, he felt under the driver's seat for his stash and took a generous fingernail full, straight up his nose and a little onto the gums. Jesus Christ, he needed that. He sucked the last grains from under his nail, and took a deep breath, trying not to think about one of those sitting-room chairs being broken over his head in a *funchait* to do with his princess. They wanted things to move fast, did they? He could do fast.

He pulled out the mob he used for family, called Auntie and Uncle and asked them to come up to Swindon, to meet a girl and her family. Mrs. Guri, triumphant and talkative after a matchmaking conference earlier that day with an anxious Desi family, was surprisingly mellow when he told her of his need to marry again.

"I love her," he said. "The other marriage, that has ended. My life is here, hers is there, in the old country, and Juri, she will never get the visa."

Mrs. Guri was silent, but the extension crackled, and Uncle's voice came on the line. "Who is this other girl," he asked. "Is she Desi? A good Muslim girl?"

"Yes, Uncle."

"Who is she?" Auntie repeated. "Who is her family?"

"Nah, nah, Auntie, I want you to see her for herself. It's a good family, a wealthy family, I promise you—"

Uncle interrupted. "What business is it that they have made, then?"

Kareem had to stop this questioning. Too much detail and they wouldn't be curious enough to come up on such short notice. "Please, Uncle, Auntie. I want your advice, your blessing on this, not some Brick Lane gossip's. You're like parents to me, you know that. I can't do this without you."

"Why now? Why so quick-quick, hurry-hurry? You were in no hurry before," said Mrs. Guri.

"Tomorrow is a very auspicious date, Auntie, the seventh, and their house is, er, number 86, so 786: the number of the prophets, the lucky number. Lucky number, Auntie. Look, I'll tell you everything in the car, but I've got to go right now, business. Sorry, sorry, Uncle, Auntie, business."

He disconnected with relief. As he had hoped, they were irritated but intrigued and willing to make the journey, if only to spread Mrs. Guri's fame as a matchmaker even further afield. Tomorrow, they would come.

Another dip into his stash and then a shorter call, to brother-in-law Ahmed, calling that village idiot Baiyya and telling him that he was in love, man, but he couldn't possibly make a decision about this girl without Baiyya's advice and moral support. And on top of everything else, he was having car trouble, yeah, couldn't trust it on the motorway right now, so he was staying nearby and Uncle and Auntie needed Ahmed to drive them to Swindon tomorrow, and he would meet them there. Sorted.

There was no way he was going back to London, not with all the official attention he'd been receiving lately. It was too risky, with the police asking after him at all his regular clubs and kebab shops. Kareem would meet them in Swindon, then have the drive to Windsor Cottage to make sure that they were in the right frame of mind to welcome the match. And he wasn't mentioning, wasn't breathing a word, of his other plans.

As soon as the *nikkah* was done and he was back from Haj, they were out of there: there was no way he was putting his princess under Auntie's thumb. His council flat was a nice little earner on the side, and would keep them going until he'd set himself up somewhere out of London. Swindon maybe. He climbed out of the car and lit a cigarette. Man, this was all happening fast, even for a Desi boy. But what a Princess she was, so high and mighty with his friends and the classiest, best-dressed *lalmunni* of anybody's. And with her family on his side, even the police would have trouble touching him. He reached into the car and flicked the silver and blue *Bismillah* talisman hanging from his rear-view mirror, so that it glittered and spun. *Inshallah*.

His cigarette finished, Kareem relaxed a little, then climbed back into the driver's seat and did a quick search on his BlackBerry for Haj travel agents in Swindon. If he got a move on tomorrow, he could book a tour, pick up tickets for everyone, and be back at Windsor Cottage with Auntie and Uncle in the early afternoon. As for tonight, he would be at the local pub. He pulled a face as he floored the accelerator and sped out of the lay-by: did it have to be called The Saracen's Head?

## Thirty-six

HENRY STRAIGHTENED UP from his near-sighted crouch over the study fax machine.

"Richard, here's something for you. Looks like work, I'm afraid. Just goes to show, you take Mondays off at your peril. You're lucky—or perhaps not—I was just about to unplug it." Standing in his socks on one of Thea's good chairs at the other end of the room, Richard paused with a bust of Thomas Carlyle in his hands. "Bloody hell this is heavy. Letter or court document?"

"Oh, ah . . . here's a second page, and a third. The first one is a cover sheet from your Chambers. Letter, I think. Wait, I need my glasses. A letter, two letters from Greengrasses. One's to the Court Registry, stamped as a copy and respectfully requesting that a date be vacated. It's headed *in re Application by the Trustees of the Reid Family Trust.*"

"What's the other one?"

"And the other one, that's addressed to you, also with the Greengrasses letterhead. It's, ah, got the same re, and it's signed Felicity something."

"Read it out," he said, and grunted as he stepped down from the chair with his arms full. Macaulay weighed even more than Carlyle.

"*Dear Richard, I refer to previous correspondence and discussions of . . .* ah, I see, it's copying the court letter to you and advising that Simon Reid, the beneficiary of the material Trust, has voluntarily agreed to admit himself to the Priory. Ohh. That's for rock stars, isn't it? *And on this basis our clients have instructed us to withdraw our application for directions.* So is that good?"

"Is that all it says?"

"*Many thanks, Greengrasses* per Felicity something. Enc. And a smiley face."

Richard moved the chair along and climbed back up. Typical Felicity: she never could text him without an emoticon either. He hoped for her sake, and Greengrasses', that she hadn't done it on the letter to the court.

"Yes, good news for me and for them. And I might be able to stay around a few more days to help out with the move."

"Oh, that is good news." Henry raised his voice and directed it out the door. "Did you hear that, Thee?"

"What?"

"Richard's staying on a bit longer. Some court case has collapsed."

There was the sound of something striking the flagstones in the hallway and not remaining intact. "*Christos!* Jonathan and Andrew, now look what you've done! Out of this hallway, upstairs, both of you!"

Sounds of complaint and resistance ensued, and the crash of something else hitting the floor and more swearing from Thea. Richard got down from the chair, Gibbon and Cicero this time, and lowered them onto the top of the study desk.

Henry walked to the doorway and peered out. "Would you like a hand out there, Thee?"

"*No!*"

Richard looked back up at the bookshelves, where Plutarch and Sir Walter Scott still eyed him smugly, as well as two busty maidens. Muses, perhaps.

"How about I take the boys to McDonald's for an early lunch. There's one on the way to Swindon, isn't there? It's eleven now, that'll get them out of your hair for a couple of hours, let you pack up your papers. I'll finish off the bookshelves tonight. Or you could take the boys?" he said to Henry.

"Oh, if you could. I think Thee's a bit tired, you know. She wants to get all this done, then we, ah, she's got an appointment in Swindon. And tonight she wants to head up to the Abbey for a bit of a look-see upstairs. That's phase two, you know, the upstairs. She's meeting with the decorator tomorrow to plan that next."

"Oh." Richard slowly brushed some dust off his shirt. "Tonight?"

"Yes. We're setting up in the main rooms downstairs first, but we won't be sleeping there until something's been done with the upstairs bathrooms and, ah, I think hanging space or something. It's all been brought forward a bit because Thea wants to start entertaining there, even if we'll still be sleeping here for the time being. Not enough space for big dos at the Lodge, and Thee says she needs a change. Anyway, she knows what needs to be done and good old Theo Kiriakis has stumped up with the cash for the plumbing now, so full steam ahead. Come to think of it, Thee told me that Mrs. Choudhury's taking the boys later this afternoon, so you could probably drop them straight there after McDonald's."

"Fine with me."

"Mrs. Choudhury's been a godsend these last few months, you know, what with last-minute babysitting and helping hold the fort." Henry returned to the study doorway. "Thee, Richard's—"

"I *know*."

"Perhaps Richard might like a cup of tea first, before he goes."

"Well, he knows where everything's kept."

Henry looked at him apologetically, and Richard grinned to show he wasn't bothered. She'd had a bee in her bonnet ever since the dinner party. But she'd had a lot on her plate, with the move, and this Hunt ball and whatever.

Richard shouted the universally recognized word up the stairs, unleashing yells of joy and a thunder of feet above, before the two boys shot into the hallway, sneakers undone, pushing each other out of the way with cries of, "I'm ready, Uncle Richard," and, "No, I'm ready first."

"Right then, into the car."

———————

AND THROUGH THE hurly-burly of the drive and the extended agony of decision-making in front of the lurid menu, the excitement and anxious comparison of the Happy Meal toys and the screaming, sweaty fun of the playground, a sense of purpose filled Richard's mind like a green flag set suddenly in motion. He knew what he had to do, and now was the time.

While he kept a weather eye on Andrew and Jonathon's relentless circling in the play area, he dialled Greengrasses. He was put through to Felicity straight away, who confirmed that he was not needed to appear tomorrow, as the court had been happy to vacate the date and allow notices of discontinuance to be filed within the week, by consent of the parties.

"Always helps if it's a cancellation in good summer weather, Richard."

"I think you're right there—judges are human after all. What made the son fold? I assume some sort of reconciliation?"

"Oh, sort of. He was bashed outside a nightclub last Friday night: the police think it was a drug deal gone wrong. Anyway he's in the London Clinic now, with a broken nose and cheekbone and some missing teeth, feeling very sorry for himself. The parents have visited, and what with one thing and another, he's apparently agreed to go into the Priory straight from there. I think the idea is he can do his, umm, *withdrawal* in a nice private room at the Clinic, then go straight on to rehab without being exposed to too much temptation in between."

Richard opened the glass door into the playground area to ascertain that the muted screaming he could hear was wilful rather than involuntary, then shut it again.

"Sorry, Felicity—that's my nephews."

"I *was* wondering. So, you're out of London today?"

"Yes."

The boys looked like they could keep going indefinitely. All he could think of was getting back to the Abbey.

Felicity burbled on. "Martin and Louise—the Reids—are thrilled of course, and *very* hopeful for the future."

He remembered to bite his tongue this time, despite recalling his father's eternal misguided optimism. He had maintained to the end that Mother had died of pneumonia. It wasn't for Richard to disabuse the Reids of their hopes.

"I assume the extra Trust payments will continue then?" he said.

Felicity bridled, as he'd known she would. "I don't think that's *our* concern anymore, is it, Richard?"

"You're right there." He was pretty sure that they both knew that Felicity was saying this now because she was still kicking herself for not having said it on the last occasion. He stopped himself from adding *till the next time they come to you*, and made noises about signing off, which elicited her usual delaying tactics.

"Well, if you have some capacity now, I've got another couple of briefs to put your way, and we could meet to discuss . . ."

"So long as it's nothing urgent. I'm taking a week off from work. Family time. Perhaps we can talk when I'm back."

"Oh. I *do* hope everything's alright . . ."

"Thank you again, Felicity."

"Don't mention it. I—"

He hung up, shoved the phone into his jeans pocket and opened the glass door. "Time to go, you two. Have you got your toys?"

The drive back to the Choudhurys was marginally quieter: a lot quieter once he had given Andrew and Jonathon his phone to play games on.

## Thirty-seven

KAREEM PULLED INTO the motorway service station near the Swindon turnoff at one o'clock, in plenty of time. It was all going like clockwork, right on schedule. Everything was sorted just as he'd promised Shunduri's family it would be, and he was on top of the world again.

Already this morning, at some god-awful hour, he'd booked the Swindon registry office and some junior mullah at the Broad Street mosque, then dealt with the travel arrangements. He'd had to pay through the nose for Haj visa applications and tickets for the three of them. And then he'd shelled out for the premium tours package with complimentary ihrams, at a cost that any fool off the street would have paid, thanks to all his useful contacts being in London.

Reluctantly, he parked the Rover in a prominent position to make it easier for village idiot Ahmed Guri to find him. Not for the first time that day, Kareem found himself wishing that he hadn't chosen such a gangsta vehicle. He'd been hunching down in his seat every time he caught sight of a police car. It would be better on the way to Windsor Cottage: just having three more people in the car made him look much more the average Asian type on the roads. Kareem climbed out hastily, located his smokes and lighter: please god, let him have time for a smoke before they got here.

A heavily laden silver Golf made a hard left into the service station, accompanied by a burst of honking and swerving from a lorry following behind. The car drew to a halt directly behind the Rover. Why Idiot had decided to take his Golf rather than Uncle's Ford sedan, only he would know. This was not the time for cultivating his delusions of having some street cred: this was about looking after the elders.

Sure enough, Uncle was already climbing out, tired and cross, his suit jacket folded up around his waist. A battered roadmap fell out with him, and Uncle trod on it with an air of revenge finally achieved. The back passenger door swung open, and Auntie's hand appeared on top of the doorframe. The car tilted and rocked as she rose up into view, along with a bulging Tesco bag and a large shiny black handbag, which hung and slid on her wrist like bracelets. When she let go of the car to swat Ahmed out of her way, the Golf visibly lifted as it was relieved of her weight. Serve Idiot right if he had to get his suspension serviced.

Kareem stepped forward and bent to touch their feet in rapid succession. "*Salaamalaikum*, Khalo, Khalama, Baiyya. I'm so glad you are here."

But no one would look at him, not even Ahmed who seemed somehow allied with them, despite what had obviously been a nightmare drive, probably with his doof-doof music up all the way. Kareem moved back as Auntie swept past, and she and then Uncle made a beeline for the Rover.

He only just managed to blip it open before Auntie's hand wrenched on the handle, and she started to hoist herself up into the back seat, the Tesco bag and handbag tagging behind. He hastened to open the front passenger door for Uncle, who climbed in without comment and almost shut the door on Kareem's fingers.

Ahmed was fussing about with the locking mechanism on his Golf, and Kareem walked over to him. "Hey, *Salaam*, Baiyya. Looks like you'll be gettin' in the back wiv Auntie. How was the drive?"

Ahmed was flustered. Usually he was too stupid to get stressed.

"Yeah, good, good. Look, Dad wants me to go back and open up the restaurant. Doesn't want to lose a day of business, yeah?"

"Eh? Is there trouble then?"

Ahmed fiddled further with the remote, and the Golf's horn gave an irritated blart. "Yeah, Kareem, you could say that. We had the police around early this morning, askin' about you, tellin' us you could help with their enquiries. Tellin' us someone had a broken nose and a broken face and you'd been seen in the vicinity of the crime, yeah."

"Jesus Christ. They came to the house?"

Ahmed looked a little happier. "Yeah. A person of interest, you are. And Mum and Dad, they really lost it, man. Dad's talkin' about going back to Bangladesh, and Mum's tellin' everyone she never should of taken you in. What did you *do*, yeah?"

"Nothing, man, nothing. They got me mixed up with someone else."

Ahmed looked smug and put his hands in his pockets. "No smoke without fire, Kareem. That's what Mum and Dad are saying. And that police visit—that really stressed them, yeah."

"Look, I'll be back soon to sort all that out. There's no need to worry."

"No rush. I don't think Dad wants you round in the restaurant, with all this happenin'. Mum doesn't even want you at home right now."

You mean you don't, Kareem thought. He swallowed his scorn and fear, gave his respects again, and walked away from the dirty dog to the Rover. If there was any justice in this world, Idiot's Golf would be cleaned up by one of those juggernauts before he got back to London.

Heading out onto the A road, the car was thick with silence. He could see Auntie in the rear-view mirror, mashing her handbag on her lap and managing to look cramped even in the spaciousness of the Rover. Vicks and Miss Dior filled the car.

Next to Kareem, Uncle, not a small man either, seemed equally uncomfortable and was, moreover, in a filthy mood. He had always hated wearing a suit on his day off instead of the soft lungi and untucked shirt he was by right entitled to when not at the restaurant.

His fingers tapped and paused spasmodically, as if calculating the exact reduction in takings that would result from Idiot running the business for a full day on his own. There was a shifting of weight in the back seat, and Kareem caught Mrs. Guri's eyes on him in the rear-view mirror, so he called out.

"Are you comfortable, Khalama? You want the radio? Stop for a rest?"

Mrs. Guri shook her head and turned her gaze out the window to disapprove of hills, cows and pebbledash. Her eyes were lidded, and her bottom lip was protruding ominously. Only half an hour to go and they were in no mood to be helpful or generous.

———

MRS. BEGUM WALKED into her husband's study and closed the door softly. Two o'clock already and everything hung on that fool Kareem doing what he had promised, *Inshallah*. He'd told Dr. Choudhury on the phone that the Guris were coming to visit mid-afternoon. If only her husband was more a figure of fear to enforce this. He was in the sitting room after an early healthy-walk, and would be asleep soon. Mrs. Begum refolded the damp duster in her hand and started to run it over mantel and desktop, keeping a sharp eye out for anything of interest.

She pushed aside a pile of yellowing lecture notes that had sat on his study desk ever since they had moved there, and riffled through the papers behind them looking for something new, something with titles, that she could take to Mrs. Darby to read. But there was no letterhead, no bills, no brochures with pictures to puzzle over and interpret.

As long as Dr. Choudhury did not *one* thing more to spoil her plans, Baby and Kareem would be married before Haj, if she had to chop off her thumbs to do it. And then she would have three or four weeks, if she was lucky, to plan the reception and negotiate with Mrs. Guri for the *walima*, with Rohimun driving her and Baby making the calls, before the men returned and started interfering again.

And her husband would have to take Rohimun back now, or risk great embarrassment with the Bournes, for all his refusing to even say his daughter's name. Henry and Thea were moving back into the Abbey any day, she had seen the boxes and the tape, and that old fool still pretending that nothing needed to change. He would have to sing a different song very soon: if Henry and Thea discovered where Munni had been living, Henry might well forget and forgive, but not that Thea. Mrs. Begum pressed her lips together and gave the cheval a mean flick with the back of her hand that set it to swinging and creaking.

If Rohimun was not present, it would be clear to everyone what her current standing was, and the Guris would have the upper hand in wedding negotiations. She needed to do something, now. It was time. She would send Tariq to his sister, have him collect her, put her things in Windsor Cottage's garage, and ask his father, seeing as they were such good friends now, to forgive her. Dr. Choudhury was on the brink of it, she could tell, with this buying of paints and brushes, for all his silence on the subject, and it could wait no longer.

Mrs. Begum put her head out into the hallway and called, in a penetrating whisper, "Tariq! Tariq!"

She picked up the cushion from Dr. Choudhury's chair, punched it with her fists until it was puffy and loose again, and dropped it back onto the seat. She would never consent to be on her knees before that fat toad, begging for Kareem to be married into their family.

Her good-for-nothing son poked his head around the study door. "I was just in the kitchen, Amma."

"Never mind that, go get your sister."

"Baby?"

"Nah, nah, nah, what are you thinking? Go get Munni. Pack her up and bring her home."

"Eh? What's Abba said?"

"Just go! Bring everything. Do it now!" She raised her hand at his surprised face, and he stepped back.

"Alright, alright, Amma. I'm going. I just hope you know what you're doing. I'm going!"

Tariq disposed of, she banged shut the doors of the sari cupboard—the only tidy place in the study as usual—and swept the other papers on Dr. Choudhury's desk into one neat pile. But they still irritated her with their messy tabs and flags, so she put one hand on top of the pile and, with the other, quickly stripped the little red and yellow tabs from the sides, and threw them into the wastepaper basket.

In the basket was a small silver sphere of crumpled-up foil. She pounced on it and lifted it up to her eyes and then her nose. So he was stealing *ladhu* balls from her kitchen now. He should know better than to keep secrets from her—she always found out in the end.

It must have come from the *ladhu* balls she had made for Munni, to welcome her back into the house: that special dinner that had never happened thanks to that fool of a man, her husband. She fingered the talisman pinned into her blouse and breathed a short prayer. *Bring her back under my roof, all-merciful Allah. Let her father forgive. Find me a husband for her.*

On Dr. Choudhury's armchair, a burgundy and gold sari lay draped across the seat and spilling onto the carpet. She picked it up and stretched her arms to their utmost to fold it into two-yard lengths. How to do this.

If Richard Bourne had been a Bangla boy in this same situation, fully grown and with no parents to tell him what he needed or that it was time to marry, he would at least have had the sense to approach an intermediary, someone like Mrs. Guri. She would have made the necessary enquiries and visited Mrs. Begum and prepared her for Bangla-Richard's interest. Mrs. Begum, as a respectable woman and not at all the matchmaking type, would have been entitled to ask from her all the natural and necessary information, about his reputation in the community, his age, wealth and unmarried status, and thus his obvious need for a wife.

The sari was folded now, and she put it away in the cupboard.

Sometimes she thought this cupboard was more important to her husband than food. But what news was this to her, who had seen him swoon over saris even before they had married?

In due course, Mrs. Guri could let Bangla-Richard know that the Choudhurys, while in the habit of rejecting first-class offers every day, were not necessarily averse to further discussions. One of those ostentatiously chaperoned meetings could then be arranged with the prospective couple. Rohimun could indicate (reluctantly, modestly) that if her parents wanted this match, she would be compliant (Mrs. Begum had a little trouble imagining this part so moved quickly on) and Dr. Choudhury (appropriately prompted) could enter into dowry and settlement negotiations with Bangla-Richard. Tariq would generally hover around, so that it was as clear as possible that their Munni was not a girl without family and protection.

Richard was clearly a man smitten: she could see that he was only interested in the rest of them as a way to know Rohimun better and to find favor with her family. But where could he go from this point, how could he promote his suit without, *Inshallah*, causing offence or loss of reputation?

Being outside of the community, Richard would just have to feel his way, directed where possible by Mrs. Begum, and within the boundaries set by Tariq and Dr. Choudhury. It could take him months: some *gora* couples took years. She tsked at the thought.

There was a muffled knocking at the front door. Mrs. Begum hurried down the hall, dragging the duster over the telephone table and hallstand as she did so, and threw it open.

It was Richard Bourne, in blue-jeans and a shirt, looking as tall and handsome and determined as a suitor should, with Andrew and Jonathon just behind, climbing out of that long dark car of his. She froze. While not normally slow to appreciate any development of advantage to her family, the dizzying speed with which Allah had answered her prayers this time found her needing a second to adjust. If Rohimun, like Diana, was to venture away from the safety of home

and community and into the uncharted, dangerous waters of a mixed
marriage, this would be the man.

"Hello, Mrs. Begum. I'm sorry to intrude, but—"

"Richard!" She beamed. "You have not gone back to London!"

"A court date has been put off, so I have a few free days to help
Henry and Thea pack up the Lodge. The boys and I have just come
from McDonald's. Henry and Thea are in Swindon this afternoon
and they mentioned that you had offered . . ."

"Yes, yes. Thea asked me to look after them today, but there is no
need to ask. Anytime." She looked at the two boys approvingly. "They
eat everything." She pointed to her right. "Andrew, Jonathon, go to the
back garden. Go see the rabbits. Go, go. Samosas are in the kitchen."

"Rab-bits! Rab-bits!" The boys took off down the side of the
cottage.

"Richard, come and have a cup-of-tea."

"Perhaps later." He hesitated. "I'm sorry to intrude, but I've just
heard and I thought you should know: Henry and Thea are planning
to go to the Abbey tonight, to have a look at the upstairs rooms, for
decorating. They're moving in a little sooner than expected."

She dropped her duster, staggered backward, narrowly avoiding
Richard's outstretched hand, and sat down on the hall carpet. What
a good thing she had hoovered this morning.

"Richard, Richard, what can I do?" she wailed, but not so loud as
to disturb her husband. She covered her face and started to rock back
and forth.

Richard was silent. She peeked through her fingers and saw him
staring down at her. Perhaps he needed some further direction.

She grasped his sleeve. "You, you will help, dear Richard. No one
so proper, so capable as you!"

His long legs bent until he was squatting before her. His hands
closed around her elbows and gently lifted her upright, putting her
into something of a flutter. She had always made a point of touching
his sleeve and patting his arm, as a mark of her seniority and to pull

him into her family circle. But his touching her was a little much. No mind, she told herself, he is virtually my son-in-law.

As soon as she was standing, she batted him away and, when he persisted in offering her his arm, said faintly, "My duster."

Richard, what a good boy, took the hint almost straight away and bent again to pick it up. He handed it to her, and she clasped it to her bosom and walked unsteadily to the hallstand's covered seat (big flowers, like Thea's new couches) and sat down. He approached again, and she waved the duster at him.

"Go, go to her, Richard. Save my Munni!"

He did not move. "Where shall I take her?"

If she told Richard outright to bring her here and Dr. Choudhury found out, after they'd had words over this very thing, her husband could ruin everything with his anger against her.

But if Richard acted on his own—everyone forgives a man in love. She made a choking sob, stuck a corner of the duster in her eye and produced a tear. He continued to wait, his tallness and wideness of shoulder blocking up her hallway. She sniffed loudly.

"Where shall I take her, Mrs. Begum? Will she be welcome here?"

He just would not take the hint. She began to feel positively irritated by his *gora* need for instruction, for every detail to be worked out in advance. This was an emergency, and Richard had to be the one to rescue Rohimun, to show the initiative of a hero. If he delayed any longer, Tariq would be the one rescuing his sister, and what would be the point of that? Rohimun needed to be grateful to Richard, and if they turned up on the doorstep of Windsor Cottage together, how could Dr. Choudhury refuse his daughter in front of the eldest Bourne?

"Oh, I cannot think, dear Richard . . ."

He was relentless in his silent waiting, she had to give him that.

"What can a poor mother do?" she sobbed.

"It's time she was home."

"Yes, yes, please bring her home." The words were out.

He was gone then, at last, like a good boy, moving with surprising speed for such a tall man.

As soon as the door closed behind him, Mrs. Begum stood and trotted rapidly to the kitchen. An intermittent rumble could be heard as she passed the sitting-room door. Dr. Choudhury was fully asleep then, and she spared a pinch of gratitude for his healthy-walk. It got him out of her way, during and afterward. And the less he knew the better.

She peered through the kitchen window for the boys, who had the rabbits out of the hutch and were trying to get them to race each other. She looked at her curtain and thought of Diana and Dodi, and of herself and the grief that a bitter and hostile elder can cause. Dr. Choudhury must be brought to a clear understanding and a wholehearted consent. Only this would truly solve Rohimun's disgrace, her exile and her dangerous unmarried state.

So there might be two extra for dinner then, as well as the Guris (if they stayed that long), plus Kareem and Baby. Her goat curry would go well for them. If she was quick she could also do a chicken korma for Richard: he'd had three helpings last time and still looked too thin.

She stopped in her tracks with another inspiration. She would invite Henry and Thea as well, when they came to pick up the boys. With all their packing up, she had seen the takeaway car go past Windsor Cottage to the Lodge twice in the last week. The more Bournes to watch and judge him, the more Dr. Choudhury would feel pressured to accept his daughter, and the greater the stamp of public approval for the future arrangement of Richard and Rohimun. She threw the duster into the kitchen sink. Perhaps an egg curry as well.

---

Dr. Choudhury snorted himself awake, surprised as always to find he had slept. It was only two-thirty so the guests weren't due yet, and he shuffled in socked feet to the study, where his most comfortable chair would be sitting in afternoon sunshine at this time. But within minutes of his settling in, there was a wifely rustling outside the door. He stood stiffly to turn the key and let Mrs. Begum in.

She was carrying half a cup of steaming tea and a flowered saucer with two green paan packages on it. He sat back down in the swivel chair and watched her arrange cup and saucer before him. There was a wooden stool next to the sari cupboard, used by Mrs. Begum to reach the topmost shelves, and she arranged herself on it, her head only a little higher than his knees.

Once he had taken his paan, she took the other. They both chewed quietly for a while. In his wife's presence and with the calming buzz of betel nut in his blood, he felt the burdens of fatherhood lift a little.

Mrs. Begum spoke, her voice thickened and slowed by the paan still in her mouth. "The boys are here. Henry-Thea coming to eat."

"Ah."

"Richard was just here."

"I did not hear him. Did he seek my counsel?"

"No, no. He did not come in." She fiddled with her talisman. "Have you noticed, my husband, how often Richard Bourne comes here now. How concerned he is for us, how much he wishes to please you."

"But of course. We have much in common. We talk of Oxford, of London, of the Abbey . . ."

His wife looked at him, as if waiting for more, then leaned closer to him with her hands on her knees and spoke in a half-whisper. "Of course you have much in common. But *he* is not married."

He stared at her and only just stopped himself from reminding his wife that she was unavailable for suitors.

She leaned even further forward. "I think, maybe, *he* is ready to marry."

"On what are you basing this. Merely on his being unmarried and wealthy and visiting this neighborhood? You know that gossip and matchmaking are no interest of mine."

His wife clasped her hands together over her talisman and leaned so far forward that her chin almost connected with the corner of the study desk. "He told me, just now, that he has seen Rohimun. He has discovered her." She hurried on before he could react. "By accident.

He saw her once, um, a few days ago. When he realized that she was your daughter, he told her that she could stay in the Abbey, and he has since taken great pains to acquaint himself further with you, with Tariq, with all of us. In a way most respectful."

Dr. Choudhury could feel a headache beginning in the center of his forehead and radiating to his eyes. He pressed his fingertips to his brow and closed his eyelids.

"Please believe me, my husband, on my life, on my children's lives, he has been most honorable, most discreet. Tariq has been watching him, chaperoning Munni at all times. Richard has now told me that he has only been waiting for the right time to approach you. A sign that you saw him as an acceptable suitor. He has such respect, such admiration for you."

He could not speak. It was many minutes before he was able to comprehend what he had just been told. At length he started to recover.

"Mr. Richard Bourne. In this family?"

So this too had been taken out of his hands. Relief and astonishment rose in his heart, but was supplanted by disbelief. It was all wishful thinking: Shunduri-and-Kareem had created, in his wife's head, Rohimun-and-Richard. The mother of his children was desperate, he knew, and most likely had concocted this ridiculous story as a last resort to get his agreement to allow Rohimun back into the house for the meeting with the Guris. Perhaps there was also a motive of one-upmanship here, given that she had gone to so much trouble to eclipse his own news of the Haj with her talk of Shunduri being betrothed. Perhaps she was also jealous of his great friendship with Richard. Hah. But . . .

"Have you spoken with him much?"

"Oh no, not before today. Just now." She fiddled with her talisman again. "Although I saw something in his eyes, I felt something in my stomach, with some of the questions that he asked about our family and our daughters, at the party at the Lodge. And, just now, Richard called to say that Thea and Henry are moving into the Lodge very-soon and are visiting upstairs tonight. He wished to warn us. He is a true friend of this family."

"What?" He stood, patting his pockets for keys. "Quick-quick. Tariq must go."

"Tariq is with his sister already, but Richard said . . . said he would also go and warn her." His wife touched the talisman on her blouse again.

"I will not have more disgrace fall on this house, wife. Even if it is Richard Bourne, there will be no boyfriend-girlfriend business in this house, in this family."

Mrs. Begum let go of his sleeve and spoke with solemn certainty. "He will marry her. I will make it happen. But this cannot be done from the Abbey. She must be here, for things to be arranged properly, for him to become part of our family in the proper way."

A wave of anger and disappointment rose in him. He had had enough of women and their scheming ways, their obsession with love and marriage. He'd thought that Richard was coming to see him, was interested in him, not some flibbertigibbet daughter. He had thought there was more to Richard than that. This house was like a marriage broker's, so completely lacking in intellectual and spiritual tone that it was.

He gestured in a dignified way for her to leave. "I will not listen to this nonsense about Richard Bourne. Hah. What next? Perhaps if any young women come for Tariq, send them in, for I am quite at leisure."

His wife exited then, without another word, and he shut and locked the door behind her. Sarcasm would of course be lost on Mrs. Begum and, besides, he had a sneaking suspicion that even with Tariq, she would get her own way in the end.

He turned to the sari cupboard with, somehow, a lighter heart, recalling that Mrs. Begum had completed the false hem on one of the new saris: a symphony in green and gold that he had prevailed upon her to purchase last spring. He would pull it out and see how it draped

406 · *Lesley Jørgensen*

with the extra weight. If what Mrs. Begum had been saying about Shunduri was correct, Baby would be wearing green and gold for her *haldi mendhi* any day now.

And if, he could not help thinking, in the unlikely event that Richard Bourne was to touch his feet and ask for Rohimun's hand, well . . . perhaps being able to say that Richard Bourne, barrister, of Bourne Abbey and Kings Chambers, London, was his son-in-law, could have its compensations.

He would dwell no more on this, he decided, except for a brief thought that if it really were true, he would be rescued from the terrible conundrum of Rohimun's future and, indeed, would be persuaded to let them marry from this house. He hummed as he draped the sari's *pallu* across his chest and turned to his friend the cheval. Summer was a lovely time for weddings.

---

KAREEM SLOWED THE Rover further and made a show of fiddling with the radio and the GPS to block his passengers' view of the speedometer. He had to somehow get Auntie and Uncle into the frame of mind they were in yesterday, when he had spoken to them on the phone. Before those dirty police had come knocking on their door this morning.

He could picture it all. The police car, angled half across the road directly in front of the house, sending flashes of red and blue onto everyone's front windows, just to make sure that every two-up two-down in the street was aware that the Guris were in trouble. The loud, tireless knocking on that modest front door, until Auntie and Uncle themselves, bleary and dishevelled and scared, opened it and were walked backward down their own hallway and interviewed in their own sitting room.

And after the police had left, and the tears and shouting between them had subsided, their great need to get out of Brick Lane, the instinctive urge for escape, to put time and geography between them and the police and the gossiping of their neighbors, would have been the only thing impelling them to still come here despite their likely desire to wash their hands of him.

"Shunduri Choudhury?" said Auntie.

He braked and swerved to avoid a nonexistent car. How the hell did she know?

"Yes, Khalama." He should have realized that she had her finger in every curry and her eye in every sitting-room window. A glance in the rear-view mirror showed Auntie's forehead pushed upward into a series of bulging corrugations.

Her eyes swivelled to meet and hold his as she spoke the words again. "Shunduri Choudhury."

"Yes, Khalama, it is her." He spoke rapidly, trying to avert any explosions. "I saw her at a wedding. I have met her family, but you have been as my parents here in UK. I would never make such a decision without your blessing."

"Why such a hurry now? Is she a good girl?"

He swallowed. "Yes, yes, she is a good girl."

Uncle cut in. "Then why the hurry to make this girl wife number two? And what of your wife in Bangladesh. Have you . . . have you divorced her? She knows? Her family knows?"

He nodded. "Yes, Uncle. I couldn't get the visa for her. That's all finished now."

"You are keeping the dowry? As you had to pay for the visa application, the agents . . . Did all the dowry arrive?"

"Yes, Khalo. I bought this car." And what was left was sitting in cash in the glovebox right in front of his uncle, along with all Kareem's other money. But he wasn't telling him that. Uncle'd invest it in that dirty restaurant. "With this family, the Choudhurys," he continued, "her father is going on Haj and he wants everything sorted before he goes."

There was a distinct sniff from the back seat and an *ahh*, as if everything was now clear. He could see in the rear-view that Mrs. Guri's corrugations had relaxed a little and her lip was pushed out a bit further, in a considering way.

"I know this family," said Mrs. Guri. "They are not in the community now. The children, very modern, I think."

Kareem tried for charm, smiling brightly and trying to meet her eyes in the mirror again. "Very connected too, Khalama. Their best friends are a rich *gora* family who live in a castle. And they have pictures of themselves shaking hands with the royal family."

Auntie's eyebrows rose even higher. "What story is this, Kareem?"

"Khalama, I tell you the truth! You will see the pictures in their house." He paused, trying to think of the right words. "They know, they are close with, many important people. If I'm part of that family there will be no more trouble with the police, no misunderstandings, *Inshallah*."

The car was silent.

He tried for a lighter note. "And I'm a modern boy too, Khalama. I respect you and all that, I respect the traditions, but I'm Desi, you know? Not Bangla."

"So you want to marry soon?"

"If you like her, if you and Uncle give your blessing. Maybe," he said, speaking with great daring, "the *nikkah* and the registry office now, because, you see, Dr. Choudhury and Tariq, the son, they're going on Haj, yeah? And they want me to go with them. And after we come back, we could have the *rukhsati*, the reception and, you know, the *walima* and everyfing."

He saw Auntie take a deep breath but she only got so far as "So now it's Haj—" when her husband cut in.

"So this family has money then? What sort of dowry will they give? What sort of wedding will they want?"

Kareem lifted his foot further off the accelerator to let a tractor pass them. "A big wedding, I think: a big *rukhsati* and a big *walima*." He raised his left hand from the steering wheel to fend off disagreement and to announce his masterstroke. "But I will pay. I will pay for it all. You have been so good to me, you have brought me up as your own son, have brought me into this country. This, this is what I wish to do."

A shocked and respectful silence followed. Uncle was looking straight ahead and blinking rapidly as if not quite able to believe his luck, a marriage being achieved without arguments with the in-laws or getting into debt. The silence in the back seat was followed by an extended period of rustling and huffing and puffing, and he peeked discreetly into the rear-view mirror to see Mrs. Guri exchanging a row of chunky gold bracelets on one wrist for a collection of thinner, more modest ones from her handbag. What was she up to? She caught his gaze in the mirror, gave a dimpled smile and shook her head at him as if he was a child performing for visitors.

Mr. Guri grunted. "Any good restaurants, takeaways, here?"

"Don't think so, Uncle. Maybe. See? See there?" Kareem pointed to his right, to the hill overlooking the village and the rear walls of the Abbey rising above it. "That's where they live: the family that they visit with. The Bournes."

"Wah," they both said, and Auntie's head went down again as she busily stowed her grander bracelets in her handbag.

"My rings," said Uncle. "My rings and my bracelet."

There was more rustling as Mrs. Guri delved into her handbag and the requisite items clinked into his hand. Auntie must carry all their gold with her, not trusting the bottom of the wardrobe like most Desi families. Or, perhaps, only since the police had visited. Kareem winced.

Uncle wedged the rings onto his fingers and grunted for his wife to do up his heavy gold bracelet. She bent forward to do so and the Rover's chassis gave a complaining squeak.

Kareem steered the Rover to the curb outside Windsor Cottage. "We're here, yeah."

Auntie clicked her handbag shut and took a good look. "See, detached," she said, pointing the cottage out to her husband.

"Yeah, well not for long." Kareem snorted at his own joke. Everyone wanted this wedding now, *Inshallah*, but he'd been around long enough to know that things could still go wrong. Please God, don't let the police come knocking at the Choudhurys' door.

He muttered the first *Fatiha* under his breath and, as the Guris got out, unfolded one end of a small foil packet, dipped his finger inside and ran it along his gums. As the wave of warm, glowing confidence rose and broke in him, he pulled the rear-view mirror around to check his lips and teeth for residue. No problem. Nothing he couldn't handle.

## Thirty-eight

FOOTSTEPS SOUNDED IN the passage, and Rohimun turned in time to see the door open and the silhouette of a man almost filling the doorway, with sword in one hand and shield in the other. It was not until he stepped forward into the room that she realized it was Richard, carrying a couple of flattened cardboard boxes under one arm and a narrow roll of bubble wrap in the other.

"Oh, it's you," she said, taking hold of her right hand with her left to stop it smoothing back her hair, adjusting her *salwar*. She went back to filling the duffel bag, which was sitting beside the great bed.

"Henry and Thea are moving in downstairs, and they're going to walk through the upstairs rooms tonight," he said.

She stared at the empty box under his arm. Was he expecting her to ask him for something, to beg him for a stay of execution? Well, stuff him.

"I know. I saw the moving vans. Anyway, my stuff's always pretty much packed up." She rubbed fiercely at a patch of dried paint on her sleeve. "Tariq'll come and get me soon. He always comes around this time of day."

Richard looked around restlessly, as if he'd expected something else. "Where will you go?"

He's already uncomfortable, she thought. He doesn't want to be here. She stared at his pale blue shirtfront, immaculate in the sunshine, and turned away, to where the empty fireplace sat, and the dingy glass jars she'd used for brushes and white spirit, ready to be thrown in the rubbish. *Sorry, different worlds, and all that. Best you were on your way then*, she imagined him saying. She bent over the duffel bag to pull the zip shut. It was overfull with extra things that she had somehow accumulated along the way.

"Tariq will think of something. He'll sort that out. He knows lots of people," she said. She wrenched on the zip until it started to move, jerked it across the top of the bag, and found the zipper teeth gaping open behind it. Nothing was working. She swore to herself and tied the two handles of the duffel bag into a loose reef knot.

"Your mother says you can come home," Richard said. He was standing next to her, and when she straightened up he reached for her hands, but she snatched them away reflexively. He sat down on the bed, close enough to touch.

She folded her arms, feeling like a child caught out in a sulk. "When did she say that?"

"Just now. She wants you home straight away."

"Was Dad with her?"

"No."

Just more of the same. She felt sick. "I'll wait for Tariq, yeah. He won't be long."

Richard just sat. When he finally spoke, he said, "I know that things are not sorted out yet with your family. Not fully. Let me take you there and if things don't work out, if you don't feel comfortable, I will help. I promise."

"There's no point. Mum's just trying to force it."

"You won't be on your own. I'll be there and I won't leave until it's all settled." His arm came around her shoulders, and she closed her eyes and tried not to think of any kind of a future with him.

Was this embrace *gora* politeness or pity, or something else, which perhaps mattered as much to him as it did to her? She felt adrift in his Western world of dating and girlfriends: she had seen, lived, the fluid dishonesty of those relationships, so much a matter of mood and whim as to whether the bond would be acknowledged or betrayed. A recipe for misery.

"I thought I could manage without my family, but I can't," she said. He squeezed her shoulder, and she fought the urge to lean into his warmth and certainty.

"Remember, they know you can't stay in the Abbey and they don't want to lose you."

"And if they forgive me, if they take me back, what will you do then?" She spoke as coolly as she could, but there was still a quaver in the last word.

"I'll visit you. I'll ask your father's permission to see you."

"What do you mean?"

"Just that. I'll visit on weekends, with Tariq or your parents chaperoning, and we can get to know each other better."

"You know about all that, do you?"

"I've done my research—Google's quite a resource."

"You're going to go all Desi on me?"

"No. But I'll respect your family's concerns. And my intentions are honorable, as they say. I won't do anything to compromise you."

"Huh." What did he think he was doing, alone in a room with her, touching her, talking to her about these things, with no family here and they not even betrothed? And what did he think he had done the other night, coming to see her at that hour?

She looked at him with a deadly seriousness. "Why aren't you married already, to some deb?"

"I never wanted to settle down." His arm dropped down, but before she could twitch away, he took her hand. "But I've realized I'm more like my brother than I thought," he said quietly. "In that respect."

What did he mean? She thought of the short, fair-haired man she had seen outside whistling to his dogs and, on one occasion, dancing with an imaginary partner, the animals looking on.

He squeezed her hand, as if making sure she was paying attention. "But my life is in London."

With her other hand she drew an arc around the room. "This, here, what you see: it isn't how I am. I can't go on like this, without my family, without being a part of them. And I can't hurt them again either."

They were both silent, and Rohimun thought of her old life: the good parts; the learning and the painting, before the pressure got too much and she became too lonely.

"I miss London too," she said. "But not like it was for me before, yeah. I want to be able to come home. And I want to do my own thing now. Not portraits."

"Isn't that a portrait?"

She turned to her painting on the easel. "No. Or, not like I've ever done before."

"I've seen some of your other works."

"Where?"

"In galleries around town. One in a friend's house. They're good, but this, what you've done here, is . . . special. Magical."

She turned toward him, and he bent his head toward hers, but there was the sound of footsteps, and he let go of her hand and reached for the duffel bag.

Tariq appeared in the doorway. He spotted Richard and glared at them both before saying, in a surprisingly mild tone, "Time to be off, yeah."

Richard walked toward Tariq, and greeted him in a voice of such calm authority that before her brother even knew it, he was shaking Richard's hand and agreeing, with a dazed expression, that yes, driving back in Richard's car would be best, save carrying everything. Rohimun watched as Tariq pulled the camp bed out from under the great bed and started to dismantle it.

Richard was now busying himself with folding out the flat-packed cardboard boxes that he had brought with him and, despite her protests, was filling them with the empty jars and dirty cloths and all the other detritus of her painting.

"You're still going to be painting, aren't you? That's not going to stop."

When it came to the painting itself, she lifted it so that the easel could be folded away, but then could not think where to put it. Richard took it from her and placed it on the mantelpiece. Its colors echoed the green in the room's draperies and the dark reflected shadows of blackened oak.

She shook her head at the bubble wrap in Tariq's hands.

"You can't do that: you can't put anything on top of it. It's oil paint—it'll take months to be fully dry."

"I think I know that, yeah." He tapped the bubble-wrap roll on the edge of the mantel. "You'll never get it in the car anyway."

Richard stared at the painting. "It looks good there. We'll leave it here for now."

She folded her arms and glared at them both. "Excuse me. It's my painting. I decide."

Eldest sons were all the same: never expecting to be challenged or questioned. She tried to think of an alternative. Honestly. They both waited, their faces neutral, as if she was the one being difficult.

"Oh, never mind. I'll think about it. I'll get it later."

Tariq turned to Richard. "What are you going to say about the painting? If someone sees it?"

"The truth. That Dr. Choudhury's daughter is a talented painter and that I'm hoping to acquire this work."

"It's finished then, is it?"

"Of course it's finished," she snapped. God, brothers were irritating.

"That's a hedge, isn't it? The hedge outside. And you, it's you, yeah."

"Sort of. Not really. Can we go now?"

Between the three of them, they picked up the duffel bag and the boxes and clumped down the main stairs. Richard nodded authoritatively as they passed the movers, and they proceeded to the front door and out onto the drive. Loading up the boot was quickly done, and she wriggled into the back seat cradling her easel, bracing herself for the sickening mixture of resentment and fear that she had felt the last time she and Tariq had gone to Mum and Dad's.

But the feeling did not come, or rather, not with the same intensity as before. Perhaps it was too short a trip by car to work herself up, or perhaps it was the solid presence of Richard in the driver's seat, which said that this time it would be different. Perhaps there was a middle path, where she could paint and be with those she loved. All of them.

Richard twisted around in his seat. "Ready?"

She would not meet his eyes. "All set," she mumbled and looked out the window at the hillside running down then rising up again, toward home. She had another painting in her head now, another full-length one: of Dad looking into a cheval, to see reflected, not himself but his mother, whom Rohimun was always supposed to have taken after. She could see herself so much better now. Perhaps it was time to test if her family could be seen as clearly.

## Thirty-nine

MRS. BEGUM STOOD on her front step and welcomed the Guris warmly, pleased that she had managed to bundle Baby upstairs in the nick of time and that Dr. Choudhury's sulking would now be cut short. Her guests stepped over the threshold of Windsor Cottage with exaggerated care, clearly mindful of omens, although in Mrs. Guri's case, the width of the doorway may also have been a matter of concern. She walked them as quickly as possible to the sitting room, considering Dr. Choudhury's liking for long-speeches-at-the-door.

Kareem came in last, looking as nervous as Mrs. Begum had ever seen him, and holding a large bunch of red and white flowers. A great believer in making use of people's talents, she set him to work lifting the big armchair forward for Mrs. Guri. And, indeed, he seemed grateful enough to be moving about and doing something after that long drive.

Mrs. Begum went to get glasses of water for their guests. When she returned, her husband and Mr. Guri were standing together at the window looking up at the Abbey, while Dr. Choudhury talked about his pride-and-joy.

"Five million pounds," Mr. Guri said, in a tone that was less question than disbelief overwhelmed.

Dr. Choudhury nodded graciously. "Yes, that was the grand total for the, ah, structural repairs, although of course the roof was another matter."

"Wah . . . of course, of course. Another matter."

"The real work, which required such close supervision by someone of my academic credentials, and, ah, aesthetic sensitivities, was the interior: the stained glass, the wood and stonework, the frieze in the great dining hall and, most of all, assessment for the cleaning and repair of the Abbey's extensive collection of manuscripts, hangings, *objets d'art* and valuable paintings."

"How, how much did that cost?"

"Well, of course, the money is immaterial when one is working with, ah, saving our national heritage."

"Of course, of course. But . . ."

"Oh, I would say in the region of three-point-five million pounds. Or maybe point six."

Mrs. Begum watched a now silent Mr. Guri slap a hand gently on his back trouser pocket where his wallet bulged, as if unable to otherwise express the strength of his feelings. His wife, however, seemed more interested in the pictures of Dodi and Diana and Prince and Princess Michael, and Mrs. Begum moved to her side, realizing that she'd never told her that it was her arm, her sari blouse, in the picture with Princess Michael. She was pleasantly aware that, as they talked, Kareem was discreetly but regularly checking his hair, his tie and his fingernails, and generally fidgeting on his seat as if it had become too hot for him. He was as sweaty and nervous and impatient to see his bride as any mother-in-law could want. It was time.

After she had promised to show Mrs. Guri her sari from the photo, Mrs. Begum turned her back on Dodi and Diana and smiled at everyone. If her husband was not going to raise the issue, and neither were the Guris, then it must be her to whom the honor would fall: there was no time to be lost.

"It has been such a pleasure to meet your Kareem." She gestured at Kareem. "He has come to us twice now, such a good boy."

"He is not my son. He does what he wants."

"Yes, but what a good boy."

Mrs. Guri shot an evil look at Kareem, who was now perched uncomfortably upright on the ottoman, his hands on his knees. "*Good?* Aah. We were the good ones. We did everything for him. Everything."

Mr. Guri turned away from Dr. Choudhury and the Abbey and pointed his index finger at Kareem. "Everything," he said with emphasis, his voice gritty and angry. "His own bed, a good job."

Mrs. Guri nodded, fluttering her eyelids in emphasis. "And even then they betray you."

"Nah, nah, nah," Mrs. Begum cried with a pleading glance at Dr. Choudhury. Why did her fool of a husband not say something? This was not meant to be a Modern Youth Today discussion, with everyone competing with their stories about the second-generation's failings and stupidities. But Dr. Choudhury's mouth was as open as Kareem's, so he was no help.

Why had Kareem brought them, if this was to be their view of things? She fiddled with her talisman, thought of Baby in her bedroom waiting for the knock on her door to bring her downstairs, and despaired.

There was movement out the front window, and Mrs. Begum saw Richard Bourne's car pull up behind Kareem's. She stood up and gasped, then Kareem stood as well, and the Guris turned toward her and then the car, with various degrees of worry and fright on their faces.

Mr. Guri was positively pale, his eyes now fixed on the *qibla* mark on the eastern wall of the sitting room, and he appeared to be muttering a prayer, while one hand cupped his rear trouser pocket as if to protect it.

Mrs. Begum was sure she heard Mrs. Guri hiss "*Police!*" as she rocked forward in her chair in an apparent effort to stand, but the chair came with her. As she sat back, she drummed her heels against her handbag until it was underneath the chair and hidden by the upholstery fringing.

Kareem raised his hands to them all, with an agonized expression.

"Stay, please stay here, Uncle. This is personal, private business. All my respects, but please stay here."

Dr. Choudhury, who had also stood and was peering out the sitting-room window, aahed to himself and started to edge toward the door. Mrs. Begum saw Kareem throw him an anguished glance, as if desiring to stop him as well but unable to think how to halt his future father-in-law in his own home.

Munni was here, Mrs. Begum was sure of it. Without further ado, she shot ahead of her husband and ran out the front door and down the path like a young girl. She saw with sharp satisfaction that Rohimun was sitting in the back seat of the car and Tariq in the front. No one could find fault with that. She tried to catch her breath. She, Syeda Begum, being a modern woman, was not at all disturbed by her daughter's arrival with a highly eligible unrelated male, who had just rescued her from her castle like something out of Scheherazade.

As soon as Tariq got out of the car, she grasped his arm. "You were with them the whole time, helping to pack. You have always been with them."

"Eh? Oh, yeah, yeah, yeah."

Richard was holding the car door open for Rohimun, and Mrs. Begum pressed her nails into her palms knowing, knowing, that Dr. Choudhury was watching all this, and praying that Richard would not place a hand in the small of her daughter's back or take her hand or do any of the other not-so-helpful touchings that *gora* men were prone to do. But in fact he stood so well clear of Rohimun that Mrs. Begum was reminded of Kareem's behavior when helping Shunduri out of his car. It could only be another good omen, *Inshallah*.

She could hear Kareem's voice behind her, loud and relieved, speaking to Dr. Choudhury—they must be on the front step together. Then Shunduri was calling down from the little dormer bedroom window, asking, "What's goin' on, yeah?"

And the next thing she knew, Shunduri had run out of the front door, flashed past her and embraced Rohimun. Mrs. Begum smiled, tears in her eyes. Shunduri never did this, would never have spontaneously been this helpful, but of course, Kareem was watching everything, and now it would be even harder for Dr. Choudhury to repulse his daughter. If only Henry and Thea were here also.

She met Rohimun's eyes and gave a small, tight nod toward Dr. Choudhury. *Please go to him, don't hesitate, not now.* Then she could embrace her eldest daughter. Rohimun disentangled herself from Shunduri's grasp and walked around the car. She was in traditional clothes, thank god, one of her old college *salwars*—turquoise with brown edging—and with her hair neatly plaited, she made a pretty sight as she went to kneel before her father.

Mrs. Begum stood halfway between house and car, trying to watch everyone at once and feeling rather like the umpire in the tall chair in the Wimbledon competition that Mrs. Darby loved so much. Balls going everywhere.

Richard stayed by the car. He was observing the scene on the doorstep intently, unsmiling, his profile outlined against the greenery behind him. And for all his *gora* ways and his tall-thinness, he suddenly seemed to Mrs. Begum as irresistibly handsome as the most heartbreaking of Bollywood heroes. One hand, resting on the roof of his car, was holding the car keys in plain sight, as if to say, if Rohimun is not welcome here, she will be welcome elsewhere. Could Dr. Choudhury see that as well? Mrs. Begum hoped so, from the bottom of her heart.

Shunduri, not one to be left out of any scene, also ran to kneel before her father to beg for her sister's forgiveness. Kareem had moved into the background somewhat, pressed against the front-door lintel, and was wiping his eyes with a sparkling-white handkerchief.

Mrs. Begum, thinking suddenly of washing powder and widowhood, could not bear to look. She leaned on the end of Richard's car and stared fiercely into its dark-blue depths. Let my husband take his daughter in his arms. Let him see he has no choice, and that it will be a blessing and a release for him, as well as for Munni and for all of us.

When she turned, her two daughters were standing on the doorstep facing her, with their father's arms around them, and Tariq had tears on his cheeks, just like his father. Richard was still by the car, as if unsure what to do next. She stared at him, not breathing, willing him to act.

Through a blur of tears, Mrs. Begum watched as Richard joined the group on the steps and held out his hand to Dr. Choudhury. Her husband was not short, but the two-steps up that he was standing only brought him to Richard's eye-level. The two men acknowledged each other, then Dr. Choudhury's hand came out and they shook hands as equals. Richard said something and gestured toward Rohimun.

Mrs. Begum was entranced and did not approach them to hear what was being said, for fear of breaking the spell. Whatever it was, Rohimun had moved away with that shoulder-slouching stance she had when she had too much attention, and was drifting toward the side of the house. Dr. Choudhury, most unlike him, so awkward with touchings, then pulled Richard up a step and into an embrace, which was over as soon as it had begun and which seemed to embarrass them both equally.

Baby was watching the men avidly, almost jealously, her eyes wide and the second finger of her right hand stroking the central part in her hair. Hah, there is a girl ready to marry, painting her own part red. Whatever happens, Mrs. Begum thought, as she wiped her eyes and hurried to the cottage, Baby must marry first; it would matter so much to her. Betrothal would have to be good enough for Munni, in the circumstances. And who could hurry a *gora* suitor, anyway?

Eventually Mrs. Begum realized that dear Richard was saying something to her about leaving, dropping Rohimun's painting things off but coming back later. She nodded and turned toward her front door. Two daughters as good as married, and her family whole again. Truly she was blessed today, *Inshallah*.

## Forty

Mrs. Begum swept back into the sitting room with Tariq, beaming. Kareem was following, as careful as any younger son, closing doors behind them, and with both (both!) daughters dispatched upstairs and Richard promising to be back soon, the ball had clearly bounced into the Guris' tennis court. She stood right next to her husband, as close as any *gora* wife, and stared pointedly at the Guris, who looked as if they had not moved since she'd left them. They must speak.

Mr. Guri was wiping his forehead and top lip with a handkerchief. His mouth was open and he was breathing heavily, as if he had been running. "Is, is everything . . ."

Dr. Choudhury hurrumphed. "Yes, yes. My other daughter is home now."

"Ah, it was . . . family-visit then? The unmarked, er, blue car?"

Mrs. Begum could not resist. "Yes, yes, and Tariq with Richard Bourne, from the Bourne Abbey." From the window, Richard's car could be seen driving away. "He will be back to visit with us later."

Mr. Guri edged forward on his seat. "You have a beautiful family. And a beautiful home. Very big." His tone was as different from before as yoghurt from chilli, but before Mrs. Begum could respond, Mrs. Guri chimed in.

"And what lovely children. Beautiful children, all grown-up. It is such a pleasure to see this generation can turn out so well. It gives me hope." There was still a something in those last few words that seemed to be directed at Kareem, but no matter. Things were now as they should be, and the men needed to be left to talk.

Mrs. Begum smiled at Mrs. Guri and gestured toward the picture of Prince and Princess Michael. "Let me show you the sari." Mrs. Guri heaved herself out of the armchair, successfully this time, and followed Mrs. Begum to the study to *ahh* and fondle the fabric that had been graced by royal eyes. Once this was done, the girls should be almost ready to be brought downstairs.

---

UPSTAIRS, SHUNDURI TURNED Rohimun's shoulders so that they were both facing the wardrobe mirror.

"You know, Kareem has lots of friends. He could be such a good brother to you."

Rohimun looked at the emerald green sari Shunduri had just persuaded her to put on, then watched as her sister also scrutinized her, as if trying to think what she could offer her that would be appreciated.

"He knows everybody. He could find you a nice husband, I mean, one that wasn't bothered about . . ."

"No, thanks," she replied. "I don't particularly like . . . you just enjoy yours. I'm very happy for you." She sat down and squinted at the two saris her sister had spread out on the other bed. "If you're going to wear pink, go for the cool pink with silver embroidery. And keep it simple, Baby: just a few bangles, no tikka or hair jewelry or slave bracelets."

"You think?" Shunduri eyed herself with a doubtful expression.

Telling Baby to lay off the jewelry was like telling a bowerbird blue wasn't its color. "You look beautiful, Baby—no need to worry about that. Here, get your *salwar* off and put the sari petticoat on."

"I just hope they like me, you know?"

"Well, they'd be fools not to, yeah?"

Shunduri flapped her hands over her chest, then seemed to become preoccupied with her nails, long and gleaming in frosted pink, as Rohimun stood to unfold the sari's length.

"Put the blouse on now, so I can start on the sari. What's he like then?"

"I don't really know, yaah."

"Oh bullshit, Baby. Come on, tell me."

Shunduri gave a sort of gasping giggle and turned for her to fold and tuck the sari's skirt. "As you saw, he's sooo good-lookin'. A bit like Gulshan Grover in *Gangster*, but wiv better teeth. He thought, first time he saw me, that I looked like Rani Mukherjee in *Kal Ho Naa Ho*."

Rohimun felt about a hundred. "So what do you know about his family? There, that's your *pallu* done now."

"Oh, his *real* family." Shunduri shrugged elegantly, then frowned into the mirror. "This blouse is so old-fashioned. They're all dead years ago, from those big floods that Mum always goes on about. He's been with the Guris, working in their restaurant since he was sixteen, though they had him down as twelve on the visa so he could come over as their long-lost nephew. He's really connected—have you seen his car?"

"If you want to please your future in-laws I'd go as traditional as you can. You'll have plenty of chances to go Bollywood high-fashion after you marry."

"You know what I'd really like to do?" Shunduri's eyes sparkled. "I'd like to get one of those houses in the new estates just out of Swindon. So brand-new, no one has ever lived in them before. They're built with conservatories, and you can choose your own wallpaper inside . . . and Mum won't be too far away to help, you know, with the kids." Shunduri giggled at Rohimun's raised eyebrows. "And you could visit, stay as long as you want."

The bright sari was put away, and they both smoothed the chiffon overlay of the chosen sari with spread fingers and smiled at each other.

The sulky defensiveness that Shunduri had always had as far back as Rohimun could remember, her jealousy of Rohimun's closeness to Tariq, and to Dad, were nowhere to be seen. Now Shunduri seemed to regard herself, finally, as the lucky one, the special one, the child that the sun shone on, favorite of all. Rohimun should be happy for her.

Shunduri reached into her beauty box, pulled out a piece of elaborately worked hair-jewelry in antiqued gold, and draped it against Rohimun's hair. "This would look great on you, and maybe some lipstick . . ."

How generous Shunduri was in her triumph, wanting to share her excitement and her jewelry.

"What shoes are you going to wear? You don't want to tower over him," Rohimun found herself saying. God, she sounded like a bitter old maid. But Shunduri was oblivious to the dig.

"You know what, when I'm married, we could go out clubbing, get you to meet some nice boys maybe . . . I've got some outfits you'd look great in."

So now it was Rohimun who was the poor unfortunate, the black sheep. She sat down again. "I'm not really into that scene, Baby."

"Maybe in the future, yaah." Shunduri sat behind her and started to play with her hair, pulling her head around to face the mirror. "It's so dry. Let me oil it for you, Affa. Richard's coming back, isn't he?"

She gave a vague assent as she looked at herself. She'd never been into this kind of thing. This wasn't her. But there she was in the mirror, wearing an emerald green sari and waiting for her younger sister, still talking a mile a minute, to rub oil through her hair. Richard had never seen her in a sari.

---

MRS. BEGUM, HAVING finished showing Mrs. Guri the sari cupboard and returned her guest to the sitting room, announced, with a certain drama, "I will make tea."

As soon as she was in the hall, she hoicked up her sari and ran upstairs. She opened the door to the girls' bedroom with a warm feeling in her stomach that she had them home with her at last: both girls together now. And with no fighting, although it was probably still not a good idea to leave them alone for too long.

The air was thick with perfume and hairspray and hair oil, and she felt a thrill of pleasure to see her beautiful Shunduri in a sari. And a sari blouse that did not show the top of her breasts.

"Baby, who put your sari on?"

"Affa did my sari. Good as you, Amma!" Shunduri twirled, staggered a little in her heels and laughed, but too loud, too high. "See?"

Mrs. Begum smiled and inspected her daughter's slim waist.

"Shush now. Be calm and quiet. You are a good girl."

Who would have thought that Rohimun even knew how to put on a sari? But then she had always been good with her hands.

"You are both good girls. Come down now. Munni, go into the sitting room. Baby, go into the kitchen until I call you. "

Shunduri pouted. "Affa's not ready yet. I want to put up her hair."

"Never mind about her hair. What has that got to do with anything? Quick! Quick!"

She hurried her youngest daughter downstairs, counting seats on her fingers and calling to Tariq to bring in three more chairs. Rohimun would not be excluded from such a meeting, and Richard had promised he would return. And Henry and Thea were due anytime soon, to collect the boys. Who said the country was dull? The way things were going, they would have just as many visitors as those in Brick Lane ever had.

But in the kitchen, Shunduri halted at the sight of the largest silver tray out on the kitchen table, its edges decorated with pink paper napkins folded into delicate fans. Her smile stiffened into a grimace of fear.

"Oh Christ," she moaned, and grabbed the back of a kitchen chair as if it was trying to escape her.

Mrs. Begum felt a stab of alarm and pulled Shunduri toward the kitchen dresser. "No time for that. Quick, quick. Tea."

Shunduri got the best cups and saucers out, Royal Albert

Country-roses, rattled them onto the tray's polished center, and followed with a teabag dropped into each cup. The kettle was full and steaming, and Mrs. Begum gave her daughter's back a gentle rub before pouring the hot water. Shunduri began to add milk and sugar to each cup.

"When you go in, make sure your *pallu* is over your head, and that you serve the men first, and then Mrs. Guri. I will help you with the rest. Take your time, no need to rush this. Be slow and graceful and keep your eyes down and everyone can look at you without your having to look back at them. Do not sit. Then, later, I will send you back into the kitchen to cut up some mangoes. Here, look, they are already cut up, you just need to bring them out after a little while."

Shunduri was silent, but when she went to adjust her daughter's *pallu* she could see tears brimming. She used one of the paper napkins to soak up the tears on Baby's bottom lashes without disturbing her make-up.

"There. There. You are my best girl. My beautiful girl. Take the tray. I will send Munni out with you to get the mangoes so you will not be alone."

———

WHEN SHE FELT she couldn't stay upstairs any longer without Mum coming after her, Rohimun entered the sitting room and tried to sit down on the couch next to Tariq's chair as quietly and demurely as any mother could wish. She sat bolt upright and with her hair scooped to hang forward over one shoulder, so that its freshly oiled strands would not mark the back of the sofa. The sari that she had only put on for Mum's sake, and her sister's, felt surprisingly comfortable. Perhaps because she'd put it on herself and with considerably fewer safety pins than Mum would have used. Or perhaps because its relative plainness was light years away from her sister's confection of froth and shimmer, and the vivid reds and yellows that Mum preferred.

Shunduri was handing out tea cups and the tantara of cup on saucer must have been audible to everyone. She looked as fragile as a butterfly in her pink and silver chiffon, and years younger without the heavy foundation and red lipstick that she usually favored.

When she reached Mrs. Guri, the older woman took the cup and saucer in one hand, and reached out with the other to stroke Shunduri's cheek with surprising sweetness. "What a beautiful girl. Beautiful!"

Shunduri froze but, just as Rohimun was about to rise to help her, seemed to collect herself and returned to the tea tray to distribute the rest of the cups. Mr. Guri was making noises similar to his wife's, and Dad was smiling at the mantel mirror as if the compliments had been directed at him.

Mum bustled in and straight out again, as the doorbell rang, and was soon ushering Richard into the room and introducing him as the owner of Bourne Abbey, that palace up on the hill there, you can see it through the window. Mr. Guri shot off his chair with his eyes bulging, pumped Richard's hand several times, and did a strange kind of backward shuffle as he waited for him to sit down first.

Richard greeted everybody and, despite a very clear direction from Mum to take the chair next to Dad, folded up his long legs to sit next to Rohimun. His weight on the sofa made her rock toward him, and she leaned away stiffly, reaching for a cup of tea that Shunduri at the last second diverted to Richard, leading to a clashing of hands over the saucer. She snatched her hand away, hot with shame, and vowed to count the fringing on the sofa's arm till her face was cool again.

Then someone, perhaps Tariq, was talking about her painting, but what with the sound of Richard's breathing and his body only a foot from hers, she could not attend. Now Richard was speaking, something about a dealer friend of his having sold on a few of her earlier portraits, of exhibitions that had come and gone.

Luckily, no one seemed too interested, and after a few polite noises, the conversation reverted to family histories and the distant blood connection between Mum's uncle the tailor and some second cousin of Kareem's, who was related by marriage to the Guris. Photos came out then, of the two Guri daughters, and grandchildren. Rohimun could not see them, but suspected from Mum's extravagant compliments and Dad's silence that they were on the plain side. Mrs. Guri got her own back by launching into a detailed description of the enormous wedding portion paid by their son-in-law's family, only eclipsed by the size of the dowry that was sent with their daughter. Dad looked a little uneasy at this last mention, but Kareem appeared to brighten.

Everyone seemed to be keen to get along despite the jostling for position, and Rohimun watched them all as if from behind a pane of glass. Did Baby really want to take this path and marry that Brick Lane coolie-boy sitting there with his shaved head and ear bling, and his wide-boy suit that looked as if it had been sprayed on?

Shunduri perched herself on the sofa arm next to Rohimun, and her fingers, sticky and warm, burrowed into Rohimun's left palm, her nails creating sharp little crescents. She was reminded, fleetingly, of Shunduri's first day at school and how tightly she had held on to her hand then.

At the time, Rohimun had thought it was fear and that she would have to scrape Baby's fingers off hers when the time came to leave her with her teacher. But when her sister had seen her class, she'd let go and joined them without a backward glance. Only then had Rohimun realized that Shunduri's tight grip had been an expression not of fear but of a desire, pitched to desperation, to take this step, to do what her brother and sister had already done.

And now she was going where neither of her siblings had ventured. Rohimun squeezed her sister's hand back and suddenly saw it all through Shunduri's eyes: the critical judgement being made; Kareem's watchful nervousness; Mr. Guri's greed; and the ominous presence of the worldly Mrs. Guri, the most notorious matchmaker in Brick Lane, who must have been part of so many compromised, rushed-through and faked arranged marriages for other Desi families.

Her father cleared his throat. "A very impressive young man, your Kareem. Such an entrepreneur already, and yet with all the traditional values. He has clearly had all of the upbringing and support and encouragement that a young man is so in need of, in a new country."

So Dad was returning compliments to Mr. and Mrs. Guri, but instead of stopping there, he started talking about travelling with Kareem to Mecca and Medina, quoting some statistics about the crowds and the tent cities of pilgrims, and praising Kareem on his enthusiasm for the journey.

"But," Mrs. Guri was saying, in accents of concern mixed, strangely, with what sounded like relief, "the month for Haj is just two weeks away."

Mum smiled and bobbed her head. "Yes, yes, they are all abandoning me and my daughters for the Haj." The smile fell from her face. "And I do so worry. Anything could happen, so far away. Anything. The Haj is such a long and hard journey and the living conditions are not what we have become used to."

All the elders laughed then, nodding reminiscently and making it clear that this younger generation had no idea what hardship was.

Mr. Guri shifted forward on his seat, serious-faced. "My uncle, you remember, wife, grandfather's eldest? He died on Haj, and only a young man too."

Mrs. Guri nodded her head, matching his seriousness. "He was in Medina, in the tent city, and everyone in his tour group became sick with giardia. They say it was from the Africans."

Mr. Guri shook his head heavily at the loss. "He had booked a first-class tour, with a four-star hotel in Mecca for afterward, for the shopping. His family had to pay for the body to be flown back to England and then, you understand, to be escorted to Bangladesh for the burial." He shifted even further forward on his seat and adopted a tone of direst warning. "There were no refunds."

"Wah," said the elders, almost in concert, but Tariq stood abruptly, his voice loud and flat as he moved to the doorway.

"It's the first step on the pilgrimage that counts. He took the first step. It doesn't matter that he didn't finish it. It doesn't matter about the money."

"What a blessing to die whilst on Haj," said Mrs. Guri over the noise of the shutting door, and wiped away a few tears, politely ignoring Tariq's outburst.

Rohimun looked wonderingly at the slammed door and then at Richard, who had straightened at Tariq's words, and was now leaning forward, his elbows on his knees, all tense attention, as if what Tariq had said held some special meaning for him alone.

Mum nodded gratefully at Mrs. Guri. "It could happen to anyone. Young or old. Who knows what Allah has in store, *Inshallah.*"

Dad cleared his throat. "It is certainly a most risky undertaking, even in this day and age, where jets fly everywhere and everyone has a telephone. I do believe that to take such a journey still requires a certain, ahem, hardiness and courage. But such a sacrifice, such a risk, is no longer acknowledged by this modern generation. In past times, the green turban and long hennaed beard of the Hajiri excited universal respect, even reverence."

Mrs. Guri studied Dad's tweed suit and clean-shaven face for a moment and then turned to Mrs. Begum. "It is so pleasant to be here seeing you again, and your lovely family. And we have so many things to talk of."

Mum cut in. "Perhaps it is time for the young people to sit on the patio for a little while. Rohimun can make tea for us, and paan."

Dad hemmed, as if not willing to abandon his subject just yet. "Family is truly the only foundation for a godly life. Family and Haj."

No one responded, and after a moment Mum threw a significant look at Mr. and Mrs. Guri. "We have a patio here, next to the kitchen. You can see it from the kitchen window, and from upstairs."

Mrs. Guri grunted her assent, and the two women ushered Kareem and Shunduri as the acknowledged couple, blushing and smiling, up and out ahead of them. Rohimun stood up to leave, uncomfortably aware that Richard had done the same.

As she turned to shut the sitting-room door behind them all, she caught a glimpse of the two fathers: Mr. Guri shuffling his chair closer to Dad's, their heads already lowered to discuss financial arrangements. How quickly it all happens, when everyone wants the same thing.

She found herself alone in the kitchen with Richard. Mum and Mrs. Guri must have gone upstairs to talk, and probably to spy on Kareem and Shunduri from Mum's bedroom window. Outside, they could see Kareem's shining scalp and the glittering pink of Shunduri's veiled head as they sat demurely on the garden patio bench, like Asian Barbie and Ken. Approaching them shyly from the direction of the rabbit hutches were the two Bourne children. Kareem spotted them first, and jumped up, smiling, as one of them toed a soccerball toward him. Kareem said something then removed his jacket, folding it neatly, and placed it on the bench after Shunduri had crossed her arms when he tried to hand it to her.

Rohimun leaned forward to watch, hearing the squeak of the upstairs window as she did so. "Are we the chaperones then?" Richard asked behind her.

"Looks like it, yeah. But I don't think we're the only ones."

She watched Kareem scoop the ball onto the toe of his shoe and start to bounce it up and down, calling to the boys. "Who's the soccer player den?"

"Me!" they both said at once, arms akimbo, tongues out, dancing around him.

Kareem kicked the ball to his left, and the boys took off after it, jostling each other violently.

"So who's chaperoning us?" said Richard.

"Oh, they won't leave us alone for long," she said, not looking at him. "Besides, we all know my reputation's rubbish, so I think we probably need Henry over here to look after you."

"Perish the thought." He took hold of a tendril of her hair and wound it slowly around his finger. "What's that in your hair?"

She could feel his eyes. "Shunduri oiled my hair."

"What sort of oil?"

"Almond, I think. I didn't notice."

"It makes your hair look different. Heavier and darker, like an old oil painting. It's almost in ringlets. Beautiful."

Her face felt hot. "Shunduri's the beautiful one."

"I disagree." There was an awkward silence. "What happens now?"

"Well, Dad and Mr. Guri are probably talking about the dowry gold and how many saris and what whitegoods they'll have to give each other, and Mum and Mrs. Guri are probably talking about where to hold the reception and the *walima*. That's like the second reception that the groom's family puts on after the honeymoon."

"Jesus Christ. That's pretty quick."

"Yeah."

"How do you feel about it all?"

"It's what Shunduri's always wanted, that's for sure."

"A good traditional girl."

She bridled, then realized that he was teasing her. "Yeah, unlike the one you've gotten yourself mixed up with."

"What about marriage itself?"

She shook her head. "It's not for me."

"No?" He looked at her musingly. "No, I don't think that kind of marriage would suit me either."

"An Asian family would always get the better of you on the wedding settlement anyway. You wouldn't stand a chance."

He smiled, startling her with the transformation. "I think I'd pay anything not to have to wear the turban."

"Oh, they'd make you pay alright. And wear the turban. And dance at the *walima*, Bhangara-style." She lifted her hands in the air and shrugged hips and shoulders to demonstrate, but felt foolish and dropped her arms. "What are you talking about marriage for anyhow?"

He hesitated. "I was thinking how much pressure there would be. To marry."

"Yeah. Well, Mum's too busy at the moment but she'll have me and Bai in her sights pretty soon."

At that instant, the kitchen door swung open, and Mrs. Guri entered, eyeing them suspiciously as she moved aside to let Mum in behind her.

"Munni, make tea and paan," her mother said while stepping

between her and Richard on the pretext of rinsing her fingertips in the sink. "Dear Richard, please go now, and ask Shunduri and Kareem to come inside. It is time."

He turned and went out the kitchen's back door. Rohimun put the kettle on the stove, laid out more cups and teabags, and sat down gloomily at the kitchen table to wrap little packages filled with paan and lime. Why was it only now, when she was back within the family home, that she realized she was thinking of him that way? What kind of person was she, to only want what she couldn't have?

She could hear Mum and Mrs. Guri behind her, who, from the oohing and aahing about how sweet they looked, must be spying through the kitchen window. Jesus Christ, what was so different about what Shunduri had done and what she had done? Yet it was all working out for her sister.

Stupid, vain Shunduri, who could lie to Mum and Dad without batting an eye, about her studies and how much she'd spent shopping, and have a boyfriend in London all this time without getting caught, was having it all. Not that she wanted to be in Shunduri's shoes: it just seemed so unfair.

Now Mum and Mrs. Guri, having agreed what a lovely couple Kareem and Shunduri would make, were ushering them both, along with Richard, back toward the sitting room, and Mum was telling her to come, hurry, leave the paan now.

Back in the sitting room the negotiations were nearly over, with the Guris even conceding that Kareem and Shunduri would not need to live with them in London. For the Guris, experienced negotiators if there ever were, to give up all the benefits of an extra body in the restaurant and an extra hand in the kitchen at home, as well as the access to the dowry and the grandchildren that it would give them, was strange to say the least. The only person who didn't appear to be surprised was Kareem.

Tariq had his camera and tripod at the ready, and the happy couple were arranged with stiff formality onto hall chairs, almost side by side.

Mrs. Guri, smiling, had worked two surprisingly delicate bracelets off her wrist and took Shunduri's right hand and slid them on, to her cries of, "Ooh, thank you Auntie!" while the two families ranged behind them with much rustling and many displays of mutual consideration. Rohimun found herself at the edge of the group, next to Mr. Guri, who carefully kept his sleeve from brushing against her. In case of contamination, she thought. Probably best to cut me out of the photo altogether.

Tariq waved her away. "Just the parents now, Munni."

She shuffled out of frame, moving to stand behind Tariq. Baiyya looked in his element now, fiddling with the tripod and directing: left a bit, smile everyone, move your veil back a bit, Baby, I can't see you. Shunduri's hand made a token tug but her face remained half-obscured by her *pallu*, which was pulled well forward, with only her trembling pink mouth clearly visible. How virginal, thought Rohimun sourly.

Just as Tariq called out to count to three, Kareem suddenly slid from his chair onto one knee, gazed up at Shunduri and grinned. Mr. Guri's exclamation of impatience was cut short as Kareem's right hand opened to reveal a red velvet box. A dramatic pause, then Kareem's thumb sprang the lid. It flicked open and, with an elaborate flourish, was angled toward the light, its contents fiery in the camera's flash.

When Rohimun looked at her brother, he was grinning as well and, completely in the spirit of it all, keeping the SLR's button depressed, its repeated flashes strobing the happy couple with a whole series of shots, while Shunduri, ever camera-conscious, did the slo-mo gasp and modest half-turn away to perfection as her mother lifted her left hand and held it out to her betrothed.

"You like it? That's two carats!" said Kareem, remembering just in time, Rohimun noticed, to look at Dr. Choudhury and at Tariq for token permission before pulling it out of the box and placing it on Shunduri's finger.

"An engagement, modern-style!" said Mum, craning to look at the ring.

Mrs. Guri nodded her head with gracious authority. "A lot of couples are doing this now. The diamond ring is traditional in Christian families."

Mum stared doubtfully at Shunduri's finger, now posed before her for the photo. "Not always. Sometimes they have a blue stone like Princess Diana and Princess Kate. Or a red stone, like Princess Fergie."

Mrs. Guri sniffed. "Nah, I have never seen *that*."

Tariq caught Rohimun's eye, and she smiled at him in recognition of Mrs. Guri's jealous denial, but he didn't seem to notice.

"Go get my other memory card, would you?" he said to her, already turning back to the seated couple. "It's on my dresser. Hey, Baby, you'll put your shoulder out with that rock!"

On the way out, she almost ran into Mrs. Guri, who smiled and pinched her cheek. "You will be next," she said, but then hesitated, as if recalling something she'd heard or seen, and started to speak across Rohimun to Mr. Guri, about visits and dates.

Rohimun noticed that Richard was watching her with what looked like pity. Prick. She left the room and took off up the hallway and the stairs, feeling as irrelevant as a servant, or a ghost.

So this was her rehabilitation. Or rather, she was on probation, to be allowed in, but carefully watched, never trusted or really listened to. Others must still be protected from her corrupting influence. She was a burden, a shameful burden that must be carried.

She ran into the tiny room that Mum had made up for Tariq, with its single bed and almost complete absence of possessions, like a monk's cell except for the Man United duvet cover and the *Bismillah* over the head of the bed. Tariq certainly wasn't irrelevant downstairs. He was in the thick of it, happy to see Shunduri married, to let Kareem call him Baiyya, because it took the pressure off him,

And, in time, he would probably join with Mum and Dad in talking about her taking a trip to Bangladesh (*Just a holiday, Munni. You need a holiday!*) because in the old country there would always be somebody who would marry her for the visa, and not be too fussy otherwise.

Her dowry would be residency and citizenship, her wedding portion all the claims to reputation in the community that her marriage would give her, with the added bonus of a likely enforcement of traditional values by a husband from the old country. Cooking and cleaning, beatings and babies.

She leaned out of the dormer window and glimpsed the Abbey. The new slate tiles were silver in the sunshine, and its yew hedge appeared more like a great green gateway than a wall to keep the world out. The Abbey had been a sanctuary, really. And she'd thought at the time that she had glimpsed the beginnings of something there.

The door opened behind her, and she recognized Richard's measured tread, so different to Tariq's light step.

She tried for cold, but came out sulky. "I'll catch it if they find you in here."

"I thought you'd like to know, Henry and Thea have just arrived. And the Guris are leaving now. Without Kareem. They had some business in Swindon apparently."

Rohimun leaned back out the window and looked down. For two fat people, they were moving pretty quickly, with no apparent desire to meet Mum and Dad's latest visitors. Perhaps they'd had enough. They weren't the only ones. "I dropped your painting things in the old stables, up at the Abbey, earlier. I was thinking that would be a good place to work. It's very light—"

"I didn't ask you to."

"I know. I want to help." He paused, as if thinking. "What you said in the kitchen, about family pressure. I just want you to know, I'm here because I want to be."

She drew back from the window and stared at him, suspicious. His face was in full sunshine and in his eyes, in the irises, there was a multitude of blues and greens and golds that flared in random streaks and arcs from the dark center like a corona at full eclipse. Without meaning to, she tilted forward.

"We'd better go back downstairs," he said.

"Yeah." She went toward the door. "I can handle it, you know. The pressure."

"Of course," he said and turned to leave.

"Yeah," she said again. But for how long? And what were they to each other, really?

## Forty-one

MRS. BEGUM FAREWELLED the Guris with an energetic wave that simultaneously welcomed Henry and Thea, who were climbing out of Thea's car, looking tired and dishevelled and not entirely ready for company. As she walked back up the garden path, she passed Kareem who was watching the Guris depart in his car as if he'd never see it again.

Andrew and Jonathon, hearing their parents' voices, ran around to the front garden, covered in dirt and rabbit fluff, to greet them. At the door, Dr. Choudhury, teary once more, embraced Henry and Thea, telling them how important family was and how welcome they were as he blocked up the hallway, preventing anyone from entering further.

She pushed past her husband and urged them all to come in, blessing her own foresight in having cooked three curries earlier and wondering if there was enough rice. She glimpsed Thea and Baby in the hallway, hugging and kissing each other's cheeks as if they were old friends, before finding herself swept up into the sitting room by the force of everyone else's progress to the kitchen. There was more noise at the front door, and she ran back to find Mrs. Darby there.

"*Salaam*, come in, come in!" Mrs. Begum ushered her neighbor into the sitting room. Overwhelmed by events and the high of plans come to fruition all at once, weddings to arrange, crying husband, she forgot herself so much as to pull her friend into a small, elbow-gripping embrace, and spun her around in the middle of the sitting room.

"Oh!" both ladies cried, then laughed, and when Mrs. Begum released her they both sat down and caught their breath.

Mrs. Darby, still smiling, patted her décolletage with a be-ringed hand. "Syeda, my dear, I am so sorry to disturb you right now, but I could not wait. My daughter, my Patricia, is pregnant at last. Three months today!"

Mrs. Begum gasped and threw up her hands. "Your very first grandchild: after so many years of eye-vee-ef!"

"So long," said Mrs. Darby. "So many cycles. And now. After all this time."

"Aah," said Mrs. Begum. "She is blessed, truly blessed, *Inshallah*. You will be a daddu, a grandmother, now. At last."

She watched her neighbor dab her eyes, with only the tiniest flicker of her own betraying the fact that a small part of her was keeping an ear on hallway and kitchen doings. Such wonderful news for her friend that even the great events of her own day she would not mention.

She clasped Mrs. Darby's hands. "You will be wanting to be with her."

Mrs. Darby nodded, her tears rising again. "I saw the travel agent this morning and I have booked a ticket. I am going . . . to Australia. For a year. Maybe more."

"Wah! You are emigrating! What will we all do without you? And so far away!" Mrs. Begum looked at her friend with pity and alarm. How was Mrs. Darby going to manage this great thing on her own? She had never been abroad, didn't even like going into Swindon for shopping and hadn't been to London since her husband had died, five years ago. She herself, Syeda Begum, had done this great thing, this emigration, but she was much younger then than Mrs. Darby now.

She thought of that terrifying train ride to Dhaka so many years ago, and later the amazement and confusion of her arrival in Heathrow, and clasped Mrs. Darby's hand anew. "You will be happy there. Tariq will drive you to Heathrow and carry your bags. And I will come. And your daughter and son-in-law will be there when you arrive in that place. I will look after your garden . . ."

"Oh, the flight doesn't really worry me."

"Nah, nah, you will be very comfortable. They feed you and are very friendly. You will be fine, *Inshallah*."

Mrs. Darby glanced toward the noise of the kitchen and rose to her feet. "I must go."

"Nah, stay and eat with us. I have chicken korma."

"No, my dear, not this time. You have a full house and"—she paused significantly—"maybe you have some news for me?"

Mrs. Begum smiled, shaking her head as well. "Stay, stay."

"No, I will go. I just had one more thing to say." Mrs. Darby drew herself up to her full height, her neatly separated grey curls trembling a little around her powdered face.

Mrs. Begum looked up at her, conscious now of further news of great import.

"In the light of these events, I will be resigning my presidency of the Lydiard-and-Stowe District Women's Institute."

"But—"

"No, no, Syeda. One cannot manage such things from a distance. Look what happened to Rhodesia when the royal family cancelled their visit. Rioting, and then a dictatorship."

She waited to hear more, but it seemed as if Mrs. Darby herself was still absorbing what she had just said.

At last her neighbor spoke again. "I want you to take my place."

"Nah, nah!" Mrs. Begum gasped, then covered her mouth, staring at her friend.

"I *insist*. You have been a tower of strength, particularly when dealing with that Upwey woman. I could not have managed without you over the last twelve months. For example, the fruit-cake incident. And when Marge went over my head. But I'm losing track. I want you to take over the presidency. There is a meeting of the executive tonight and I want to nominate you, my dearest friend. Eileen and Ailsa will support me on this, and I think I can count on the two Julies and that funny woman from the post office. And you don't need to worry about the paperwork—Ailsa is an excellent secretary and will do all that side of things. She just needs direction."

Mrs. Begum could not speak. There was more noise from the kitchen, and Mrs. Darby patted her hand, then moved toward the hallway door.

"I know I can rely on you, Syeda. You know how things should be done and it will be one in the eye for Audrey Upwey and her nuddy-calendar fund-raising ideas. I'll report back tomorrow. Come over to my house in the morning and we'll have a cup of tea, and you can tell me your news then too."

Mrs. Begum, reeling with the events of the day (she had not even asked Allah for the presidency), saw her neighbor out and bustled to the kitchen, slightly delayed by the two boys who shot into the hall-way and pulled at her skirts, asking about *ladhu* balls. What more, what more could happen on this blessed day, *Inshallah*?

---

As RICHARD FOLLOWED Rohimun downstairs, they passed Tariq, who glared at his sister, pointedly ignored Richard, and said it was too late for the memory card now, they were done with photos. There was a clamor from the kitchen, and Richard decided, in the light of Tariq's reaction, to delay his entrance a little, hanging back in the hallway so there was a respectable gap between his arrival and Rohimun's.

When he felt it was seemly to go in, there was barely space to do so. Thea and Henry, Kareem and Shunduri, Dr. Choudhury and Mrs. Begum, were all talking at once, and the boys were running in and out. Mrs. Begum was telling Rohimun, who was at the counter pour-ing milk into cups, to be quick, quick.

"Tea for everyone, then?" he said as he approached her.

"Yeah." She turned back to her task, smiling, and as he watched her, it occurred to him that perhaps it was being the center of atten-tion she'd hated outside on the steps, not what he'd said. There was a muttered apology behind him, as Tariq squeezed past Richard and then Rohimun, pulling on her plait as he did so.

Kareem was fussing Shunduri into a kitchen chair in a way that oddly mirrored Henry's actions with Thea, who, for once, didn't seem to mind. Mrs. Begum smiled at Henry and Thea, and beckoned Rohimun toward them.

"My other daughter, Rohimun, she is home now. She has come back."

Rohimun stood there awkwardly while Mrs. Begum beamed and tucked a strand of hair behind her daughter's ear. "You are a *good* girl."

Richard edged down the kitchen counter, keeping out of the way as Andrew and Jonathan hopped around the table, then crawled underneath it, making rabbit sounds. Henry was standing behind Thea, his hand on his wife's shoulder and her hand resting in his. He bent to whisper to her, and she looked up at him and squeezed his hand.

Henry straightened and caught Richard's eye. "We've got some news. Just been for the scan . . ."

Shunduri gave a loud gasp, her eyes theatrically wide and one hand, fingernails tipped with pink, over her mouth. Thea, of all people, went distinctly pink as well.

"We're, ah, pregnant. Twelve weeks today. Couldn't quite believe it till we saw the scan."

"Henry, Thea, congratulations. You've caught me completely by surprise." Richard maneuvered around the table to embrace his brother and kiss Thea on the cheek. "I had no idea."

"Well, neither did we actually. Thee's had a dodgy tummy for a while, been, you know, a bit teary, dropping things, but we never thought . . ."

"Ohhh!" cried Shunduri, as if it was a surprise that Henry and Thea had put on especially for her. "I can't believe it. I can't *believe* it!"

Thea was more relaxed than Richard had seen her in ages as she leaned back against her husband, saying something to Kareem about paradise gardens. Richard watched them, feeling again the outsider. He had never even suspected. How long—and how much work— does it take to get to that level of unspoken, happy companionship, that perfect trust? He felt as if he should be apologizing for having so underestimated the solid reality of their marriage.

He caught Thea's eye. "You feeling well?"

"Oh, yes, now that I know."

Shunduri was sitting breathlessly forward, as if trying to absorb every detail. "Do you know what it will be?"

Henry shook his head. "Not till the twenty-week scan, the obstetrician says. I don't mind, just healthy is all I ask."

Thea smiled. "A girl. I'm sure it's a girl. And we're going Greek this time—we're going to call her Aphrodite."

"Does old Theo Kiriakis know yet?" Richard asked his brother.

"We're telling him tonight. Must say, good timing and all that. We told him about the mihrab last night and he was pretty upset about it, having had bad memories of the Turks, you know. Refused point-blank to fund further excavations until Dr. Choudhury said that Saudi money was likely available for this sort of thing, then he came through. Good old Theo." Henry chuckled. "The first Bourne girl in three generations, you realize. Our great-aunt was the last one. Richard, remember Great-aunt Caroline with the nose, whose fiancé was killed in the war? Never could figure out which one."

Dr. Choudhury, who had been sitting quietly, still wiping his eyes, chimed in. "Yes, those Saudis are very wealthy and have fingers in all sorts of pies."

Rohimun placed a half-full cup of tea in front of her father and moved toward Richard. She slid a full cup onto the countertop next to his elbow, without looking at him. He thanked her, trying to catch her eye, but she had already turned away.

Tariq reached for a cup his sister was handing him, and his mother swung a playful hand at his cheek. He flinched.

"*You!* What am I going to do with *you!*"

He grinned but kept his hands protectively around his ears. "Don't hit me, Amma."

Rohimun, ignoring Tariq's dramatic pose, passed his tea, poured cups for Henry and her mother, and set up the paan tray while everyone talked babies, and the two boys did circuits of the table before stopping to talk to Kareem, who seemed to be the new favorite, about their ghost trap for the Abbey.

Richard could see the differences between the two sisters more clearly now, brought out by Shunduri's high-pitched drawl and expansive gestures, and her acquisitive air, even seeming to covet Thea's impending motherhood. When Shunduri wasn't staring at Thea, she was throwing Kareem pointed looks, and he eventually said, as if continuing an argument, "Look, I'll miss you too, yeah, but it's only a few weeks. Big picture, Princess, big picture." Shunduri tossed her hair at this, hair styled as short and shiny as Deirdre's, and as different as anyone's hair could be from Rohimun's.

Shunduri was as tall and lean as her brother, but there the similarity ended. Rohimun, and indeed Tariq, had a gravitas that loud and needy Shunduri seemed to be without: life experience perhaps. His eyes rested on Rohimun again, and he wondered about what life had brought her, and how he would get to know her better.

---

MRS. BEGUM WAS glowing inside and out. Ahh, the ways of Allah, Peace be upon Him, were truly beyond all understanding, all planning and thinking. Everyone was sitting down and talking, laughing and crying as they should, except for Munni and that Richard, as quiet and awkward as if it was the day of a funeral, not a day of miracles. She tried to make Richard sit at the table, but he would stand, so she talk-talked to him about small things and he answered her, as slow and considered as always.

Rohimun could be married from Windsor Cottage and, if Richard insisted, Tregoze Church as well: perhaps, first, with just his family, before the mullah arrived. And she would make sure that they used an older mullah, perhaps visiting from Bangladesh, who would not ask any awkward questions. She was no Bora Khalo, no Prince Philip, determined to obstruct things rather than accept that this generation had different rules, different needs.

They would suit each other very well, *Inshallah*, both being university-clever. Far better than one clever but with no schooling, and the other merely learned, but a fool in the world. That was a far harder balancing act than between Christian and Muslim.

She looked at her husband sitting at the kitchen table, wiping his eyes and smiling—at her, at his children, at everybody—and thought of their own perpetual swinging triangulation of love, frustration and dependence, all conjoined. She and Babru Choudhury had grown into each other until they were one being and no more able to separate from each other than a yolk from its white in an omelette. How had all this sprung from Syeda Begum's fifteen-year-old pity and some-time contempt for the lonely skinny boy in her uncle's shop?

So much to do, so much to plan, and the great need for things to happen as soon as possible. She turned to her curries, her dahl, her rice, standing ready on the stove to sustain them all, and spared a moment to brush her fingers over her talisman and breathe, *Inshallah, Inshallah. Allhamdu-Lillahi shukran wah hamda.* Praise be to Allah, gratitude and praise. We have come so far in so short a time, let me not fail my children now.

# Acknowledgments

To the 2007 RMIT Novel I and Editing I group of talented students and teachers, particularly Rob Williams, who listened to and critiqued early parts of this book, and whose own writings were a source of inspiration as well as setting a high bar for us all.

To my children, Shareef and Shakira, who have dealt with my preoccupation with humor and tolerance (most of the time) and passionate interest (some of the time).

To my friends and relations who have shown interest, made suggestions, praised the bits I hated and hated the bits I loved, laughed at the sad bits and couldn't understand the funny bits, were insulted or flattered by a fancied resemblance to characters they had nothing in common with, and couldn't relate to the ones they did, you have all made me a better writer. And hopefully a thicker-skinned one.

To Manik Meah, whose invaluable knowledge of Bangla and Desi language and culture was so generously shared. Any mistakes which remain are my own.

To my brave editor Aviva Tuffield, her doughty assistant Ian See, and the whole crew at Scribe with Henry Rosenbloom at the helm: many thanks for what became a marathon exercise in editing and authorial guidance. And for seeing it through to the very end when lesser hearts may have failed.

I am also grateful for the financial assistance and moral support provided by the 2011 CAL Scribe Fiction Prize. It came at a time when I was down on my uppers, and gave me expectations beyond my station.

READERS GUIDE

— ⧉ —

# A Matter of Marriage

by Lesley Jørgensen

## Discussion Questions

**1.** Shilpi steals Shunduri's thunder at the cafe when she shows up in a "flowing Saudi-style *abaya* and *niqab*, as black as night." This is just the first instance where a character uses traditionalism for dramatic effect. Where else in the novel does this happen?

**2.** Our introduction to Simon casts him as a villain because he suppresses Rohimun's creativity and expects domesticity. But throughout the book we learn that Dr. Choudhury also expects Mrs. Begum to be the housekeeper and hates the progressive influence of Mrs. Darby. Discuss this irony.

**3.** When reflecting on his daughters, Dr. Choudhury thinks, "There was bound to be trouble when both temper and talent were given to a woman." Which woman is he referring to?

**4.** Coolie-girl that she is, Shunduri's beauty is described as flashy in the opening chapters of the book. But when Thea and Henry see her, Shunduri is described as "a negative print of Grace Kelly," and her demure beauty can be appreciated. Discuss each character's take on beauty throughout the book.

**5.** Discuss the opium story line in chapter twelve. Were you surprised that this didn't come up again?

**6.** Do you think that the trip to Mecca will happen?

**7.** Syeda Begum never had a traditional wedding because she was pregnant. Babru Choudhury had an affair with his doctoral supervisor. In this case do these two "wrongs" make a right?

**8.** Pregnancy (her own and the pregnancy of others) indirectly plays a role in getting Mrs. Begum what she wants. How does pregnancy move the story line along?

**9.** Royalty is mentioned throughout the novel. Rohimun is compared to Princess Di. Discuss Mrs. Begum's fixation with Dodi and Diana, and the relationship of royalty to each character.

**10.** Dr. Choudhury can be elitist; he has an odd obsession with the sari cabinet and his own wife calls him a cockroach. At the end of the story, do you feel animosity toward him, or are you sympathetic? Does the fact that Mrs. Begum uses his full name on the last page change your feelings?

**11.** Dr. Choudhury thinks of Tariq as perfect combo of East and West. Is that true? Is he the only one?

**12.** Richard and Rohimun's relationship quickly moves from an initial meeting to Richard buying a pricey rug that reminds him of her— even though at that point he's still not sure if she's in the Abbey as the lover of Dr. Choudhury or Tariq. At what point were you convinced that they had a connection? How did you feel about the pace of their relationship?

**13.** Mrs. Begum is an extraordinary female figure whose power is in many ways linked to her prowess in the kitchen. Is she "the only one trying to fix this family," as she proclaims? How do her skills add to her power to help? How do others help, if they do?

**14.** Dr. Choudhury says that Saudis are "number-one villains": "You know, these Saudis. Ignorant people, thinking that they can buy anyone and anything with their dirty money." Who else could he be talking about?

**15.** Mrs. Begum approves of Kareem because of who he is on paper. Do you believe that Kareem has had a very Jane Austen–esque moral awakening?

**16.** Rohimun reflects on Western relationships: "Was this embrace *gora* politeness or pity, or something else, which perhaps mattered as much to him as it did to her? She felt adrift in his Western world of dating and girlfriends: she had seen, lived, the fluid dishonesty of those relationships, so much a matter of mood and whim as to whether the bond would be acknowledged or betrayed. A recipe for misery." Is the Desi way easier? Better?

**17.** One of the funniest uses of Jane Austen's humor is evoked by Jørgensen with a third-person perspective on the marriage of Mrs. Begum and Dr. Choudhury. What other scenes made you laugh?

# Notes

—⟨∞⟩—

# Notes

# Notes
—⦃∞⦄—